DOGWOOD HILL

Center Point
Large Print

Also by Sherryl Woods and available from
Center Point Large Print:

The Christmas Bouquet
A Seaside Christmas
The Summer Garden
An O'Brien Family Christmas
Beach Lane
After Tex
Angel Mine
Temptation

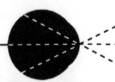

**This Large Print Book carries the
Seal of Approval of N.A.V.H.**

DOGWOOD HILL

DOGWOOD HILL

Sherryl Woods

CENTER POINT LARGE PRINT
THORNDIKE, MAINE

This Center Point Large Print edition is published in the year 2015 by arrangement with Harlequin Books S.A.

The text of this Large Print edition is unabridged. In other aspects, this book may vary from the original edition. Printed in the United States of America on permanent paper. Set in 16-point Times New Roman type.

ISBN: 978-1-62899-504-6

Library of Congress Cataloging-in-Publication Data

Woods, Sherryl.
Dogwood hill / Sherryl Woods. — Center Point Large Print edition.
pages cm
Summary: "When former pro football quarterback Aidan Mitchell comes to Chesapeake Shores to take a high school coaching job, he's embraced by the town—especially the O'Briens. But Aidan has a secret that could alter all their lives"—Provided by publisher.
ISBN 978-1-62899-504-6 (library binding : alk. paper)
1. Large type books. I. Title.
PS3573.O6418D64 2015
813'.54—dc23
2015002320

Dear Friends,

When a family is as strong as the O'Briens, there's not a lot that can shake them to their very foundation. But when Aidan Mitchell comes to Chesapeake Shores as the new high school football coach, he brings with him a secret that's definitely going to stir things up.

Add in a woman, newcomer Liz March, who has a few secrets of her own, and there's plenty of drama on the horizon for those morning gabfests the O'Brien women like to have at Sally's Café.

There's nothing I enjoy more than spending time with the O'Briens, and this chance to cause a little stir in town was just too good to pass up. I hope you'll enjoy how all the secrets unfold and how these two newcomers are embraced by the O'Briens. Once again, I think they prove that family is what counts, no matter how it's cobbled together.

All best,

Sherryl

❯• 1 •❮

Standing outside Chesapeake Shores High School on his first visit to this quaint small town on the Chesapeake Bay, Aidan concluded he'd never seen a more beautiful sight in his life.

Not the hillside covered with a forest of flowering pink and white dogwood trees, though that was spectacular and unexpected in the middle of town. Not the nearby bay, which was sparkling in the spring sun, though it made him yearn to go fishing despite the fact it was something he'd done only once before in his life. Not even the state-of-the-art football stadium with its pro-level electronic scoreboard, its lush grass and impressive permanent bleachers, all of which should have knocked his socks off as the school's prospective coach.

Nope, what caught his eye was the slender woman with her blond hair tousled, her laugh carrying on the breeze as she chased a puppy that was trying valiantly to herd a flock of unhappy Canada geese.

Just then the dog, some sort of black, white and brown Aussie shepherd mix from the looks of him, spotted Aidan, bounded over and tried to corral him into joining the geese in the nice tight group he was apparently envisioning in his instinctive puppy brain. With a black patch of fur around one eye, he bore a striking resemblance to a pirate, causing Aidan's smile to spread.

"Stop it! Archie, that's enough," the woman commanded, fighting hard, but unsuccessfully, to swallow another laugh. "Sit. Be nice."

Archie obediently sat, tongue lolling, and gave Aidan a hopeful look.

"I'm so sorry," she said. "He got away from me."

"No problem," Aidan replied.

"Actually it is a problem. The town has very strict leash laws," she explained as she snapped Archie's leash to his collar, "except for the dog park on the other side of the hill. It's fenced in, so the dogs are allowed to run free, but Archie here spotted the geese, instinct kicked in and the second someone opened the gate, he took off on a mission to round them up. He thinks it's his job."

"He's very good at it. Where do I fit in? Not being a goose, that is."

When she smiled, amusement setting off sparks in her deep blue eyes, it quite simply took his breath away.

"Oh, he thinks anything that moves is fair game," she confided. "He's very diligent."

Aidan, who'd never owned a pet, regarded the dog warily. "What happens now? If I move, does he try to snag me by the hand to drag me back?"

"I think you're safe for the moment, though if you happen to have a dog treat in your pocket, you'll make a friend for life."

"Sorry. No treats."

As if he understood, Archie stared at him dolefully, then inched closer, finally butting Aidan's hand.

"He'll take a good head rub, instead," she told him. "Don't worry. He really is harmless. I've only had him for a couple of weeks, but he's been a real gentleman. His owner had to give him up because he was too energetic for her, so he's looking for a new person and a new purpose."

"Thus the geese," Aidan guessed.

"Exactly."

"Are you his new person?"

"Oh, no," she said at once. "I already have two dogs and a cat, none of which I intended to have, but people know I take in strays and try to find new homes for them. When something like this comes up, they bring their pets to me. Cordelia's grandchildren meant well when they gave her a pet for her birthday, but they didn't really think about her being close to eighty. It happens a lot. People think the elderly need companionship, but they really have no idea which animal might be best suited for the job."

"And you do?"

"I'd like to think so. Cordelia now has a beautiful cat whose owner died. Fluffy sits in her lap and purrs. They're both content with their new arrangement."

"What about the three animals still with you?" he asked, sensing that she was a woman for whom compassion probably overruled good sense on many occasions.

"I'm afraid I got attached," she admitted with a rueful expression. "I'm Elizabeth March, by the way. Most people call me Liz. I own Pet Style on Main Street a few doors up the street from Sally's Café. I opened just before Christmas last year."

Aidan couldn't stop the grin that threatened. "Pet Style?" he repeated. "I had no idea pets were fashion conscious." He glanced pointedly at Archie as he spoke. The dog was happily sniffing a buttercup. His leather collar looked as if it had been given a good chew on more than one occasion. The serviceable, but unremarkable, leash was equally worn.

"They're not, but their owners sure are," Liz said. "You'd be amazed. Just last week I sold a fancy rhinestone-studded designer dog collar for $150. I'd expected to be stuck with it, but thought I should give a couple of high-end items a try. Sure enough, a tourist grabbed it up an hour after I put it on display."

Aidan shook his head in astonishment. On a beginning coach's salary, he'd be lucky to buy dog food and pay vet bills. Thankfully, he'd spent frugally and invested wisely during his couple of years as a pro football player. When he glanced back at Liz, she was regarding him speculatively.

"You wouldn't, by any chance, be looking for a dog?" she inquired, turning those bright blue eyes on him in a way that would probably get most men to agree to do just about anything she requested. "He's up to date on all his shots and he's housebroken. Best of all, Archie already likes you."

Archie was, indeed, happily sprawled across his feet, apparently having concluded that he was no longer going to be allowed to run free, so Aidan shouldn't be allowed to budge, either. He promptly perked up at the mention of his name. For half an instant, Aidan was actually tempted to say yes, if only to make this woman happy. Fortunately, given his circumstances, common sense kicked in.

"You're very good at finding new homes for your strays, aren't you?" he said.

"So it seems," she said, beaming.

"Sorry. Not this time. I don't have room in my apartment for a dog this size, and if those paws are the indicators they're supposed to be, Archie here is bound to get bigger. I may be moving soon, anyway."

"*To* Chesapeake Shores, not away," she said, as if it was a fact he'd already revealed. "You're going to be the new football coach."

Aidan just stared at her. "Are you psychic, too?"

"Nope, but the town loves its team, and the

13

word on the street is that an ex-pro player is going to be coaching next season. Everyone has high hopes we'll stop being the laughingstock of the region. Since you look like a jock and you were standing out here admiring the stadium, I just put two and two together."

He gave her an amused look. "How does a jock look?"

Color tinted her cheeks. "You know, fit, well-toned."

He laughed. "I see. Well, I am Aidan Mitchell," he confirmed. "And I'm interviewing for the job, but I don't have it yet."

"Oh, you'll get it," she said confidently. "Everyone's very excited. You'll be the second pro player in town. Of course, Mack Franklin grew up here, and he only played professionally for a season before becoming a sports columnist, but the town loves him. He started a local weekly newspaper a couple of years back. It's a very tough business, if you know anything about newspapers these days, but he's beaten the odds because it's the best way to find out what's going on in town." She paused for breath, then amended, "Aside from sitting in Sally's and listening to the gossip, anyway. At least Mack tries to bring some journalistic credibility into play."

After growing up in New York, Aidan was astonished by this insight into small-town ways. Or perhaps it was just Liz March, who chattered like a magpie. "Does Mack know that his competition is a local café?"

"Of course he does. Sally's his best source. But mostly he'd be the first to find out what's going on, anyway. He's married to an O'Brien, which makes him practically royalty in Chesapeake Shores."

Aidan instinctively stiffened at the comment, though he hoped she hadn't noticed. "Why is that?"

"You don't know the town's history?" she asked, looking startled.

"Is it a criteria for living here?" he asked, mostly in jest. "Do they give a test at the Realtor's office?"

"Not really," she said, apparently taking him seriously. "It's just a local legend, so people tend to know it. As I understand it, the land originally belonged to an O'Brien who came here straight from Ireland. His family farmed it for years. A couple of decades ago, three of his descendants—Mick, Jeff and Thomas O'Brien—built Chesapeake Shores from scratch on that land."

She paused for breath, then added, "Mick's the famous architect who designed the town. He might not be an elected official, but his word still carries a lot of weight around here. Jeff manages properties and sells real estate." Eyes twinkling, she gave Aidan a pointed look. "So it wouldn't really surprise me if he does spread the story himself, though I imagine he'd consider testing potential residents to be ill-mannered."

Aidan chuckled. "Touché."

"There's another brother, too. Thomas is a well-respected environmentalist who runs a foundation that fights to protect the bay."

Aidan's brain seemed to shut down at the casual mention of Thomas O'Brien. Maybe coming to Chesapeake Shores had been a huge mistake, after all, if just hearing that name made him flinch. He'd gotten a tip about the coaching job and been drawn here as if fate were stepping in, but now all he felt was the familiar bitterness and anger crawling up the back of his throat. That it might be unwarranted was a concept he struggled with from time to time.

He suddenly realized that Liz was studying him with a worried expression.

"Are you okay? Did I say something that upset you?"

"No, not a thing, I'm fine," Aidan assured her. "Thanks for the background information." He deliberately took a quick glance at his watch, then added, "I need to get going."

He turned and quickly walked off in the direction of his car.

"Aidan!" Liz's concerned voice carried on the breeze. "The school office is the other way."

He gave her a wave of acknowledgment and kept right on going, thankful there was no set time for his interview. He'd intentionally scheduled it that way, promising to call once he arrived in town and got settled into the room the school had reserved for him at The Inn at Eagle Point. Maybe after a shower and some food and a little more time to think about what he was doing, he'd be ready to make that call. Or maybe not.

It was a big decision, deciding whether to stay and take a risk, or go. If his friends could see him now, they'd be stunned by his indecisiveness.

On the field, he'd been a quick-thinking quarter-back, reading a defense and making split-second adjustments that determined whether a play succeeded or failed. He hadn't struggled for even a minute with his decision to retire when he'd realized that an injury had slowed him down, ruining his effectiveness on the field. He'd always wanted to coach at the high school level. He'd gotten his teaching credentials in college in anticipation that this day would eventually come. At the end of his season last November following a second knee injury that had taken him out for the year, he'd made the call. Sure, it had come a lot sooner than he'd anticipated, but fate was funny that way. He wouldn't be one of those players who hung on past his expiration date.

But this decision? This was different. This was a twenty-eight-year-old man trying to decide not only whether a job and town might be a good fit but if the time was right to meet his biological father—Thomas O'Brien—for the very first time.

Liz held a cup of coffee in her hands to warm them as she sat in a booth at Sally's with Bree O'Brien Collins, who owned Flowers on Main, the store next door to hers. Bree was also a playwright who ran a local theater, but she still loved spending the occasional day making flower arrangements, especially for special occasions. Today she'd been so busy with the decorations for a baby shower that they'd postponed their morning coffee break until afternoon when Liz's high school helper could cover for her.

"I'm telling you, it was very strange," she told Bree. "We were just talking. I should say I was chattering away, filling him in on this and that." She regarded Bree with a rueful expression. "I really do have to stop doing that, going on and on, I mean."

Bree's grin suggested she was doing it again.

"Okay. Sorry. I'll get to the point. I promise. I'd tried to convince him to take Archie, but he wasn't interested. Then I admitted that I'd guessed who he was. We talked about the job for a couple of minutes, or maybe I did all the talking. Anyway, he took off, and not toward the school, as if he'd realized he was late for a meeting or something. He headed in the opposite direction."

"Well, that is weird," Bree said. "Maybe he

18

doesn't like dogs. Archie is a sweetheart, but not everybody notices that when he's trying to herd them."

Liz chuckled. "Yes, I'm familiar with the reaction. The poor thing can't help himself, though. But the Archie issue was resolved. Aidan wasn't interested, and that was that for me. Pets belong with people who'll love and appreciate them. Actually I was filling him in on local history, how O'Briens built the town, when he got this kind of glazed look on his face, then took off."

"So you think his reaction had something to do with the O'Briens?" Bree asked, frowning.

"It felt that way, but how could that be it? Everybody loves your family."

Bree made a face. "That's a slight exaggeration. Dad's made his share of enemies over the years. Heck, for a long time, he didn't even get along all that well with his own brothers. He, Jeff and Thomas clashed over every detail when they were building the town. It's only recently, thanks to my grandmother's determination, that peace and family harmony have been mostly restored. If you force people to sit around the same table on Sunday long enough, sooner or later they have to start talking civilly. I doubt Nell envisioned just how long that process would take, though."

Liz nodded distractedly. She was still perplexed by Aidan's behavior. "Then I must have misread his reaction," she said eventually. "I guess we'll see when word spreads about whether he's taken the job at the high school."

"Well, whatever Aidan feels about the O'Briens, it's one-sided," Bree said. "Dad is determined to get him hired as the coach. He practically hand-picked him from the list of candidates, so there's no bad blood there, at least on his side. And you know Mick O'Brien. When he wants something, he usually gets it."

Bree sat back and studied Liz with a speculative expression. "So, what was he like? Aidan, I mean."

Liz blushed under the friendly scrutiny. "I suppose he was good-looking in that well-built, jock way." She wished she hadn't noticed just how toned and fit he seemed to be, or the way his eyes had sparked with wit, or the dimple that occasionally appeared in his cheek when he was teasing her.

"In other words, you wouldn't kick him out of bed," Bree concluded.

Liz frowned at the lighthearted remark. "I wouldn't let him *in* my bed," she corrected, though she hoped he wouldn't make a liar of her. She had a feeling he could. To bolster her resolve she reminded both of them, "It's way too soon for me to be even thinking like that."

Truthfully, she hoped she never thought that way ever again. Her past had left her beyond skittish when it came to relationships. She was fiercely independent these days and determined to stay that way. Once burned—especially as badly as she had been—twice shy.

Bree's expression immediately sobered. "Liz, sweetie, it's been a year since the accident. I know you loved your husband. I also know you moved here to get away from the memories and to start over. It's time to do that. Meeting someone new is part of the process. You don't have to feel guilty if you find Aidan Mitchell attractive."

"It's not about guilt," Liz said defensively.

"It sounded that way to me."

"It's about time. I have a new business. I need to focus on that. I have new friends, to say nothing of a houseful of pets. There are barely enough hours in the day for all I have to do. A relation-ship is out of the question right now."

Bree clearly didn't agree. "Archie and all the rest are no substitute for letting another human into your life," she scolded.

"I have plenty of humans in my life," Liz retorted. "Right this second I'm thinking there might be one too many." She tried to force a light, teasing note into her voice, even as she prayed the barb would strike home and end the conversation.

Bree immediately backed off, her expression stricken. "I'm sorry. Meddling is a family trait. I just care about you. We all do. Even Dad's started asking questions about why no one's come up with a good match for you yet. Now that all of his children, nieces and nephews and even one granddaughter are married, he seems to have gotten this crazy idea that it's his civic duty to work on marrying off every single person in town."

"I've barely been in town six months," Liz protested.

Bree grinned. "In his opinion, that's plenty long enough. Trust me, you do not want Mick deciding to find a man for you."

"Heaven forbid," Liz replied with heartfelt emotion. "I've heard the stories. Next time the subject comes up, you tell your father that he can find me a date right after he agrees to take in Archie. That ought to shut him down."

That earned a chuckle from Bree. "Now, why didn't the rest of us come up with a threat like that?"

"Maybe you weren't as eager to evade his matchmaking as I am," Liz said, standing up. She hated lying to her friend, to anyone, in fact, but she didn't think she'd ever be ready to share the real story behind the night she'd lost her husband. Better to escape now before Bree coaxed her into revealing something she didn't want to remember, much less talk about.

She reached into her purse for money to pay for her coffee and raspberry croissant, treats she allowed herself only after strenuous outings with her animals. Chasing Archie all over Dogwood Hill today definitely qualified.

"No. It's on me today," Bree protested. "It's the price I pay for sticking my nose where it doesn't belong." She stood up and hugged Liz. "We may be well-meaning, but don't you dare hesitate to tell any of us to butt out, okay?"

Unexpected tears stung Liz's eyes. "I won't, but to be honest, knowing that you care enough to butt in means the world to me."

It was almost as if she'd found a whole new family after losing her husband on a rain-slicked road one terrible night a year ago. The pitiful truth was, though, that she'd apparently lost him long before that and never known it.

After his disconcerting conversation with Liz, Aidan drove around town trying to convince himself that Chesapeake Shores wasn't the place for him. He diligently focused on the downside.

It only had a tiny district of shops and restaurants, for one thing. There were more businesses and a greater diversity of fancy and take-out food options within two blocks of his apartment in Manhattan's Upper West Side than there were in this entire town, maybe even the whole region without going all the way to Annapolis or Baltimore.

He picked up a copy of the local weekly Liz had mentioned and compared it to the daily New York newspapers, then shook his head. When a meeting of the town's beautification committee was front-page news, he was definitely in the wrong place.

Then, of course, there was the insight Liz had given him into a town where seemingly everyone knew everyone else's business. In New York, though he had plenty of friends in the city, he was barely acquainted with most of his neighbors. That had always suited him just fine. There were enough real celebrities around town that a professional athlete could easily avoid the limelight if that was his choice. In his case, it had been.

How could this possibly be the best match for him? Even if the town didn't come with a whole slew of emotional baggage attached, small-town living probably wasn't right for him. He'd go stir-crazy in a month, quite probably sooner.

Sighing heavily, he came to what had to be the best decision. He'd set up an interview for tomorrow, because he'd made a commitment and commitments meant something to him. He'd even try to listen with an open heart, but his mind was already made up. He'd decline the job, wish them well, then take off right after the interview.

There were bound to be other coaching jobs, jobs that wouldn't put him anywhere near a man he'd now convinced himself he didn't really need to know or even meet. Thomas O'Brien was a name on a piece of paper, an important piece of paper to be sure, but meeting him wouldn't change the fact that he'd been nothing to Aidan his entire life. At least he knew where to find him if some genetic health issue cropped up years from now.

An image of Liz crept into his head and he felt a moment's regret. Not only was she beautiful, she had a good heart. He'd felt an instantaneous connection to her, something that rarely happened with the women who tended to flock around professional athletes. Liz was real.

Still, he couldn't allow a momentary attraction to a woman to sway him into making a decision that was so obviously all wrong. He'd have a nice dinner, get a good night's sleep, meet with the high school principal and then go on his way.

Satisfied with his plan, he checked the directions and headed toward The Inn at Eagle Point. As he drove along the winding road, he couldn't help noticing the nearby bay, and once more Liz's mention of Thomas O'Brien's passion for that body of water slipped past his defenses. He pieced her words together with what little his mother had told him over the years and wondered what it must be like to be so idealistic that a cause mattered more than people, more than a son. If he left, he'd never know the answer to that.

"Stop it!" he muttered, as emphatic with himself as Liz had been with Archie earlier. The decision was made.

Somehow, though, it didn't seem quite as valid as when he'd first reached it.

• • •

When Liz got home that night, Archie, Sasha and Dominique met her at the door of her little bungalow across the street from Dogwood Hill. The two terrier mixes that she'd rescued soon after coming to Chesapeake Shores might be small compared to Archie, but there was little question about who the alpha dogs were in her home. Girls ruled! After a few failed attempts to herd them, Archie had acquiesced to their dominance.

Now he sat quietly by and waited for his turn to get Liz's attention. Then all three dogs trailed her into the kitchen, where her imperial majesty, a one-eared Siamese known as Anastasia, regarded them all with a superior look as she sat beside her kitty dish awaiting dinner. When Liz once again tried a less-expensive brand of cat food, Anastasia regarded her with an accusing look and turned up her nose.

"I don't even know why I try," Liz grumbled. "Other than the fact that this other stuff is going to bankrupt me." Even so, she dumped the rejected food in the garbage and replaced it with the cat's preferred brand.

As she looked around her small, but nicely updated kitchen, the mismatched group of strays brought a smile to Liz's lips.

"Bree's wrong," she told them emphatically as she doled out more hugs and scratches behind the ears, then dished up dinner for the dogs. "You guys are all the companionship I need."

But even as she said the words, an image of Aidan Mitchell crept in to make her blood pump just a little faster. And that was exactly why she had to stay far, far away from him.

⇉· 2 ·⇇

Aidan was staring out the window of the restaurant at The Inn at Eagle Point with its unobstructed view of the bay, nursing his second cup of coffee after a surprisingly excellent breakfast, when a shadow loomed over the table. He looked up to find a man standing there, hand outstretched, a welcoming expression on his face.

"Mick O'Brien, son. And you're Aidan Mitchell," he said confidently. "Welcome to Chesapeake Shores." Without asking, he pulled out a chair and sat. "I've been expecting your call since yesterday."

For an instant Aidan couldn't find his voice. This man was his *uncle!* He had absolutely no experience with extended family beyond his maternal grandparents, and no experience at all when it came to his paternal family. Obviously his decision to get out of town without crossing paths with any O'Briens hadn't taken into account Mick O'Brien's determination to court him for this job. Aidan wasn't sure what his real role had been in the search for a new coach, but he'd been aggressive once Aidan had submitted his application.

When Aidan had called the school yesterday to confirm the appointment with the principal for this morning, he'd been told yet again how eager everyone—especially the town's founder—was to close the deal. The enthusiasm had been rewarding, but disconcerting given his determination to leave without signing on for the job.

Mick glanced around for a waiter, then stood up and grabbed a cup from a neighboring table and poured himself some coffee from the pot the waiter had left earlier. As he stirred in some sugar, Aidan surreptitiously studied him, wondering how much Mick might resemble his brother and trying to decide if he saw anything of himself in the man.

After years of wondering and getting only evasive answers from his mother when it came to his father's identity, Aidan had finally found the O'Brien name when he'd come across his birth certificate while cleaning out his mother's dresser after her death last summer. There were a couple of clippings about Chesapeake Shores and the bay preservation foundation, as well.

Over the years he'd been told that his father had been a good man who had important things to accomplish. His mother had never mentioned what those things might be. Those clippings she'd tucked away were the first clues he'd had.

Nor had she ever hinted that they'd parted as anything other than friends. To Aidan's knowledge his father had never contributed a dime to his support. In fact, given his mother's independent streak and a few indiscreet comments from his grandparents about her pride, he'd concluded that she'd never even told him about the pregnancy. Surely, though, if he'd been such a paragon, Thomas O'Brien must have suspected. Then again, Aidan had known his share of men who were capable of being oblivious to anything that didn't fit conveniently into their plans.

So even though Anna Mitchell had tried to impart an image of a mysterious but kindly individual, resentments had simmered inside Aidan. He'd grown up wondering why he and his mom hadn't been more important than some idealistic goal in his dad's life. And, since his mother had never had another serious relationship to his knowledge, he had to wonder about the man who'd meant so much to her that she'd never moved on.

"You okay?" Mick asked, regarding him with concern. "You look a little pale. You're not coming down with something, are you? We have a real good doctor here in town. I can take you by his office if you want to be checked out."

Aidan quickly shook his head. "No, sorry. I'm

fine. You just caught me by surprise. I spent yesterday getting to know the town. I gave the principal at the school a call late in the day to confirm our appointment for this morning. He must have told you I was here."

Mick grinned. "Not necessary. There aren't a lot of secrets in Chesapeake Shores and you're big news. I knew five minutes after you drove into town." He shrugged. "Besides, my daughter Jess owns this place. She gave me a call right after you checked in. I would have popped in right then, but she told me you seemed a little distracted and to give you time to relax. For once, I listened to her—and my wife—and didn't come barging right over. To tell you the truth, Megan—that's my wife—is usually right about these things, though if you tell her I said that, I'll deny it."

Aidan recalled the friendly woman at the desk. So, that had to be Jess, another O'Brien, a cousin apparently.

Before Aidan could respond, Mick glanced pointedly at his empty plate. "If you're ready to go now, I'll drive you over to the high school. We're all anxious to get the ball rolling, get a contract nailed down. Then I can show you a couple of places around town that are for sale. There's not much to rent. Buying makes more sense, anyway."

Aidan couldn't help wondering if Mick was such a successful architect and developer because

he was part bulldozer. "There's no offer on the table, and I haven't agreed to anything yet," he reminded Mick, thinking that saying no was going to prove a lot trickier than he'd anticipated.

"I think you'll like the terms," Mick said confidently. "It's a great little town. The school has resources to pay you decently and get you whatever you need. The stadium's first-rate. I did my homework and brought in a top-notch designer, since it's beyond my area of expertise. I put my best contractors to work on it a few years back, but if there's anything we missed, you just let me know. I've got some grandkids who're going to want to play ball and I want the best for them and that includes a coach who can turn this team around. I know it's politically correct to say that winning's not everything, but these lopsided losses are discouraging."

Aidan imagined that was a serious understatement. He'd studied the team's record, not a win in the past five years. He decided to focus on the stadium, which was a real positive.

"To be honest, I've seen a few college and even pro stadiums that weren't that impressive," Aidan told him. "You did a great job."

In fact, if it hadn't been for all the peripheral angst attached to this particular job, it would have been a dream, no question about it. Aidan couldn't imagine anyplace else where he'd be given carte blanche to invigorate a high school football program with whatever it took to make it successful. Those resources usually came at the college level.

Still he said, "One step at a time. Let's have that meeting and see how it goes. You know I don't have a track record coaching high school football. You may decide I'm not right for the job."

"Not a chance," Mick said. "I've done my homework. I know you were a leader in the locker room and not just on the field. That, along with the recommendations from your coaches, speaks highly of you."

Aidan couldn't help feeling flattered, but he couldn't let himself be swayed. "Okay, let's say I do say yes, I have one question for you in the meantime." He was hoping the answer would solidify his resolve. The last thing any coach needed was too many bosses micromanaging his decisions.

"What's that?" Mick asked as they walked outside into the warm spring sunshine and headed toward a large and surprisingly muddy truck that had obviously seen some time on a work site recently.

"If I take this job, exactly who do I answer to? The principal, the school board or you?"

Mick's booming laugh filled the air. "I won't be the person signing your checks," he replied candidly. "That doesn't mean that folks in town don't tend to listen to what I have to say."

Aidan nodded. "Good to know. Any other tips for getting along in Chesapeake Shores?"

Mick gave him a long look. "You stick around. Come to Sunday dinner at my place. All the O'Briens will be there. We'll be happy to fill you in on everything you need to know. If you're not already convinced, we ought to be able to seal the deal."

Aidan's pulse began to race. Could it possibly be that easy? A few days in town and he'd come face-to-face with his father? Could he sit at Mick O'Brien's table and keep what he knew to himself, at least as long as it took to decide if he wanted to reveal the truth? Would he be able to look into Thomas O'Brien's face without unleashing all the vitriol he'd stored up? A meltdown over a roast and mashed potatoes would certainly put an end to his coaching career in this obviously close-knit town.

He drew in a deep breath and made yet another of those quick decisions, this one fraught with all sorts of disturbing potential consequences. Fate had brought him here. Until he gave the school his answer, he might as well make the most of it.

He met Mick's gaze. "I'll do that, sir, if you're sure it's not an imposition."

"Nothing my family likes better than seeing a new face at the table," Mick assured him.

Aidan couldn't help wondering if they'd still feel that way after his visit.

· · ·

Aidan immediately liked Rob Larkin, the principal of the high school, who seemed to have no qualms at all about standing up to Mick O'Brien and taking charge of the interview. With his crew cut and preppy attire, he looked to be in his forties, but there was a steely resolve in his eyes that suggested he ran a tight ship. Mick actually sat back and let the principal run the show.

"Although your football credentials are what got you here today," Rob said, "I'm interested in hearing what you think a high school coach's role should be."

Aidan leaned forward. "I had the best possible model as a coach when I was in school. He was an excellent motivator. He had strict rules—he wanted to win, but more important than either of those things, he wanted to teach the players to be better men. If I can be half as effective as he was, I'll do a good job for you."

Caught up in his enthusiasm for the topic, he forgot for a minute that he wasn't 100 percent sure he really wanted this job.

"What about grades?" Rob asked him.

"At the top of my list," Aidan said readily. "Nobody plays if they're failing. I'll get them whatever help they need, but I won't tolerate them slacking off when it comes to academics."

He saw the principal and Mick exchange a satisfied look.

"Why don't we take a walk around the school so you can see the gym, the locker room and our equipment?" Rob suggested.

"Sure," Aidan said, already knowing what he'd find—the absolute best of everything.

"Would you like to meet a few of the players?" Rob asked. "I can arrange to pull them from classes."

Aidan quickly shook his head. It wouldn't be fair to get their hopes up, and it would be harder for him to say no if he'd seen the young men who might be pinning their hopes on him.

"Another time," he said. "But let's take a look around."

As they toured the school, Aidan was more and more impressed, not only with the facility, but with Rob Larkin. He was a dedicated educator, no question about it. He was also happily surprised by the principal's interactions with the students that he witnessed. There was friendly respect on both sides.

It seemed the students all knew Mick, too, and their easy camaraderie with such an important man spoke well of Mick's relationship with all of the town's residents. Aidan couldn't help wondering if Thomas, with his lofty ideals, related half as well to average folks.

When they'd made their way back to the principal's office, Rob said, "There's one other thing I should mention. In addition to teaching a

35

few physical education classes, you'd also be expected to handle one after-school activity. Coach Gentry loved the outdoors, so he organized a group that spent time cleaning up the bay. He worked closely with Mick's brother Thomas on that project. We'd like you to continue that. It's important to get these kids to appreciate the environment, to understand that there's a whole big world outside of sports."

Work with Thomas—his father? Aidan wasn't sure he could do that. He swallowed hard and tried not to let his immediate reaction show. There was no point in making an issue of it now, since he didn't intend to take the job. He needed to nod and let it go.

"Of course," he said. "If I stay, I understand that an after-school activity beyond coaching would be part of the job. It sounds like a worthy cause."

"Not much matters more around here," Mick chimed in. "You'll see. Just get my brother started when you meet him on Sunday. He'll talk your ear off." He leveled a look at Aidan. "So, do we have a deal? A five-year contract. We know it's going to take time, though none of us would be unhappy to have a winning record a lot sooner than that."

"I'd like some time to think about it," Aidan said, clearly startling Rob Larkin and stunning Mick.

"What's to think about?" Mick asked, a hint of indignation in his voice. "Opportunities like this don't come along every day. Most schools wouldn't give you half that long to make a difference."

"I know that, and I appreciate it," Aidan told him. "But Chesapeake Shores is a big change for me. I want to be sure it can be mutually beneficial. That long-term deal is a sweet one for me, but I'm not so sure it's in your best interests. After all, this is my first coaching job. I could be terrible. And Chesapeake Shores is a big change from New York. It might not be the best fit for me. Let's all give it some more thought."

"Of course," Rob said, before Mick could step in. "It is an adjustment. I came here from DC, so I know. For me, it's been a welcome change, but it's not right for everyone." He glanced at Mick. "It's no reflection on the town."

"Of course not," Aidan said.

Mick seemed to take his cue from the principal. "We'll talk some more on Sunday," he said eventually. "I'll drive you back over to the inn now."

"That's okay. It's not that far. I'd like to walk, if you don't mind." He stood up and shook Rob's hand. "It was very nice meeting you."

"You, too. I hope we'll have the opportunity to work together."

"Thanks for the ride over, Mr. O'Brien."

"That's Mick, son. I'll see you on Sunday. Just ask Jess for directions."

"I'll do that."

Outside, on another glorious spring day that showed off the town's best attributes of blue skies and sparkling water, Aidan drew in a deep breath. Saying no was going to be a whole lot harder than he'd ever anticipated. The size of the town and the length of that contract were still issues, but the real hang-up was the prospect of getting closer to a man he'd dreamed about for years, but wasn't really sure he wanted to know. That was especially ironic now that the possibility seemed within reach.

Liz wasn't surprised when she spotted Aidan walking up the driveway to Mick's for Sunday dinner. Nor was she especially startled when Bree pulled her aside and asked if she'd mind sitting next to the newcomer at the table.

"He's bound to feel more comfortable if there's a familiar face nearby," Bree said. "Someone other than my father needs to take him under their wing. Since you two have met and you're a recent newcomer to town, you're the obvious choice."

"And of course that's the only reason you've chosen me for the job," Liz remarked, her skepticism plain.

Bree gave her a look that was all innocence. "Of course. What other reason could there be?"

Bree glanced across the room and watched as Mick led Aidan around making introductions to his family. Liz couldn't seem to keep her gaze off him, either. With Bree's siblings and their spouses in the room, grandchildren underfoot everywhere, plus a couple of nephews and their families, it was bound to be a little overwhelming for anyone.

"He's looking a little shell-shocked already," Bree commented.

"I remember what that was like," Liz acknowledged. Even now, after being included for several Sunday and holiday meals, she needed the occasional time-out to get her bearings. "Okay, I'll do what I can to keep Aidan from running for the hills. Mick really does want this job to work out, doesn't he?"

"He's gotten a little obsessed about it," Bree conceded. "Especially since Aidan didn't sign on the dotted line right off the bat. Dad's not used to anyone holding out, especially when money's not the issue. It's frustrating him." Bree grinned. "Mom thinks it's good for him. The rest of us are just wondering where Aidan got the backbone to stand up to him. We might ask for lessons."

Liz gave Bree a pointed look. "I might want a couple of those lessons myself."

Though it was evident Bree got her message, she merely waved it off. "Stop. You know I'm just giving you a push in the direction you want to go, anyway." Then she literally gave Liz a gentle shove. "Go. Save him."

Liz crossed the room and caught Aidan's eye. "Could I speak to you a moment?"

Mick gave her a startled look that quickly turned speculative. "We can talk more later," he told Aidan at once. "Never turn down a pretty woman's invitation."

Aidan regarded her with an expression of relief. "Thank you," he said as Mick moved away.

"I wasn't sure you needed rescuing, but I recall how I felt after my first half hour with a houseful of O'Briens. Would you like a little fresh air?"

"I'd love some," Aidan admitted, following her outside to a porch lined with rockers and Adirondack chairs facing the bay.

Liz gestured toward the chairs. "We could sit here or we could walk. Dinner's not for another half hour and since most of the kids are outside playing, Nell always rings a very loud bell to get everyone's attention."

"Then let's walk," Aidan said. As they reached the edge of the wide expanse of lawn and stood looking out at the bay, he turned to her. "Who's Nell? I don't think I've met her. Mick's wife is Megan, right?"

"Exactly. Nell is Mick's mother. This may be his house, but, trust me, when it comes to meals, she's in charge. And her food is worth whatever chaos guests might have to deal with."

"You must be a regular," he said. "How'd that happen?"

"I take in stray animals. The O'Briens take in stray residents. Bree brought me home one Sunday right after I opened my shop and I've been coming ever since. Not every week, but enough to feel more or less comfortable with the intrusive questions and well-meant advice."

She studied him as he stood beside her, hands shoved in his pockets, his well-toned shoulders looking oddly tense. "You're not nervous about all this, are you? It's clear you have the upper hand. Mick really wants you to accept this job. Or is that the problem? Are you feeling pressured?"

"Of course not," he scoffed. "It might be my first coaching job, but I have the credentials. I'm up to it. I'm just not convinced it's the right fit."

"Why is that?" she asked, startled. "You don't like Chesapeake Shores?"

"I'm sure it's a great little town," he responded.

"*Little* being the operative word, I imagine," she said, taking offense on behalf of the town. "This is not some backwoods community in the middle of nowhere. We have great people and great restaurants. We have a playwright whose work has been produced on Broadway, Mick's daughter Bree, in fact. We have a top country music songwriter, too, and her husband is a Grammy-winning singer. They keep a home here and come back from Nashville whenever they can."

Aidan smiled. "Do you belong to the Chamber of Commerce?"

41

"Yes, of course, but I'm telling you this so you'll understand that Chesapeake Shores is a wonderful place to live, even if it's not New York."

"I never meant to imply that it wasn't," Aidan told her. "It just may not be right for me. We'll have to see."

Liz didn't entirely believe his declaration of open-mindedness, but she had no idea why. Nor did she think these nerves she sensed were about his capability as a coach or whether the town was a good fit for him. Still, she let the subject drop.

"Have you met the whole family?" she asked instead.

He relaxed a little and laughed. "I have no idea. I met what seemed like a hundred people in there. Is that all of them?"

"I think most of Mick's immediate family was there, but his brother Jeff and his family were just coming up the walk when we came outside. Come to think of it, I didn't see Jo—that's Jeff's wife— with them. I don't think I saw Thomas inside, but he could have been in the kitchen with Nell or somewhere in the yard playing catch with his son and some of the other kids."

An odd expression passed over Aidan's face, just as it had the other day. This time she knew she wasn't wrong about what she was seeing. She hesitated, then asked, "Do you already know some of the family?"

"No, why?"

"Because you reacted just now when I mentioned Thomas. You did the same thing the other day when the O'Brien name came up. What am I missing?"

"You're imagining things," Aidan said, though his tone wasn't the least bit convincing.

"Aidan, if there's something you're not saying, if there's some history here or bad blood or something, maybe it is the wrong place for you. The town is overrun with O'Briens and they stick together. You need to understand that and be sure of your decision."

He gave her a long, inscrutable look before answering. "I'm not sure of anything," he said quietly.

And, just like before, he turned and walked away, leaving her with a whole slew of troubling questions.

Though she sat next to Aidan at dinner, Liz was all too aware that he carefully avoided making conversation with her. In fact, he was fairly quiet, responding only when asked a direct question. He seemed content to let the nonstop chatter and laughter swirl around him.

She also thought she caught his gaze straying more than once toward Thomas O'Brien, but maybe that was because her imagination had gone into overdrive following their talk outside.

As soon as the meal ended, she went in search of Nell to thank her for another incredible meal, then to say her goodbyes to Megan and Mick. She thought she'd be home free and able to make a quick escape after that, but Mick drew her aside.

"So?" he asked. "How's Aidan leaning? Is he going to take the job or not?"

Liz regarded him with amusement. "What makes you think I have any inside knowledge?"

"The two of you were outside for a while. Looked to me as if you were talking pretty seriously about something."

"You were spying on us?" she asked with a scowl, though she wasn't the least bit surprised. Of course Mick had been keeping a close eye on them. That was who he was, a man who paid close attention to the things that mattered to him.

"I don't spy," he objected, then sighed. "You know how much the school needs him, Liz. Did he give you any hint about which way he's leaning?"

"Not really," she said, though her gut was telling her Aidan was going to walk away. She didn't want to be the one to break that news to Mick, not when she wasn't certain of it. Who knew what sort of pressure he might decide to pour on the poor unsuspecting man?

"Can I give you a bit of advice?" she asked Mick.

"Why not? You're practically part of the family,

and heaven knows, not a one of them keeps a single opinion to themselves."

Liz laughed, knowing it was a genetic predisposition of the O'Briens to share advice whether it was wanted or not.

"Give the man some space," she suggested to Mick. "He seems to be weighing this decision. Too much pressure might have the opposite effect of what you're hoping for."

"He'll never find a better opportunity," Mick said. "He needs to understand that."

"That may be," Liz conceded. "And I'm hardly an expert on Aidan Mitchell, but I think overselling the job could backfire."

She glanced across the room to where Aidan was talking to Mack Franklin. Whatever the conversation, his expression was animated and he looked more relaxed than she'd ever seen him. She had a hunch that while Mack might be talking football, he wasn't pushing the coaching job. In fact, whatever he was saying had Aidan laughing. That sound made her feel surprisingly good.

Mick followed the direction of her gaze, his own gaze narrowing. "You think Mack's approach, whatever it is, is the right one, don't you?"

"Looks that way to me," she said.

Mick's focus returned to her. "You seem awfully concerned for a man you barely know. Any particular reason for that?"

Liz scrambled for an answer that wouldn't give

away this odd connection she felt to a man she'd barely met. "I just know how much you want him to stay and what it would mean to the town to have a winning team."

Mick didn't look as if he bought the reply, but he didn't pursue it. Liz thought she was off the hook, until he added, "I imagine it won't break your heart, though, if he decides to stick around."

No, she thought with a sigh. It wouldn't break her heart at all, even if she wasn't quite sure why.

⇒• 3 •⇐

In the end, despite a boatload of reservations, Aidan surprised himself and decided to take the job *if* he could win one big concession. He wanted a one-year deal, not five. He figured that would be long enough for him to prove himself as a coach and short enough for him to escape if it got too difficult being around Thomas. He'd take an option for another four years, but that was the best he could do.

He'd made the decision during dinner, after he'd had a chance to observe Thomas O'Brien from a distance at the crowded table. He'd concluded that despite his own simmering resentment, the man didn't seem to be the devil incarnate he'd imagined. He was just a man who seemed crazy about his wife and who adored his little boy. In fact, watching Thomas with Sean had set off a flurry of mixed emotions with envy beating out resentment. He'd had a great life, thanks to his mom, but he couldn't help wondering how much better it might have been if his dad had been in the picture.

Despite Mick's suggestion that he speak to Thomas about preserving the Chesapeake Bay, Aidan deliberately steered clear of him. He never exchanged a single word with him beyond a polite hello when introduced. Truthfully, he wasn't sure what he might say when they inevitably met again.

By taking the job, he knew he'd have to face Thomas eventually. Perhaps getting to know him through his work would pave the way for a different kind of bond. Maybe he'd even come to understand the man his mother had loved and respected enough to release from any obligation to her or their child. Surely as an adult he could grasp such strong emotions and dedication in a way he hadn't been able to as a young boy longing for a father.

With his mind finally made up, Aidan drew Mick aside as the family began to leave.

"May I speak to you?"

Mick studied him closely. "Good news or bad?"

Aidan smiled. "I hope you'll think of it as good news. I've decided to accept the job, if you'll agree to a modification of the contract. I'll call Rob in the morning to talk that over, but I wanted you to know now."

"What sort of modification?" Mick asked.

"I only want a one-year deal. I think that's fair to the school, the town and to me. It gives us all time to evaluate how things are working out."

"And then what?" Mick asked irritably. "You'll get a little experience under your belt and cut and run? What's fair about that?"

"I could be a terrible failure and you'll be rid of me in a year without having to give me some huge payoff to go. Maybe that's the way you should look at it," Aidan suggested.

"Son, you can't go into a job thinking you're going to fail."

Aidan smiled. "I'm certainly hoping not to, and I believe I can turn this team around, but nothing in life is a certainty. I'll be a lot more comfortable if we all take the time to evaluate this carefully."

Mick sighed. "I suppose I can't argue with that logic, but people are going to want to know you're committed to the job, that you're a part of the community, that you believe wholeheartedly in the team. They won't be happy you'll have an out at the end of a year."

Aidan leveled a look into his eyes. "It's the best I can do, sir. I would certainly understand if that's not good enough."

Mick remained silent, clearly debating with

himself. Eventually he said, "I suppose I should be grateful that I didn't scare you off altogether."

"No, if anything, meeting your family convinced me of the kind of values I can expect to find in Chesapeake Shores. It made me want to give this a try," Aidan said. "I was an only child, so today has been a real revelation."

"You're close to your parents?"

"It was just my mom and me, and she died last summer."

Mick's expression reflected real dismay. "I'm so sorry to hear that. Well, you come here and you can consider us family," he said generously. "There's always room for one more. You ask Ma about that. Next thing you know, she'll be dropping off food every time you turn around to make sure you're eating properly."

Aidan chuckled. "I wouldn't say no to that. The meal was the best I've had in a long while."

"You get a craving, you can get the same thing anytime at O'Brien's, the pub on Shore Road. My nephew Luke owns that, but Ma has trained his chef. It's a real friendly place, like a home away from home."

"I'll keep that in mind."

"How soon can you start?" Mick asked returning to business. "It might be good to get y[...] back here and in place before the end of the sch[...] year, so you'll have time to assess your player[...]

"I was thinking the same thing, if that suits [...]

I know sometimes contracts start in August, though."

"They do, but don't you worry about that. I'll take care of it. We'll set up something separate for these last couple of months of this school year. Now, let's talk about getting you settled in town. There's still some daylight left. How would you like to take a look at those houses I mentioned the other day?" Mick asked eagerly.

"I think an apartment might be better, given the terms of our deal," Aidan said. "I thought I spotted a for-rent sign on one of those places above the shops on Main Street."

"Renting is the same as throwing money down the drain," Mick objected.

"Or into your pocket," his brother Jeff commented dryly as he joined them. He turned to Aidan and explained, "Mick and I split the income on those rentals."

"Which is why I'm telling him he should buy," Mick argued. "You and I are doing just fine. We don't need his rent money. He'll have something to show for those monthly payments, if he makes them on a nice house."

Aidan had a hunch the bickering was as much of a habit as these Sunday dinners. He knew it when Nell marched over and stood between her two towering sons.

"Enough!" she said sternly, winking at Aidan. 'I'm sure the man knows what's best for him. If

you're so sure he's wrong, give him a month-to-month lease in case he decides later he wants to buy a home. Come to think of it, you could put that rent money in escrow toward his down payment."

Aidan regarded her with astonishment. "That's a very generous idea, but it's not necessary."

Mick's expression, though, turned thoughtful. "Ma's right. We could do that. It would give you this year you're so dead set on to look around for a house and have money in the bank when you're ready to buy. No need to make a snap decision. Jeff, you okay with that?"

Jeff laughed. "If Ma's starting to make our business deals, it's going to cost us money, but I'm not going to be the one to argue with her."

"Then it's settled," Mick said happily, shaking Aidan's hand. "I'll meet you in Rob's office first thing tomorrow and we'll hammer out all the details, then we can go by the real estate office and sign that rental agreement." He glanced at his brother. "You'll have Susie make the appropriate changes about that escrow business?"

"Of course," Jeff said. He turned to Aidan. "And just so you know, my wife teaches PE at the school and coaches women's soccer. Jo couldn't be here today, but she wanted you to know how excited the staff is that you might be coming."

"I'll look forward to meeting her," Aidan told him, reminded yet again of how integral the

O'Briens were to this town. Liz had definitely been right about that. "I'll see you in the morning, Mick."

"Did you have a chance to speak to Thomas?" Mick asked.

"Not yet."

"Well, there's plenty of time for that," Mick said. "He's going to be eager to put you to work, too."

Aidan bit back a sigh. That was the mixed blessing in all of this, but the die was cast now. One of the lessons his mom had taught him was never to look back.

Make your choice and live with it the best way you know how, she'd said.

He recognized now that was exactly what she had done. She'd let Thomas O'Brien off the hook all those years ago and learned to live with it. If she'd had regrets, she'd never once let on to him. Now he had to do the same.

It had taken less than an hour in Rob's office to nail down the details of Aidan's contract. Though Mick had made one last pitch for a five-year commitment, Aidan had held out and Rob had backed him.

On the drive back to New York, he returned a slew of unanswered calls from his former teammate Frankie Losada, who'd been leaving messages for the past couple of days.

"What's up?" Aidan asked when the call connected.

"Well, when I first called, it was to talk you into going to the big opening-night party at a new club in SoHo. A-list all the way. I figured we'd meet some very sexy ladies. When I called again, it was to tell you that model you used to date, Donatella, was asking about you. The last five times were to try to figure out why you weren't taking my calls. It's not like you to fall off the radar."

Aidan smiled at the evidence of Frankie's never-ending quest for pretty women and a front-of-the-tabloids social life. Aidan had rarely been interested in that scene. When he had shown up, it was usually because Frankie, who protected his blind side on the field, had twisted his arm.

"I told you I was going down to Maryland to look into a coaching job."

"At some backwoods school that hasn't won a game in how long? Five years or something?" Frankie scoffed. "I thought you had to be joking."

"Not joking, Frankie. I took the job."

His friend fell silent, then said, "Man, I think you need to take Coach up on that offer to get you counseling. That knee injury did something to your head."

"I do not need counseling," Aidan said. "I need to work. I need to feel as if I'm doing something worthwhile."

"New York is chock-full of worthwhile causes," Frankie argued. "Why do you think we're up to our eyeballs in appearances when we aren't at practice or playing games? Coach is all about good deeds."

"My celebrity ended the day my career ended," Aidan reminded him. "When I'm not throwing winning touchdowns, I'm just some normal guy who used to play ball."

"Are you having some kind of pity party? Do I need to get you back out on the town, set you up with a new woman to prove you're still *the* man here in the city?"

"Look, I'm on my way back to the city to pick up my stuff. How about dinner tonight? You can see for yourself I'm perfectly rational."

"Dinner's good. Want me to give Donatella a call, invite her along?"

"Only if you want to date her," Aidan said adamantly. "I'm not interested in going down that road again."

"Up to you, man, but she is *h-o-t,* if you know what I mean."

"I always know what you mean," Aidan said, his own thoughts going to a little blonde chatterbox, who was hotter without trying than Donatella ever dreamed of being. "See you tonight. I'll call for a reservation at Luca's."

"Hot damn!" Frankie said. "I love that place. You can't move without bumping into a real babe."

"I like the food," Aidan said.

"You keep telling yourself that," Frankie said. "You might talk all noble, but you like the women just as much as I do."

There had been a time, Aidan thought, when that had been true, right up until he'd realized how shallow many of them were. Not a one could hold a candle to Liz. Her presence in Chesapeake Shores was like a huge signing bonus, though he had a hunch he'd have to work awfully hard to earn her affection. And with his plan to stick around for only a year, maybe it would be best if he didn't even try.

Two weeks later, Aidan had moved his belongings into a one-bedroom apartment overlooking Main Street. It had not escaped his notice that Pet Style was just downstairs, assuring routine encounters with Liz, who'd proven to be as disconcerting and intuitive as she was beautiful.

Now, on his second morning after settling in, he was standing by the open sliding glass doors in his living room enjoying the view across the town green and breathing in the clean fresh air. The green's open space was surrounded by blooming beds of red tulips. He glanced into the distance and spotted Liz heading his way, juggling a purse and a couple of huge boxes. As she neared, the boxes tumbled from her arms, spilling out an assortment of pet toys. She dropped her purse in a misguided attempt to grab the boxes and, when everything scattered, a mild curse crossed her lips, immediately followed by a guilty expression and a quick look around.

Aidan grinned, set down his cup of coffee, jogged down the steps out back and around the side of the building. He reached the green before she'd picked up even half the toys. He found her cell phone several feet away in the dew-dampened grass, along with a lipstick and several brightly colored pens. He gathered them up and joined her.

She gave him a startled look. "Where'd you come from?"

"Up there," he told her, gesturing toward his apartment and the open sliding doors that led to a tiny balcony.

"Oh, dear. You didn't . . ." A blush tinted her cheeks bright pink.

"Hear you?" he said innocently.

"You did, didn't you? I normally don't use that kind of language. Really. I was just exasperated with myself for trying to haul all of this on foot. I should have driven to work, but it was such a nice morning, I decided to walk. I love this time of year when the air is soft and scented with spring flowers."

Aidan continued gathering up the packages of squeaky toys and put them into the second box. "If this is store inventory, why didn't you have it delivered to the store?"

"I did, but I ran out of time to price it yesterday. This coming weekend is the first of the season. I need to have everything on display today. Chesapeake Shores is always swamped for the long Memorial Day holiday weekend. The other store owners have told me that most of their income comes in between Memorial Day and Labor Day, when we're crawling with tourists. This will be my first summer season, so I want to be sure I start off right."

"Didn't you mention that you'd opened just before Christmas?"

She nodded, then sighed. "Big mistake. I did okay over the holidays, but the winter was deadly. I should have guessed it would be, but once I made the decision to move here and open the store, I was anxious to get started. Plus, spaces on Main Street don't come along that often. When I spotted one for sale, I grabbed it." She shrugged. "No point in looking back, though. I just have to make this summer season count."

"Or?"

She regarded him blankly. "Or what?"

"Will you quit? Do something else? Move away?"

She looked taken aback by the alternatives he'd mentioned. "I can't let myself think like that. This has to work, and that's that."

"So failure's not an option?"

"Absolutely not."

He admired her determination. In an odd way, it reflected the lecture he'd given himself when he'd decided to take the coaching job. He picked up the last of the toys, then grabbed the two boxes.

"I can carry them," she protested.

"So can I. Lead the way."

After a momentary hesitation, she crossed the street and opened the door of her shop. Aidan took a quick glance around at the colorful array of everything from pet accessories to toys and some organic pet food. There was even a fancy Victorian-style doghouse, large enough for the adult Archie would become, in one corner.

"That is for a dog, right? It's not a playhouse?"

Liz tilted her head slightly and studied it with a smile on her lips. "I suppose it would work okay for a toddler, but no, it's meant for a dog. Believe it or not, it's another one of those outrageously expensive items that seem to be selling. It's a custom design by Mick's nephew Matthew. I'm sure you must have met him at Sunday dinner. He's an architect like Mick, but he started this as a fun sideline. I'm taking them on commission or he'll custom design them for people if they want one that looks just like their home or something like that."

"Good grief."

She laughed. "I know. Crazy, isn't it?"

Aidan glanced at his watch. It wasn't yet seven-thirty, surely too early for the store to be opening.

"Do you have time for a cup of coffee at Sally's?" he asked impulsively.

She seemed flustered by the question. "No," she said a little too quickly. "I mean, I do, but I usually meet Bree there around eight-thirty."

Something told him there was more to her refusal than a prior-standing commitment, but he shrugged it off. "No problem. Another time."

She seemed to be struggling with herself before finally saying, "If you're right upstairs and don't have other plans, you could join us."

"That's okay. I don't want to intrude."

"You wouldn't be intruding. Half the people who own shops around here stop in. Of course a lot of those people are O'Briens, so you'll already know them from dinner at Mick's. You'd be welcome."

"I need to get over to the high school before nine," he said. "I'm meeting with Coach Gentry and Rob Larkin to make some plans for next season. I want to do some unofficial spring training to assess the players before school's out and assign their workouts for the summer. Maybe another day. See you, Liz."

He was almost to the door when she called out. "Aidan, is it true what I heard, that you only signed on to coach for a year?"

He nodded.

"That doesn't seem to give the team much of a chance to get its act together."

So, Mick had been right. People were going to be upset by what they viewed as a lack of commitment.

"I think it's long enough for both the school and me to see if we're a good match," he replied.

"Or is it a way to hold the town up for a lot of money if they want you to stay?"

Aidan frowned at the suggestion it had anything to do with money. "Any idea what a successful pro football player makes, Liz?"

She blinked at the question. "Not really."

"Then let me reassure you, I don't need to take advantage of the town. My career may have been cut short, but I did okay and most of what I made is doing just fine in investments. I took this job because I've always wanted to coach at this level. This seemed like a great place to start."

"Then why not commit?"

He studied her closely. He sensed there was a lot more behind the question than the obvious. "Is commitment a particularly touchy subject for you, Liz?"

The direct question seemed to take her aback. "Isn't it for everyone?"

"I suppose, but this seems to matter an awful lot to you."

"I just think people should keep their promises."

"No question about it, which is why I made a commitment for the amount of time I thought made sense for me and for the school. At the end of the year, we'll both decide how it's working out." He gave her a knowing look. "Sort of like dating for a year before committing to marriage."

The blush on her cheeks told him he'd hit the nail on the head. Somebody had run out on her, leaving her particularly sensitive to the whole commitment thing.

"You're right," she said tightly. "Sorry if it seemed like I was judging you. I'll see you around. Thanks for the help just now."

For the first time since he'd met Liz, Aidan realized that she wasn't just a perpetually cheerful advocate for the joy of living in Chesapeake Shores. He recognized that there were things she was hiding, a skittishness he couldn't explain. He couldn't help wondering if her life was every bit as complicated as his. She might make his pulse race and his imagination take off in some steamy directions, but his life was unsettled enough right now without taking on her secrets, too.

"Was that Aidan I saw coming out of your shop a little while ago?" Bree asked, her curiosity in full swing.

"Yes, but you can wipe that look right off your face," Liz replied. "He saw me spill some stuff as I was crossing the green. He came down to help."

"Then the rumor's true?" Shanna O'Brien, who owned the bookstore, said. "He's taken one of the apartments upstairs?"

"I guess so," Liz said.

"Your old one," Bree told Shanna. "Much to my father's dismay. Dad wanted him to buy a home."

"Which is why the rent money is going into escrow for a house," Susie chimed in. "I drew up the paperwork myself. Dad told me it was Gram's idea and that Uncle Mick actually went along with it."

Liz looked around at these women who'd become her friends, every one of them either born an O'Brien or married to one. Only Heather, Connor O'Brien's wife and the owner of Cottage Quilts on Shore Road, was missing this morning.

"Where's Heather?" Liz asked, hoping to steer the conversation away from Aidan and her connection to him. "Come to think of it, she wasn't at Sunday dinner the last time I was there, either."

Shanna glanced at Bree. "It's not a secret, is it?"

Bree shook her head, but glanced worriedly at Susie before answering. "Morning sickness," she finally revealed. "It's apparently hit her real hard."

"Don't look at me like that when you mention morning sickness," Susie grumbled. "People in this family are going to have babies. Just because I can't doesn't mean I can't be happy for them."

Bree reached over and squeezed her hand. "But we all know how hard it's been for you waiting to hear if you and Mack will be able to adopt."

"Sure it's hard," Susie said, "but please don't tiptoe around the subject of babies and pregnancy. That just makes it worse. And, so help me, if you don't ask me to be a part of planning for the baby shower, I'll never forgive you."

A devilish grin spread across Bree's face. "Great! You're in charge. That works out perfectly."

"I guess that'll teach me to open my big mouth," Susie said with feigned dismay.

Liz laughed. "I'll help," she promised.

"We can get Jess's chef at the inn to bake those scrumptious cupcakes with mounds of buttercream frosting," Shanna suggested. She looked around the table. "That's a hint for *my* baby shower, in case you didn't recognize it."

"Of course you can have cupcakes," Susie said. "And Bree will do her magic with the flowers," she added, giving her cousin a triumphant look. "Won't you, sweetie?"

"Of course," Bree said readily.

"There you go," Susie said. "Two baby showers under control."

"Since Heather's not due for months yet, maybe we shouldn't get ahead of ourselves," Shanna cautioned.

Bree's expression sobered. "Especially after the miscarriage Heather had last year. I know she's really nervous. She and Connor want so badly to give Little Mick a baby brother or sister."

Again, a shadow of despair crept over Susie's face. "At least they have Little Mick," she said softly.

Bree swore under her breath at the unmistakable tears that threatened to overcome Susie. "I knew we shouldn't have started talking about this. Change of subject, please. Anything."

"I want to hear more about Aidan rushing to Liz's rescue this morning," Shanna said. "I'm so sorry I missed that. That man is some serious eye candy."

Liz flushed.

"He is that," Bree agreed, even as she held tightly to Susie's hand.

Susie managed a watery grin. "So, give, Liz. What's the scoop?"

"There is no scoop. We've bumped into each other a couple of times."

"And the cozy chat I saw you two having at Mick's before Sunday dinner a couple of weeks ago?" Shanna teased. "What was that about?"

Liz shot a poisonous look in Bree's direction. "That was me trying to be friendly, per the directions of an O'Brien busybody. Nothing more."

Bree chuckled. "Tell me you didn't enjoy yourself. There's not a woman here right now who wouldn't like being the center of that man's universe even for a couple of minutes."

"Then I invite you all to take your turn," Liz

responded. "Aidan's a friendly guy. I'm sure he'd love to get to know you all a little better."

"I'm thinking our husbands might object," Shanna said, then shook her head. "Nope, I'm afraid he's all yours, Liz."

"But I don't . . ." Liz began, then frowned. "Oh, what's the use? Not a one of you will believe me no matter how many times I tell you I'm not interested."

And sadly, after the way her pulse had done a happy little hop, skip and jump at the sight of him this morning, she wasn't entirely sure she believed it herself.

Aidan stood on the sidelines after school as Coach Gentry put his players through their paces. He'd included a couple of graduating seniors in the workout, explaining to Aidan that none of the younger men had yet demonstrated the sort of leadership skills needed to be the team captain.

"They've looked up to these boys for a couple of seasons now," the coach said. "You're gonna have guys who can pass, catch and block and a few decent tacklers, but they're not a cohesive unit on offense or defense." He gave Aidan an apologetic look. "I probably shouldn't be telling you this. It's likely to scare you right off."

Aidan chuckled. "Nope, it just adds to the challenge. I want any insights you can give me about their strengths and weaknesses."

"Keep an eye on Hector Santos. He has good hands and good instincts, but he's a pretty raw talent. As a freshman he didn't get much playing time, but I suspect he could be a standout. Trouble is, he's a shy kid, and it doesn't help that he's still struggling a little with English. His family's only been in this country a couple of years."

Aidan's instincts went on high alert. "Legally?"

Coach nodded. "As far as I know. I didn't ask for documentation. He's enrolled in school and that's good enough for me." He leveled a look at Aidan. "I should probably warn you, though, that if he's as good as I think and you decide to play him more, there's going to be trouble with Porter Hobbs."

"Which one is he?" Aidan asked, surveying the field.

"He's Taylor Hobbs's daddy," Coach Gentry said, gesturing toward a lanky young man, who was throwing moderately accurate passes down-field. "The boy's okay, but the father is a real piece of work."

"I'll keep that in mind," Aidan said, making a note on his cell phone about that as he had with all the other tips the coach was sharing. He'd reach his own judgments over the next three weeks before school let out, but for now Gentry's insights were helpful.

He took another look at Taylor Hobbs and spotted the serious-looking boy who'd been catching his wobbly passes talking to him. From their intense expressions, it seemed the Hobbs kid was getting advice he didn't much like.

"Any idea what that's about?" he asked the coach.

"Henry's a real good friend of Hector's, but he's also like some kind of team mediator. He gets that Taylor's the quarterback for now, so he keeps trying to give him pointers. Surprisingly, Taylor listens to him, but not without giving him some grief."

"Still, it sounds like the boy might have that leadership quality you said was lacking," Aidan suggested.

Coach Gentry nodded. "Could be. It's up to you to make that call now." He studied Aidan. "You seen enough?"

Aidan nodded.

"I'll call 'em over, then, and introduce you. You can take it from here and I'll take off."

"That's not necessary," Aidan told him.

"Yes, it is. Some of them have been listening to me for four years now, for better or mostly for worse. They need to know you're in charge from here on out. You need me for anything, though, you know where to find me. I won't be leaving town." He gave Aidan a solemn look. "I love these kids. I want to see them reach their potential. I truly believe you're the man who can make that happen."

"Thanks. I'll try not to let any of you down."

The coach blew a sharp blast on his whistle and waved the boys over. "Have a seat," he instructed, gesturing toward the bleachers. "I know you all are aware that I'm retiring. This is Aidan Mitchell. Some of you will recognize him as the rookie of the year in the NFL a couple of years back."

An enthusiastic cheer went up from the players.

"Well, you can start right now thinking of him as your new coach," Craig Gentry said. "And I expect you to show him the same respect you've always shown me. I think together you're going to turn this team into something special. Take it away, Aidan."

He stood there a moment, clearly fighting some powerful emotions before adding, "I'll be seeing you boys around. My door's always open."

He turned then and walked quickly away to a loud ovation, deliberately led by Aidan.

When silence fell, Aidan saw the young men regarding him intently. He took a deep breath, trying to figure out what to say.

"Hey, Coach," the boy who'd been working with Hobbs called out. "Don't look so terrified. It's not as if we could do any worse."

The comment was greeted by nervous laughter that broke the tension.

"Well, it's my belief that we're going to do better next year and even better the year after that," Aidan told them. "To do that, though, you're going to have to train hard, listen to what I tell you and play your hearts out."

"We can do that," the same young man said. "Can't we?"

A surprisingly emphatic roar greeted his claim. Aidan grinned. "What's your name?"

"Henry, sir."

"Have we met?"

"At Sunday dinner a couple of weeks ago at Grandpa Mick's," he said. "He's not my real grandpa, though. I'm not actually an O'Brien, but Kevin and Shanna adopted me after my real dad died."

"What position do you play, Henry?"

"When the family plays on Thanksgiving, I'm a quarterback," he replied, then grinned impishly. "Around here, though, I mostly sit on the bench."

It probably made sense given his slight build, but Aidan sensed something in him that none of the other boys had yet demonstrated, a willingness to step up and a real ability to lead.

"Well, Henry, here's the deal. I can't say for sure what these practice sessions will reveal to me about each of you or how this fall's team will shape up, but for the next few weeks until school's out, you're the team captain. How's that?"

The boy's face lit up. "Seriously?"

To Aidan's relief, no one voiced an objection. In fact, there were a surprising number of high fives from the surrounding boys, proving that his instincts, at least for the moment, were right on target.

"Okay, then, here's the plan. Starting tomorrow I want you here fifteen minutes after the final bell, ready to work your butts off. Nobody's position on the team is guaranteed. You'll each be earning the right to play next year. If you're not strong now, you will be by the end of summer. Understood? I want you eating right, working out, acing your finals and on this field every single day doing your absolute best. I'm going to set up individual meetings with each of you so I can learn more about you. I'll want your suggestions for making the team stronger. All of this may take more time than you're used to putting in, but it's mandatory."

He'd expected a few grumbles, but heard none.

"Coach?" a boy asked hesitantly. "Are you going to cut any of us? My dad will kill me if I don't stay on the team."

"Then we'll do our best to make sure you're good enough to stay on here," Aidan promised him. "But you have to do your part."

A grin spread across the boy's face. "I can do that."

"That's it for today, then," Aidan said. "I'm really looking forward to getting to know each one of you."

Henry was on his feet first. "Go, Lions!" he shouted.

Soon feet were pounding on the bleachers and the refrain echoed across the field. Aidan smiled. If that enthusiasm carried over to their play, he had a hunch he could turn these young men into a team with a fighting chance.

⇒· 4 ·⇐

Liz had just popped into the bookstore to pick up this month's book club selection when Shanna's adopted son, Henry, came bursting through the door, his face alight with excitement.

"Guess what!" he called out, tossing his backpack onto a chair and shoving his glasses up the bridge of his nose.

"Must be something good," Shanna said, grinning at him.

"Hi, Ms. March," Henry said politely, then turned back to his mom. "Coach made me captain of the team. It's mostly honorary since we're not playing right now and it could only be for a few weeks till school's out, but I'm *captain!* Can you believe it?"

"Oh, sweetie, that's wonderful!" Shanna told him. "How'd that happen?"

"I'm not sure exactly," Henry admitted. "We had a workout and then there was a team meeting with Coach Mitchell. Coach Gentry introduced him, then took off. It was kinda weird. Nobody was saying anything, so I spoke up. I made a joke, and then I got the other guys to show a little team enthusiasm, too. Maybe that impressed him. It didn't seem like all that much at the time. I just felt bad for him. He seemed kinda nervous."

Liz held back a smile at Henry's bemused expression. She couldn't be sure, though, if it was over being named team captain or recognizing nervousness in an adult, especially a football hero.

"I'm sure he appreciated what you did to break the ice," Shanna said, then added loyally, "And you deserve to be captain. You have loads of leadership abilities."

"But I'm a lousy player," Henry said candidly. "I'm fast, but my throws aren't accurate, probably because those stupid contacts still make my eyes water, so I can't see downfield. Or maybe I should start lifting weights seriously so my arm's stronger. What do you think?"

"Beyond my pay grade," Shanna said. "But I'm sure Coach Mitchell will make the most of your talents and suggest what you can do to improve on them. That's why he's here." She gave him a stern look. "Just remember one thing—"

"No steroids," Henry recited dutifully before she could finish.

Shanna laughed. "Okay, I've said it a few times before."

"About a million," Henry confirmed. "I get it.

Really. I'm not going to put my body at risk just to play a sport."

Shanna regarded him with a triumphant expression. "And that is why I love you so much. You actually listen to me."

Henry gave her an innocent look. "Aren't kids supposed to listen to their moms?"

Shanna gave him a hug. "Yes, my darling son, but not all of them do, especially once they hit their teens. As for playing sports, there are plenty of healthy ways to get stronger. Ask Coach Mitchell."

"I will," Henry agreed, his expression turning serious. "I thought I was probably wasting my time playing football, but maybe not. I guess it's worth at least trying to make the team again. It's actually fun, when we aren't getting trounced." He sighed. "Not that *that* happens often."

Liz took her package from the counter, then paused to give Henry a kiss on the cheek that had him blushing.

"Congratulations!" she told him.

Back in her own shop, she straightened up and checked end-of-the-day receipts as she watched for Aidan to come home. Oh, she wasn't admitting, not even to herself, that over just two short days, she'd figured out his schedule, but the truth was she'd all but memorized the time of day when he took off in the morning and the time when he generally returned. Those quick glimpses had to satisfy her, though, because she was not—absolutely not—going to pursue him or open her heart to him.

Today, however, the second she saw him crossing the town green, she opened the door and waited to catch his eye, then beckoned him over. There was one thing she needed to say.

"You did a very good thing today," she told him, trying not to gape at the way his T-shirt stretched across his chest or the way his worn jeans hugged his long legs.

He looked surprised by the compliment. "What did I do?"

She forced her attention back to his face. "You made a young man start to believe in himself. Or maybe I should say in his athletic promise."

"I did that? In one very brief team meeting? Who are you talking about?"

"Henry. I happened to be next door when he came in after school and told Shanna about being named team captain. Even if it's only a token title just for now, you made that boy's day. He knows he's smart, but sports are still new to him. He was never encouraged to play anything before he came to live with Shanna and Kevin. If you're even half as good at motivating the other players, your team will win the state title next year."

Aidan laughed. "I think it's way too soon to get carried away. Having a good leader as captain is a long way from putting a strong team on the field."

"Why did you choose him?" she asked curiously, then frowned. "It's not because he's Mick's grandson, is it?"

"Absolutely not. I made the decision before I even realized that. He took some initiative at the team meeting that spoke well of his leadership abilities. The other boys responded well to what he said. I made a snap decision, though I did make it clear the title could be temporary." He frowned. "He does understand that, right?"

"No question about it," Liz confirmed. "Still, Henry's a pretty serious kid who's had some tough breaks in his life. You gave him a real boost in confidence today. Seems to me that's the mark of a great coach, not that I have a lot of experience determining what it takes to be an effective coach."

"Thanks for saying that," Aidan said. "I know I understand a lot about playing football and I have a whole notebook filled with plays and game strategy, but working with boys this age is new to me. For all their bravado, their egos are still pretty fragile. I'm not so old that I can't remember what that was like. I don't want to do anything to shatter their confidence and self-esteem. I think that's as much a part of my job as turning them into decent players."

"Well, I just wanted to tell you the impact you had on one boy today," Liz said, backing away. "Have a good evening, Aidan."

She turned to go inside her shop to finish closing up and was surprised when he followed her.

"How was your day?" he asked, glancing around. "I see you got those toys on display. Are you going to be ready for the flood of tourists by Friday?"

Liz sighed. "I hope so, but there's no way of telling. I've never run a business like this before."

"You mean one that depends on seasonal tourism?"

She smiled sheepishly. "I mean any business. I used to teach elementary school, which is one reason I know a little bit about motivating kids."

Aidan looked surprised. "Boy, when you make a change, you do it in a big way. What made you decide to open a pet store?"

Though she'd had to come up with an answer for a lot of people over the past few months, she still took a moment to frame one for Aidan. "When I decided I wanted to make a fresh start, I decided to embrace it wholeheartedly."

"Didn't you enjoy teaching?"

"I loved it, but if I'd just changed cities, it wouldn't have felt like that much of a change." She didn't want to mention that being around young children would have been a stark reminder of the family she'd longed to have, the one she'd anticipated being just around the corner, only to discover that it wasn't in her husband's plans at all.

"I grew up with pets and I thought it would be fun to have a store, so I could meet new people all the time. I deliberately chose Chesapeake Shores because it's a tourist town, yet it's small enough to get to know your neighbors well."

"Any regrets?"

She laughed. "At the end of almost every month all winter when I was trying to balance the books," she admitted. "But I'm eager for summer and the onslaught of customers everyone has been promising me. The other business owners have provided a real support system, so I'm far from discouraged. I came here for a change and a challenge. So far I haven't been disappointed."

"Are you always this upbeat and optimistic?"

She frowned at the question. "You say that as if it's a bad thing."

"Not at all. I'm a big believer in choosing to look at the bright side, but not everyone can pull that off."

"It is a choice, isn't it?" she said quietly, thinking of the weeks after her husband's death when bright spots had been few and far between. If there had been any at all, she'd chosen not to see them, deliberately wallowing in her pain.

And then a very wise friend had suggested she could decide whether to live her life mired in grief, self-pity and regrets, essentially ending her own life right along with her husband's, or whether she wanted to live as fully as possible.

She'd started making plans for the future the next day, eventually choosing a path that excited her in a way nothing else had for weeks. Perhaps even longer, if she were being entirely honest.

Aidan seemed to be studying her closely. To her shock, he reached out and touched a gentle finger to what she knew were shadows under her eyes.

"What put these there?" he asked.

Shivering a little at the tender touch, she backed away a step and forced her brightest smile. "No idea what you mean."

He gave her a skeptical look. "Seriously?"

"Hey, don't you know it's never polite to point out that a woman looks as if she hasn't slept in days?" she asked brightly. "I have about a million lists of things to do running through my head. That's not nearly as effective for getting to sleep as counting sheep."

"No, I imagine it's not," he agreed. "Maybe you need to take a quick break, get your mind off all those details for a little while. How about taking a walk around the corner to O'Brien's? I hear Nell trained the chef, so the food's bound to be good. I'm getting sick of my limited culinary skills, which tend to rely too much on frozen entrées. If I'm going to preach to my players about the right nutrition, I should practice what I preach."

She hesitated. "I really shouldn't," she protested, thinking not only of all she had to do, but that spending more time with Aidan was

definitely a bad idea. He had a way of sneaking past her defenses when she least expected it. And, the real kicker, he wasn't planning to stick around all that long.

"An hour at most," he countered. "And I'll stay and help you unpack inventory or whatever you need after we eat. I'm a stranger in Chesapeake Shores. It's probably your civic duty to see that I don't eat dinner alone."

She laughed at that, then thought of all the people who'd taken her under their wings when she'd first moved to town. There had been very few nights when she'd had to eat alone unless she'd chosen to do so.

"Okay, fine. An hour, though, and I expect you to haul all the empty boxes to the recycling center for me, so I can get them out of the back room."

"You'll just have to point me in the right direction," he agreed.

"I can certainly do that. Give me a second to wash up and grab my purse."

As they left the shop, she couldn't help saying a little prayer that Bree and Shanna were both long gone from their own businesses, because if either of them caught a glimpse of her with Aidan, she was going to face an onslaught of questions at tomorrow morning's gathering at Sally's.

Aidan thought he heard Liz groan when they walked into O'Brien's on Shore Road.

"Something wrong?" he asked, glancing around at the packed room. He noted then that Liz's gaze was locked on the bar, where several O'Briens were seated and gesturing for the two of them to come over. He grinned. "Ah, another center for town gossip, I presume?"

She sighed. "You have no idea. I should have thought of that before I agreed to come here with you."

"Liz, we're two friends and neighbors having dinner. What's the big deal?"

She gave him an incredulous look. "Two *single* friends," she pointed out. "In a pub filled with O'Briens, who have taken matchmaking to new extremes."

"Well, it seems we have no choice but to join them or cause a major stir by taking off. What's your preference?"

"We'll have to go over there," she said, clearly resigned.

When she looked as if she was bracing to face a firing squad, he put a hand on her arm to hold her back. "First, remind me of who's there."

"That's Luke behind the bar. This is his pub. He's Jeff's son, Mick's nephew. That's Susie, his sister, on the stool at the end."

"That's right. She drew up my lease, though I didn't meet her when I signed it. She's also the one who's married to Mack Franklin," Aidan recalled, then recognized the man on the neighboring stool. "And he's right next to her."

"And Megan O'Brien is next to him, which means Mick is bound to be here shortly."

Aidan chuckled. "I'm beginning to see the problem."

"I doubt it," Liz responded direly, then led the way to the bar, where Mack had vacated his stool so she could sit next to Susie.

"Interesting," Susie murmured to Liz, regarding her with a grin.

Aidan noted that Liz's cheeks flushed bright pink, but before he could mention that to her, Mack started questioning him about his meeting with the team earlier. Knowing that the ex-player had a real interest in the game and his prognosis for the team's next season, he filled him in.

A moment later, Mick appeared and slapped him enthusiastically on the back. "You surprised me today," Mick said.

"How so?"

"Making Henry captain of the team till the end of the year," Mick said.

Apparently this was the first some of the others had heard about it. Megan regarded Aidan approvingly. "I don't know a thing about football, much to the dismay of my husband and my sons, but I do know Henry. That boy was born to be a leader. I'm so glad someone had the sense to see that."

"Agreed," Mick said. His gaze narrowed. "You

did see that in him, right? It didn't have anything to do with who he is, did it?"

"I honestly had no idea who he was when I appointed him captain," Aidan said for the second time that afternoon. "He stepped in, showed some initiative and spirit, and I decided on the spot to recognize that. I wanted to send a message to all the boys that they'll be rewarded for their actions on and off the field." He shrugged. "Punished, too, for that matter, but we didn't get into that."

Mick nodded. "I like that. I know Kevin and Shanna appreciate it, too. Kevin called me right before I came over here to tell me how excited Henry is. Do you know anything about how he came to live with them?"

Aidan shook his head.

"Shanna was married to the boy's dad. Henry adored her, but when she and his father divorced, she was forbidden from having any contact with Henry. It about broke that woman's heart and left a little boy with no one he could count on except a couple of strict grandparents who didn't know what to do with him."

Aidan frowned. "What about his father?"

"He had a serious problem with alcohol. It tore up his liver. After Shanna moved here and got together with Kevin, Henry's grandparents saw that Henry's best chance for a normal life was with Shanna and Kevin. They kept him in touch with his biological daddy, but when he was gone, they adopted Henry. He's blossomed since he's been with them. We're all real proud of him and glad to count him as an O'Brien."

The story reaffirmed what Aidan had already guessed, that the O'Briens were good people whose lives centered around family, no matter how that family might have been cobbled together. Once more he had to wonder if there would have been room in their hearts for him if only his mother had paved the way years ago by telling Thomas O'Brien he had a son.

Aidan was still thinking about his connection to Thomas O'Brien the next day when Coach Gentry pulled him aside before that afternoon's practice session.

"Rob mentioned to you about the after-school club you'll be sponsoring next year, right?"

"The one that works with the bay preservation foundation," Aidan said.

"That's the one. I know you have practice with the team this afternoon, but the club's meeting after school. It's the last meeting of the year. Thomas O'Brien's going to be speaking to the students to thank them for their work. I thought you might like to stop in and say hello. Any chance you could get there by four? That's when we'll be winding down. Thomas has arranged for refreshments to be sent over from the inn. You won't want to miss those."

Aidan knew there was little to be gained by postponing the inevitable. He had to be in the same room with Thomas at some point. Just like that Sunday dinner at Mick's, it might be best to be surrounded by other people.

"I'll do my best to make it," he promised the coach. "It may just be for a couple of minutes, though. I don't want to cut practice short and set a bad precedent. The team needs to take these sessions seriously, even if the season is months away."

"Understood."

Though the meeting was on Aidan's mind the rest of the day, he managed to push it aside long enough to get the team started on a series of drills. He asked Henry and another PE teacher, who'd volunteered to help out, to record the results while he ran over to the school to drop in on the end-of-season party.

Thomas had just wrapped up his speech and, while a table was set up with refreshments, the kids were all gathered around him asking questions, clearly inspired by whatever he'd said to them before Aidan's arrival. With their serious expressions and earnest questions, it seemed they thought of him as a sort of rock star of the environmental world.

Aidan hung back, watching Thomas and listening to him as he interacted with the students. He wasn't even the tiniest bit condescending, but rather took their questions seriously and answered them thoughtfully. When he caught sight of Aidan, he sent them off toward the refreshment table, then made his way over to Aidan. He held out his hand.

"I hear you're taking over with this gang next fall," he said, shaking Aidan's hand with a firm grip. "It's an incredible group. They've done a good job this year."

"I may be new to the area, but I already understand what a great cause it is," Aidan said. "I'll do my best to encourage the kids to continue doing whatever they can to help."

"Awareness is always the first step with something like this. People tend to be careless with our resources until they understand the consequences. Then most people are more than willing to do their part to protect them."

Aidan had the feeling Thomas was just warming up, so he was grateful to have a team outside waiting for his return. "I'm going to want to hear a lot more about this and what activities you'd like us to take on next fall, but I've got a bunch of players on the field doing drills. I need to get back to check on them. I just wanted to say hello and let you know you can count on me."

"I'll do that," Thomas said. "Maybe we can get together a few times over the summer to brainstorm."

"Sure," Aidan replied, though the prospect filled

him with a sense of dread. Suddenly it felt as if everything was moving too quickly. He'd wanted to find his father, maybe even see him from time to time, but this was already more intense than he'd envisioned.

Of course, he thought with a sigh, maybe that was because of the huge secret that stood between them. He knew exactly who Thomas was, but the older man knew him only as the new football coach and sponsor of an after-school club. Once the truth was out and that dynamic changed, who knew what might happen?

Liz opened the shop's doors on the Friday morning of Memorial Day weekend not knowing what to expect. There was a familiar trickle of regular locals who stopped by before noon, mostly to pick up the organic pet food she stocked. Cordelia was among them.

Liz smiled at the older woman, who was wearing a flowered print dress and bright yellow sneakers. "You look very perky and springlike today," she told her. "How are you, and how is Fluffy?"

"That cat does something every day to put a smile on my face," Cordelia told her, then confided, "But I do miss Archie. I know he was too much for me, but he's such a special dog. I named him for my late husband. Did I tell you that?"

"No, you hadn't mentioned it," Liz said. "Would you like me to bring him by to visit?"

Cordelia's face lit up. "Would you? Please do, if it's not a bother. We always had Aussies, Archie and me. I know that's why the grandchildren chose him, but none of us thought about how much energy it takes to keep up with one, especially a puppy. Are you going to keep him?"

"I've been looking around for a good home, but so far no one's stepped up."

"And he's growing on you, isn't he?" Cordelia said knowingly. "I suspected that would happen or at least I was hoping it would, so he'd stay close by."

"Please don't count on it, Cordelia. I'm not sure I can keep a third dog," Liz lamented.

Cordelia immediately looked disappointed. "I would so hate it if he moved away," she said with a sigh, then forced a smile. "I suppose placing him with the right family matters more than whether I get to spend a little time with him occasionally."

Seeing the older woman's disappointment, Liz knew right then that Archie wasn't going anywhere. "We'll take it one day at a time. Unless the perfect owner comes along, he'll stay with me."

Cordelia gave her a sly look. "Someone told me they saw him with that handsome young man, the new high school football coach. They said Archie seemed to take a real shine to him."

Liz laughed. "He did, but Aidan can't take on a dog right now."

A speculative expression crossed Cordelia's face. "I had a conversation with Nell after church the other day. Word is that you might have taken a shine to the same man. Any truth to that?"

Liz felt heat climbing into her cheeks. "Cordelia Ames, please tell me you are not going to start matchmaking, too," she chided. "Believe me, there are more than enough meddlers in this town already."

Cordelia regarded her with an unrepentant look. "It's hard to say how many nudges it might take before people do what they've been wanting to do all along."

Liz was about to protest that she didn't need any nudges, at least not in Aidan's direction, but several chattering customers came into the store. She clamped her mouth shut. Arguing with a customer, no matter the topic, couldn't be good for business.

Thankfully, Cordelia seized on their arrival to give Liz a bright smile. "You have a good weekend, you hear. And I'll look forward to a visit with you and Archie sometime after the holiday when you have the time."

Liz shook her head as Cordelia left the store, clearly satisfied that her mission was complete. It was hard to say, though, if her real mission had been arranging that visit with her former pet, assuring that Archie stayed with Liz permanently or poking her nose into Liz's business and giving her a less than subtle shove in Aidan's direction. No matter which, Liz feared it was going to take all her concentration not to fall into the sneaky woman's trap.

Come to think of it, with Liz already promising to keep the dog and to take him by for a visit, Cordelia was batting an impressive two for three.

5

After his Saturday morning run, Aidan showered, then sat on his balcony with a cup of coffee, enjoying the soft morning air. It struck him as a picture-perfect start to the holiday weekend. To lend credence to his assessment, he noted that Main Street and Shore Road were both crowded with shoppers and with locals pausing literally in the middle of the street to catch up, while drivers waited more or less patiently.

There wasn't a parking space to be had, which made him grateful that most places he might want to go were within walking distance. Customers had been leaving Pet Style and the other stores laden down with packages. He counted that as a good sign for Liz's business. The fact that he was suddenly interested in how the weather might impact Pet Style's sales was a little too telling for his comfort.

At one o'clock, tired of his own company, he went downstairs to Sally's to grab a sandwich for lunch, but the café, too, was jammed. Sally signaled to him that a booth in back was about to open up, then led the way there even before the dishes could be cleared.

"I'll get back to you in a few minutes. Anything I can bring you to drink when I come?" she asked, her expression harried.

"Iced tea would be great," he said.

"Sweetened?"

Aidan had forgotten that most people around here preferred it that way. "Unsweetened, if you have it."

"Of course we do," she said. "Hang in here. I'll get back to you when I can. Haven't had a day like this in months, so I'm not complaining."

"Take your time," Aidan told her. "I'm in no hurry."

When she finally made her way back to him, she dropped down wearily on the seat opposite him. "Two minutes off my feet, that's all I ask."

He grinned. "Are you suggesting I should take my time ordering, maybe discuss the specials?"

"Smart man," she said approvingly. "I recommend you order the crab cake sandwich with coleslaw and fries before we run out, but could you please ponder that for a few minutes?"

He laughed. "You got it."

She studied him for a minute, then asked slyly, "Have you dropped in on Liz today?"

The question probably should have surprised him, but he'd already grown used to how fast news of relationships—real or perceived—rocketed through town. "No, why? I imagine she's as swamped as you are."

"Exactly. And since she's never been through a holiday crush before, I imagine she didn't think to bring her lunch. How about I fix her one of those crab cake sandwiches, too, and you can take it by when you leave. I'm sure she'd appreciate it."

Aidan nodded at once, probably a little too eagerly if the satisfied expression on Sally's face was anything to go by. "I can definitely do that," he responded.

Sally chuckled, her expression smug. "Thought you might grab the chance. I had to see for myself if the rumors were true."

"What rumors are those?" he asked, though it didn't take a genius to figure it out.

She gave him a pitying look as she stood up. "Oh, please. Don't try that innocent act on me. I've been around too long. I'll get right on those specials. You can take your order next door while you're at it and vacate this booth so I can cram in more customers—how's that?"

"Sounds like a plan," Aidan said. "I'll wait for you at the register."

She patted him on the shoulder. "Good boy. I like a man who can take a hint."

Maybe what she really liked, Aidan thought as he headed to the register, was a man so easily swayed into going along with her devious plans. He was beginning to see what Liz had been trying to tell him about Chesapeake Shores being a haven for well-meaning matchmakers. For the moment, though, that suited him just fine. Sally had just shoved him in a direction he'd been wanting to go all day without being willing to admit it.

Liz was trying valiantly to keep her cool as she rang up sales, answered questions and tried to guide people toward merchandise. She'd always considered herself to be decent at multitasking. With a roomful of elementary school students, she hadn't had much choice. They, however, could be ordered into a time-out when she started to feel overwhelmed. The customers and the unruly wave of questions just kept coming. She had no choice but to keep smiling and cope.

Not that she wasn't grateful. Today was going exactly as she'd hoped it might. She'd just had no idea how exhausting success might feel a few hours into it. Her cheeks actually ached from keeping that smile in place.

To top it off, she was starving. She hadn't thought to bring so much as an apple with her today. Until now, she'd always had time to at least call in an order to Sally's, then run over to pick it up. Not that she would have had two seconds to eat something today, unless it could be consumed through a straw while she was ringing up sales and putting things into uncooperative plastic bags that seemed deliberately impossible to open. She barely had time to look up and make eye contact with the customers.

"Did you find everything?" she asked automatically, even as she handed off two bags to the previous customer.

"I was looking for the owner," a male voice announced.

Her head snapped up. "Aidan! What are you doing here?"

He held up a bag. "Sally thought you might be hungry. Judging from the chaos in here, I'm guessing she nailed it."

"You have no idea," she said, eyeing the bag with longing. "What's in there?"

"A crab cake sandwich and coleslaw. French fries, too. I've been here a few minutes, but it should still be warm."

She closed her eyes and imagined it. Chunks of lump crabmeat seasoned perfectly and lightly fried with creamy coleslaw on top. Crispy french fries. She nearly moaned with pleasure.

"It sounds heavenly," she murmured.

"I can attest to that. I slipped into your back

room and took a couple of bites of mine, hoping the crowd out here might thin out any minute, but it seems pretty steady."

"It has been all day," she said wearily, then grinned. "It's exhausting, but absolutely wonderful, even better than I expected."

"How about this? I'll take over at the register long enough for you to go in back and eat something. I left an iced tea back there for you, too. Sweet with lemon. Sally said that's how you like it."

She eyed the bag with real regret. "It is, but I can't possibly take a break."

He lifted a brow. "Are you worried I'll take off with your cash?"

"Of course not. But you don't know the system."

"Is everything priced?"

"Of course."

"And it has a bar code?"

"Sure."

"And the register calculates the sales tax?"

Liz nodded.

"Then go. If I run into a problem, I'll come and get you."

Still she fretted. "Can you do a credit card sale?"

"I earned my spending money for college by working at Bloomingdale's during the holidays." He glanced around the store. As busy as it was, it hardly qualified as a holiday madhouse in New York. "I think I can handle this."

Before Liz could think about what she was doing, she put her hands on either side of his face and kissed him soundly. "You're an angel sent from heaven." The impulsive gesture was a shock to her system, but she didn't have time to linger over the sensation. She could do that just before bedtime.

Aidan chuckled. "There are some who'd dispute that," he said, then handed her the bag with her lunch. "Enjoy your break. I promise not to give away the store."

Since there were several customers in line, she left him to it and hurried into the tiny back room, kicked off her shoes and sat down with a sigh of relief.

Even as she noted that Aidan had come nowhere close to finishing his own meal, she opened her bag, took out a French fry, then took a long sip of the ice-cold tea. Nothing she'd ever eaten had tasted better, at least until she took her first bite of the sandwich.

"Oh, sweet heaven," she murmured. Aidan might not be an angel, but he'd surely been sent by one. Sally couldn't have chosen a better meal to send over. Liz would have to thank her profusely tomorrow morning.

As much as she wanted to stay off her feet and savor the delicious food, she hurried through it, washed her hands and headed back to the front of the still-packed store. Aidan was handling sales with an easy charm that had those in line laughing as they waited patiently for their turns.

As Liz was heading to the register to relieve Aidan, a woman stopped her to ask about the custom doghouses. She pulled a picture of a Great Dane from her purse along with a picture of her sprawling home.

"Do you think the designer could do something like this for my Petunia?" she asked Liz hopefully.

Petunia? Liz thought, barely stifling a laugh. "I'm sure he could. Why don't I give Matthew the pictures and your number and ask him to give you a call? You can work out the details directly with him."

"Will you still get a commission if I do that?" she asked worriedly. "I like to support small businesses whenever I can."

"Matthew and I will work that out," Liz promised her, appreciative of her thoughtfulness. She jotted down the woman's name and phone number to pass along to Matthew. "Is there anything else I can help you with?"

The woman beamed. "Not a thing. That nice young man has already rung up my purchases, but he said I needed to speak to you about the custom doghouse." She shook her head. "I don't know how he did it, but I'm leaving here with at least three things I'm sure I didn't intend to buy. You have a wonderful selection. You can count on me being a regular. I'm afraid I pamper Petunia outrageously. That dog is like a child to me."

As the woman left, a satisfied expression on her face, Liz glanced in Aidan's direction. He was smiling at a group of women in a way that could have gotten anyone—or at least any female over the age of consent—to buy just about anything. Maybe he was more than an angel. Perhaps he was a secret weapon she ought to consider using on a much more regular basis.

But, she told herself sternly, only as long as she could find some way to inoculate herself against all that charm that seemed to come so naturally. Her husband had been a lot like that, charming everyone he met. She'd learned way too late to distrust that, but it was a lesson she wasn't likely to forget.

"How was lunch?" Aidan asked when Liz eventually made her way back to the front of the store.

"Delicious," she said. "Thank you. And thanks for the break, too. I think I can handle things from now on out. You should go back and finish your own lunch before it's ice-cold."

"I had plenty," he insisted. "Do you have help coming in?"

She shook her head. "There's a high school girl who comes in after school a few days a week, but her family was going away for the weekend."

Aidan frowned. "It wasn't very responsible of her to bail on you on a holiday weekend."

Liz shrugged. "I didn't think it was a big deal at the time. I know better now. Tess is hoping for more hours this summer and now I can safely tell her she'll get them."

"How about I hang around, at least until the crowd slows down. You can work your magic answering questions and I can stay up here at the register."

"I can't ask you to do that," she protested.

"You didn't ask. It's not as if I have other pressing things to do. I've been enjoying the chance to talk to people." Unsaid was that he liked watching her in action, too. She had a quiet sales manner that seemed to make people instinctively trust her. And her enthusiasm for the merchandise was plain. It was a potent combination that excited people, but assured they never felt pressured.

Glancing around at the number of people still milling about, she seemed to reach a conclusion. "If you're sure you don't mind, I'd be grateful for the help, but only until things quiet down."

"Agreed," he said at once. "Now go. There's someone else looking longingly at that doghouse. I think you can sell another one."

Liz immediately scurried off in that direction, leaving him to ring up sales and chat with the tourists, who seemed to have come from all over the region. Many were staying at The Inn at Eagle Point and raving about the food. Others were asking for tips on other shops and restaurants.

"I'm new to town, but I've heard good things about Brady's seafood," he told them. "And I can testify firsthand that O'Brien's has a terrific, authentic Irish pub menu. If you're looking for something simple, like a burger or a crab cake sandwich, Sally's right up the block is terrific. It's very popular with all the locals."

He was amused to realize he was starting to sound like a spokesman for the Chamber of Commerce. Not that he was likely to do this on a regular basis, but he really did need to get around more if he was going to be passing out recommendations.

As that tourist left, he started ringing up yet another sale, when he realized the woman was studying him intently.

"You're the new football coach, aren't you?" she said.

"Aidan Mitchell," he confirmed.

"I'm Pamela Hobbs. My son is the team quarterback. He'll be a senior next year, so his father and I are expecting great things from him."

"I'm still getting to know the players," Aidan told her, wise enough to word his response carefully. "We're a long way from settling how next fall's team will shape up, but Coach Gentry definitely told me about your son. I'm looking forward to seeing him in action. I hope to get in a couple of scrimmages before school's out."

She frowned at his response. "Surely you're not considering making any changes to the roster."

Aidan saw the minefield. "It's much too early to say."

She looked as if she was about to argue, but instead she gave a tug to her tight, scoop-neck T-shirt to display even more cleavage before fluffing her perfectly highlighted chestnut hair. Holding his gaze, she suggested, "Perhaps we could have a drink and discuss this further."

He bit back a smile. "Sorry. As you can see, I'm busy."

She frowned at that. "You're not working here, are you?"

"I'm helping out a friend."

"Well, I'm sure she won't mind if you take care of something that is related to your job as the coach."

"She might not, but I do. I made a commitment. Besides, any decisions I make about next year's team will be based on what I see on the field."

She drew herself up, her expression hardening. "Then I imagine my husband will want to have a chat with you Tuesday morning."

Aidan nodded, keeping his expression pleasant. "I'll look forward to it."

As much as he didn't want to get into it with any player's father, the prospect of tangling with a mother who was so obviously on the prowl was a whole lot less appealing.

Even though Pet Style was supposed to close at six, it was after seven by the time the last customer left. Liz's feet ached and she was even more exhausted by having to keep a smile plastered on her face, especially with a couple of customers who'd been rude and demanding. She'd also been out of sorts since she'd noticed Pamela Hobbs, a notorious flirt, flaunting her ample chest in Aidan's face.

"I noticed you made a conquest earlier," she said in what she hoped was her most casual, disinterested tone as she turned the lock on the door and put the closed sign in the window.

Aidan glanced up curiously from the display he'd started straightening. "What are you talking about?"

"Pamela Hobbs," she said. "I should probably warn you, though, that she's married, but has a reputation for not paying much attention to that fact."

A slow grin spread across Aidan's face. "Thanks for the heads-up, but I knew exactly who she was and what she was after, which is why I turned down her invitation to leave here and go out for a drink." He gave her a wink. "Thanks for giving me the perfect excuse."

Liz wasn't sure if she was more impressed by

his intuitiveness or appalled by Pamela's lack of discretion. "Does that happen a lot?" she asked. "Women coming on to you?"

"When I played pro football, it happened all the time," he said in a way that suggested he was more bewildered than pleased by it. "Since I've been coaching less than a week, this is a first that a mom has tried to assure her son's spot on the team by offering herself up as an incentive." He held her gaze. "And just so you know, I wouldn't have been interested even if I hadn't known she was married. She's not my type."

Liz couldn't seem to keep herself from asking, "What is your type?"

"I'll let you know when I figure it out, but definitely someone a whole lot less obvious than Pamela Hobbs."

"You've never been in a serious relationship?"

"Define *serious*."

"One you thought might lead to marriage," she said at once.

He shook his head. "I've had a couple of long-term relationships, but in college I was too focused on making it into the National Football League. Once I was drafted, I was determined to put all my energy into getting better. Anything too serious would have been a distraction. The women I knew got tired of waiting around."

"You don't sound terribly distraught over that," she noted.

"Which tells me I wasn't that serious about any of them," he said. "I was certainly sad to end things with a couple of them, but I wasn't ready to make the commitment they wanted." He shrugged. "Then my mom got sick, I had a career-ending injury and I didn't have a lot of time to think about anything else."

"Is your mother better now?"

A deep sadness darkened his eyes as he shook his head. "She lost her battle with cancer last summer."

"Oh, Aidan, I'm so sorry."

"Me, too."

"And your father?"

He seemed to still at the question. Avoiding her gaze, he shrugged. "Never knew him. And before you ask, there were no siblings."

Liz couldn't imagine what that was like. She might not have the perfect family, but she'd grown up with two loving parents and a couple of sisters who could get on her last nerve, but whom she adored. None of them had understood it when she'd chosen to move away from Charlotte, North Carolina. They'd wanted her to stay close, where they could support her, but what they'd seen as genuine caring to her had felt a lot like smothering. She'd needed to make a clean break to start over.

She realized Aidan was watching her intently.

"Where'd you go just then?" he asked. "You looked sad."

"I was just trying to imagine what your life must have been like with only your mom around," she said.

He laughed. "If you'd ever met my mom, you wouldn't look so distraught. She was amazing. She worked hard and she turned every day into an adventure. She loved New York, so whenever she was off we took advantage of all the city has to offer. We spent hours at the Museum of Natural History or the Botanical Garden or just walking through Central Park with her pointing out every tree and flower until I'd memorized their Latin names."

"Sounds as if she would have loved Chesapeake Shores and the way people here care about the environment. I'll bet she and Thomas O'Brien would have been kindred spirits."

Aidan looked startled by the comment, but he nodded slowly. "You're absolutely right," he said, that faraway expression back in his eyes. "She would have loved it here."

Not for the first time, Liz got the impression that there were things Aidan wasn't revealing, some part of the story of his past that he was keeping to himself. Still, it wasn't in her nature to pry, especially not when whatever it was seemed to make him so sad. She understood all too well that there were things people needed to keep private. She had plenty of demons of her own carefully locked away.

"Not to change the subject," she said lightly. "But I am absolutely starving yet again, and you must be, too, since you never did have time to finish your lunch. I need to get home to let the dogs out. If you're interested, I could order a pizza. I owe you more than that for the way you pitched in today, but I'm not sure I can muster up the energy to cook or go out. I just want to take a shower, kick back and be off my feet."

"A pizza sounds fantastic," Aidan agreed at once. "Why don't you head home to deal with the dogs and I'll pick it up? Anything to drink?"

"Beer if you want it. I only have tea and diet soda in the house, but I'm good with that."

"Either one suits me, too," Aidan said. "I may not be in training, but I mostly steer clear of alcohol except at a summer barbecue or on the occasional night hanging out with the guys."

Liz thought of Shanna's remark to Henry about good player nutrition. "That reminds me. Do you plan on getting into the whole diet and exercise thing with the players?"

"Of course. Why?"

"Henry mentioned something about needing to get stronger. Shanna's apparently a little freaked that he might turn to steroids, even though Henry says he's gotten the message about how bad those are."

"My players won't go near steroids," Aidan said flatly. "I'll make sure of that. Tell Shanna she doesn't have anything to worry about. I'll start hammering that message home first thing at Tuesday's practice. I hope to work with each player next week and come up with an individualized training plan for the summer. And just because school's out doesn't mean I won't be following up to make sure they stay on track."

Liz regarded him with approval. "I was right," she said with satisfaction.

"About what?"

"The kind of coach you're going to be. It's great that you care so much. The high school is very lucky to have you."

"We'll see if the players agree once I start getting serious about their workouts," he said.

"I think they're going to take to it like ducks to water," she said at once. "Those boys want so badly to prove themselves and start winning. Nothing against Coach Gentry. He's a great guy, but he didn't have what it took to motivate them or to teach them what it would take to improve."

"And you think I do?"

"I know it," she said with confidence.

She also thought he had what it took to heal her heart, if only she weren't so terrified that he could just as easily break it.

❄· 6 ·❄

Aidan was halfway up the walkway to Liz's when she opened the front door. Archie bounded out with an ecstatic bark, paused to pick up a tennis ball, then almost knocked Aidan to the ground in his exuberance.

"Is it me or the pizza he's excited about?" he called out to Liz, who stood where she was, laughing and leaving him to extricate himself from the situation.

"Let's just say I've never seen him get that worked up over pizza before, and it's a staple around here," she said. "Archie, behave! Get back here."

Instead of obeying, Archie sat down in the middle of the sidewalk blocking Aidan's way, dropped a tennis ball at his feet and looked up at him with adoring eyes. Despite himself, Aidan couldn't help chuckling.

"If you want me to play with you, you have to let me inside so I can put dinner down," he scolded.

The dog's response was to pick up the ball, then drop it again in an attempt to get his own message across.

Aidan cast a helpless look in Liz's direction. "I

think we're at a stalemate. Can you grab this pizza?"

She came out wearing shorts and a tank top that almost caused him to swallow his tongue. With her feet bare, he couldn't help noticing that her toenails were painted a pale pink that reminded him of seashells. Though her hair had been pulled back neatly all day, tonight she'd swept it up on her head in a careless knot that left damp blond tendrils framing her face. She looked as if the weight of the day had been washed away by a quick shower.

"You look . . ." Words failed him.

"Clean?" she suggested.

He laughed. "Way better than that."

"I needed to get out of those clothes and into something comfortable," she said. "A shower helped, too. I was feeling pretty grungy."

"You looked great before, but you look even better now. Being relaxed suits you."

"Doesn't it suit everyone?" she replied, reaching for the pizza. "You have five minutes with Archie or I can't promise there will be any of this left by the time you get inside."

Aidan dragged his attention away from her fresh-scrubbed face and glossy lips long enough to say, "Did you hear that, Archie? Five minutes and not one second longer. I'm not giving up dinner with a pretty woman to enter-tain you."

Woof! the dog responded, head tilted as if he understood completely.

"I'm telling you, he has a real connection to you," Liz said. "Are you sure you don't want a dog?"

"Have you seen that apartment upstairs from your shop? It's barely big enough for me to turn around, much less have Archie underfoot."

"I suppose I can't argue with that," she said with obvious regret. "I certainly wouldn't want him to be cooped up in a small space all day. See you inside in a couple of minutes. Tea or soda? I'll pour that before you come in."

"Tea's good," he said. "Unsweetened, though."

She shook her head. "You Northerners don't know what you're missing."

Aidan watched her walk up the porch steps, his gaze pretty much glued to her shapely bottom in those shorts. There was a good chance the woman was going to make him a little crazy if he wasn't careful, especially since she'd made it pretty clear she wasn't interested in dating anyone right now. He wasn't sure he believed her, but he had little choice but to take her at her word and act accordingly.

Friendly banter and no sudden moves, he warned himself, then turned his attention to the dog, which was much safer territory.

Liz put the pizza and drinks out on the kitchen table, then stood at the dining room window, where she could watch Aidan and Archie in the yard. The dog ran in excited circles waiting for Aidan to toss that grungy tennis ball again and again. More times than not, Archie managed to catch it before it ever hit the ground.

"Okay, that's it," Aidan said at last. "It's time for a rest."

Liz scurried away from the window and back to the kitchen as she heard Aidan coming up the steps. He tapped on the screen door, then opened it. Archie raced ahead of him into the kitchen. The dog went straight to his water bowl and began lapping it up, splashing more of the water onto the floor than he could possibly have drunk.

"Seems to me it's too bad Archie isn't human," she commented, glancing up at Aidan as he washed his hands at the sink.

"Oh?"

"He was doing a darn fine job of catching your passes in midair."

Aidan glanced at her. "You were watching?"

"I caught a glimpse," she claimed.

A smug smile spread across his face. "You were watching!"

"Okay, maybe I was just a little fascinated. I always like to be sure humans aren't mistreating my pets."

"I don't suppose it mattered if Archie was wearing me out?"

She gave a deliberate shrug. "You can take care of yourself, I'm sure."

"Nice to know what your priorities are."

She held his gaze. "I've tried my best to make them clear."

Aidan sighed. "Message received." He kept his gaze locked with hers. "Just so you know, though, I've been known to break a few rules in my time."

Liz shivered at the intensity in his voice and the daredevil spark in his eyes. Yeah, she could definitely believe that.

Overnight the springlike weather changed. Sunday morning dawned with a chill in the air and rain in the forecast. Liz couldn't imagine that would be good for business, but when she got to Sally's for her morning coffee and croissant, Shanna didn't look the least bit distressed. Nor did Heather or Megan, who joined them a few minutes later.

"Why don't you all look more upset by this rain that's about to come down in buckets?" Liz asked.

"Because rain means most people won't be going out on their boats or swimming today," Heather said. "Since they've come for a long holiday weekend, they won't take off for home, either. They'll be shopping!"

"After the rush yesterday, how many people can possibly be left?" Liz asked.

"Just you wait and see," Megan told her. She gestured at the line already waiting for tables at Sally's. "See what I mean? Have you ever seen it this busy before at this hour? Everyone's already out and about. I predict Ethel will sell out of puzzles and games before noon and you'll be down to the last of your merchandise before the end of the day."

Liz regarded her with wide eyes. "You can't be serious. I ordered what I thought would be enough to last through the Fourth of July."

"And how did the shelves look at the end of the day yesterday?" Shanna asked.

"Pretty bare," Liz admitted. "I'll be restocking for the next couple of hours till I open the doors."

The women exchanged an amused look.

"Will Aidan be helping with that?" Shanna asked slyly.

Liz felt her cheeks turn pink. "Why would you ask that?"

"Because he was there till closing last night," Heather said. "Just so you know, I wasn't spying. Connor walked by your shop on his way to meet me for dinner and he mentioned it to me."

"And Mick noticed Aidan was in the yard with Archie when he was driving past Dogwood Hill on his way home," Megan added, then patted Liz's hand sympathetically. "Don't freak out. It's not as if we're all nosy, just observant, especially when it involves someone we like. In this case, two people we like."

Bree came in just then, grabbed a chair and pulled it over. "What did I miss?"

"Liz looking like a deer caught in headlights when we mentioned all the attention Aidan is paying to her," Shanna said, her grin unrepentant.

"Oh, yeah, about that," Bree said, a twinkle in her eyes. "I heard Pamela Hobbs had him in her sights at your store yesterday."

Liz frowned. "Did you also hear he turned her down? Emphatically, I gather."

"Smart man," Megan said. "I'd say I can't understand what gets into Pamela, but that's not true. If I were married to Porter Hobbs, who knows what I might do to keep from drinking myself into a stupor every night. He's not only a big blowhard, he's terminally boring."

"Why don't you tell us what you really think, Mom?" Bree said, laughing.

Megan looked momentarily taken aback, then laughed. "Tell me I'm wrong."

"I surely can't do that," Bree said. "He was in Abby's class, not mine, but he was no better back in high school." She turned to Liz. "Ask my sister next time you see her. Porter made a few passes at her before she and Trace got serious. Pamela was his fallback girl and she always knew it. Still, she likes that big fancy car dealership he has in Annapolis and the money it brings in."

Heather sat back, a grin on her face. "Sometimes it hits me just how much fun it must have been to grow up here. I lived in a fairly small town, but it was nothing like this."

"It didn't have O'Briens," Shanna suggested.

Megan laughed. "Yes, I'm sure that made all the difference. Chesapeake Shores was definitely shaped by my husband and his brothers."

"Don't forget Gram," Bree said, her expression turning thoughtful. "Nell is the one who made them into the men they became, and she still has a firm grip on the rest of us. I'm so glad she's still around to impart those values to the next generation."

"Amen to that," Megan said, her own expression turning serious.

Bree frowned. "Mom, what's wrong? Is Gram not well?"

"As far as I know, she's fine," Megan insisted, though her smile was clearly forced. "I just worry about how much things might change when she's gone. After that scare she gave us a few years ago, losing her is never far from my mind."

"I think we all worry about that," Heather said. "Which is why we need to treasure every minute."

Liz thought of the O'Brien matriarch and her role in this amazing family. She was so glad that she'd arrived in town in time to get to know her just a little. She lifted her cup of coffee.

"To Nell," she said quietly.

"To Nell," the others echoed.

"She would hate it if she could hear us," Megan said. "She'd say it sounds as if we're already mourning her, when she has a lot left to give and a lot left to live for, especially since she and Dillon found each other again in Ireland. I think that romance and their marriage revitalized her."

"You're right," Shanna said. "Let's toast that."

This time the toast was far more upbeat and followed by a good bit of laughter.

"There now!" Megan said, setting down her cup. "She'd approve of that. What she's not going to be happy about is how many of us are missing from the table for Sunday dinner today."

"It's the one weekend all summer that she tolerates us playing hooky, though," Bree explained to Liz. "We just won't hear the end of it till the Fourth of July!"

"Maybe not till Labor Day," Megan amended. She glanced outside. "Looks as if the rain's stopped temporarily. I'd better seize the opportunity to get to the shop without getting drenched."

The gathering broke up, though Shanna and Bree walked with Liz to her shop as Megan and Heather hurried off to their businesses around the corner on Shore Road.

"You did okay yesterday?" Shanna asked.

"Better than I could possibly have imagined," Liz said, thinking of the hefty amount she already had totaled for Tuesday's deposit.

"I don't suppose Aidan had anything to do with that sparkle I see in your eyes," Shanna teased.

"Absolutely not," Liz claimed. "I'm all about the cash."

Bree laughed. "Keep telling yourself that."

Liz intended to. This was no time to lose focus on her goal of making Pet Style a success.

Aidan spotted Liz on the sidewalk downstairs, chatting with Shanna and Bree before they left for their own shops. He'd made her agree the night before to call him if she needed help today, but his gut told him she wouldn't do it even if there were customers hanging from the rafters. He made her nervous and he wasn't entirely sure why. Maybe it was because she wanted so badly to ignore those sparks that kept sizzling between them.

To keep himself from stopping in just to say hi, he deliberately forced himself to grab the Sunday *New York Times* and head for Panini Bistro, where he could read the paper and linger over a cappuccino.

Despite the rain, Shore Road was already hopping just like Main Street. Panini Bistro was crowded with tourists who'd had the same idea he'd had. He was about to turn around and leave when he heard his name being called out from a table in the back. He spotted Connor and Kevin O'Brien waving in his direction. Kevin was already dragging an empty chair over from a neighboring table. Aidan stopped at the counter to order his drink, then joined them.

"If you were hoping for peace and quiet, you've come to the wrong place," Kevin said, glancing around at the crowd. "It's not even Memorial Day and I'm already eager for the tourist season to be over."

Connor laughed. "My brother doesn't really hate tourists, because he knows they're very good for the businesses our wives run," he said. "He just sees every one of them as a potential threat to the bay."

Kevin scowled at him. "You would, too, if you saw the amount of trash they leave behind."

"It sounds as if you're as dedicated to preserving the Chesapeake as your uncle is," Aidan said, concluding this was the perfect opening to pick up a few more tidbits about his father.

"I think he's even more of a fanatic," Connor said, nudging his brother. "You know how it is with the recently converted."

Kevin's scowl deepened. "Bite me."

"Seriously," Aidan persisted, "were you drawn into your work by Thomas?"

"Of course," Kevin said. "Much to my father's dismay. He and Thomas hadn't gotten along all that well for years, so Dad viewed it as a betrayal when I decided to go to work with him."

"Dad actually pouted," Connor said, then

grinned. "I believe Mom finally got tired of it and told him to stop being a baby, that we all had the right to pursue our own dreams."

"Yeah, Connor's dream back then was to save the world's men from the evil women divorcing them. He handled some pretty messy divorces. It left him jaded. He wasn't a big proponent of marriage back then."

Aidan studied him curiously. "What changed? Meeting Heather?"

"Oh, no," Kevin said before Connor could reply. "He already knew her. They already had Little Mick. He thought love was enough, that marriage was the problem."

"Well, you have to admit that Mom and Dad didn't set the greatest example," Connor said. "And Uncle Thomas was no better. Connie's his third wife."

It was all Aidan could do not to let his jaw drop. Maybe his mom had been a whole lot smarter than he'd realized, if the man was that fickle.

"They both seem happily married now," he ventured cautiously.

"Mom and Dad are great," Kevin confirmed. "And Connie was exactly the right woman for Thomas. They share the same passion for preserving the bay. A common passion like that can bind two people together."

Definitely food for thought, Aidan concluded.

"Change of subject," Connor said. "How's the team shaping up? Can we expect to win the regional championship?"

Aidan gave him a wry look. "We've run drills and had a couple of team meetings. It's a little early for me to start bragging on their prospects for next year."

"Can you please just tell us that they won't suck again?" Kevin pleaded. "Those boys have had about as much heartbreak as they can handle. I'm amazed some of them have stuck with it. We had a real promising defensive tackle a few years back, but when his folks saw the handwriting on the wall after his first season, they transferred him to a private school that had a halfway decent team. I'd hate to see us lose any more players with potential or the cycle will never end."

"Losing all the time really is discouraging," Aidan agreed. "I've been through a couple of losing streaks in my career and it took a lot to motivate the team to get back on the field and keep trying, especially at the end of the season if there was no hope for the play-offs."

"Your last season you had a winning record," Connor scoffed. "And the team made the play-offs."

"True, but only after we lost the first three games," Aidan reminded him. "Coming back from that pitiful start is what I'm talking about. It builds character."

"I think the character of these kids has taken all the *building* they can handle," Kevin commented.

They spent the next few minutes talking about teams that had bounced back after a losing start and what had made the difference.

"They had heart," Aidan suggested.

"I'm not sure these boys have any heart left to give," Kevin said.

"Have you spoken to your son? Henry's the temporary captain because he still believes in the possibilities and he was able to spur the other boys into the same mind-set. I'm not saying they won't backslide if we start off with a couple of losses, but right now, I think they're starting to feel optimistic. It's my job to make sure they keep on believing in themselves, even if they falter along the way."

Kevin gave him a long look. "Do you believe in them?"

"Let me put it this way," Aidan said, meeting his gaze. "I wouldn't have taken the job if I didn't think I could make a difference."

"One win would make a difference," Kevin replied.

Aidan laughed. "I'm counting on a few more than that."

The brothers exchanged a look.

"I guess we need to have a little faith," Connor said.

"Or at least keep our skepticism to ourselves," Kevin suggested.

Aidan nodded. "Couldn't hurt for them to think the community's behind them."

"Hey, we've always been behind them, win or lose," Kevin said. "But it sure would be nice to leave that fancy stadium after a victory. I think the last time we won, Connor was still playing, and the old stadium had temporary bleachers and a makeshift refreshment stand."

Connor's expression turned nostalgic. "I loved that old stadium. Stole my first kiss under those bleachers when I was twelve."

Fascinated, Aidan sat back to listen.

"You did not, you little dreamer," Kevin retorted.

"You ask Janie Lofton," Connor replied indignantly.

Kevin's mouth gaped. "Janie was in my class. She was already in high school when you were twelve."

Connor's grin spread. "Don't I know it! Best night of my life, at least till I met Heather," he added dutifully. He sighed. "I don't know what Dad was thinking when he made those permanent stands. There's not a decent place anywhere to steal a kiss."

Kevin laughed. "Maybe that was deliberate. He has a lot of granddaughters to protect."

"All I have to say is that it's the most impressive high school stadium I've ever been in," Aidan said. "Your father has done this town proud. Now I need to put together a team that's worthy of such a fancy facility."

"Amen to that," Kevin said.

"On that note, I'd better take off," Connor said. "I left Little Mick with his grandfather. It's never a good idea to let Dad have free rein with him for long. He spoils the kids rotten." He glanced at Kevin. "What about you? You'll be at Sunday dinner, right? It'll mostly be men and kids today, since most of the women are working. That'll give Gram fits, but she doesn't like to break tradition even if half the family can't be there."

"I'll be along," Kevin said. "Unlike you, I'm perfectly content to let Dad spoil my kids. They wear him out so he's more mellow by the time I show up."

Connor laughed. "Good point. Aidan, you want to join us? There's plenty of room at the table today."

"Why don't you?" Kevin said.

Aidan shook his head. He couldn't bring himself to take advantage of their hospitality, not when there was so much he was keeping from all of them.

"Not today, thanks. I'm going to spend some time looking through Coach Gentry's notes and watching some videos he gave me of the games from last season."

Connor regarded him sympathetically. "Well, if

that gets too depressing and you change your mind, just come on by."

After Connor left, Aidan noticed Kevin seemed to be nervous. To give him time to collect his thoughts, he got up and got himself another cappuccino.

"Something on your mind?" he asked when he returned to the table. "Are you worried about Henry if I decide not to keep him on as team captain?"

Kevin shook his head at once. "No way. That kid is amazing. Sometimes I think he was born thirty. Or maybe it was just all he went through before he came to live with us, but he takes things in stride. He's repeatedly reminded us that the job's not his for good. He's just excited that it's his right now. You gotta love a teenager who thinks that way."

"It is admirable and unusual," Aidan agreed. "If it's not that, what is it?"

"I had a talk with Thomas at work the other day. He was telling me you're taking over with the school club that's been working with us on bay preservation."

Aidan nodded. "I've spoken to him about it, yes."

"He got the sense that you might have reservations."

Aidan frowned. "I'm sure I told him I was eager to help out, that I recognized how worthwhile the cause is," he said, wishing he'd delivered that message with more conviction than he apparently had. Just being polite clearly hadn't covered his misgivings.

"He said you said all the right words, but when he wanted to schedule some time to brainstorm plans for next fall, you seemed evasive," Kevin reported.

Aidan sighed. "I probably did," he admitted. "Right now, my focus is on football and trying to shape up the team. I only have a couple more weeks before school's out. I won't get these kids back on the field till late summer. You know as well as I do that's not a lot of time to get them fully prepared for next season."

"Understandable, but you have to see where my uncle is coming from," Kevin replied. "Preserving the bay is an all-consuming obsession for him. He wants to work with someone who's equally committed."

Aidan's temper stirred. "So he's decided I'm not committed after a single conversation?"

"It's not that," Kevin said hurriedly. "I don't want to put words in his mouth. I guess I just wanted to hear for myself that you're interested in working with us. Otherwise, maybe you should speak to Rob about assigning another teacher to the club."

Kevin couldn't possibly know how badly Aidan wanted to do just that, but his annoyance with

Thomas for leaping to such a conclusion kept him from admitting it. Pride and his upbringing insisted that he stick with the commitment he'd made.

"You can tell your uncle that when fall rolls around, I will give this obligation my all, just the way I intend to do my best for the football team."

Kevin looked taken aback by his sharp tone. "Hey, man, I'm sorry. I just wanted to give you an out if you wanted one. We'll be glad to have the support. You just need to understand how Thomas is."

"Believe me, I've heard a lot about his dedication and idealism," Aidan said, fighting to keep any hint of bitterness from his voice. "I can respect that. As for those get-togethers he wants to have, there will be plenty of time once school's out. I'll give him a call and schedule something. Let him know that."

Kevin regarded him with a guilty expression. "I didn't just create an awkward situation for you, did I? All I really meant to do was clear the air and give you a chance to opt out if you weren't interested in the project."

"Got it," Aidan said. "No harm, no foul. Honestly."

Kevin didn't look entirely convinced, but clearly he decided he'd done enough damage. "I probably should get over to Dad's, too. You sure you don't want to come along? I understand

Gram's made pot roast. It's not to be missed."

"Another time," Aidan told him. "Enjoy the rest of your day. I've got the *Times* crossword to do and all those game videos to watch."

He didn't add that those would be enough frustration without trying to evade Thomas and his uncomfortable insightfulness. He was going to have to do a whole lot better at covering his emotions if he wanted to get to know the man without inadvertently revealing what he knew about their connection.

≫· 7 ·≪

Though she hardly had five minutes to think the rest of the holiday weekend, Liz was forced to admit that when she did have a second, her thoughts kept straying to Aidan. She hadn't caught so much as a glimpse of him since they'd had pizza on Saturday night. It had been a comfortable couple of hours, though trying to ignore those sparks between them had taken a lot of willpower, more than she'd imagined ever needing again.

It was one thing to be attracted to the man, she told herself sternly. That just proved she was alive. Acting on it, however, was something else, something she wasn't prepared to do, because allowing her defenses to come down opened her up to a load of potential hurt. She'd already been through more than enough heartache to last a lifetime.

Even with all of those very stern lectures she'd delivered to herself mentally, more than once her gaze had gone to the slip of paper she'd tucked into her pocket with Aidan's cell phone number written on it. She'd been sorely tempted to call and plead for his help, but that fierce independent streak of hers had convinced her that was more about wanting to see him than it was about needing help in the shop.

By the time she closed on Monday after the holiday crowds had left for home, she was glad she'd done those last two days on her own. She'd proven something to herself. And totaling the receipts in her kitchen on Monday night gave her an amazing sense of satisfaction. She was going to pull this off. She could honestly say now that she believed that Pet Style had been the right decision for her future and not just some crazy escape from the past, as her family thought of it.

How had they not been able to see that her entire life had been leading up to something just like this venture? Not only had she started taking in strays as a child, but she'd volunteered at a vet clinic as soon as the family vet thought she was old enough. She'd volunteered to help with a shelter's pet adoption Saturdays, too. Rescuing animals in distress was every bit the passion that teaching had been, and while going to veterinary school hadn't been a realistic option after her husband died, a shop like this had been.

When her phone rang, a tiny part of her was hoping it would be Aidan so she could share the good news of the weekend's success with him, but instead it was her mother's voice she heard on the other end of the line.

Even as she mentally chided herself for not checking caller ID, she said, "Hi, Mom. How was your holiday?"

"The more important question is how was yours? Not that it was much of a holiday, I'm sure. I imagine you were putting in ridiculously long days."

Liz let the familiar refrain wash over her, pretending that the attitude didn't hurt.

"I honestly don't know why you thought any of this was a good idea," Doris Benson continued. "Everyone I've ever known who worked in retail says it's incredibly demanding, and that's without the added pressure of it being your own business. I've left a couple of messages over the weekend, but I assume you were too exhausted to call back."

Though her mother never meant to instill guilt in her offspring, she managed to do it just the same.

"To be honest, I haven't even checked my messages," Liz told her, her face as flushed as if she'd been caught with her hand in that old chintz cookie jar that had sat on her mom's kitchen counter for years. "You're right about the exhaustion. Being on my feet all day has been tougher than I thought it would be. I thought being in a classroom would have prepared me, but it didn't come close."

Even as she made the admission, she knew it had been a mistake. Of course, her mother seized on it.

"If this is turning out to be so difficult, are you still sure it's what you want?" Doris asked, her voice finally filled with genuine concern, rather than judgment. "There's no harm in changing your mind. I'm sure you could get your old job back. I ran into your principal the other day, and she said they would absolutely love to have you whenever you're ready. Everyone at that school loved you, you know."

Liz sighed at the exaggeration. She'd butted heads with parents, other teachers and that very same principal on too many occasions to count. The only thing she'd truly loved about the job had been the kids, most of them so eager to learn and open to new ideas.

Hanging on to her patience by a thread, she said, "Mom, I'm not coming back to Charlotte, and I don't want to teach again. This is the life I want, and this is where I want to be. This weekend may have been exhausting, but it was in a good way. Seeing a dream come to life and realizing that the shop was going to be a success was amazing."

"But, sweetheart, your family is here. We miss you. And you shouldn't be alone right now."

"I'm hardly alone. I've made a lot of friends."

"That doesn't make up for family."

"No, it's not the same," she agreed, though right this second she rejoiced that it wasn't the same. That wasn't something she was about to tell her overprotective, easily offended mother, though. "Why don't you and Dad come for a visit some weekend? You'll fall in love with Chesapeake Shores the same way I have. And I'm dying to show off my house and the shop. Maybe then you'll understand."

"You know how your father hates to travel."

"Then bring LeeAnn and Danielle. We could have a girls' weekend."

"Won't you be too busy for that?" Doris asked, though she did sound tempted.

Her reaction was enough to encourage Liz to press a little harder. "I'll have to work during the day, yes, but you could shop or just enjoy being by the bay. There are some wonderful restaurants you could try. We'd have our evenings together. We could play Scrabble or poker, the way we used to when we'd go to the beach on vacation."

Her mother sighed. "I'll think about it and speak to your sisters. You know how busy they are, though. The kids keep them hopping. I'm not sure their husbands would be willing to take over, even for a couple of days."

"Then they're married to the wrong men," Liz said without thinking.

"What a terrible thing to say!" her mother replied. "You know better."

Liz didn't know better, but it was an argument she wasn't likely to win. Besides, her sisters seemed happy enough with their marriages. It truly wasn't her place to suggest they'd settled, too eager to walk down the aisle to wait for the right men to come along. Seriously, how could she even hint at such a thing when her own supposedly perfect marriage had turned out to be such a sham?

"I'm sorry," she apologized. "Please don't mention it."

"Of course not," her mom said. "I'm not going to stir up trouble."

"I hope you can come, though," Liz said. "Promise me you'll try."

"I'll do my best, sweetheart. You take care of yourself. Don't work too hard. And don't forget to call me once in a while. Otherwise I'll worry."

As Liz hung up, she couldn't help noting that her mom had never actually asked how the holiday weekend at the store had gone. Even if Liz had shared the final sales tally with her, she doubted her mother would have been pleased. She sometimes wondered if her family wasn't hoping that she'd fail just so she'd come home again.

Well, that, she thought with renewed determination, simply wasn't going to happen. The doubts she'd harbored over the winter had been wiped away by the weekend's success. A glance at her very healthy deposit slip for tomorrow morning, which didn't even include the credit card sales, reassured her once again that she was right where she belonged.

Aidan had been expecting a visit from Porter Hobbs on Tuesday morning, but he hadn't expected Rob Larkin to accompany him. Now the three of them were crammed into the small coach's office.

Rob gave Aidan a sympathetic look, then sat back. "Okay, Porter, say your piece. We need to let Coach Mitchell get back to work."

The big man, whose face Aidan recalled seeing plastered on a few auto dealership billboards out on the highway, stood up. He clearly wanted to pace, but there was no room for that. Instead, he bent down, put his hands on the desk and scowled directly at Aidan, deliberately invading his space. Aidan refused to budge an inch, making sure that Porter knew the intimidation tactic wasn't going to work.

"I heard some mighty disturbing news from my wife over the weekend," Porter said. "I'm hoping she got it all wrong."

"What's that?" Aidan asked mildly.

"She says you're thinking of replacing our boy as the team's quarterback." His scowl deepened. "Now that can't possibly be right, can it? Not with all the money I've donated over the years to help out this team. They'd still be playing in that old, rinky-dink stadium if I hadn't written a sizable check."

Aidan wondered how Mick O'Brien might view that sizable check. It was his impression that Mick had paid for much of the construction out of his own pocket. He glanced at Rob, who merely shrugged.

Aidan held Porter's gaze. "What I told your wife, Mr. Hobbs, is that I'm in the process of evaluating all of the players right now to get a sense of what their talents might be and what positions they're best suited to play. I haven't made any decisions at all. My goal is to put the best possible team on the field in the fall." He kept his gaze steady and unblinking, as he added, "I'm sure you feel as strongly about that as I do."

"I know I do," Rob chimed in. "I think that's a sentiment the whole town would agree with."

Some of the bluster seemed to drain out of Porter, but that didn't stop him from declaring that Taylor was meant to be a quarterback. "I've been working with that boy myself since he could hold a football. You might not know this, but I put in some time on the field at the

University of Maryland back in the day, so I know a good quarterback when I see one."

"I'm sure you do," Aidan said, vowing to himself to look up exactly what sort of playing time Porter Hobbs had put in and in what position. "And you have the advantage of all those years of working with Taylor to see how talented he is. If he's everything you say he is, I'm sure I'll recognize that, too. During my days in the NFL, I played with some Pro Bowl athletes myself, so I do have some idea of what to look for."

He wasn't proud of himself for the one-upsmanship, but he figured Porter had it coming.

Rob stood up, clearly satisfied with where things stood. "Porter, I told you Aidan would reassure you. He's being open-minded."

"I just want to be sure he gets the picture," Porter said, clearly not ready to let it go. "Taylor belongs in that quarterback position. I won't see it go to the likes of that Santos kid."

Up until that instant, Aidan had been fairly sympathetic to a father wanting to protect his son, but the hint of bias in Porter's disdainful use of the boy's Hispanic last name set his teeth on edge. Apparently Rob sensed that the situation was about to deteriorate, because he put a hand on Porter's back and steered him rapidly toward the door.

"Thanks for taking the time to see us," the principal told Aidan.

"Not a problem," Aidan said, clenching his fists, but out of sight.

Five minutes later the principal was back in his office. "I'm sorry," Rob said. "I had to bring him in here and let him say his piece. He has an overinflated sense of his contribution to this football program, and he also has a big mouth. It's not worth it to have him running around town stirring up trouble. Just know that whatever your decision is, I'm behind you."

"Understood," Aidan said, not envying Rob for the position he'd been put in. "By the way, have you seen Hector Santos on the field?"

Rob nodded. "He's got raw talent, no question about it. Are you leaning in that direction?"

"Too soon to say after just a couple of practices and drills," Aidan said. "But if it's best for the team, I won't hesitate to make that call."

"You do what you need to do. I'll deal with Porter." He grinned. "So will Mick O'Brien, if he ever hears Porter bragging about funding that stadium. His check might have covered the snack bar. O'Brien money built the rest."

"I wondered about that," Aidan admitted. "I'd sure hate to offend a major donor, when the team's not even on the field yet."

"No worries about that. I think he's been neutralized for now," Rob said. "You handled the whole thing with amazing tact."

Aidan wasn't entirely reassured. "Are there

other people in Chesapeake Shores who'll react the way he did, just because Hector's Hispanic?"

"I'd be surprised if there are," Rob said candidly. "I've never seen any hint of prejudice in this community. Mick O'Brien might not hold any formal position in this town, but he'd never tolerate that kind of an attitude. Obviously he can't control people's private thoughts or even their actions, but I think people look up to him. They tend to follow his lead."

Aidan nodded. "I'll have a chat with him next time I see him. I want to get his take on how much ruckus I'm likely to stir up if I make a change."

"Seems like a smart idea," Rob said. "How are the other players getting along with Hector?"

Aidan allowed himself a smile at last. "I noticed there was a little tension the first time we got on the field, but then he threw a couple of long spiral passes that were dead-on. They would have been easy touchdowns. Even Taylor Hobbs went up to congratulate him. And Henry's taken him under his wing and been working with him on his English. He even offered to tutor him over the summer to keep his grades up."

Rob looked pleased. "Henry is a constant source of amazement to me. He has such a well-developed sense of kindness and maturity."

"Naming him team captain was an impulsive move on my part that first day," Aidan replied, "but nothing that's happened since has given me cause to regret it."

Rob grinned at him. "If all your instincts are on track like that, I'm predicting it's going to be a good year."

"Let's not get ahead of ourselves," Aidan cautioned. He wanted the community to be excited, but not so optimistic that disappointment was bound to follow.

Because Shanna always had a coffeepot going in her bookstore for her customers, Liz occasionally popped in there to grab a quick cup to go, especially when she didn't have time to wait at Sally's. Shanna's coffee might be weak, but at least it had enough caffeine to keep her going for an hour or two.

As she walked in late on Tuesday afternoon, she found Henry in the seating area with an unfamiliar boy with an olive complexion, dark hair and big brown eyes. Henry looked up, pushed his glasses back into place and grinned.

"Hi, Ms. March. Are you looking for Mom?"

"I'm actually looking for coffee. Any left?"

"I guess so," he said with a shrug. "I'm just keeping an eye on the store because she had to run around the corner to help Grandma Megan with some pictures she was trying to hang in the gallery."

"How was practice today?" Liz asked as she

checked the fancy coffeemaker, then poured herself a cup.

"Awesome," Henry said excitedly. Then his expression turned apologetic. "I'm sorry. This is Hector Santos. Hector, Ms. March owns the pet store next door."

The boy greeted her shyly, his English heavily accented.

"Hector, are you on the football team, too?"

"*Si.* I mean, yes, ma'am."

"He's going to be a superstar quarterback," Henry declared as color stained Hector's cheeks.

"Not so," he said. "Taylor is quarterback."

"Not for long," Henry argued. "Wait till you see Hector pass, Ms. March. He's awesome, and he can scramble out of the pocket like a pro. Taylor can't do that."

Liz chuckled at his enthusiasm. "Are you sure you're not his agent?" she teased. "You sure do know how to sell his skills."

Henry took her quip seriously, his expression immediately turning thoughtful. "Maybe that's what I should be," he said solemnly. "I'll never be good enough to play professionally, but I recognize real talent just like Mr. Mitchell."

"Something to consider," Liz said. She glanced at Hector. "Do you have a pet?"

He shook his head. "I would like a dog, but my parents have said no."

Liz recognized the real longing in his voice.

"Well, you have Henry bring you by my house one day. I have three dogs and a cat. They'd all love some extra attention."

Hector's face lit up. "Is true? We could do that?"

"Anytime I'm home," she assured him. She put a dollar in the honor jar by the coffeemaker and held up her to-go cup. "Henry, tell your mom I said thanks. Study hard, you guys."

By the time she reached the door, she could already hear Hector chattering excitedly, half in English, half in Spanish, about the chance to play with her dogs. She had a hunch she'd have company before the week was out.

After so many long days in the store, Liz was in desperate need of some exercise. She also needed to do something to work off that caffeine she'd had late in the day just to keep her eyes open till closing.

Since the dogs had been cooped up too much as well, she got all three of their leashes and headed to the dog park. As soon as she unsnapped the leashes, the dogs barked exuberantly and took off. Fortunately they were all socially well behaved and got along well with the other dogs who were there, giving her a chance to chat casually with the other owners.

"Uh-oh," Kitty Fawcett said, laughing. "There goes Archie!" A shouted warning to the man just leaving wasn't in time to keep Archie from making his escape through the open gate.

Liz sighed. "Can you keep an eye on the other two for a few minutes while I round Archie up?" she asked Kitty.

"Sure," the other woman said at once, then added with a chuckle, "But I do want to be home before dark."

Since dark was at least an hour away, Liz made a face at her attempt at humor, then took off running.

As she raced out of the dog park and over Dogwood Hill shouting for Archie, she reminded herself that tonight had been about getting exercise not just for the dogs, but for her. Archie had definitely assured that she'd get more than she'd bargained for.

As she emerged from the dogwood trees, she spotted her traitorous speed demon of a dog sitting calmly at Aidan's feet.

Aidan shot her a grin that made her already-racing pulse scramble just a bit more. Apparently all those lectures she'd delivered to herself over the holiday weekend hadn't had any effect at all. She was alive, all right!

"I figured you'd be along soon," he commented. He gestured to the dog, who was ecstatically wagging his tail. "Does he belong to anyone you know?"

Liz bent over at the waist trying to catch her breath, but she still managed to feign a scowl for

Aidan's benefit. "Very funny. This is all your fault, you know."

"How so? I was nowhere near the dog park. I assume that's where he was since he's not dragging a leash behind him." He glanced pointedly around. "No geese in sight, either."

"No, but he seems to have some sixth sense when you're around. He obviously came straight to you."

"Shouldn't you be thanking me?" Aidan teased. "If it weren't for me, he could be down by the bay by now going for a swim."

"You're right. I should be thankful for small favors," Liz said as she clicked the leash into place on Archie's collar. The dog regarded her with what she could only interpret as disgust. Making an impulsive decision, she handed the leash to Aidan. "Here. He's all yours."

She turned around, allowing herself a small smile as she deliberately walked away.

After a moment of stunned silence, Aidan and Archie caught up with her.

"What's that supposed to mean?" Aidan said. "I've told you before there's no way I can have a dog."

"You already have a dog," she said. "He may be staying with me, but he's adopted you. I'll give you a bill for room and board."

Panic seemed to flit across Aidan's face, and she sensed it had nothing to do with being charged for Archie's care.

"Liz, be reasonable. It's a tiny one-bedroom apartment, barely bigger than a studio, when you get right down to it."

"And I have a two-bedroom house with two other dogs and a cat. What's your point?"

"It's just not fair for him to be shut in all day while I'm at school," Aidan told her.

"He seems to be doing okay at my house all day when I'm at the store. Besides, school will be out in a couple of weeks." She beamed at him. "You'll have lots of time to take him out for runs then. If you want, I'll even keep him till school is out. That should work out perfectly. Any more objections?"

Aidan frowned. "I thought you didn't want to place pets with people you didn't think would be good owners."

"True," she said readily, as they reached the dog park. "I think you're going to be an excellent owner. You just need to get used to the idea."

Liz claimed the two dogs that Kitty had been watching, tried to ignore the other woman's amused glance at Aidan and a now-docile Archie and headed toward home. Aidan was still arguing with her when they reached her house. This time, though, she was determined not to listen. Whether he realized it or not, he and Archie were meant to be together.

Inside the house, she released all three dogs. Hers headed for the kitchen for water, but Archie stayed right at Aidan's side as if sensing that something significant involving his future was about to change.

Determined to seize the moment and not allow anything to dissuade her from this decision, she added, "You should probably come over early Saturday morning."

Aidan frowned. "Why? Aren't you working?"

"Of course, but if you're here by seven, we'll have time to take Archie for a visit to Cordelia. You should probably get to know her."

He stared at her blankly. "Who's Cordelia?"

"I told you about her," she reminded him. "She was Archie's original owner. She misses him. I want her to know that he's going to a good home and, best of all, that it's with someone right here in town so she can still see him. You'll enjoy spending time with her, I'm sure." And Cordelia would be in her element with a handsome man coming around with Archie in tow. She'd have bragging rights at the seniors center.

Aidan looked as if he might argue, but instead he sighed deeply. "You're not going to change your mind, are you?"

She glanced pointedly at the dog, who hadn't taken his eyes off Aidan during the entire exchange. "How can I? This was clearly meant to be."

"He has to stay here till school's out," Aidan said, as if clinging to one last shred of hope that he could eventually change her mind.

"Agreed," she said, fighting a smile. "But not one second longer."

"We'll see," Aidan murmured, but even as he spoke, he was stroking Archie's head.

"I have to go," he said suddenly, and turned toward the door.

"Have a good night," she called after him, holding tight to Archie's collar when the dog whimpered and clearly would have followed him.

When Aidan was out of sight, she petted the Aussie. "Don't fret. You'll be going home with him soon. I'll see to it."

Even as the promise crossed her lips, she found herself chuckling. It might not involve people, but apparently she was turning into something of a matchmaker herself. There must be something in the Chesapeake Shores air that made people want to see everyone they knew happy . . . one way or another.

⇒ 8 ⇐

"I swear to God, I don't know how she did it," Aidan told Connor the next morning when he bumped into him at Sally's. He'd come in earlier than usual, hoping to avoid Liz for a change, because last night's interaction had proved to be even more disconcerting than usual. As he waited for his coffee, he filled his friend in.

"I was out for a run, minding my own business,"

he continued. "Next thing I knew Archie came bolting out of nowhere with Liz hard on his heels. She jumped to the conclusion that meant he belonged with me. Now she's determined to move him into that tiny apartment upstairs the second school lets out."

Connor chuckled. "Is this the first time in your life you've crossed paths with a woman who's determined to get her own way?"

"Hardly," Aidan said. "But usually they've wanted to move themselves in, not a dog."

Connor gave him a disbelieving look. "And it was easier to say no to that than to a dog?"

"We're talking about women. It's never easy," Aidan said in a resigned tone.

"So, help me out. Is it the dog or Liz who's complicating your life?" Connor persisted.

"It's the combination, man. Liz, *plus* that dog looking at me as if he understood every word she was saying."

Laughing, Connor glanced at his cell phone, then shook his head. "Darn, it's only June 1. I thought for sure you'd hold out till the Fourth of July at least. I owe Kevin twenty bucks."

"You had a bet with your brother about Liz and me?" Aidan asked incredulously.

"Not just Kevin. Dad was in on it, too," Connor revealed. "As a matter of fact, he was the first one to pick up on the vibes between the two of you. I have to give him credit. When it comes to this kind of stuff, he's usually right. I have no idea how a man who was so clueless about what my mom needed from him can recognize love—"

"Love?" Aidan echoed, panic setting in. "Who said anything about love? Liz is a beautiful woman. She's sassy and charming and generous, but recognizing all that does not mean I'm falling for her."

"Okay, maybe it's just lust. Call it whatever you want to, but Dad seems to get it. Maybe it's *because* he and Mom got a divorce and he had to win her back. Anyway, my point is he tends to nail these things. He sure did his best to get Heather and me together. And he saw what was going on with Kevin and Shanna before either of them were ready to admit it. Heck, he has a whole long track record I could cite."

He gave Aidan a commiserating look. "I almost feel sorry for you."

Aidan blinked at that. "Why?"

"Because when Mick O'Brien sees two people he thinks are right for each other, he stops at nothing to make sure they fall into line," Connor told him, an amused gleam in his eyes.

"Sweet heaven," Aidan murmured. "And your wives? Were they in on this bet, too?"

"They didn't bet, but they thought you'd cave even faster. In fact, they've been counting on it. They're all anxious to see Liz happily settled."

Alarm once again made Aidan's pulse race.

"Happily settled? As in married? To me?" This just kept getting worse and worse. Liz was still balking at the thought of a date, and he was only a step or two ahead of her. Marriage? That was so far down the road, he couldn't see it with binoculars.

He sighed. "This isn't good," he said as he grabbed his cup of take-out coffee and started outside. He paused and gave Connor a curious look. "Why did they focus on me?"

"Well, to be honest, you weren't in the picture when they got up a full head of matchmaking steam, but the minute you turned up in town and they spotted a couple of sparks flying, the handwriting was on the wall as far as they were concerned."

"Can't you tell them to butt out?" Aidan asked plaintively. "Heather, at least?"

"My wife is in a hormonal state these days," Connor lamented. "I try not to argue with her about anything. It's a no-win proposition. Same with Kevin and Shanna. Sorry, pal. You'll have to take a stance all by yourself, at least if that's what you really want to do."

Aidan heaved yet another sigh. At this rate they were going to have to treat him for hyperventilating in another couple of minutes. "Living here is going to be a challenge, isn't it?" he muttered.

"Only if you fight the inevitable," Connor said,

not even trying to hide his amusement. "By the way, I know you're the football coach, but I'm guessing you can hold your own in a game of hoops. Want to join us tonight? I'm thinking you might need to work off some of that frustration. You've met most of the guys already. After we play, we hang out, drink a couple of beers and tell tall tales about how athletic we used to be."

Aidan finally let himself relax again. Any sport was familiar turf, and a much better topic than women in general or Liz in particular. "Used to be?"

"I played college baseball," Connor reported. "I wasn't half-bad, but there was no chance I'd make it professionally. Mack, of course, played professional football till he was sidelined by an injury. The whole family plays touch football every Thanksgiving. It used to be men-only, but then my cousin Susie got into the game one year to make a point to Mack, and things haven't been the same since. We had to stop playing dirty."

"How annoying!" Aidan said dryly.

"You have no idea," Connor said with real regret. "But Mack is crazy in love with his wife and he's not about to tell her that she can't play. She had a tough battle with cancer a few years back. She's been in remission for a while now, but nobody wants to deny Susie anything. We've all had our share of successes in one way or another, but Susie's the real hero in our family. She's as tough as they come."

Aidan heard the note of genuine admiration in Connor's voice and tried to imagine how incredible the woman must be to have earned that. From what he knew, Connor had been a pretty hard-nosed divorce lawyer in Baltimore, who was trying to mellow out with a general practice in Chesapeake Shores.

"I'm a little rusty when it comes to basketball, but I imagine I can hold my own," he told Connor as they walked along Main Street in the direction of Connor's office. "I'd love to play. What time and where?"

"There are outdoor courts in the park on the far side of Dogwood Hill. You can see them just past the dog park. You should be able to find them with no problem, or I can stop by and pick you up."

As Connor perfectly well knew, given their conversation just now, Aidan was well acquainted with the location of that blasted dog park. "I'll find them."

And just like that he suddenly had the potential for a group of real pals. As much as he'd enjoyed his first weeks in town, he missed the camaraderie with his teammates. He missed getting together with Frankie, even though he heard from him almost on a daily basis, checking to see if Aidan was ready yet to come back to New York where he belonged.

Still, as much as he was looking forward to getting together with Connor and his relatives for

149

a game of hoops, guilt nagged at him. He couldn't help wondering just how friendly they'd be when they discovered he was family and he'd kept that from them. The longer he kept the secret, the less likely they'd forgive him for it. And, surprising as it was to him, he realized that was starting to matter.

Liz sat on the porch at Susie Franklin's beautiful home on Beach Lane relaxing at the end of the day. On the nights when the guys played basketball, the women in the O'Brien family got together at Susie's for what was purported to be a book discussion. To the total frustration of Shanna, no more than fifteen minutes ever seemed to be devoted to talking about whatever book they'd chosen. Tonight all the talk was about Aidan Mitchell and, to her everlasting regret, Liz's connection to him.

"So, Liz, now that you've spent some time with Aidan, what do you think of him?" Susie asked as if they'd never before had this conversation. There was a mischievous gleam in her eyes that suggested she hoped this time they'd get a different answer.

"There have been plenty of other sightings of the two of them together," Bree reported.

"All of which we've discussed, ad nauseam," Liz reminded them to no avail.

"I wonder if he deliberately rented my old

apartment over the shops just because your store is right downstairs?" Shanna speculated, a grin tugging at her lips.

"I've wondered the same thing," Susie claimed. "And let's not forget that I lived there, too, so I know what an incredible view it has of the green and whoever might happen to be walking by."

"Stop it!" Liz said, laughing. "How many times do I have to tell you there is nothing between Aidan and me."

"Until you make it sound convincing," Bree said. "So far, not so much, especially when he seems to be underfoot every time we turn around."

Liz frowned at her friends. She needed to set them straight before they manufactured a romance that was doomed before it even started.

"There's not going to be anything between Aidan and me, except maybe a friendship. My only goal is to get him to take Archie off my hands, and just last night I finally found a way to do that."

Bree gave her a triumphant look. "See what I mean? They were together again last night. You might as well admit the truth, Liz. There's something going on."

"I'm not admitting anything," Liz said very firmly. "I talked him into taking the dog—that's it."

"Did it involve holding him hostage and torturing him till he agreed?" Shanna asked. She grinned. "That could be fun. Fur-lined handcuffs. Maybe feathers or whipped cream."

Liz rolled her eyes at the suggestive comment, though it did stir up a few steamy images. She imagined those would be stuck in her head all night long.

"Absolutely not," she said. "I just pointed out a few inescapable facts."

"Such as?" Shanna asked.

"Archie already adores him. He's more Aidan's dog now than he is mine, even though I'm the one who's been feeding him and taking care of him."

"Okay, I hear what you're claiming about Aidan not being in your life as a potential lover, but I'm not sure I understand it," Heather said. "Do you have something against good-looking and sexy? I swear if I weren't happily married to Connor, I'd give him a second look, I can tell you that."

Shanna, who was pregnant with what would be a fourth child for her and Kevin O'Brien, patted her belly. Everyone knew they were desperately hoping for a girl this time. They already had Davey, Kevin's son from an earlier marriage, plus Henry, and then Johnny, the son they'd had together just two years ago. She'd flatly refused to learn the sex of this baby in advance.

"Okay," Shanna said, glancing around with a guilty expression as if she feared being over-heard. "I should not even be looking at other men these days, but every time Aidan walks by the book-store, I have to admit I admire the view. Kevin caught me the other day and dragged me into the back room and kissed me senseless. He said he just wanted to be certain if I was thinking about sex, he was the one on my mind."

"And I'm sure you told him there was no question of that," Bree protested with exaggerated dismay. "That's my brother's baby you're carrying, after all."

"Which means my hormones are in overdrive," Shanna reminded her. "It's a side effect of pregnancy I'd never anticipated. Liz, you really do need to go out with Aidan, so you can tell us all about it. We long to live vicariously."

"And since I'm in the throes of morning sickness most days, I could use a good distraction, too," Heather chimed in.

After a quick glance at Susie to see how she was reacting to all this talk of pregnancy, Liz frowned at Shanna and Heather. "I am not going out with Aidan just to satisfy your curiosity. Seriously, that would be crazy." To say nothing of dangerous to her own mental health, she thought to herself. It would not take much for her to forget all these noble resolutions she'd made and see if he was half as clever with those lovely, strong hands of his as he was with charming words.

"Then go out with him to satisfy yours," Bree suggested. "I know you want to. I've seen the way you look at each other whenever you cross paths at Sally's."

"Which seems to be every morning lately," Heather commented, her expression innocent. "Quite the coincidence, wouldn't you say?"

"Definitely," Susie agreed, then reached over to give Liz's hand a squeeze. "You do know we're only interested in making sure you're happy and stay right here in Chesapeake Shores forever, right?"

"What do I have to do to convince you that I am here to stay and that I am happy?" Liz asked in exasperation. "Just because you've all married the men of your dreams doesn't mean I need a man in my life. Been there, done that."

Bree frowned. "Hold on. What was that tone all about? It's the first time you've even hinted that your marriage was anything other than perfect."

Liz cursed herself for the faint slip of the tongue. "You're imagining things. I just meant that I'm nowhere near ready to get involved with anyone again. It's possible I will never be ready."

"There it is again," Bree said. "Happily married women don't swear off men when they're widowed. They grieve, to be sure, but eventually they usually open their hearts to someone else."

"Says who?" Liz retorted. "There are plenty of women who don't think any man could possibly live up to the one they lost."

"And you're one of those?" Bree asked, her

skepticism plain. "That's not how it sounded."

Susie frowned. "I agree. I heard the same thing. Liz, you certainly don't have to tell us anything you don't want to, but we are your friends. If there's ever anything you need to talk about, we'll listen. No judgments and no advice."

Liz lifted a brow in disbelief. "As if you could pull that off."

"We can just listen," Heather insisted. "We've had some practice."

"Oh, who are you guys kidding?" Shanna said, siding with Liz. "The O'Briens have rubbed off on all of us. We couldn't shut up if we wanted to."

"But we will try," Bree said, belatedly regarding Liz with genuine concern. "Remember that, okay?"

For just an instant, Liz was tempted to open up and reveal the secret she'd been keeping to herself ever since the night she'd lost her husband, but when it came right down to it, she couldn't. She knew it would change the way they looked at her. That night and everything that had led up to the accident had certainly changed the way she'd looked at herself.

She was very much afraid, in fact, that no amount of time passing would ever diminish the pain of that night, not just the accident itself and losing her husband, but every awful revelation that had come before it. How could she possibly think of moving on when she'd failed so terribly as a wife the first time?

• • •

Aidan wasn't entirely shocked by the discovery that the O'Brien men and their friends were a very competitive group. They took to the basketball court as if they were the Miami Heat and LeBron James going up against San Antonio in the NBA finals. Not that a one of them possessed the same skill level, of course.

Despite the intensity of the game, however, they still found plenty of time to taunt each other as only friends of long standing and family could. They knew each other's weak spots and exploited them. It was only a matter of time before their attention turned to Aidan.

Maybe it had something to do with the fact that his gaze kept straying toward the dog park, but Connor was the first to pull him into their sights.

"Something interesting going on in the dog park, Aidan?" Connor teased. "Your attention seems to be wandering."

"I noticed the same thing," Mack chimed in. "That wouldn't have anything to do with Liz, would it? You hoping to catch a glimpse of her? Or maybe it's that dog I understand you're about to adopt, though it would be a pity if you found that to be more interesting than a beautiful woman."

"I am not watching for Liz or Archie," Aidan claimed. "It's just that this game is moving so slow, my mind's had plenty of time to wander."

Kevin regarded him incredulously. "Men, did you hear that? He just accused us of being sluggish and boring on the court."

"I heard the same thing," Connor said.

Aidan grinned as he dribbled the ball and watched for an opening. "Truth hurts, doesn't it?" He dodged Connor's attempt to block him and drove past him to make the basket. "So does losing. Not that I would know about that, since last time I checked my team was winning."

Will Lincoln, a shrink who was married to Jess O'Brien, the owner of the inn, winced at the comment. "Would you mind a little advice from a mental health professional?" he said to Aidan. "Do not take pokes at a sleeping lion. We might have these guys on the ropes right now because they're distracted by all the trash talk, but I guarantee they can pick up the intensity in a heartbeat."

"Ain't that the truth," Kevin said, grabbing a rebound and charging past Aidan for a quick dunk shot that brought them within six points of Aidan's team.

Aidan didn't much care if his comments cost his team the game, as long as it changed the direction of their thoughts from his love life.

For a full ten minutes, the two teams were silent except for their panting and the sound of their sneakers slapping against asphalt as the battle on the court escalated. As the buzzer on their kitchen timer ticked down, Aidan stole a ball from Connor, took it down the court and sank the shot, just as the timer went off.

"And that," he said with a triumphant grin, "is how it's done."

Kevin and Connor exchanged a look.

"Bet I can wipe that smug look off his face," Connor taunted.

Kevin grinned. "You mean by mentioning that Liz just hit the dog park wearing short shorts and a very tight tank top?"

Recalling precisely how hot she'd looked the other night in just such an outfit, Aidan's head whipped around, but there was no such vision in sight.

"You dog," he said to Kevin.

Kevin and Connor gave each other satisfied high fives.

"Knew you'd look," Kevin said.

"And why is that?" Connor teased, his expression innocent.

"Because he's in *l-o-v-e,*" Bree's husband, Jake, said.

"Hey," Aidan protested. "You were on my team. Aren't you supposed to be on my side here?"

Jake chuckled. "Not when it comes to this. It's too much fun watching you squirm. All of us have paid our dues. We've taken the heat, made it to the altar and are now living happily ever after. We want everyone to share in our joy."

Aidan shook his head. "What you really mean is that misery loves company. You're jealous that I can date any woman I happen to find attractive."

Will winced for the second time that night. "Please tell me you did not just suggest that we're miserable because we're married. If that remark makes its way to our wives, you'll be run out of town."

Right this second, Aidan wasn't seeing the downside of that.

After she left Susie's, Liz couldn't seem to shake the old memories that had been stirred up by their conversation. Once she'd left North Carolina, she'd resolved to put her marriage and all the rest where it belonged, in the past. Most days she'd been successful doing that. Josh March rarely crossed her mind, or when he did, she immediately found some way to drive him out again.

That determination to keep those thoughts at bay was one of the reasons she'd taken up running. With her earphones in and music blasting as she ran, to say nothing of just trying to breathe, those memories couldn't creep in, not the good ones or the bad.

Since it wasn't that late when she got home, she changed into jogging shorts and shoes, grabbed her iPod and turned on a mix of songs with a fast beat and cheerful lyrics. Ignoring the plaintive looks of all three dogs, she went out alone.

She instinctively avoided Dogwood Hill and headed toward the bay, where the winding road would take her toward The Inn at Eagle Point. From there, she wound her way back toward town and Shore Road, which would probably still be bustling on the warm late-spring evening.

With the music playing and her concentration focused on her breathing, she was startled when someone stepped in front of her and blocked her path. Shaken, she looked up into Aidan's face.

Pulling the earbuds from her ears, she scowled at him. "You scared me to death!"

"I've been calling your name for the past block," he said.

She gestured to the iPod. "Sorry. I was listening to music."

"It's a little late for a run, isn't it?" he asked. "Even in Chesapeake Shores, you probably shouldn't be out alone at this hour."

She gave him an incredulous look. "It's barely ten."

He tapped his watch. "Check again. It's going on midnight."

Liz regarded him with shock. "That can't be. I know when I got home it was going on ten."

"And then you, what? Changed clothes? Ran— where exactly?"

"Up to the inn," she conceded, then sighed. "I guess it was farther than I realized. Or maybe I'm just slower. I'm a little out of practice."

"Any particular reason you decided to go for a run in the first place at this hour?"

She shrugged. "It clears my head."

"Of?"

She smiled. "This and that."

"Ah, the woman has secrets," he said.

She held his gaze. "Don't we all?"

"I suppose you're right," he said, looking vaguely uncomfortable. He gestured across the street. "Panini Bistro hasn't closed yet. Want to grab something to drink before you head home? It doesn't seem to be crowded with O'Briens at this hour."

"I wouldn't mind some bottled water," she admitted.

"Come on, then," he said, taking her elbow and guiding her across the street. "You grab a table out here. It's too nice to sit inside. I'll get the drinks."

Liz nodded. "That works."

She sat down gratefully, suddenly aware in every muscle that the run had taken her farther than she usually went. At least it had served its avowed purpose of clearing her head of thoughts of Josh. Sadly, though, it seemed Aidan was now front and center once again. Why couldn't she just give in to the inevitable and engage in some hot, steamy sex? That would definitely clear her head, at least temporarily.

And that, of course, was precisely why she couldn't. Sex was easy. It was fun. It was after sex that emotions could get all tangled up and life could get really complicated.

When Aidan returned with two cold bottles of water, she studied him and noted that he was dressed more casually than usual. In fact, she thought, hiding a smile, it looked as if he'd grabbed that T-shirt straight from the dryer.

"Did you get dressed in a hurry?" she asked.

He glanced down at his shirt and grimaced. "You'd think that, wouldn't you? But no—I played basketball with a bunch of the O'Briens tonight. This shirt is a little the worse for wear. In fact, if I were you, I'd stay downwind of me."

Liz laughed. "I've always thought men were kind of sexy when they sweated."

He regarded her incredulously. "Seriously?"

"Must be all the pheromones they exude."

He laughed. "Well, to hear my mom tell it, it was a cardinal sin, especially if I expected to be in the company of ladies."

"So, what does that make me?"

"A lady, no question about it," he said quickly. "But I spotted you running as I was coming home and didn't want you to get away. I figured this was an exception."

"So, how was the game?" she asked.

"The game was great. My team won."

"The only critical point of the evening, I gather," she said, chuckling.

"Well, of course. It's a guy thing. Winning

matters, though if you tell any of my players that, I'll swear I was misquoted. How'd you spend your evening?"

"With the O'Brien women. They weren't nearly as competitive, unless you count the degree of their meddling."

He slanted a surprising look of commiseration in her direction. "Must be genetic."

She gave him a sharp look. "You, too?"

"Oh, yeah."

"What did you tell them?"

"To take a hike."

Liz regarded him hopefully. "Did that work?"

"Are you kidding me? Not a chance," he said ruefully. "What about you?"

"Ditto," she said.

"Any thoughts about what happens next?"

She smiled at the hopeful note in his voice. "Just remember that we're in control of our own destinies. They're not."

Aidan nodded, then stared toward the bay, his expression thoughtful. When he finally turned back to her, he asked quietly, "Are you so sure about that?"

Something in his tone suggested he was more resigned than convinced.

"We have to be," she said flatly.

"Okay, then. Come on. I'll walk you home."

Liz stood up. "You don't have to do that," she protested. "It's a few blocks."

"Another of those lessons from my mom," he said simply. "This one took."

She smiled. "In that case, who am I to argue?"

And at least with Aidan by her side and his words still ringing in her ears about them possibly not being in charge of anything, there wasn't a chance in the world she'd be thinking about Josh.

⇒ 9 ⇐

The chance encounter with Liz was still very much on Aidan's mind Friday afternoon, though he was trying to keep his attention focused on the team as it ran through drills in preparation for a final scrimmage before school let out next week for the summer.

Between his wandering thoughts and the actions on the field, he didn't notice Mick O'Brien until the practice session ended. As soon as Aidan dismissed the boys, Mick headed in his direction.

"I'm no expert, but seems to me there's a big improvement already," Mick said.

"They're still learning," Aidan told him, then grinned. "But I think they're catching on, too. What brings you by?"

"Henry's been bugging me to check out the Santos kid," Mick said. "Are you as high on him as my grandson is?"

"Funny you should mention Hector," Aidan told

him, grateful to finally have an opportunity to get Mick's take on the community's likely reaction to any quarterback change he might make. "I've been wanting to discuss the quarterback situation with you. I could use some advice."

Mick laughed. "Porter's been trying to intimidate you—am I right?"

"You're right," Aidan said, not all that surprised by Mick's perceptiveness. "I'm just wondering how much of his attitude is being protective of his son, something I can totally understand, and how much might be a prejudice that's going to be shared by the whole community."

"Porter believes his boy is talented," Mick responded slowly. "And I can see some potential there."

"Taylor understands the fundamentals," Aidan agreed, trying to be fair. "But Hector? He's something special."

"My grandson certainly thinks so," Mick conceded. "Not that Henry's the expert you are. He's just recently decided he wants to be a sports agent and Hector's his first big find."

Aidan chuckled. "If he could find a few more with that much talent, I'd be very appreciative."

Mick studied him. "Hector really is that promising?"

Aidan nodded.

"Then I don't see that you have much choice," Mick said. "You were brought in to make this team the best it can possibly be. You don't put a boy on the field if you don't think he can do the job. At least you don't when there's someone you know can do it better."

"I'd just hate to stir up some sort of community backlash that will only wind up hurting Hector."

Mick's expression turned thoughtful. "I think that can be avoided," he said carefully. "What do you have in mind for Taylor?"

"Truthfully, he's got decent hands and the speed to be a receiver, if he's willing to make the transition."

"Does he get along okay with Hector?"

Aidan nodded. "I don't think Taylor will be the problem. I've had them practicing together and it's gone surprisingly well considering they're rivals for the same position."

"Then you leave Porter to me," Mick said. "I think what he wants most is for his boy to have playing time and to be a star. If Taylor can do that in another position, I think I can convince Porter that there's not a downside. It takes twenty-two men on offense and defense to make a team. Hardly matters where they excel, as long as it's a winning combination."

Aidan regarded him with appreciation. "Agreed."

Henry came running back onto the field just then with Hector alongside. "Grandpa Mick!" he shouted. "Did you see practice?"

"I saw," Mick said, giving him an affectionate

pat on the back, then holding out his hand to Hector. "I've been hearing very good things about you, son."

"Henry's my friend," Hector said shyly. "He is, how do you say, biased."

Mick smiled. "And your coach? Is he biased, too?"

Eyes wide, Hector looked up at Aidan. "You told him about me?"

"I did," Aidan confirmed. "And whatever Henry said is true, Hector. You're very, very talented."

"*Muchas gracias*," Hector said. "I do my best."

"You certainly do that," Aidan agreed.

"Now, how about a couple of burgers and some fries at Sally's?" Mick asked the boys. He glanced at Aidan. "Any objections?"

"Not from me," Aidan said. "I'd join you, if I could."

"Why don't you?" Mick said, his expression sly. "Might give you a chance to stop in and visit a friend."

Given what Aidan knew about Mick's sneaky intentions, he was quick to decline. Besides, just last night he'd determined to give Liz the space she claimed to want. He could hardly argue against it being the smart thing to do for both of them. The less fodder these matchmakers had to work with, the better off they'd both be. And with his own uncertainty about how long he'd stick around Chesapeake Shores, why start something he might not be around to finish?

Of course, that said, it was a whole lot easier to say no to Mick now, when he already planned to see Liz first thing tomorrow morning for the promised visit with Cordelia.

Liz was still asleep and having a lovely dream on Saturday morning when she was awakened by someone pounding on her door and the earsplitting sound of Archie's ecstatic barking. That could only mean one thing: Aidan, the very man at the center of her dream.

Muttering under her breath, she dragged on a robe over the shorts and tank she wore for sleeping, then went to the door. Aidan regarded her with a stunned expression.

"I woke you?" he asked as Archie danced around him.

"What was your first clue?" she asked, well aware of how grouchy she was before her morning coffee, especially when awakened from a sound sleep.

Aidan unsuccessfully tried to hide a smile. "I thought we had a date this morning."

"A date? I thought we'd concluded that dating was a nonissue. You have your reasons. I have mine. Yada yada."

"Okay, bad choice of words. I thought we were taking Archie to see his former owner. You told me to be here by seven."

Liz groaned. She'd completely forgotten about the command visit she'd insisted he pay to Cordelia.

"Give me ten minutes," she said at once.

"Take twenty. I'll make coffee."

"If I had decent coffee in the house, do you think I'd drink so much at Sally's?"

"Okay, then. I'll make a run to Sally's. You still get twenty minutes. How about some eggs to go with the coffee? Toast? Anything? Frankly, I'm starving, so I wouldn't say no to breakfast before we go."

Liz studied his cheerful expression, then sighed. "We're back to giving me ten minutes. Then we'll both go to Sally's."

He grinned. "That works for me. What about Archie?"

At last she found a reason to smile. "He can go upstairs and investigate his new home while we eat. He's much better these days about chewing up the furniture."

Aidan stared at her. "Am I supposed to take comfort from that?"

She beamed at him. "You probably should. He still has a few other habits you'll probably want to break him of. I hope you have plenty of room on the top shelf in your closets for your shoes."

Aidan's heartfelt sigh followed her into the bathroom.

A few minutes later, they had Archie and his

crate in Aidan's car and were parking behind the shops on Main Street. Upstairs, which truly was a lot smaller than Liz had imagined, the dog went dutifully into his crate, though he gave Aidan a look of betrayal as he did it.

"We'll be right back," Liz promised. "You be a good dog. No barking."

Woof! Archie barked, but without much energy behind it.

Downstairs at Sally's Liz cursed her lack of foresight when they walked in to find the usual assortment of O'Brien women already assembled.

"There you are," Bree called out. "We saved you a seat." She grinned at Aidan. "We had no idea you were coming, but we can fit you in, too."

Liz noted that Aidan looked as if he'd rather eat dirt, but he dutifully took the space Bree had indicated next to Heather in the booth, while Liz took the chair that had been pulled up to the end of the table. Aidan immediately grabbed a menu and hid behind it, which gave all of the women the chance to give Liz a less than subtle thumbs-up.

This morning just got better and better, Liz thought with a sigh. She was never going to hear the end of it. Her endless denials were already falling on deaf ears. She was starting to not give much credence to them herself. She was just about as smitten as they all thought she was.

When they'd played basketball, Connor O'Brien had told Aidan to feel free to borrow his boat anytime he felt like going out on the bay to do a little fishing.

So, after that uncomfortable breakfast accompanied by less than subtle grilling and a visit to Cordelia, who seemed thrilled about the new arrangement for her beloved Archie, Aidan made a quick call to Connor to make sure he didn't have plans to use the boat. Some alone time on the water, where no meddlers could find him, held a lot of appeal.

At Mick's, Aidan walked out onto the sun-drenched dock and launched the sturdy little row-boat. It had a small engine, but since he'd decided on doing this for the exercise, he stuck to using the oars. He was glad there was no one around to witness his awkward attempt to maneuver even such a tiny craft on the calm water.

He rowed steadily for a half hour or so until the muscles in his shoulders cried out, then rowed back to the dock, aware that it had been a pitiful testament to his inexperience on the water.

As he was tying up the boat, he glanced up and spotted Thomas O'Brien sitting on a bench at the end of the dock, his son Sean nearby with a fishing pole in his hands and his feet dangling in the water. Aidan fumbled with the rope he was using to tie the boat to the dock. Thomas caught it before it fell into the bay and tied it securely.

"How's the fishing?" he asked Aidan.

"I couldn't say. I was just testing to make sure I could get out on the water and back. Did you come over to take the boat out?" Aidan asked. "Connor said he wasn't planning to use it this morning."

"Sean's perfectly content right here," Thomas said. "So am I. Nothing I like better than being around the bay on a day like this. It's a reminder of why I spend all those hours locked up in my office in Annapolis or making the rounds to visit all the power brokers trying to prod them into making tougher laws."

As Aidan stood there awkwardly, trying to figure out something to say, he realized Thomas was studying him intently.

Maybe there was nothing more to the look than simple curiosity, but it made Aidan nervous. What if Thomas saw something familiar in his face? None of the other O'Briens seemed to have noted any family resemblance, but Aidan wasn't 100 percent sure there wasn't one.

"Since I ran into you, would this be a good time for you to tell me a little more about your foundation?" he asked, mostly to divert Thomas's attention. He figured it wouldn't hurt to reassure Thomas of his interest while he was at it.

To be honest, since coming to town and hearing so many extol Thomas's virtues, he'd become increasingly curious about the mission that had kept the man from wanting to be a dad twenty-eight years ago. He seemed to have settled into the role quite comfortably now with Sean, who looked to be about seven.

"We do what we can to protect this amazing estuary," Thomas explained readily. "It's a never-ending task. Seems as if there's always someone who wants to loosen the laws to allow more farm or industrial runoff. If we're not strict about the limits on fishing, crabbing and so on, the supplies will dwindle dangerously. If we're not vigilant about all of it, we'll lose the battle and this estuary will be destroyed. That would be a crying shame."

Aidan could hear the passion in his voice and followed his gaze toward the sparkling waters. An eagle chose just that moment to soar into the air. "It would be," he found himself saying as he watched the magnificent bird's flight. "How did you get interested?"

"I spent my life on these waters. I caught my first rockfish right off this pier, or the old rotting one that preceded it, I should say. I caught crabs, even hauled in a few oysters from time to time. Then I started reading about the decreasing supplies for the watermen to harvest every year. I hung out with some of them and listened to their stories. I could see for myself that the ecosystem was changing and not for the better. I couldn't sit by and watch that happen, not just for my generation, but for the generations to come."

"Sounds like an all-consuming goal," Aidan said. Thomas's words were no salve for years of resentment, but Aidan was forced to admit he was beginning to understand just a little.

"If you're really interested, I have some books you could read," Thomas said, then grinned. "I try to turn everyone I meet into a convert when it comes to the environment around here. I figure no one could be a harder sell than my brother, and I've finally gotten Mick on board."

"He didn't agree?"

"Not when it interfered with his plans for building the town," Thomas revealed. "Had to take him to court."

Aidan's mouth gaped. "You took Mick to court? I'd heard there was bad blood back then, but no one mentioned why."

"We're past it now," Thomas said, then chuckled. "Mostly, anyway. He claims he even sees my point. This town probably sticks to the spirit of the Chesapeake Bay Act more closely than any other community along the water in any of the states where it applies."

Aidan began to see just how deep Thomas's convictions ran. He couldn't help admiring that, even if it also confirmed that in the past he and his mom would have been no match for such dedicated idealism. He tried to imagine what it would be like to be so passionate about a cause that people didn't matter.

And yet Thomas appeared to be happily married now, a contented family man. How had that happened? What powers of persuasion had Thomas's wife, Connie, had that his mom hadn't. Bitterness, never far from the surface especially since he'd come to town, reared its head. It was complicated by the school principal's insistence that he take on the after-school assignment of working with the kids who'd organized a junior support group for Thomas's foundation.

A one-year commitment, he reminded himself. Not forever. For now he needed to embrace this opportunity to get to know his father on his own turf.

"I imagine I'll have to get up to speed if I'm going to be working with the kids at the high school," he finally said. "They probably know a lot more than I do at this point."

Thomas regarded him with what seemed to be real pleasure and maybe even a hint of relief. "They're a fine group of young people. It's been wonderful to see them dedicated to a cause that's so important to this town and this entire region. I guess that means we'll be working closely together, too, since I try to come to as many of the meetings and activities as I can."

Aidan bit back a sigh. He'd known that would be the case, but hearing it rattled him more than he'd expected. Somehow he'd envisioned crossing paths with his father only on rare occasions. Surely Thomas was too busy to spend much time with one high school club, or so he'd convinced himself. He'd had some crazy idea about being able to glean the kind of man he was from limited contact, just enough to fill in the gaps without forming any real relationship.

Still, maybe it was a good thing, becoming immersed in his father's cause. He was already convinced about what a good cause it was. If he ever hoped to bond with the man, this was an excellent way to start.

"I imagine I'll be wanting those books you recommend and perhaps a short course in what we need to do to be effective and helpful," he told Thomas.

"Anytime you're ready," Thomas responded cheerfully. "As you can already tell, it's a topic I never tire of discussing."

"I'll be in touch, then," Aidan said. He gave a wave to Sean, his half brother, a concept he couldn't even begin to wrestle with right now. "Hope you catch something."

Sean gave him a beaming grin. "I always do. Mom's counting on me bringing home dinner."

"You could join us," Thomas suggested. "I can pass along a couple of books."

"Thanks. Another time. I have plans for tonight."

He had no idea what those plans might be, but anything would be better than pretending that this man hadn't had the power to make Aidan's life very different from the one he'd had.

Not that it had been a bad life. His mom had been amazing. She'd worked hard and they'd been okay. But even in a few short weeks in town, he'd come to realize that a childhood as an O'Brien would have been something very different, indeed.

Liz was standing in the doorway of her shop when she saw Aidan ambling in her direction. Her heart did a little flutter. Apparently it was not getting the message about avoiding him or keeping him in a tidy little box labeled "friend."

As Aidan drew closer, she noted the troubled expression on his face and instinct kicked in.

"Everything okay?" she called out.

He glanced in her direction as if surprised to see her. "Hey. I didn't notice you standing there."

"I opened the door to let in a little fresh air. It cuts down on AC bills and when the weather's this beautiful, I like to enjoy it. Where have you been?"

"After we left Cordelia's, I took Connor's boat out."

"Catch anything?"

He chuckled. "I didn't even try. Trying to keep the boat from going in circles was about all I could cope with."

"Is that what put that expression on your face? Doing something at which you didn't excel?"

"Believe me, there are plenty of things I don't do well. And I don't know what expression you thought you saw, but being on the water was nice. It was a new experience, and I'm always open to trying new stuff." He gave her a lingering look. "On that note, how about dinner tonight? We can plot our anti-matchmaking strategy. And I've been hearing really good things about Brady's."

"It's excellent," she confirmed, tempted.

"Is that a yes?"

She couldn't think of a single good reason to say no, other than panic at the thought of spending an evening with him in the romantic ambience of Brady's. Since she tried really hard not to avoid things just because they were scary, she nodded.

"Sure. I'd love to go. I'll want to go home and change first."

"You close up here at six, right? How about I pick you up at seven? I'll make a reservation."

"Good idea. It's the summer season, so it can be packed."

He gave her another long look, one she couldn't quite interpret. It made her toes curl just the same.

"Thanks, Liz. I'll see you at seven."

And, as he had too many times before, he bolted before she could make sense of exactly what was going on. The man was a mystery, and as anyone in their so-called book club could testify,

Liz was a real sucker for a good mystery. This time, though, she had a hunch that even with her well-honed detective skills, the ending might be totally unanticipated.

Mick was sitting on the porch smoking his pipe, something he'd been forbidden from doing inside, when he spotted his brother and nephew coming up from the pier.

"Catch anything?" he asked Sean, who promptly beamed at him.

"Two big rockfish," he said proudly. "And I reeled 'em in all by myself." He glanced up at his dad, then amended, "Well, mostly by myself. Wanna see?"

"Of course I do," Mick said as the boy lugged the heavy bucket filled with seawater over to him. The water sloshed onto the porch, causing Sean's eyes to widen with dismay.

"I'm sorry," he said. "I'll clean it up."

"Hey, it's not a big deal. Maybe you could run into the kitchen and ask your aunt Megan to give you some clean water to rinse it off."

"Sure," Sean said eagerly, running off.

"Connie's doing a real good job with that boy," Mick said.

Thomas feigned a scowl, just as Mick had anticipated.

"Hey, I know a thing or two about manners," Thomas protested. "Ma saw to that."

Mick laughed. "She did, indeed."

Thomas sat down in the rocker next to Mick's, drawing in a deep breath. "That pipe tobacco still reminds me of Dad."

Mick nodded. "I know. It's the only reason I smoke the thing. It brings back memories."

They sat there for a few minutes in surprisingly companionable silence given their sometimes contentious relationship.

"Thought I saw Aidan coming up from the pier earlier," Mick finally said.

Thomas sighed. "You did. He'd apparently taken Connor's boat out for a while."

Mick studied his brother. "Now, why does that put that particular look on your face? Did he toss some trash into the bay? Let some oil spill out of the motor?"

Thomas frowned at him. "He did neither one. I'm just finding him hard to read. I saw him here at dinner and once since, and he seemed to get along well with everybody, but when I've spoken to him, he gets real uptight."

"You must be imagining things," Mick said.

"I thought so, too, at first, but it's happened more than once. He's supposed to replace Coach Gentry with that bay preservation club at the high school, but when I spoke to him about it at the school and again just now, I sensed he wasn't very enthusiastic about the idea. I even mentioned that to Kevin after the first time we spoke. He said he talked to Aidan and that he swore he was committed to the project. Even today, he said all the right words, but there was no passion behind them, if you know what I mean."

Mick gave him an amused look. "Do I need to point out that there's probably nobody on God's green earth, and I use the term advisedly, who's as devoted to the cause as you and my son?"

Thomas chuckled, visibly relaxing. "You're probably right about that."

"Stop your worrying," Mick advised. "Give him time to get up to speed. If Aidan doesn't seem to be coming around, you can insist on a new adviser for the group. Or you can talk to him about it, see what his reservations are. It could be as simple as being single-minded about getting the football team into shape. That is why he was hired, after all."

"That's pretty much what he said to Kevin. I just wish I didn't have this sense that there's something I'm missing."

"Such as?"

"I don't know exactly," Thomas admitted. "He reminds me of someone, but I can't put my finger on who it might be."

"Now you really are imagining things," Mick said. "That boy's never been anywhere near Chesapeake Shores before. I've seen his résumé. He grew up in New York, went to school there, played ball there. In fact, that's probably why he looks familiar. You probably saw him play a time or two on TV, that is if you ever glanced up from one of your books long enough to watch football."

Thomas ignored the gibe and nodded. "That's probably it."

Sean came back just then with water and a mop. He could barely lift the bucket, so Mick dumped the sudsy water on the porch to wash away the salt water, then reached for the mop. "I'll take care of this. You get those fish home to your mama, so she can fix 'em for dinner."

Sean made a face. "Dad and me have to clean 'em first."

Thomas didn't look any more pleased about that than his boy did. "Yes, we do," he said.

Mick slapped his brother on the back, but grinned at Sean. "Go on, you two. Cleaning fish will make a man of you."

Thomas scowled at him. "When was the last time you cleaned one?"

"I've cleaned more than my share over the years," Mick claimed, then shrugged. "You and Jeff were always too squeamish."

"Squeamish?" Thomas echoed indignantly as his son laughed.

"Squeamish," Mick repeated, then looked at his nephew. "And don't you let him tell you otherwise."

"Come on, Sean," Thomas urged. "Let's get out

of here before my brother completely ruins your idealized vision of me."

Sean blinked. "Huh?"

"I'll explain on the way home," Thomas said, scowling at Mick.

As Mick watched the two of them cross the lawn, his booming laugh trailed after them. Nothing much he liked better than getting under his brother's skin from time to time. It beat most of those hobbies his wife was always telling him he should try.

⇒· 10 ·⇐

Even though her planned dinner with Aidan was emphatically *not* a date, it felt a whole lot as if it was, Liz concluded as she yanked one outfit after another from her closet, then tossed them aside as all wrong. Brady's wasn't fancy, but it did seem to require something dressier than her old teaching wardrobe of slacks and tailored blouses, which she also tended to wear at the store because they were comfortable.

Okay, dressier wasn't exactly right, either, she admitted to herself. She wanted something more feminine and just wanting that scared her because it seemed to prove that this *was* a date, after all. Otherwise, it wouldn't matter to her how she looked.

Women always care how they look, she mentally defended herself as she tossed aside a perfectly acceptable dress that she would have worn out with anyone else.

"Oh, just pick something," she grumbled finally, reaching back into her closet. Her hand landed on a sundress that came with a saucy little midriff-length sweater that was perfect for a night that promised to be a little cool. So what if the dress had a slightly revealing neckline? The bright blue color and sprinkling of daisies across the fabric made it cheerful and feminine. It was meant to be worn on an occasion just like this one. In fact, she'd bought it on impulse on sale last summer on the off chance she'd ever again have a special evening planned. It still had the price tags attached, which probably proved just how dull she'd allowed her social life to become.

Satisfied at last, she was dressed in minutes. She picked up a bottle of her favorite perfume, then found herself debating whether perfume suggested a date. Thoroughly impatient with herself for regressing to the behavior of an unsophisticated teenager with a first boyfriend, she spritzed the light scent into the air and walked through the mist.

When Aidan knocked, Archie went nuts as usual, racing impatiently between her bedroom and the door and back as if to hurry her up.

"Would you please just calm down?" she

ordered, laughing, "before I trip and wind up on the floor."

She was still laughing when she opened the door. Aidan's eyes widened appreciatively, his gaze never once leaving her as he petted Archie distractedly.

"You look amazing," he said at last.

Liz smiled. Exactly the effect she'd been going for, even if she hadn't wanted to admit it. "Thank you."

"You ready to go?"

Not really, she thought, fearful of the way her pulse seemed to be suddenly scrambling and of the long-missing hum of excitement that had stirred in her blood. "All set," she forced herself to say.

Even though she argued that Brady's was close enough to walk there, Aidan insisted on taking his car.

"You've been on your feet all day." He glanced down at the strappy, sexy heels she'd put on at the last minute. "And those shoes don't look to me as if they're meant for long strolls."

"Probably not," she admitted. They were pretty and very feminine, but not especially practical.

At the restaurant, they found the foyer jammed with people waiting for tables, just as she'd predicted. Aidan slipped through the crowd to claim their reservation, then returned to her side.

"They told me it would be about ten minutes. Want to wait here or in the bar?"

"Here's fine," she said.

"So, how was business today?" he asked. "Any letdown after the holiday weekend last week?"

"Maybe a little, but it was still surprisingly busy. More locals came in, I think. I'm discovering they tend to avoid the big holiday crowds. Several mentioned to me that they prefer the quieter weekdays when the tourists have gone home. I can't say I blame them. That's when Chesapeake Shores is at its best."

He studied her, then smiled. "You really love it here, don't you?"

Liz nodded. "I do, more and more. How about you? You regretting that you didn't commit to being here longer?"

To her regret, Aidan shook his head.

"One year was the right thing to do. That said, this is starting to feel like home. Or maybe I've just found my comfort zone now that I'm working with the team."

Liz was about to ask how that was going when Porter and Pamela Hobbs walked out of the main dining room and straight toward them. She noticed Aidan tensing at their approach.

"Mitchell," Porter said tersely.

"Mr. Hobbs," Aidan said stiffly. "Mrs. Hobbs. How was your dinner?"

"Overcooked," Pamela said sourly. "I don't recommend you have the prime rib. I had to send it back twice."

186

Liz fought to hide a smile. Little wonder it was overcooked, if the waiter had taken it back to the kitchen twice. It was a wonder he hadn't thrown it in her face. Brady, however, was known for training his staff to accommodate the customers' wishes, no matter how unreasonable or demanding.

"I'll definitely keep that in mind," Liz told her.

Porter scowled at Aidan. "I had a talk with Mick O'Brien the other day," he reported.

"Is that so?" Aidan said mildly, not sounding especially surprised.

"I gather you'd run to him tattling on me," Porter said derisively.

"Actually I didn't," Aidan said. "Mick stopped by practice. He saw the boys in action and wanted to know how the team is shaping up. I told him."

"I know what you told him," Porter said irritably. "You're going to pick that Santos kid over my boy. I warned you about that."

Liz noted that Aidan didn't back away. Nor did he seem intimidated by the man's bluster.

"And I told Mick the same thing I told you, that I was brought here to do what's best for the team. Taylor and I've had a talk about putting him in a different position, one where he can make a real contribution to the team. He's eager to try that. You should come by. He and Hector have a real connection on the field, probably because Taylor has played at quarterback. He understands the routes. He can anticipate exactly where Hector intends to throw a pass. He's got not only the instincts, but the hands to make the reception."

Porter didn't seem the least bit pacified. "The boy was meant to play quarterback," he said, refusing to back down.

"Let me ask you this," Aidan suggested, his tone reasonable. "Would you rather have him develop as a mediocre quarterback who won't get the attention of a single college scout, or a star receiver who can take his pick of some of the best football programs in the country?"

Porter finally looked intrigued, as well he should, Liz thought, impressed with Aidan's argument.

"You think he can do that?" Porter asked, a noticeable gleam in his eyes.

"Porter, honey, don't let him try to sweet-talk you into changing your mind," Pamela argued. "We know what's best for our son. Everyone knows it's the quarterback who gets the money and attention."

Liz wanted to step in and remind her of who had the pro football experience and the coach's job, but she kept quiet, mostly because it was obvious Aidan didn't need her help. Porter seemed to be wavering at last.

"I asked you a question," Porter reminded Aidan, shooting a quelling look at his wife that silenced her.

"Come by and watch the two of them," Aidan suggested. "Then you tell me."

"I'll be there Monday afternoon," Porter said. "I'd better be impressed by what I see."

"I think you will be," Aidan replied.

"I'm coming with you," Pamela said, not looking nearly as convinced as her husband. "I want to see for myself what all this hype is about that Santos kid." She frowned at Aidan. "You'd better hope this is not about some liberal, knee-jerk attempt to play favorites because the boy's Hispanic and deserves a break he hasn't earned."

Liz spotted a muscle tic in Aidan's jaw and knew the limits of his diplomatic skills were being sorely tested. She'd held her tongue up to now, but she couldn't let Pamela's ill-considered remark slide.

"I've spent a little time with Hector," she told the couple. "He's a very nice young man. He's humble, smart and eager to help the team. So is Taylor. You should be proud of that."

Pamela frowned at the suggestion by someone they barely knew that they weren't taking pride in their son's willingness to be a team player. "Of course we're proud of Taylor. We want the best for him."

"As all parents want the best for their children," Aidan said. "My job is to go beyond that and figure out what's best for the team. Ultimately that will make each of these kids shine, too."

"Can't argue with that," Porter conceded reluctantly, though Pamela still didn't look satisfied.

"We'll be there Monday afternoon," Porter repeated, almost as if it were meant as a warning. "Come along, Pamela."

Just then the maître d' came to take Liz and Aidan to their table. Only when they were seated did Liz meet Aidan's gaze.

"Well, that was fun," she commented as she took a sip of her water. Her mouth seemed to have gone dry as a result of all that tension. "Is that what it's been like for you the past couple of weeks? Are you getting pressure from every direction?"

"To be honest, Porter's the only one who's made any kind of a fuss," Aidan said. "Hopefully, once he sees what those two boys can do on the field, he'll back off."

Liz studied him closely. "Any regrets now about going into coaching? Dealing with Porter would be enough to send me packing."

Aidan laughed. "You never met my mom. I think dealing with Porter is some kind of karmic payback for me. I'm pretty sure she came close to driving my high school coach into an early grave. She watched the Giants and the Jets every Sunday, studied them, in fact. She thought she knew everything there was to know about the game and about my ability to play it. I'm surprised she didn't insist on sitting on the bench and naming herself assistant coach. I keep reminding myself about that whenever I have to deal with Porter."

He grinned at her. "Thankfully, by the time I went to college, I'd convinced her to back off."

Liz stared at him. "You're kidding. It took that long? You must have been humiliated."

"Not really. I suppose I was embarrassed from time to time, especially when my teammates would get on my case, but I got what she was doing. No kid ever had a bigger advocate than Anna Mitchell. It started when I played in a Pop Warner league and never let up. I think she was determined to fill the role she imagined a father would have filled if my dad had been around. Trust me, there were dads whose behavior was a whole lot more humiliating."

"Was it tough?" Liz asked. "Not having your father in your life?"

An odd expression washed over Aidan's face, one she couldn't quite read. There was a hint of sadness, yes, but also something else. Bitterness, maybe. Since he usually seemed so upbeat about his upbringing, it surprised her a little.

"As a little kid, I had a lot of questions about why I didn't have a dad around," he revealed eventually. "Mostly what my mom did was remind me that we were so lucky to have each other."

"She never told you about your father, not even when you asked?"

"She had a standard response, one that painted a

rosy picture of an incredible man who simply hadn't been ready to be a dad. I tried my best to take my cues from her. She didn't seem to hate him for that, so how could I? Besides, I could see how sad it made her to think that she wasn't enough for me."

"So even as a boy, you were intuitive and kind," Liz surmised.

"I loved my mom," he said simply. "I didn't want to make her unhappy. Don't get me wrong. I wasn't a saint. I lashed out from time to time and accused her of trying to keep me from my dad. I even threatened to take off and find him, but mostly I kept my questions and my resentment to myself."

"That's very noble. Didn't you ever want some genetic history or a name?"

"Sure, and more than once as I got older I thought about digging around and trying to find answers on my own, but I thought about how disrespectful that might seem to her. And I told myself, when it came right down to it, what did it matter? Why would I want to know someone who didn't care enough about either of us to be in our lives."

Liz didn't entirely buy that he'd been that mature about it. Oh, she believed he loved his mom and hadn't wanted to distress her, but a teenager's curiosity about who'd fathered him wasn't usually pacified by logic.

She saw Aidan studying her, a faint smile on his lips. "You think I'm glossing over how much this bothered me, don't you?"

"Are you?"

"Okay, I've been resentful and bitter at times, no question about it, but I covered that up with my mom. There were times as I got older when I wanted to demand answers, but just when I might have pushed for them, my mom got cancer. After that my whole focus was on trying to support her." His expression turned sad. "And then it was too late." He gave her a wry look. "There was no deathbed confession of the truth, in case you're wondering."

"So you still don't know any more about the man who fathered you?"

Instead of a direct answer, he gave her a puzzled look. "Why are you so concerned about this? It's ancient history. *My* ancient history."

Liz was taken aback by his sharp tone. "I guess I was just trying to picture myself in your shoes, having all these huge questions left unanswered."

He held her gaze. "I know who I am, Liz. I know the kind of man I am, and it was Anna Mitchell who made me into that man, not some guy who provided sperm."

The heated response made her squirm. What had she been thinking, digging into such a private topic and suggesting he'd handled it all wrong? She was the one who'd been putting up walls, and now she was climbing over them herself, trying to turn this into a more intimate relationship than she herself had claimed to want.

"I'm sorry," she said sincerely. "I really didn't mean to upset you. I grew up with my family intact. I had lots of friends whose parents were divorced, but at least both parents were in their lives to one degree or another. It's hard for me to picture growing up without ever seeing a parent or knowing anything about the kind of person they are. I guess I was projecting what I imagined my reaction would be onto you."

Aidan stared out at the bay, then took a drink of his water before he finally faced her again. "I took my mother at her word, that he was a good man. For most of my life that was enough for me. It had to be."

Liz didn't believe for an instant that he still felt that way, because the shadows in his eyes when he said it told another story entirely. Clearly, though, it was a story he didn't intend to share with her. And hadn't she had enough of men with secrets to last a lifetime? It was just one more reminder about the wisdom of keeping Aidan at arm's length.

Once dinner came—neither of them had the prime rib—the conversation turned casual and Aidan finally allowed himself to relax. All that talk about his dad had left him jittery and uncomfortable.

Sure, he'd had questions, maybe a million of them. He still did, but he was finally in a position to get a few of them answered. He just wasn't ready to share that information with anyone, not even this woman who seemed to be genuinely concerned about him.

He glanced across the table, noting the color in Liz's cheeks, possibly put there by the one glass of wine she'd allowed herself. Strands of blond hair had escaped her topknot to curl carelessly about her face. She looked relaxed and infinitely more approachable than she probably intended.

"Dessert? Coffee?" he asked, not eager for the night to end, despite those earlier uncomfortable moments.

She studied the dessert menu, then put it aside with a sigh of regret. "Not for me."

He grinned. "You don't even want to share that chocolate lava cake with me?"

Her eyes lit up, just as he'd anticipated. He'd learned that women could resist a lot of treats, but that one seemed to call to them. It usually became irresistible after just the tiniest bit of encouragement from him.

"You promise you'll eat most of it?" she asked.

"Promise," he said solemnly, beckoning for the waiter. When he'd placed the order for the decadent cake and two decaf coffees, he sat back and studied her.

She was a mass of contradictions tonight. That dress with its revealing neckline sent out one message that contradicted every word she spoke about what she was looking for in her life. Or more specifically, what she didn't want. Even as she held him almost literally at arm's length, her demeanor and questions invited him into a more personal relationship. Aidan didn't know what to make of her. He certainly couldn't see that they were headed in the direction that was expected by a whole slew of O'Briens.

And yet there was that undeniable spark of electricity, the one they were both so determinedly ignoring.

When the waiter returned with the warm cake with its dark chocolate interior and ice cream melting into that fudgy moistness, he watched as Liz dipped her spoon into the gooey concoction, then put it into her mouth, closing her eyes with a moan of pleasure.

Desire ricocheted through him like a heat-seeking missile. Dessert—at least this particular one with this particular woman—had definitely been a bad idea. It was putting thoughts into his head that had nothing to do with food. That was something that had never happened before. Usually he was content just to observe his date's enjoyment of something she usually denied herself.

Liz had eaten several bites before she noticed

that he'd had none. "Hey, you promised to eat your share."

"It's more fun watching you savor every spoonful," he admitted candidly, though he did pick up his spoon and take a tiny bite. The dark chocolate burst on his tongue in all its promised decadence. He could see why it had sent her into raptures. "Not bad."

She laughed at the understatement. "I defy you not to take another bite. It's addictive. Admit it."

Aidan put down his spoon to prove a point, but Liz waved hers under his nose. The aroma alone was enough to have his mouth watering. He snagged it from her hand. "Okay, you win. It's addictive."

She sat back, seemingly satisfied with his response. "How on earth will I ever work off all those calories?"

"Not that you need to worry about that," he said, "but how about a walk on the deck out back? It looks as if it runs along the waterfront far enough to give us a little bit of a workout."

"Perfect," she said at once.

"I'll get the waiter."

Aidan paid the bill and held out his hand. After a faint hesitation, Liz slipped hers into his, then followed him outside. She paused long enough to remove her shoes, leaving her barefoot as they strolled side by side.

"It is so beautiful," she whispered, pausing to stand by the railing.

A full moon glistened in a silvery path across the bay. As Aidan stood beside her, he couldn't seem to keep his gaze off her face. She looked especially soft and radiant in the moonlight. Her pale pink lips were more tempting than any of the decadent desserts on the menu had been, and that was saying something. Even that chocolate lava cake couldn't compare when it came to pure temptation.

Before he could resist, he touched her cheek, then leaned down, brushing his mouth across hers. Unsure of his welcome, it began as a gentle, tentative touch. In less time than it took for their breath to mingle, though, it changed into something more, something hot and demanding, as darkly delicious as that chocolate. The air seemed charged with electricity. His blood hadn't pumped this hard after his five-mile run first thing this morning.

Reluctantly, he pulled away and looked into her dazed eyes.

"You okay?" he asked.

"A little stunned," she admitted. "It wasn't supposed to be like that."

He smiled at her unexpected candor. "So, Miss Liz, you've been imagining our first kiss? What was it supposed to be like?"

"No, of course not," she claimed, clearly flustered. "I meant it wasn't supposed to happen at all." A frown settled on her face. "We can't do that again, Aidan." She said it with as much starch as a librarian trying to quiet an unruly patron.

"Oh, I think we will," he corrected, convinced that the barriers they'd been putting up had just come crashing down around both of them. Knowing how quickly a fire had flared between them wasn't something either of them was likely to forget or ignore, no matter how hard they tried.

She backed up a step, shaking her head. "No. I mean it, Aidan. This just can't happen."

It suddenly registered that she wasn't just being coy. "Why not? You're single, right? I thought I heard you were a widow, in fact."

"That doesn't mean I'm fair game," she said with surprising ferocity.

Aidan was startled by her angry reaction. "Of course not." He regarded her with worry, fearing he'd crossed some line he'd never even imagined was there. "Liz, what's going on? If you're genuinely not interested in anything more than being friends, just say so."

"Haven't I said that more than once?" she asked with real frustration.

"I'd like to know why, if you're willing to explain."

"Can't you just accept that's the way it has to be?" she asked plaintively.

"If that's the way it has to be, then of course I can," he conceded. "But that kiss said something else. I think it would be a shame not to share a few more of those to see where this might lead."

"I disagree."

"Is this about that one-year deal I signed? You don't think I'm capable of commitment?"

"Maybe a little," she said. "But it's more than just that."

"Please explain. I might be able to put your mind at ease." A sudden thought struck him. "Is it the tabloids? I know they made me out to be a playboy when I first played professionally, but that was so far from the truth it was laughable."

"I don't follow the tabloids," she assured him. "This is just for the best, Aidan. Let's leave it at that."

He bit back a sigh at her stubborn refusal to explain. He could sense a real fear of some kind behind her reaction, but he was at a loss to interpret it. In the end, though, it was her decision. He had to respect that.

"Okay, then," he said quietly. "If you don't want to pursue this—"

"I don't want to pursue it," she said emphatically, though her voice was shaking. She couldn't seem to meet his gaze, which suggested she might be lying to him, maybe even to herself.

Still, Aidan wasn't about to force the issue. Sometimes people just didn't click. Given everything else in his life, devoting time to figuring out Liz was probably a lousy idea anyway.

He dared to touch her cheek again. "Liz, sweetheart, don't look so miserable. No broken hearts here, okay? We'll stick to being friends."

Her eyes were surprisingly bright as she directed her gaze everywhere but toward him. He realized with a sense of shock that she was close to tears.

"Thanks for understanding," she said, still not meeting his gaze as those tears tracked down her cheeks.

"Sure," he said. But the truth was, he didn't understand at all. And he had a hunch he wasn't going to forget that kiss half as easily as he'd claimed.

⇒ 11 ⇐

Liz avoided Sally's the morning after her dinner with Aidan, even though Sunday-morning breakfast there was her favorite. Sally made outstanding waffles with real Vermont maple syrup and served them with bacon that was perfectly crisped. There were usually a few other people there whom she knew, not as many as there might be on a weekday, but enough that she usually had company. The comfort of those waffles and her friends was probably what she needed most. What she didn't need, though, was a chance encounter with Aidan after that ground-shaking kiss and the downhill evening that had followed.

Liz kept right on avoiding the café during the next week and the following weekend, even though Shanna, Bree and Heather had all called her on it. They clearly recognized there was something more behind this change in her routine than the flimsy excuses she kept offering. Liz, however, was determinedly not talking. Satisfying their curiosity was not her top priority. Getting her equilibrium back was.

She'd been doing just fine building a new life. The attraction to Aidan had been an unanticipated distraction from her goal of becoming the independent woman she wanted to be. And, no matter how hot those kisses had been, two people with secrets they were intent on keeping could hardly have any sort of future, not when trust and honesty had to be at the core of any relationship.

So, instead of the routine she'd come to love, she ate a bowl of cereal standing up at her kitchen counter, then took the dogs for a walk, hoping the exercise would wipe out the memory of that amazingly romantic moment on the deck at Brady's with moonlight spilling over them.

Unfortunately, it seemed it would take more than a daily walk to accomplish that. That kiss had been every bit as magical as Aidan had believed, no question about it.

Maybe, she thought with a hint of wry humor, it could be excised from her brain with some sort of Gamma Knife procedure. Until then, though, she had to keep moving and trying to dodge all the questions that kept coming her way from her friends.

On the second Sunday of her self-imposed exile, she was almost home when Archie started straining at his leash, then broke free and bounded toward the house. She understood why when she spotted Aidan sitting on the front porch. Her traitorous heart leaped with almost as much joy as Archie was expressing. She closed her eyes for an instant and prayed for guidance.

"Good morning," Aidan said quietly, then held out a large take-out cup of coffee from Sally's. "You weren't at breakfast. It's not the first time you've missed it. Since the absences started the day after we kissed, I've gotten the feeling you're avoiding me."

"Why would I do that?" she said, as if the thought had never crossed her mind. "I just changed up my routine. I like taking the dogs for a walk instead. They need the exercise before being cooped up in the house all day."

Hoping to divert his attention from whatever

his mission might be, she said, "By the way, isn't school out this week?"

"Tuesday's the last day," he confirmed.

"Then you'll be getting Archie on Wednesday," she said flatly, not allowing any room for argument. "I'll have all his things ready by eight, so you can pick him up."

Aidan's gaze locked on hers. "I didn't come to discuss the arrangements for Archie."

A flash of panic washed over her. She'd been hoping that he'd gotten the message, that the words she'd spoken that night at Brady's and her subsequent actions had finally gotten through to him that she wasn't interested. Or, to be more precise, wasn't going to *allow* herself to act on any wayward interest she might feel.

If only they'd never shared that blasted kiss, she thought, remembering it in exquisite detail— the softness of his lips, the mingling of their breath, the heat that had tracked right through her bloodstream. Good thing she wasn't like most men, she concluded wryly, since they thought with their hormones. A dynamite kiss was all it took to wipe reason straight out of their heads. Fortunately, she was less susceptible. Well, not to the kiss, but to the urge to follow up on it with more.

She accepted the coffee Aidan held out to her, but made herself frown at him. "I thought we weren't going to pursue this, whatever *this* might be. Didn't we decide that just the other night? I thought I'd made myself clear. Have you forgotten that conversation and your promise already?"

Aidan didn't seem impressed by the reminder or the snippy tone in which she delivered it. "I brought coffee, Liz. *Friends* do that sort of thing, especially when they sense they might have upset a *friend* and that the *friend* might be deliberately avoiding them because of it."

The way he delivered the word *friend* made a mockery of it. Still, he allowed the words to hang in the air until she finally sighed, pretty much acknowledging that he'd gotten it right. Darn the man for being so intuitive. Under other circumstances, it was a trait she'd appreciate.

"Do you want me to go?" he asked.

"I suppose not, especially since you've brought coffee," she said, sounding more like a petulant child than a grateful woman. And truthfully, she was grateful. She'd been caffeine deprived for days now. The weak, if convenient, coffee she'd been begging from Shanna just didn't compare to Sally's strong brew.

Filled with reluctance, she sat next to him. All three dogs flopped down in the sunshine, though Archie's spot was once again as close as possible to Aidan. Liz got it. Despite her very strong resolve, she wanted to throw herself straight into his arms. She had a feeling all that solid muscle and masculine heat would prove irresistibly comforting, and right this second, she was in desperate need of reassurance. Unfortunately, though, he was the last man she ought to be getting that from.

They sat in silence for a while, sipping coffee. She had to give him credit. He apparently wasn't going to push for answers, even if he claimed to have come here to get them. She appreciated that more than she could say.

"Do you want to talk about it?" he asked eventually.

She immediately stiffened. So much for not prying. "Talk about what?"

"Whatever happened that made you so determined to keep men in general, or me in particular, at arm's length."

"Do you really need to dissect the whole thing?" she asked. "I thought most men hated that sort of discussion."

"I'm not most men," he said. "And despite these walls you want to keep up between us, I do care about you."

She studied him curiously. "Hasn't anyone ever turned you down before?"

The question seemed to amuse him. "More times than you can probably imagine. I can take rejection, Liz. It's not about that."

"Then what is it about?"

"I made you cry," he said simply.

"I did not cry," she said fiercely.

"Close enough," he said. "I saw the tears in your eyes, even as you were saying no to us spending more time together."

"You're imagining things," she said, a note of desperation in her voice.

He held her gaze, then said quietly, "I don't think so."

"Why can't you just take what I said at face value and leave it alone?"

"Because that kiss was amazing. I don't know about you, but that kind of chemistry doesn't come along every day for me. I felt it the first time I saw you. It seems like a shame not to see where it could take us. Believe me, I have a whole slew of reservations about it, too. The timing is lousy for one thing. I have a lot to prove in this town. Still, I can't help thinking that some things are worth the risk."

She gave him a long look. "You don't know what you're talking about, Aidan. There are plenty of risks not worth taking."

He frowned. "What happened to you, Liz? You're not a cynical person. In fact, you may be the most positive person I've ever known. Anyone who knows you would say the same thing."

She could tell that he intended to keep pestering her until he got some answer that satisfied him, no matter how much she was hurt by having to reveal things she wanted to leave buried.

"I got my heart broken, that's what," she blurted

before she could question the wisdom of responding at all. "Not just broken, shattered. I came here to put it back together, not to risk it being broken all over again." She leveled a look into his eyes. "I won't allow that to happen, Aidan. Do you get it now? I will not allow it!"

And with that, she got up, went into the house with the dogs racing in after her. She slammed the door emphatically behind her, hoping to finally convey the message she'd tried to send all along—that she wanted him to stay away.

Aidan sat where he was after Liz had gone inside, too stunned at first to move. Instinct told him to go after her, to try to get to the bottom of her heartache. That's what a real friend would do. A true friend wouldn't leave someone in the sort of pain she was obviously in.

Unfortunately, he was the source of at least some of that pain. His determined prodding had forced her into revealing something she'd clearly kept private from everyone in Chesapeake Shores. He knew if she'd revealed her secrets to any of her friends, someone would have alerted him, maybe not to the details, but to the fact that he needed to treat her with extra care. Instead, the whole town thought of her the same way he did, as a strong, perpetually cheerful woman who was 100 percent contented with her life.

Though a part of him thought it cowardly, he

forced himself to go back into town in search of someone better suited to help Liz through this crisis. Observation suggested she was closest to Bree, but Aidan couldn't seem to find her anywhere. Shanna, however, was in the bookstore, the closed sign still on the door. He tapped to get her attention.

Frowning, she came to the door and unlocked it. "Everything okay?"

"Not really," he said. "Do you have a minute before you open?"

"I have an hour. I just came in early to reshelve some books that were scattered around by customers yesterday. Coffee's on, if you want some."

"Thanks."

She poured him a cup, then gestured toward one of the comfortable upholstered chairs that had been strategically placed to encourage customers to relax and read. She pulled over a nearby straight chair from one of the tables set up in the tiny coffee area.

"Shouldn't you be sitting here?" Aidan asked worriedly. "That chair doesn't look very comfortable."

She grinned. "It's not, but I can still get up from it. If I sit where you are, I'll be there till I call in a tow truck. Something to keep in mind if you ever have to deal with a pregnant woman. Straight chairs are our friends."

He laughed. "Not in my immediate future," he said.

"The time will come," she said with confidence. "Tuck the advice away till you need it. So, what's on your mind, or do I need to ask?"

"It's about Liz."

"Of course it is. You're worried she's avoiding you."

"I *know* she's avoiding me," he corrected. "And now I have some idea about why."

"Were you getting too close?" Shanna asked gently. "We've all noticed she seems a little gun-shy about the idea of forming a new relationship."

"Has she mentioned why?"

"Not a word," Shanna said, then frowned. "Did she tell you?"

"Not the whole story," he conceded, "but enough to know that something bad went down in her past."

Concern settled on Shanna's face. "How did you get that much out of her? The only picture she's ever painted of her past for us was pretty rosy."

"I'm not surprised. That's what she seems to want everyone to think." He sighed. "But I pressed too hard and she snapped. I don't think she meant to tell me anything, but the words came out before she could stop them. Then she ran into the house and slammed the door."

"And you left?" she demanded, regarding him incredulously.

"I know it sounds cowardly, and it probably was, but I honestly think I'm the last person who can help her right now. I thought maybe you or Bree could check on her. Whatever happened, she may need to talk about it."

Shanna stood up at once. "On my way," she said. "She'll probably be here soon to open the store, but it would be better if I caught her at home. I'll call Kevin and ask him to come in and cover for me till I get back."

She hesitated. "I don't know what to do about Pet Style, though. She's going to use opening up as an excuse not to talk to me."

"Do you have a key?" Aidan asked.

She nodded. "She gave me one for emergencies."

"I helped her out Memorial Day weekend. I know the system. I can cover. Just give me a heads-up when you're on your way and I'll figure out a way to make myself scarce in case she doesn't want to cross paths with me."

Shanna finally gave him a more approving look. "I take back all those mean thoughts I was having about you five minutes ago. You're a very considerate man. You didn't just run screaming for the hills when she had a meltdown, you had the good sense to come for me."

Aidan shrugged, not sure he deserved the praise. "I care about her, Shanna. I know she doesn't want me to, but I do, even if it never develops into something more."

"Give me your cell number," Shanna said. "I'll call when we're leaving the house or to let you know that she's not coming in at all, if she decides she wants her part-time employee to finish out the day."

Aidan wrote it down for her. "Thanks, Shanna."

"Don't thank me. I'm her friend. So are most of the women around here. We've got her back." She handed Aidan the key to Pet Style. "I'll let her know that you do, too."

He stood in the doorway to Liz's shop and watched Shanna hurry off to her car, talking on her cell phone as she went. She might have been calling Kevin or rallying the troops. Either way, he knew Liz was going to be in good hands, with a much better support system than he might have provided in his own bumbling, if concerned, way.

The doorbell rang again and again, sending the dogs into a frenzy. Liz pulled a pillow over her head, but she couldn't seem to block out the commotion.

"Oh, for heaven's sake," she finally muttered, dragging herself off the bed and going to the door. Enough time had passed since she'd abandoned Aidan on the porch that she doubted it was him.

She threw open the door, startled to see both Shanna and Bree there. She frowned at them.

"Why are you here?" she asked as they marched determinedly right past her as if fearful she'd shut them out. Truthfully she'd been tempted to do just that.

"Where else would we be in a crisis?" Bree asked.

"What crisis?" Liz replied, though she was very much afraid she already knew. Aidan had gone for help, which, if she thought about it, was very sweet of him, but totally unnecessary. Her crisis was over.

"Aidan told me he upset you. He thought you could use a friend," Shanna told her. "From the looks of those puffy, red eyes, the least you could use is some help with makeup."

Liz was startled when a chuckle erupted. It was the first time since she'd found Aidan on her front steps that she'd felt at all like laughing.

"Thanks for pointing out that I'm a wreck," she said to her friend.

Shanna grinned. "Always glad to help."

"Now, talk to us," Bree commanded. "What did that slimebag do to upset you?"

"Aidan is not a slimebag," Liz said, rushing to his defense.

Bree looked smug. "I wasn't actually referring to Aidan, but it's telling that you're so very quick to defend him."

"This has something to do with what happened

to you that sent you fleeing from North Carolina," Shanna said, regarding her with a worried expression. "You didn't leave just because your husband died in an accident, did you?"

Liz closed her eyes. She really, really didn't want to talk about this. "Not entirely, no," she said eventually.

"Sweetie, don't you want to talk about it?" Bree asked. "It might be easier to move on if you got it off your chest. Who better to share this with than two people who care about you?"

"What did Aidan tell you?"

"Not a blessed thing," Shanna said with unmistakable frustration. "Just that you were upset and might need a friend."

"So we both came," Bree said cheerfully. "You need a friend in this town, you get a twofer. Sometimes more, but we decided not to over-whelm you by dragging everyone else who cares along with us."

Thank heaven for small favors, Liz thought. "Aidan really didn't say anything?"

"Honestly, no," Shanna repeated. "Whatever you said to him, he kept to himself."

As badly as Liz wanted to hate him for forcing her to drag up old memories, she couldn't help being impressed by his discretion and by his decision to send her friends over here in his place. "Look, if you're worried that we're going to share whatever you tell us with all of your friends, I promise that won't happen," Bree said. "We all love you and want to help, not to make things worse. You get to decide who knows what and when."

"I appreciate what you're trying to do, but I really don't want to talk about it with anyone," Liz told them. "I've worked hard to put that time in my life behind me. Talking about it will only make it fresh."

"Or maybe it will help to share the burden and get a new perspective," Shanna told her gently. "We don't want to pry. And if you say that's not what you need, we'll respect it."

"But you need to know we're here anytime you need us," Bree added. "You're not alone."

Tears welled up in Liz's eyes yet again. "Thank you," she whispered.

Shanna and Bree were by her side at once, pulling her into a fierce group hug that had the tears flowing even harder.

"I swear if your husband weren't already dead, I'd go after him myself," Bree said.

"How do you know what happened was his fault?" Liz asked, surprised by the ardent statement. "Maybe I'm the one to blame for everything that happened."

"Not buying that for a second," Bree said. "We know who you are, Liz March. You're a good person through and through. Whatever he did was all on him."

Liz regarded her friends with wonder. "How did I get to be so lucky?"

"You came to the right town for your new life," Shanna said simply. "I know all too well just what that means. Chesapeake Shores gave me a fresh start when I was down and desperate, too."

Liz knew Shanna was exactly right. Chesapeake Shores—and the O'Briens—were filled with healing warmth and compassion.

Aidan thought he was handling things at the store reasonably well, despite being distracted by worries about what might be going on at Liz's.

When Shanna finally poked her head in, he frowned. "I thought you were going to give me a heads-up when you left the house so I could take off. I need to be gone, if Liz is coming in."

"Actually she specifically asked that you stay. She wants to thank you."

"For what? Upsetting her?"

"Probably not that," Shanna said, smiling. "I'll leave it to her to tell you what's on her mind. She was taking a shower and getting dressed when Bree and I left. She should be here soon."

Aidan couldn't seem to stop himself from asking, "How did it go over there? Did you get to the bottom of whatever's going on?"

"Even if we had, I wouldn't share her private business with you, any more than you told me what she said that got you to send me over there.

I think she's feeling better now. That's all that matters."

It wasn't all that mattered, Aidan thought, but it was obviously all Shanna was prepared to say. She waved goodbye and headed on to her own business. Bree popped in two seconds later.

"You have good instincts, Aidan. Don't give up on Liz."

He frowned at her. "She doesn't want me in her life, at least not as anything more than a friend. She's been pretty clear about that."

"And I'm telling you to stay the course," Bree said, then winked at him. "I'm very wise about these things. Trust me."

Aidan wasn't sure he could do that, but he might as well see how things played out. He'd already been drawn in, and, like it or not, that kiss had pretty well sealed the deal.

He paced nervously behind the counter, regretting that it had been a slow morning so there were no customers to provide a distraction as he awaited Liz's arrival.

When she finally came in the door, he studied her intently. He could still detect traces of her tears, but otherwise she looked far more composed than she had the last time he'd seen her.

She walked over to the counter, set down her purse and met his gaze. "I'm sorry."

He frowned. "Why are you apologizing to me? I'm the one who inadvertently reminded you of a bad time in your life. I should be apologizing."

A faint smile crossed her lips. "That's the point. It was inadvertent. You couldn't possibly know you were going to trigger an outburst like that just by suggesting that you thought we might have something special."

"Well, it's true that your reaction was pretty unexpected," he said, venturing a smile of his own. "Are you feeling better now?"

"Less hostile, anyway," she assured him. "In fact, I owe you big-time for sending Shanna to the house. She dragged Bree along. Their support was just what I needed."

"Did you talk to them?"

"If you're asking if I bared my soul, no. I really do want to leave my past where it belongs. I don't see the point of dragging it out and dissecting it."

Aidan regarded her with regret. "I'm hardly an expert in this area, but it seems the past is right here, right now, standing between us. It's not allowing you to move forward."

For an instant, she looked startled, but then she slowly nodded. "I hadn't thought of it that way, but you're probably right. I am allowing it to affect the choices I'm making. That's probably not fair to you."

Aidan shook his head. "No, the person it's most unfair to is you," he corrected. "I know a thing or two about letting the past haunt you, Liz."

She frowned at that. "So, what are you suggesting? Should I spend years with a shrink trying to get to the bottom of it? Spill my guts to every person I meet until it no longer has the power to hurt me?"

"I don't know the answer to that," he said candidly. "I just know that keeping it bottled up doesn't really seem to be working all that well for you, not if it's cutting you off from having the full life you deserve."

"Meaning a relationship with you?" she said, an edge back in her voice.

"Meaning a relationship with anyone. How can you honestly have a real friendship with someone, much less anything deeper, if you're holding some huge part of yourself back?"

Even as he said the words, he realized they applied to him, as well. Shaken, he stepped out from behind the counter.

"I'm glad you're feeling better now," he told her. "There were a few sales earlier, but it's been pretty quiet. If you have any questions, you know how to find me."

She gave him a puzzled look as he headed for the door. "Aidan, are we okay?"

He turned back. "You mean do we understand each other?"

She nodded.

"Probably even more than you realize," he said quietly. "Take care, Liz."

This time he was the one who walked away with a whole slew of conflicting emotions plaguing him, leaving Liz to stare after him with confusion written all over her face.

» 12 «

Aidan had very mixed feelings about the end of school. Even though he'd scheduled a few team meetings over the summer and arranged, for the players to follow training and nutrition guidelines, he couldn't help feeling as if way too much was being left until summer's end. He suspected every high school coach, faced with the challenge of getting his kids ready for the new season, felt the same way.

It helped a little that Porter Hobbs was finally on board with the change Aidan had recommended for Taylor. He'd stood on the sidelines at three straight practices and seen the way his son and Hector connected to make the kind of plays that could win a regional championship if the rest of the team played at their level. Of course, at this point that was a very big *if*.

On the last day of practice, Hobbs had actually congratulated Aidan for spotting Taylor's potential. Aidan knew it helped that Taylor was genuinely excited about the change and had become friends with both Hector and Henry.

Aidan wasn't sure how Hobbs felt about the friendship, but the trio were proving to be real team leaders.

Aidan was in his office on Tuesday afternoon making his final notes for the year when the door opened and the three boys stuck their heads in.

"Coach, do you have a minute?" Taylor asked.

"Of course," he said, leaning back and noting that they seemed to be surprisingly hesitant. "What's on your mind?"

"The team's been talking," Henry said, glancing at the others for affirmation. Hector and Taylor nodded.

"We'd like to keep practicing this summer," Henry continued. "I know it's your vacation, but we know we have a lot of work to do. Team meetings won't be nearly enough. Would you mind setting up a real training schedule and working with us?"

"Just a couple of days a week," Taylor suggested, then grinned. "It is summer vacation, after all, and we want to do fun stuff, too."

Hector followed up, his expression worried. "Only if it's no trouble," he added.

Prepared for some sort of bad news, Aidan was stunned by the request and the initiative they'd shown. He regarded the three of them with astonishment. "Whose idea was this?"

"Mine," Taylor said, looking embarrassed. "I should have thought of it last year."

"You'd just made the varsity team," Aidan reminded him. "You'd probably barely found your way to the locker room."

Taylor laughed. "Are you kidding me? My dad's been taking me through the locker room and the stadium since it was built. I think it was a hint."

"More than likely," Aidan agreed, imagining all the ways Hobbs had gone about putting added pressure on his son. "Is the entire team on board with this?"

Henry nodded, his whole demeanor suggesting their eagerness for him to agree. "We want to win next season and we're starting to believe we can."

"Good," Aidan told him. "Because I believe it. Let me speak to Rob about the policy. I don't know if official team practices are allowed or any of the other implications about holding a school activity during summer break. I'll do my best to figure out something that won't break any rules."

The boys immediately exchanged excited high fives.

"No matter what I find out," he told them, "I'm very impressed by your enthusiasm. That's the kind of commitment it takes to be winners. I want you to tell your teammates that. I'll be in touch in a day or two, as soon as I see what can be worked out."

"Thanks, Coach," Taylor said, leading the others from Aidan's office.

He leaned back in his chair, a smile spreading across his face. If enthusiasm and commitment were the only keys, this team was going places. Best of all, he'd seen glimpses of the raw talent it would take to get them there.

Liz thought a lot about what Aidan had said about the inability to truly move forward if the past maintained a stranglehold on her emotions. She found herself wanting to talk to him more about that, and about why he seemed to know so much about it. Was it because of whatever she'd sensed he was holding back about some prior relationship with the O'Briens? He claimed not to have one, but more than once his body language and odd reticence when the name was mentioned suggested otherwise. Still, it was hard for her to imagine bad blood that no one on the O'Brien side seemed aware of.

On Wednesday morning, Archie was freshly bathed, his toys assembled in a big basket. All of the dogs seemed to understand that today was a momentous day. They sat watchfully by on the warm June morning as she waited for Aidan's arrival to pick up Archie.

At eight-thirty, just when she was beginning to think he'd either forgotten or was intentionally avoiding her deadline, she spotted him coming up the street. Archie, of course, made a dash for him. For once she saw no point in reprimanding him.

From here on out, Archie was Aidan's responsibility.

Tail wagging, the dog happily followed him back to the porch, then dutifully sat down as Aidan settled into a chair next to Liz.

"You ready to become a pet owner?" she asked, smiling.

He glanced at her. "Do I have a choice?"

She frowned at the glib response. "Of course. If you really, really hate the idea, Archie can stay here," she said, then turned to the dog. "But look at him."

Archie was regarding Aidan with that familiar look of pure adoration. "Can you really turn your back on that?" she asked.

Aidan instinctively reached out to pet the dog's head. "No, of course not, although I think you're underestimating his attachment to you."

"Of course he loves me," she said with a laugh. "I've been feeding him and taking care of him. You're the one he's truly bonded with, though. I think he knows you'll take him on runs and give him treats from the table that he shouldn't have."

Aidan laughed. "Exactly what I intended."

His expression sobered as he studied her. "You seem better today. It's not just because you're losing a houseguest, is it?"

Liz wasn't sure she was ready to get into this, but she did shake her head. "I've been thinking a lot about some of the things you said the other day. I'm not sure what I intend to do about it yet, but I can admit you made a couple of valid points. I have been stuck in the past."

She deliberately held his gaze and opted to be pushy for once. "Have you considered taking your own advice?"

He seemed genuinely startled by the question, but then his expression shut down. "No idea what you mean," he claimed.

"Of course you do," she said, calling him on the deliberate evasion. "I don't know what your secrets might be and you certainly don't have to share them with me, but I do know they have as firm a grip on you as mine do on me."

"And how did you reach that conclusion?" he asked, his tone disparaging. "I thought Will Lincoln was the only professional shrink in town."

"True. He has a degree and actual office hours," she replied, refusing to take offense. "But I have a woman's intuition and sometimes that's just as good in certain circumstances. I caught your expression during that pretty little speech you made to me on Sunday. It suddenly dawned on you that you're carrying some burden you're keeping secret, too. When you realized you were being hypocritical, you couldn't get away from me fast enough."

She managed to catch his gaze and hold it. "Can you honestly tell me I'm wrong?"

For a minute it seemed he might not answer at all, but then he sighed heavily. "Not really," he confessed.

"Care to share?"

"Not really," he said.

A twinkle came and went in his eyes so quickly she might have missed it if she hadn't been watching him so closely. She couldn't help feeling pleased with herself for pegging his likely reaction.

"Then I guess we both have some thinking to do and some decisions to make," she said quietly. "It's actually kind of nice to know I'm not the only one who's not an open book."

He gave her a long, serious look, then chuckled. "I wonder if we both wouldn't be much better off hanging out with people who can't see right through us."

Liz laughed with him. "What would be the fun in that? I like people who keep me on my toes."

"Only up to a point," he suggested.

This time she was the one whose expression sobered as she sighed. "Yes, but only up to a point."

It suddenly seemed as if this habit she had of trying to solve riddles was about to drag her even more deeply into a sea of complications. Lately, though, since she'd met Aidan, it seemed it might be worth going there.

• • •

After thinking about that disconcerting conversation with Liz for most of the day, Aidan really needed to work off some steam. Since vigorous sex was definitely off the table, he decided to see if the guys were playing basketball anytime soon.

"Come on, Archie, let's go for a walk," he said, grinning when the dog immediately found his leash and brought it to him, tail wagging.

As he hit Main Street with Archie already tugging on his leash and eager to run, Aidan caught the gloating expressions on Shanna's face and on Bree's when they caught sight of the two of them. Obviously they shared Liz's sense of triumph over getting him to adopt the dog. Susie was the next to step outside when she saw them. She stood in the doorway of the management office, a grin on her face.

"New addition to the family?" she inquired with a cat-that-swallowed-the-canary look.

Aidan nodded.

"You do know that there's a No Pet clause in your lease, don't you?" she said solemnly.

Aidan came to a complete stop and stared at her. "You can't be serious?"

She nodded. "Oh, but I am."

"And you never thought to say a word about it before now? I know you were well aware that Liz has been trying to pawn Archie off on me."

"I assumed you'd read the lease," Susie said innocently. "Seems to me that's the first thing a man who really didn't want a pet might have done."

"Well, I obviously never read the fine print," he grumbled. "Are you going to be the one to tell Liz I can't keep Archie?" He looked at the dog, whose attention was going back and forth as if he knew he was the topic of conversation. "For that matter, are you going to tell Archie he doesn't have a new home, after all?"

For just an instant, Susie looked vaguely guilty. Then she chuckled. "Got you!"

Aidan frowned. "Got me? What does that mean?"

"There's no pet clause in the lease, and even if there were, Uncle Mick and my dad would never enforce it. I just wanted to see for myself if Liz was right and you really are attached to that dog."

The level of relief that washed over him startled him. Apparently it was true. He liked the dog. And, as much as he'd grumbled about taking him in, he wanted Archie to stay.

"You are a sneaky, sneaky woman," he told Susie.

She looked surprisingly pleased by the comment. "I'd almost forgotten how much fun that could be," she told him. "I'll have to work on honing that skill again."

Somehow Aidan doubted that Mack or anyone else in the family would encourage it.

"So, are you through getting me all worked up over nothing?" he inquired lightly.

She tilted her head thoughtfully, then said, "Yeah. I think that will do it for now. Stay alert, though. You make such an easy mark, I might be tempted to try something else."

Given what Aidan knew about her health history, he couldn't get truly angry over her prank. It was nice to see this playful side of her. He suspected even though they might not want it directed their way, most of the family would agree.

He gave a gentle tug on Archie's leash. "Come on, boy. We've got places to go." He waved in Susie's direction as they walked away.

At Connor's office, he was forced to endure yet more teasing the instant Connor spotted Archie tied up to a post on the porch of the house that had been converted into a law office.

"So, the rumors are true? Liz won, and you now have a dog?"

"Seems that way."

"You don't seem as distraught by that as you did when she first backed you into a corner," Connor observed.

"Archie and I have an agreement," Aidan explained. "We're not going to do anything to make each other's lives miserable. I think it'll work out. In fact, it may be a whole lot less complicated than most relationships with humans."

Though he'd made the remark lightly, Connor's

expression turned serious. "Does that mean you're giving up on Liz? I know a whole bunch of people who are going to be unhappy about that."

"I'm not giving up. It's just on hold," Aidan told him, then quickly amended, "by mutual agreement, so tell all those women in your family not to get their drawers in a knot."

Connor didn't seem pacified. "Mutual agreement? You sure about that?"

"A hundred percent," Aidan insisted. "That's the way we both want it. Liz even more than me, if I'm being honest."

Connor regarded him doubtfully. "Okay, if you say so. And since you apparently didn't come by here for my expert commentary on women not always meaning what they say, what did bring you by?"

"Basketball," Aidan told him. "Are you all getting together to play again anytime soon?"

Connor's lips twitched. "I'm sensing a desperate need to work off some frustration."

"Bingo."

"The kind of frustration generally brought on by woman problems," Connor continued as if Aidan hadn't spoken.

"I never said that," Aidan protested.

"You didn't have to. I'm a guy. I've been where you are. I played a lot of basketball." He grinned. "I imagine I can make a few calls and put a game together for tonight. Seven o'clock?"

"That'll do," Aidan said. "I appreciate it." He glanced out the window and noted that Archie was straining on his leash, trying to get to a window, apparently so he could spot Aidan. The dog probably wasn't strong enough to pull down that post he'd been tied to, but better not to find out for sure. "I should go." He gestured toward the window. "Archie seems impatient and that's probably not good."

Connor nodded, a grin tugging at his lips. "See you tonight. Prepare to sweat."

Aidan laughed. "As if you 'girls' present any real challenge," he taunted.

Connor shook his head. "Did you learn nothing last time? Trash talk only gets us all riled up."

"Not enough to beat us, though. I'm just hoping to make it more interesting this time."

"I'll be sure to pass that along," Connor promised. "When O'Brien pride is on the line, things can get ugly."

Aidan wasn't impressed by the implied threat in his tone or the words of warning. "You do whatever you need to do."

He gave Connor a casual wave on his way out the door, untied his dog, then jogged back to his apartment. All in all, he considered his first day out of school to have been an interesting one. Tonight he'd find out what sort of price he'd pay for his possibly ill-advised taunts. It didn't much matter, though, as long as it kept his mind off Liz.

Liz was going through catalogs looking for new inventory to replace everything that had sold out already when Susie Franklin came in.

"Where were you earlier?"

Liz regarded her with confusion. "I've been here all morning. Why? What did I miss?"

A broad grin spread across Susie's face. "I really got Aidan."

"Got him how?" Liz asked.

"I told him there was a No Pet clause in his lease. There's not, of course, and Uncle Mick would have given him an exception if there were, but you should have seen his face. I don't care what he says to you about not really wanting that dog, he's totally attached to Archie."

Liz laughed. "Of course he is. I knew those two were a perfect match from the first moment I saw them together."

"And so much less complicated than claiming Aidan for yourself," Susie commented slyly.

Liz frowned at her. "No idea what you mean."

"Oh, of course you do, but I won't push. That's not why I came in. Apparently the guys are having an impromptu basketball game tonight so Aidan can work off some sort of stress." She looked even more amused by that. "I can't imagine why, can you? I mean, school is out, so where's the pressure?"

"Are you heading somewhere with this observation?" Liz asked her, though it would probably have been wiser to let it pass.

"Just saying," Susie said, her eyes sparkling with barely contained laughter. "Anyway, it gives us the perfect chance to have a book club meeting at my place."

"Has anyone actually read a book lately?" Liz inquired, amused as always that they still insisted on calling it a book club.

Susie shrugged. "Probably not, but we're well-intentioned. Shanna's always reading something. She can give us the condensed version and we can move on to other topics."

Liz laughed. "I'm sure she'll appreciate that."

"Oh, she'll hate it, but facts are facts. In summer especially, none of us has a second to actually read a book." She regarded Liz hopefully. "Are you in?"

"I'm in," Liz said. "But only if you can assure me that Aidan and I won't become the main topic of conversation."

"No promises," Susie said blithely. "The two of you are awfully fascinating, but I'll do what I can."

Short of avoiding her friends for the foreseeable future, Liz figured that was the best she could hope for. "What time?"

"Seven. I'm going to make a huge salad and a big bowl of fresh fruit. That's my contribution to healthy. The rest of you can bring the decadent stuff."

"I call dibs on bringing ice cream," Liz said. These days it was a wonder she hadn't become the sole support of Ben & Jerry's. She had a hunch that Aidan's approach to handling stress by playing an energetic game of basketball with the guys was probably a whole lot healthier. Too bad the women didn't seem similarly inclined.

With the cool breeze blowing off the bay a refreshing change from the day's earlier heat and humidity, Liz and the O'Brien women had gathered on Susie's porch with its amazing view of the water.

"I swear, I don't know how you ever get anything done, much less make yourself leave the house with a view like this," Liz told Susie as she sipped a glass of sweet tea.

Susie glanced up and looked around as if it was all new to her. "It is pretty incredible, isn't it? I'm afraid there are too many days when I take it for granted. When I was so sick and Mack was having this house built, all I did was pray that I'd live long enough to move into it with him. The day he carried me across the threshold here was one of the happiest of my life. I was so afraid things would go badly with my treatments that I spent every minute I could right here, in this very chair, soaking it all in."

She looked around, tears in her eyes. "And now I take it for granted. How awful is that?"

"That's the way life is, sweetie," Bree said, moving her own chair closer and giving Susie's hand a squeeze. "We don't dwell in the past. We keep looking ahead. Sometimes that means we forget all those promises we made to God when times were tough."

Susie sighed. "It shouldn't be that way, though. I have so much. I have my health back. I have this beautiful home. I have the man of my dreams, and yet I want more."

Heather and Shanna immediately exchanged a guilty look. Susie caught it.

"Stop that! Being pregnant is a wonderful thing and I am so, so happy for both of you," Susie told them, but the sadness in her eyes suggested something else.

Liz understood that dream in a way none of the others could. She'd gone into teaching because of her love for children and their curious minds and clever imaginations. She'd been so sure she and Josh were ready for that step. Learning otherwise on that terrible night of the accident had devastated her.

Sure, unlike Susie, physically she was still able to have children, but since she couldn't envision a time when she'd allow a man back into her life, it seemed children were off the table, as well. So, to some degree, she could relate to Susie's longing for something that seemed so far out of reach.

"You and Mack are hoping to adopt, right?" she asked.

Susie nodded. "But it's a long process, a lot longer than I ever imagined. I was delusional, I guess. I thought we'd fill out all those forms, go through a ton of interviews and a baby would miraculously appear a few weeks or months later." She made a face. "Not so much."

"Don't you dare give up," Jess told her. The owner of the inn had taken a rare night off to join them. Usually once the summer season was in full gear, she didn't allow herself many breaks.

"Of course I won't give up," Susie said. "But trying not to be discouraged is a little beyond me." She forced a smile. "Enough of that. Mack's probably sick of listening to me. I'm sick of listening to me, for that matter. I don't want to drive you all away, too."

"You couldn't do that if you tried," Heather said. "You're stuck with us, especially since you have the great view and the excellent snacks. I say we bring on the ice cream."

Liz stood up, as eager as the rest of them for a change in topic. "I brought three kinds, along with enough toppings to stock an old-fashioned ice-cream parlor. I'm thinking sundaes. How about the rest of you?"

Shanna moved with surprising agility for a woman in her eighth month of pregnancy. Heather was up just as quickly.

Five minutes later, the granite countertop of the island in Susie's kitchen held a spread of everything from hot fudge sauce and peanuts to melted caramel, sprinkles and whipped cream. Double dips of ice cream had been doled out, accompanied by teasing remarks and plenty of laughter.

When they were finally back on the porch with the desserts, sighs of contentment could be heard all around.

"Shouldn't we be talking about books?" Shanna asked between bites. "When I get home, I need to be able to tell Kevin that we really are a book club and say it with a straight face."

"So talk," Heather said.

Shanna shook her head. "I can't. My mouth is full of ice cream. Anybody else?"

"I read a book on Australian shepherds the other day," Liz volunteered without thinking.

A hoot of laughter greeted her comment.

"Australian shepherds?" Susie echoed. "Not boxers or cocker spaniels or terriers?"

Liz frowned at her. "What's your point?" she asked irritably, though she knew perfectly well what they were all thinking.

"We just find your fascination with that particular breed interesting, that's all," Bree said, her eyes sparkling with amusement.

"Personally I was thinking she was looking for an excuse to see Aidan so she could pass along information she thought he might need," Susie said. "You know, since they've agreed not to see each other that way anymore." She drew dramatic quotation marks in the air around *that way*.

"And why aren't you seeing each other that way?" Shanna asked. "I don't get it."

Liz looked from one expectant face to the next, noted the barely contained laughter, then sighed.

"Okay, I'm pitiful," she acknowledged. "Aidan's never had a dog before and I thought the book might be helpful, but that isn't the reason I ordered it. I wanted an excuse to see him."

"Why do you need an excuse when the man clearly wants to see you, too?" Bree asked.

"Because we agreed," Liz said.

Every woman there burst into laughter.

"Idiots," Shanna murmured.

"Delusional," Jess added. "And given how long it took me to figure out I was in love with Will, I am very familiar with that tendency."

"Aren't we all?" Laila O'Brien murmured. "I was still fighting my feelings for Matthew all the way to the altar on that trip to Dublin."

"Thank you so much for the support," Liz griped to the whole unsympathetic lot of them.

Bree patted her hand. "Don't worry, sweetie. Our amusement really isn't directed entirely at you. Just like Jess and Laila said, we've all been there, every one of us, living in the land of denial."

Despite her friend's attempt at reassurance, Liz

didn't feel one bit better. She knew their lives had all turned out okay. Right now, she couldn't imagine any such outcome for her own, at least not one that included Aidan.

⇒ 13 ⇐

The basketball game didn't work as an effective stress reducer. Aidan was as edgy and off-kilter after the game as he had been before they'd played. Oh, he'd worked up a good sweat and had even scored a few baskets, but his concentration had been shot. He was hoping no one had noticed, but these were O'Brien men. They might not be sensitive, but they were intuitive, especially when it was obvious that some distraction had kept his head out of a game he'd been so anxious to play.

Though he'd probably gotten closer to Connor than any of the other men, it was Kevin who'd apparently been designated to get to the bottom of whatever was on his mind. Aidan supposed he ought to be grateful Will hadn't been chosen for the assignment. He had a hunch a good shrink could peel back his defenses in less time than it took to say *Liz March*.

As Aidan sipped from a bottle of lukewarm water, he watched as the other men dispersed. Even their parting catcalls were muted. Kevin stayed dutifully behind.

Aidan studied him warily. He didn't envy the guy. This was the second time he'd been put in an awkward position. The last time it had been Thomas who'd put him there with questions about Aidan's interest in the bay preservation project.

Seizing the initiative with the vague hope of getting the cross-examination over with, Aidan looked Kevin in the eye. "Something on your mind?"

Kevin was clearly startled by the question. "Actually I was wondering, we all were," he began uncomfortably, "if there was something you wanted to get off your chest. Maybe problems with Liz?"

"No problems," Aidan declared flatly, hoping to put an end to that line of speculation.

Kevin looked perplexed by his adamant response. "The word is that you're not seeing each other anymore."

"We were never seeing each other in the first place," Aidan told him, avoiding any mention of the kiss that might have made a liar of him.

"Not the way I heard it," Kevin said. "And the grapevine in this town might be annoying, but it's usually as accurate as it is fast."

"Not this time," Aidan insisted. "Liz and I are friends. Period. Mutual agreement."

"A mutual agreement doesn't usually drive a man onto a basketball court to get his tail whipped,"

Kevin noted. "Now a one-sided agreement, that's something else entirely."

Aidan studied him incredulously. He'd spent enough years in a locker room to know there were few boundaries among guys, but he'd never before had his love life dissected with quite this much fascination or seemingly genuine concern. There'd been a few bawdy remarks when he'd gone out with a model a couple of times, more when he'd been linked to an actress, but that was it. He didn't know how to handle the real worry that seemed responsible for Kevin's probing. His solution was to try, yet again, to deflect it.

"What is it with the men around here, or at least the O'Brien men?" Aidan asked, trying to sound curious, rather than impatient. "I've never known men to want to dissect relationships the way you all do."

Kevin laughed, looking relaxed for the first time since the conversation had begun. "It comes from having Mick in the family. My father meddles, as you've been warned. We've all been the victims of that meddling, so we like to pass along the favor whenever we get the chance."

"Is there any way to get you to back off?" Aidan asked in frustration. "Short of coercing Liz to walk down the aisle, that is?"

"Truthfully? Probably not," Kevin said with a shrug that suggested many things had been tried and that all had failed. "You could try giving us another focus for all our energy. Do you have one of those?"

How about his relationship with Thomas, Aidan thought. That would surely do the trick. Of course that was not a topic he intended to share with anyone except the man in question. And he had no particular timetable for doing that, yet another worry that was weighing on him these days. He seemed to be putting off contact with his father, even with that self-imposed one-year clock already ticking.

With school out and no answers yet about whether he could call any unofficial practices, he had too few distractions himself. Maybe that was the cause of his restlessness and not Liz at all. Wouldn't that be a relief?

"Sorry, nothing," he told Kevin, then grasped for the first straw that came to mind. "How's Shanna feeling?"

"Huge," Kevin said, then quickly amended, "Not that I think she's huge. That's her perception and I will call you a stinking, flat-out liar if you ever say otherwise."

"Wise man."

"You have no idea," Kevin said. "The last pregnancy—her first actually—went pretty smoothly. It sort of caught us off guard. This time, though, she's been sicker. She's gained more weight. And there are days when she's mad at the whole world, but especially at me for thinking another baby would be a great idea. There was about a minute there when the doctor thought we might be having twins. You should have seen the look on Shanna's face. I swear if she'd had a weapon, I'd be dead."

Aidan laughed, even though he knew he probably shouldn't. "Sorry, man."

"No, you're not. No one is," Kevin said, sounding resigned. "Every single person in my family is taking great delight in this. All I know is that Shanna's due date can't get here fast enough. I want my cheerful, contented wife back."

"She's seemed cheerful enough every time I've seen her," Aidan said.

"Sure. You're not the enemy. That's reserved for me. All I did was suggest one night that we have one more. I guess I did it long enough after the baby had started sleeping through the night that it seemed like a good idea to her, too. I might have mentioned something about Henry being old enough to babysit, not that he's around the house much these days. The only thing he cares about is football." He gave Aidan a hard look. "Thanks for that, by the way."

Aidan couldn't help it. He laughed again. "You might be the only person in this entire town whose life is as crazy as mine is right now. Thanks for reminding me that things could be worse."

Of course, Kevin O'Brien had one very important thing that Aidan didn't. He knew exactly who his father was and there was nothing complicated about acknowledging it. In fact, it was a source of pride, rather than a potential scandal.

With the Thomas situation, as Aidan was starting to think of it, very much on his mind, he was thrown completely the morning after his conversation with Kevin when he walked into Sally's and found Thomas there with Connie and Sean. Thomas waved him over.

"If you're not meeting anyone, join us," he suggested. "We're celebrating the end of the school year."

"It's a tradition," Sean said, then beamed. "I get all the pancakes I want."

Aidan chuckled. "That sounds like an excellent tradition."

"Then you definitely need to join us," Connie said. "After all, your school year just ended, too."

Seeing no polite way around it, Aidan pulled over a chair and sat at the end of the booth. Crowding in beside Thomas was not an option.

"Keep in mind that the school year only lasted a few weeks for me," Aidan said. "I'm not so sure I deserve to celebrate."

"Then you only get half as many pancakes as Sean," Connie said, regarding him with a twinkle in her eye. "Not to worry. He's ordered a lot. Our son's eyes are way bigger than his stomach, so Thomas will wind up finishing every last bite of them. He hates waste. I've tried to explain that those calories don't magically not count just because he's being frugal, but he doesn't seem to care."

Thomas shrugged. "Sally makes excellent pancakes, and since you don't give me anything but bran flakes at home, I'm going to indulge when I can." He met Aidan's gaze. "Take it from me. Do not marry a woman who has the avowed intention of keeping you healthy."

Connie scowled at him. "So I should sit back and wait for you to die of a heart attack? I was a single mom for a long time. I'd like to stay married long enough to enjoy it."

Thomas laughed and reached for her hand, lifting it to his lips. "I'm glad to know your reasons are totally unselfish."

Aidan listened to the lighthearted exchange with a sense of wonder. Would Thomas and his mother have gotten along half as well? Had they teased each other when they were dating? He tried to imagine the two of them together and couldn't. He hoped by the time Sean was his age, he'd realize what an amazing thing their loving, attentive relationship was.

Even as he thought about that, he considered what impact his own news was likely to have on these two people who had no idea of the bomb he was preparing to drop on them. Did he have the right to turn their lives upside down? He was no longer quite as eager to exact some sort of revenge on Thomas, but he still believed the truth needed to come out, if only to provide some closure on the past for him.

Since he couldn't grapple with that at the moment, he faced Connie. "You were a single mom?" he asked.

She nodded. "A divorced single mom. My daughter's grown and married now. She lives in Nashville, where she writes for some of the top country singers."

Aidan recalled what he'd heard about her. "She's married to Caleb Green, right? I'm a big fan of his music."

"Well, Jenny's written a lot of it," Connie said, her pride evident.

"And I can sing most of it, too," Sean piped in. "And Caleb's been teaching me to play guitar."

Connie regarded her son with amusement. "Sean and his cousin Emily Rose—that's Bree's daughter—would very much like to tour with Caleb. If I don't stay on my toes, Caleb might actually let them. He claims he's had worse opening acts."

Aidan glanced at Thomas, who was regarding his wife with a besotted expression. "How do you feel about your son going on a concert tour?"

"We'll talk about it when he turns eighteen and not a moment before," Thomas replied without hesitation.

"Dad!" Sean protested. "That's, like, forever."

Thomas shrugged. "Education first."

"There's no school in summer," Sean pointed out just as his pile of pancakes arrived. As he drowned them in syrup, he added, "That's why we're celebrating, remember?"

Connie winked at her husband. "I told you not to bother arguing with him. He's got an answer for everything, just like his dad."

Thomas chuckled. "But I'm older and wiser *and* I'm the dad," he said triumphantly. "I win!"

Observing the tight-knit family, it was all Aidan could do not to sigh with envy. This was what he had missed. This was what his mom had missed, though she'd apparently given up the chance at it willingly. He'd had no choice in the matter. And for the first time, he allowed himself a brief little moment of surprisingly strong resentment directed toward his mom, then immediately felt guilty for it.

He might not understand her reasons, but he had to respect that Anna had done what she thought was best by keeping him and his father apart. Maybe Thomas really hadn't been a good candidate for marriage or fatherhood back then, and as Aidan had learned, there were two failed marriages in Thomas's past to add proof to that. Aidan needed to remember that, because casting blame now was a wasted effort.

As he looked around at the man who was his

father, the woman who had no idea she was his stepmother and at his half brother, Aidan felt for the first time in his life as if he had no idea of who he really was. All these years he thought he'd known himself. He was, first and foremost, Anna Mitchell's son, her pride and joy. He'd been a smart student and an excellent athlete who'd become a professional football star for a short time. He'd even thought, given time, he'd be a solid high school coach. He'd envisioned a future with a wife and kids. Those were all the things that mattered to Aidan Mitchell.

But Aidan Mitchell *O'Brien?* He didn't know that man at all. And every time he envisioned trying to fit into the family he was coming to know, he felt as if he'd be turning his back on the man he'd always believed himself to be.

He was relieved when Thomas slid out of the booth and announced he had to get to a meeting. Connie and Sean followed his lead, leaving Aidan alone with his increasingly confused thoughts and a cup of coffee that had gone cold.

Liz passed Thomas, Connie and Sean as they were exiting Sally's and paused to say hello. Inside, she spotted Aidan sitting at the end of an empty booth. Since the table was still cluttered with dishes, she jumped to the conclusion he'd been eating with Thomas and his family. And since his expression was anything but cheerful, she concluded it hadn't gone well. Once again her sense that there was something going on between Thomas and Aidan stirred to life.

"Want some company?" she said, slipping into the vacated booth before Aidan could even think about trying to stop her.

He regarded her with amusement. "It's a little late for me to say no now, isn't it?"

"Pretty much. All the other seats are taken, anyway. You can't hog this whole booth to yourself. I assume you had breakfast with Thomas."

He nodded.

"How'd that go?"

"Fine. Why wouldn't it?" he asked, an edge in his voice that suggested she'd touched on a sore point.

Liz waited until Sally had cleared the table, then brought her coffee and her usual croissant, plus a fresh cup of coffee for Aidan, before saying another word. She kept her gaze on Aidan, who finally gave her an apologetic look.

"Sorry. I didn't mean to snap your head off."

"Why did you? Just because I asked an innocent question about the meal you'd shared with Thomas?"

"I'm pretty sure there was nothing innocent about the question," Aidan contradicted. "You've been hinting for a while that you think something's up between the two of us."

"Because that's the way it seems to me," she said agreeably. "Is there?"

"I never laid eyes on Thomas or any other O'Brien before I moved to Chesapeake Shores," Aidan said, his gaze steady.

"That's not exactly the point, though, is it?"

"What is the point?"

She tried to think of a reasonable explanation for his behavior, but couldn't come up with a thing. The situation didn't really seem to call for guesswork. "I don't know. It just worries me to keep detecting these strange undercurrents and observing how unhappy you seem to be over something."

"Let it go, Liz."

"The same way you've let go of trying to figure out my past?" she inquired.

He smiled. "Yes, just like that. I may have a whole slew of questions, but I've stopped asking. I've accepted that you'll tell me what you want me to know when you want me to know it."

She doubted he was as accepting of that as he claimed. Studying him over the rim of her cup, she asked, "Do you remember what you said to me the day you brought a cup of Sally's coffee to my house?"

"I'm sure I said a lot of scintillating things," he retorted glibly.

"Of course you did," she said, her tone dry. "I was specifically referring to your insistence that dropping by with coffee and checking on me was something a friend would do."

"Ah, that."

"Well, my poking around in your business to try to figure out this mystery is also what a friend would do."

"Is that so? I thought maybe a friend would take my word that it's not a topic I intend to discuss."

Liz seized on the comment. "So there is something," she said triumphantly. "You just don't want to talk about it."

"Whether there is or there isn't, we're pretty much at an impasse, since I've declared it off-limits."

She recognized the stubborn set to his jaw and knew she'd pushed as far as she could. She couldn't help feeling a little deflated, though. Didn't he know by now that he could trust her with his secrets?

Even as that thought crossed her mind, she sighed. Talk about a double standard. She supposed Aidan would trust her with his secrets right about the same time she started trusting him with hers.

Mick had just returned from checking on one of the Habitat for Humanity projects he was overseeing in his volunteer capacity as a contractor when he spotted Thomas sitting in one of the Adirondack chairs at the far end of the porch. As it frequently was, his gaze was directed toward the bay. He had a notepad in his lap, but whatever he'd been working on had apparently been forgotten. In fact, he seemed lost in thought.

"You plotting a strategy for getting rid of some uncooperative lawmakers?" Mick asked, only partially in jest. He knew there were a few folks in the state capital his brother would love to see run out of office.

"Not today," Thomas said, his smile halfhearted. "I was just jotting down some notes for Aidan about projects I thought the high school kids might want to be involved with in the fall."

"So he's come around?"

"He's still saying all the right words," Thomas corrected.

Mick frowned. "You don't believe he's sincere?"

"Oh, who knows? I'm probably imagining problems where there are none," Thomas grumbled and grabbed an oatmeal raisin cookie from the plate beside him.

Mick promptly reached over and snagged the last one. "Ma was here baking today?"

Thomas nodded, then grinned. "I got here just in time to do a taste test."

"Since when has Ma ever baked a bad batch of cookies?"

"Not once that I can recall," Thomas replied, then winked. "But it never hurts to hint that this might be the first time."

Mick laughed and nodded approvingly. "You're turning out to be sneakier than I imagined."

Thomas lifted his half-empty glass of milk in a silent salute. "And didn't I learn from the best?"

"That you did," Mick agreed. He studied his younger brother with concern. "What's really on your mind? Something tells me for once it's not the bay or those school projects."

"I've mentioned this before but I keep getting this weird vibe from Aidan," he admitted.

"Weird how?"

"I can't put my finger on it, but there's definitely something . . ." His voice trailed off and he shrugged. "I can't explain it. I wish we knew more about him."

"Such as?" Mick asked. "I can show you his résumé. We did the usual background check. Nothing turned up or we'd never have called him about an interview, much less hired him."

"I'm not talking about some criminal past he's hiding," Thomas said impatiently, then shook his head. "I don't know what I'm talking about exactly. It just hit me again this morning that something's off."

"This morning? Where did you see Aidan this morning?"

"He came into Sally's when I was there with Connie and Sean. I asked him to join us."

Mick chuckled. "The end-of-school pancake bonanza?"

"That was it," Thomas confirmed.

"Did Aidan turn you down? Take off?"

253

"No, he joined us."

"Was he quiet? Rude?" Mick asked, struggling to understand.

Thomas paused, clearly giving the question a surprising amount of thought.

"It wasn't either of those things. If I had to describe his behavior, I guess I'd say he was observant."

Mick stared at his brother incredulously. "Observant? Since when is that a bad thing?"

"It's not bad. It was just a little intense." Thomas looked at him. "You think I'm overreacting."

"Since you haven't given me a blessed thing to go on that doesn't sound perfectly normal, then yes, I think you're overreacting."

Thomas sighed. "Maybe I am." Still, he turned to Mick. "He doesn't act that way around you, though, does he?"

"Not that I've noticed," Mick said.

"He seems to get along just fine with Kevin," Thomas conceded. "They've been playing basketball with Connor and some of the other guys in the family. The only thing Kevin says he's noticed is that Aidan seems to have a thing for Liz and that it's not going so well."

"I've taken note of that myself," Mick said. "I might have to step in and give those two a push."

"And what do Megan and Ma have to say about that?" Thomas asked, looking amused.

"Oh, what do they know?" Mick grumbled. "My meddling's turned out okay so far. I gave you and Connie a gentle nudge, didn't I? You complaining about that?"

Thomas regarded him indignantly. "Now you're taking credit for my getting together with my wife?"

"I am," Mick said unrepentantly. "You were having a ton of second thoughts, as I recall. Two failed marriages. Connie being younger. Connie's daughter not exactly being on board. You remember any of that?"

"It sounds vaguely familiar," Thomas admitted. "But Connie and I would have worked through those things in time. She's a smart woman. Patient, too."

"At your age, I figured you didn't have any time to waste," Mick retorted.

Thomas laughed. "Well, there is that. Okay, thank you. Now, what do you suggest I do about Aidan? You're the one with all the ideas."

"I have his résumé inside. You can take a look at that and see if anything pops out at you."

"Is that legal?" Thomas asked. "Aren't personnel files closed to the public?"

"I was on the hiring committee," Mick responded. "I asked your opinion since he'll be working with you and the environmental club at the school. Who's going to argue with that?"

"In this town, probably nobody," Thomas acknowledged.

"Okay, then. I'll be right back."

Mick returned with Aidan's file and handed it to his brother. "Read it here, though. I probably shouldn't let it wander all over town."

"Of course." Thomas hesitated, as if he weren't sure he wanted to know whatever might be in the file that could confirm this uneasiness he felt around Aidan. Finally, visibly drawing in a deep breath, he opened the folder and glanced at the top page, then moved on to the next and then the next.

Mick saw the exact moment when something registered. Shock settled on his brother's face and his color drained away.

"Thomas, what the hell is it? What did you find?"

"The boy's mother," Thomas said, sounding thoroughly shaken.

"What about her?"

"I knew her, Mick. I knew her really well."

⇒ 14 ⇐

Mick stared at Thomas incredulously. "Are you sure about that? What's it say her name is?"

"Anna Mitchell," Thomas said without so much as a glance at the résumé.

"It's a common enough name," Mick said, waving off his brother's concern. "You're probably imagining things."

"I'm not," Thomas insisted with surprising certainty. "All along I've thought there was something familiar about Aidan, but I couldn't pin it down. It's Anna. He has her eyes, her coloring. I'm sure of it."

Mick remained unconvinced. "If you and Aidan's mom were friends, don't you think he would have mentioned the connection when he first got to town?"

"Maybe he doesn't know," Thomas suggested. "Or maybe he does and that's why he reacts so oddly around me. I have no idea what his mother might have mentioned about that time in her life. Do parents tell their kids about old college love affairs?"

"You've always had a great relationship with your exes," Mick reminded him. "Was it different with Anna?"

"I didn't think so," Thomas said, his expression troubled. "We were young, just kids really. I had so many things I wanted to accomplish, and she knew that. She had a long list of ambitious goals for herself, so she understood. We parted as friends, at least that's what I remember."

"Did you stay in touch?"

"No, she moved back to New York right after we broke up. She told me she'd decided to finish college there, that she missed her family and missed New York, that she thought her future was there. I never heard from her again."

"You never thought about contacting her?"

"It crossed my mind, but I convinced myself it was best left in the past. You know how I was back then, single-minded about my goals. Anna meant the world to me, but she was a distraction."

"How serious was it? Before the breakup, I mean."

Thomas lifted a brow. "You asking for details, Mick?"

Mick frowned at him. "Of course not. I'm just trying to follow what you're saying. Had you talked about marriage, anything like that?"

"No, never," Thomas said. A faraway look crossed his face. "She was amazing, Mick. She was smart and as dedicated to environmental causes as I was. That idealism was something we had in common."

Mick recalled Thomas's first two wives. Anyone could have told him they were all wrong for him. Neither understood his passion for his career. Connie, though, she got it. Maybe this Anna woman had, too.

"It sounds as if she might have been the perfect woman for you," Mick said.

"In retrospect, she may have been," Thomas said wearily. "I do know that I loved her, or at least thought I did. But, like I said, we were too young to be so serious. She knew that, too. In fact, she's the one who called it off."

His expression turned nostalgic. "I thought

about her for years. I'd be in the middle of some thankless fight with the politicians, half-ready to give up, and I'd hear Anna in my head telling me not to dare do that."

"So, on some level you've always regretted losing her?" Mick concluded.

"I knew breaking up was the right decision at the time, but, sure, I had regrets. I thought it was more about my ego than anything else, though. I mean, really, what did I know about love at twenty?"

"You didn't know that much when you hit forty," Mick taunted. "Not till Connie came along. You know," he added thoughtfully, "everything you said about Anna could describe Connie, too. She's as passionate about this environmental stuff as you are, and she's smart as a whip."

Thomas gave him a startled look. "You know, you're right. I never once made the comparison before, probably because Anna was so far in my past it never occurred to me. Connie and Anna would have had a lot in common. The other trait they shared was an admirable strength. I think that drew me to each of them."

Mick sat back, trying to absorb his brother's news. "You going to confront Aidan about this?"

Thomas nodded slowly. "Confrontation's the wrong way of looking at it, but I do think I have to at least mention it, ask if I'm right. If he's been harboring some sort of misplaced ill will toward me, we need to get that out in the open, especially if we're going to work together."

"And how will Connie feel about your dredging up your romantic past?"

"It has nothing to do with her," Thomas said.

Mick gave him a disbelieving look. "Even I know better than that."

"Come on, Mick. It's ancient history," Thomas replied. "Connie knows I was married twice, and she didn't freak out about that. She'll handle an old college relationship just fine. It's no threat to her. Besides, the form says Anna is deceased. She can't cause any trouble for us."

Mick regarded him worriedly. "You may be minimizing the impact of this news. Just look at how it's shaken you up knowing that Aidan's mom was a woman you used to know."

"Connie will be fine," Thomas insisted. "I'll speak to her before I ever have a word with Aidan. Like I said, though, it's been years, Mick. It's over and done with. I'll make that clear. I'll tell her I just need to tie up these loose ends, so Aidan and I can clear the air and work together."

"Up to you to decide how to handle it, of course," Mick said, for once not the least bit interested in inserting himself into the middle. He had a hunch the minefield was a lot more dangerous than his brother was envisioning. In his experience, women weren't quite as predictable as Thomas clearly thought Connie to be.

"I need to go," Thomas said, still looking shaken as he handed over the folder with the stunning information.

"You need me, I'm here," Mick said.

"Thanks, Mick."

Mick watched his brother walk away, shoulders slumped in a way he'd never seen before. Whatever Thomas said about this thing with Anna Mitchell being no more than a distant memory was a lie. It had been dragged right smack into the middle of the present. To his way of thinking that was never good.

Aidan had eaten cold, leftover pizza for dinner and was trying to settle down with a book when someone knocked on the door of his apartment, sending Archie racing in that direction to help announce the arrival of company.

Aidan laughed. "I heard it," he told the dog, grabbing his collar to hold him back as he opened the door. He was stunned to see Thomas O'Brien standing there.

"Am I interrupting anything?" Thomas asked, looking uncomfortable.

"No, come on in," he said, his tone polite, but hardly welcoming.

"Maybe we could go for a walk, instead," Thomas said, hands jammed into the pockets of his well-worn jeans.

At the mention of a walk, Archie barked excitedly and ran for his leash.

"Well, one of us is clearly enthusiastic about that idea," Aidan said, laughing. "A walk does sound good, though. I just finished way too much leftover pizza."

He followed Thomas down the stairs and around the building to Main Street. The older man didn't say a word as they turned onto Shore Road and walked along the waterfront. The restaurants seemed to be crowded with customers, but they had the walkway by the water mostly to themselves. The breeze off the bay was surprisingly chilly for June. Aidan was glad he'd thought to grab a jacket, but Thomas was shivering without one.

"Maybe we should stop somewhere," Aidan said. "It's cooler out here than I thought it would be."

Thomas laughed. "You haven't spent a day on the water when it's freezing and the wind is whipping. Now, that's cold. This is just a wee nip in the air."

"Are you sure? You can have my jacket."

Thomas shook his head. "I'm used to this." He kept right on walking, his pace deliberate and steady.

When Aidan couldn't stand it another minute, he glanced over at Thomas's profile and took note of his troubled expression. "Is there something on your mind? It's not about the school club, is it, because I have the time now to get some of those books from you. In fact, Shanna sold me one earlier today and I was just starting to read it when you showed up."

"It's not about that," Thomas said.

The weariness behind his words had Aidan's heart skipping a beat. "Then what?" he asked, filled with trepidation.

"Your mother," Thomas began.

Aidan stiffened at the totally unexpected reply. "What about her?"

"She went to the University of Maryland, didn't she?"

So, Aidan thought, Thomas had finally figured out the connection, or at least some of it.

"She did."

"And we dated," Thomas said flatly, no hint of doubt in his voice.

"I believe you may have," Aidan said, choosing his words very carefully.

Thomas regarded him with a surprised expression. "She never mentioned me?"

Aidan shook his head. "Not really, no."

"But you had some inkling we had a past, am I right about that?"

"Yes."

Thomas regarded him impatiently. "Aidan, I'm trying to figure out some things. Help me out."

"I'm being honest," Aidan said, his defenses in

place. "My mom mentioned there had been someone in her past, but she never mentioned you by name."

His reply only seemed to leave Thomas more confused. "Then why the attitude when you got to town and we first met?" Thomas asked. "If she'd told you about me, it might make sense, but if my name never came up, then I don't get it."

"I found your name after she died last year," Aidan explained.

"Okay," Thomas said, still looking vaguely bewildered. He was silent, as if waiting for more.

"How well do you remember her?" Aidan asked to fill the silence. He decided to probe for a few answers of his own before giving anything more away.

"Very well," Thomas said without hesitation. "When I saw her name and realized that's who your mother was, so many memories came flooding back to me." He met Aidan's gaze. "They were good memories, Aidan."

"Tell me," Aidan pleaded, suddenly wanting to hear every detail about their time together. He had to wonder if Thomas would share his memories so readily once the truth was out there. "I don't really know anything about that time in her life."

Thomas's expression softened. "She was beautiful, but I'm sure you saw that for yourself. Not just on the outside, but the inside, too. She was as idealistic as I was, so we had that in common. I don't think she'd found a real focus for all that energy yet the way I had, but I knew she would eventually. She had such passion for anything that interested her."

"She said the same about you," Aidan admitted, drawing another puzzled look.

"I thought you said she'd never mentioned me."

"Not by name, no. I put the pieces together after she died."

"I'm so sorry you lost her," Thomas said with apparent sincerity. "I wish we'd stayed in touch, that I'd kept up with her life, known about you before now."

"Me, too."

"What about your father?"

The charged words seemed to hang in the air. Answering that question was going to change everything. Aidan wondered if Thomas knew that, if he suspected, but his expression when he asked the question so innocently suggested nothing more than curiosity.

"I never knew him." Aidan swallowed hard, then looked directly into Thomas's eyes. "Until now."

There it was—the truth that had been weighing on Aidan's mind ever since he'd arrived in Chesapeake Shores. He waited for a reaction, any reaction, but Thomas just stared at him, clearly stunned.

"I need to think a minute," Thomas said, making his way to a bench and sinking down on it as if he'd suddenly aged.

Aidan followed, unsure of what to do next. He sat down, too, and waited.

"You have to be wrong," Thomas said eventually.

Aidan had expected the shock, but not the denial. "You think I'd lie about something like this?"

"I'm not saying you're lying," Thomas said quickly. "Not at all. I think perhaps you jammed a few pieces of a puzzle together to make them fit and came to the wrong conclusion."

"Are you saying you never slept with my mom?" Aidan asked bluntly. "That it's not possible for you to be my father? Because if you are, I think maybe you're the liar."

Thomas's face flushed. "Let's go back and start over before we both say things we're likely to regret. What makes you think I'm your father? You said your mother never once mentioned me, that she only talked about your father in general terms. Is that right?"

Aidan nodded. "She told me how idealistic he was, how committed he was to the cause that mattered to him, all things I think we can agree describe you perfectly."

"We knew other idealistic people during that time in our lives," Thomas suggested, sounding more desperate than defensive. "College kids become passionate about a lot of things."

Aidan knew he held the one piece of information that would end the argument. It was safely locked away back in his apartment. "But their names aren't on my birth certificate," he said quietly.

This time the color drained out of Thomas's face. "You have a copy of that?"

"I have the original. My mom had it hidden away, but I found it last summer when I was cleaning out her apartment after she died. She obviously didn't put your name on there to trap you into paying child support since she never even mentioned my existence to you." He frowned. "Or did she? Did she tell you she was pregnant? Did you turn your back on her?"

"Of course not," Thomas said with what appeared to be genuine indignation. "That's not the kind of man I am. I take responsibility for my actions. I may have made mistakes in my life, but I never run from things."

"Now," Aidan agreed readily enough. He'd seen enough to accept that Thomas O'Brien today was an honorable man. "But back then?"

"I did the same back then," Thomas said. "If Anna had told me she was pregnant, I'd never have let her walk away."

This time it was Aidan who was startled. "She broke up with you?"

"She did. She said she didn't want to hold me back from the things I was meant to do and that a serious relationship at that stage of our lives would do that. I didn't want her to go back to New York, but I couldn't argue with her, either. We were too blasted young. And she seemed excited about finishing up her college degree in New York."

"She never finished her degree," Aidan revealed. "She didn't have the time or money for it, not with a baby on the way. My grandparents helped out. We lived with them until I was two, but their apartment was too crowded and I was too noisy and disruptive. Plus, if you knew my mom so well, you know how independent she was. She worked two jobs sometimes, until she finally found one in the city with an organization that gave grants to environmental protection projects."

Thomas regarded him with what seemed to be real regret. "I'm so sorry it was so difficult for her, and for you. If I'd known about what was going on, I'd have found a way to make things easier."

His expression filled with sorrow. "I wish I had known, Aidan. I really do. Her decision to leave came out of the blue. I thought we were happy as we were. I suppose I should have asked more questions. I'm sorry now that I didn't."

"But at the time you were relieved when she

was gone, weren't you?" Aidan said, his words sounding more like an accusation than a question. And maybe he'd meant them to be just that, one of the many accusations he'd wanted to direct at this man who'd allowed him to grow up without a father.

"I was confused," Thomas replied slowly, as if giving his response real thought. "I was unhappy. But looking back, maybe I was a little relieved. She was right about the intensity of what we shared. We were in love, or thought we were. That kind of youthful passion can be a distraction and I didn't want to lose focus."

He finally looked in Aidan's direction, studying him as if searching for proof that they shared DNA. "I can't believe she would have kept a son from me, not the Anna I knew."

"Not even to keep you from losing focus?" Aidan asked, his tone mocking as he echoed Thomas's words.

"Look, son—"

"Don't call me that," Aidan said sharply. "You haven't earned the right."

"But isn't that the point?" Thomas asked. "If you are my son, we have to figure out where we go from here, how to build on that truth."

"*If?*" Aidan said, his anger stirring. "Are we back to calling me a liar? Or my mom?"

"I'm just saying that the situation is complicated," Thomas replied, his tone surprisingly calm. "Neither of us knows why your mother did what she did. If she never told you my name, maybe that's because she only wanted me to be your father, but couldn't be certain."

Aidan was on his feet. "Are you suggesting that my mother, the woman you claim to have loved, that you claim loved you, was cheating on you?" he asked, outraged by the suggestion. "That she put your name on my birth certificate to what? Trap you into paying support for a child who wasn't yours? Odd, then, that she never bothered to tell you about me or to go to court to ask for anything."

Thomas looked shocked by the angry words Aidan was hurling at him. "Of course not. She wasn't that kind of woman. But maybe, for your peace of mind and mine, we should be sure about this before we go broadcasting the news to everyone else."

"You want a DNA test?" Aidan said, his voice empty of emotion. "Sure, whatever. I suppose I even get why you'd doubt me, though I can tell you here and now that I don't want or expect anything from you. I'm not here to make any claims on you or your family."

"It's not about doubting you," Thomas insisted. "But this was what, twenty-eight years ago, right? It's too important to leave something this huge to chance."

"And then? When the test proves what I already

know, what will you do about it? It's not as if I need a father at this stage of my life. And you obviously don't need another son."

Thomas's expression softened for just a minute. "But I would very much like to know the one I had with Anna, if that's how this turns out. For whatever reasons she thought she had, your mother denied me that chance. I'm not condemning her for that, but I'm not the one who created this situation, Aidan. Based on what you said, you've known since last summer about me. Give me some time to catch up. Then together we can figure out what happens next."

The request was too blasted reasonable and Aidan was in no mood to be reasonable. He sighed, knowing Thomas was right. "And until we know, nothing changes. No one knows," he agreed.

"To be honest, when I saw your mother's name, I told Connie that I knew your mother a long time ago, but this?" He shook his head. "I won't mention that you're my son until we have the test results. Not a word to anyone else, either." He regarded Aidan intently. "You'll do the same?"

"Of course. Liz suspects there's some connection, but she has no idea what it might be. She certainly doesn't suspect this. I'm sure of that."

"Would you mind if we went to Johns Hopkins for the tests?" Thomas asked. "We could probably have the samples taken right here, but even as discreet as I know the doctor and his staff to be, word can get around."

Aidan nodded. He didn't want to risk any leaks, either, not until they had the proof that his claim was valid and had decided how they—both of them together—wanted to handle it. Maybe it could remain their secret, but he couldn't envision the likelihood of that in Chesapeake Shores, where private business seemed to be fair game, especially among O'Briens.

A thought suddenly occurred to him. "What does Mick know? I imagine he's the one who showed you the résumé with my mother's name on it."

"I acknowledged to him that I knew your mother, but that's all. The possibility that you were my son hadn't even crossed my mind then," Thomas said, then smiled. "I can see why Mick knowing would worry you. He'll be determined that we forge a bond whether it's what we want or not. That's his way. My mother, Nell, she'll feel the same way. If there's any doubt in your mind, she'll welcome you as another grandson. I'm the one who'll be answering her questions and listening to her lectures for days on end."

"Something to look forward to, then," Aidan said, amused by the image of Nell scolding this grown man for his past mistakes.

"Then we'll move forward with the tests. I'll make the arrangements," Thomas said. "Tomorrow, if possible. There's no reason to drag this out and leave us both wondering. I imagine you're exhausted enough by keeping this inside."

"You'll be wondering," Aidan told him. "I already know, but yes, it will be a relief to end the secrecy."

A faint smile tugged at Thomas's lips. "You have the O'Brien stubborn streak, that's for sure. I guess we'll see if that's only coincidence."

Aidan could have reassured him on that point, but Thomas clearly didn't want to leave something this momentous to chance. After spending time with his happy family, Aidan could understand why.

Liz sat in her usual booth at Sally's stirring sugar into her coffee, her mind wandering.

"I'm pretty sure that sugar dissolved at least five minutes ago," Bree commented, watching her.

Liz's head snapped up. "What?"

Bree gestured toward the coffee. "It's probably cold by now. Do you want Sally to warm it up?"

Liz sighed and pushed it away. "I don't really want coffee."

"Seems to me what you could really use is a stiff drink."

Liz blinked at that. "Excuse me? At eight-thirty in the morning?"

"You're upset about something," Bree said. "Of

course, it probably is a little early to start in on martinis."

"I've never had a martini in my life. Nor do I rely on alcohol to solve my problems," she said indignantly.

"There," Bree said with satisfaction. "Taking me to task put some color back into your cheeks. So what's going on, Liz? Everything okay with you and Aidan?"

"There is no me and Aidan," she said, the response automatic.

"I know that's what you keep telling yourself," Bree said mildly. "You may even believe it, but the rest of us aren't so easily convinced. Maybe it would help if I told you that you seem to have him twisted into knots, too."

"Hardly likely," Liz said, dismissing the possibility. "Aidan has too much going on right now to be worrying about me. There's a lot of pressure for him to get the high school team to perform well this year."

"And to hear Henry tell it, they're going to be awesome," Bree said, chuckling. "I swear that kid could do PR for the Baltimore Ravens. He knows football and his enthusiasm is contagious, especially with his friend Hector taking over as quarterback."

Liz finally allowed herself a chuckle. "I've heard him go on and on when I've run into him in the bookstore. I imagine there's a lot of football talk around the Sunday dinner table these days."

"Especially since he's brought Hector along with him a couple of times. I think the poor kid is a little overwhelmed by O'Brien exuberance, but last week he actually spoke up and argued with my dad. I'm not sure who was more stunned, Mick or Hector." She grinned. "The rest of us actually gave Hector a little cheer. You should have seen Dad's face."

"I can imagine," Liz said, laughing for what seemed like the first time in days.

"Now, back to Aidan," Bree said, quickly killing Liz's improving mood.

"Do we have to?" she begged.

"Just answer one question for me and then I swear I'll drop it, at least for this morning," Bree said.

"If that's the best deal I can hope for, go ahead."

"Is your ambivalence about getting involved with Aidan because you really, honest-to-goodness don't want a relationship with anyone, because you're not even remotely attracted to Aidan specifically or is it because of something the rest of us don't know about him, something that worries you?"

Liz saw the trap. Any answer she gave was going to bring on a full-court press for more answers than she was prepared to give. She couldn't explain why she didn't want to risk her heart again. She could hardly say she wasn't attracted to Aidan, because she was, way more than she wanted to be, in fact. She'd come to appreciate all of his good qualities, his caring side, his character.

But there were still the things she didn't know. And if she brought up these vague suspicions about Aidan having some sort of past connection to Thomas, well, who knew what sort of hornet's nest that might stir up? And if she were wrong about it, she'd have caused trouble for no reason.

"I'm waiting," Bree said.

"Maybe it's all of the above, or none of the above," Liz said, hoping to be just confusing enough that Bree would conclude she really didn't know her own mind and would give up in frustration.

Unfortunately that didn't allow for the fact that Bree was an O'Brien. Vague replies only provoked more questions. Several more tripped off her tongue, before Liz held up her hand.

"Enough!" she commanded. "I can't do this. My mind's spinning. And I need a clear head if I'm going to get anything done at work today. Plus my mom called last night and announced that she and my sisters are arriving this afternoon."

"You don't sound excited about that," Bree noted, studying her closely.

"I asked them to come," Liz said, then sighed. "But I'd been hoping for a little more notice, like maybe a year."

Bree laughed. "I get to see my family just about every day. Sometimes I'd be content with just twenty-four hours' notice before some of them poke their noses into my business. Yours will be gone again in a few days. Mine never leaves. Try to remember that when they're driving you crazy."

"I'll do my best," Liz said.

"I've got a new play opening at the theater tomorrow night. Bring them. I'll leave tickets at the box office."

Liz's eyes lit up. "What a great idea! Two hours of blissful silence." She grinned. "From them, not the people on stage."

"Good save," Bree said. "If there's anything else I can do to help out, let me know."

"You have more than enough on your plate with a new production opening. The tickets are plenty. I owe you for making the suggestion and holding four seats. I know you're usually sold out these days."

"I always have seats for friends and family," Bree said. "I like to stack the deck with a friendly audience, especially on opening night. Now I'd better run. We have a dress rehearsal and a last costume fitting this morning. One of the kids in the show has been growing like a weed. Unfortunately, she's mine."

"Emily Rose is in this?"

Bree nodded, her eyes shining with maternal

pride. "She's even singing a song. I've created a little diva, I'm afraid."

"I can't wait to see her. I promise to clap wildly."

"All I could ask," Bree said, leaning down to kiss her cheek. "That, and that you reconsider opening your heart just a tiny bit to let Aidan in."

Liz sighed. "How did I know you weren't done with that?"

"Because I'm me," Bree said readily.

Liz watched her go, then looked around for Sally. "Could I have a large cup of coffee to go?" Something told her she was going to need all that caffeine and probably a lot more before the day was out.

⇛ 15 ⇚

Aidan had made the trip to Baltimore for the DNA test. Now the only thing left to do was to wait for the results. He desperately wanted to see Liz. He wanted to share all of this with her and get her take on it, but he'd promised to keep silent. On top of that, he recognized that she wasn't exactly open to taking on his secrets, not when she was so clearly struggling with her own. That was a hurdle they'd have to face later, at least if he wanted to pursue his growing feelings for her. He hadn't had any experience at falling in love, but what he was feeling for Liz, even without much encouragement from her, seemed like the real thing to him. He wasn't prepared to give up on seeing where it led.

Right now, though, he hoped maybe the sight of her might prove distracting, that it might quiet his nerves or spur a different sort of restlessness entirely. Maybe she'd even agree to go out for a quick dinner or at least a drink, anything to keep his mind off that blasted test that could change everything. With results days away, he needed a distraction, and basketball with O'Brien men clearly wasn't the best choice. There would be too many chances for him to blurt out something he'd regret.

He put off dropping into Liz's shop by settling onto a bench by the bay and calling Frankie. Frankie was always good at providing a couple of stories to keep Aidan's mind off whatever was troubling him. What he hadn't considered, though, was just how well his old friend could read him.

"Hey, I've given you some of my best stuff," Frankie complained. "What do I get in return? Not so much as a chuckle. What's going on down there? You thinking you made a mistake? You know management here would take you on in a heartbeat."

"Doing what? Babysitting you oafs in the locker room? No, thanks."

"What about being a quarterback coach?"

"The team already has a great one," Aidan reminded him. "That's who trained me."

"Yeah, well, they'd come up with something."

"I made a commitment here," Aidan reminded him. "That means something to me."

"What I still don't get is why Chesapeake freaking Shores, or whatever it is?"

"If you'd come for a visit, you'd have some idea. It's a great little town."

"Any clubs? Hot babes? A great nightlife?"

"No," Aidan admitted.

"Then it's not for me. Why don't you get your butt in gear and come to New York this weekend?"

For an instant Aidan was tempted, but going out on the town with Frankie didn't hold nearly the appeal of getting even a glimpse of Liz. That was probably yet more evidence of just how hard he'd fallen. He might as well resign himself to it and chase the dream.

"Thanks, but I have things to do here," he told Frankie. "Stay out of trouble, okay?"

"Always," Frankie promised. "You do the same, though it sounds as if you don't have many opportunities to get into trouble in the first place."

Aidan hung up and headed for Main Street. When he walked into Pet Style, he found three unfamiliar women wandering around in the store while Liz finished a sale at the register. The older of the three kept firing questions in Liz's direction, seemingly oblivious to the fact that Liz was busy with a customer.

"Mom, please," Liz said, clearly fighting for patience after making an apology to the customer. "I'll be finished here in a minute."

Ah, Aidan thought. Her family had come to visit. As he walked in her mother's direction, he caught the look of panic on Liz's face, but he didn't allow that to slow him down.

"You must be Liz's mother," he said, holding out his hand. "I'm Aidan Mitchell."

Liz's mother gave him a long look, her gaze narrowing, caught somewhere between suspicion and disapproval. "Doris Benson," she said eventually as if debating whether to say anything at all to this impertinent stranger who'd approached her without a proper introduction.

The younger women displayed no such hesitation. They hurried over and introduced themselves as Liz's sisters, LeeAnn and Danielle.

"I wonder why Liz hasn't mentioned you," Danielle said, unabashedly giving him a thorough once-over. "You're definitely noteworthy."

"Danielle!" her mother chided, her suspicious gaze never leaving Aidan. "How do you and Liz know each other?"

"We're friends," Aidan said. "We met when I first arrived in town about six weeks ago to coach the high school football team. I live in an apartment right upstairs, so we run into each other a lot."

Liz's other sister's eyes widened. "You're *that* Aidan Mitchell! I recognize you now," LeeAnn gushed, promptly pulling out her cell phone to snap a picture. "Wait till I text this to Teddy. That's my husband. He's going to be so excited. We're big Carolina Panthers fans, of course, but he thought you were about the most promising quarterback to come along in years." Her expression sobered. "Too bad about your injury. I had no idea you were in Chesapeake Shores." She shot a critical look toward Liz. "No one thought to mention there was a celebrity right here in town."

"As I mentioned, I've only been here a short time," Aidan said. "And since my football career is behind me, I doubt anyone in town thinks of me as a celebrity these days."

"Well, any football fan surely does," LeeAnn contradicted. "And you and my sister are friends. Imagine that." She winked at Danielle. "Liz always did know how to snag the most handsome guy around. You should have seen Josh."

"That's enough!" Liz said, her sharp tone finally snagging her sister's attention as she rushed in their direction.

"What did I say?" LeeAnn asked.

Her expression was innocent, but Aidan didn't think there was anything innocent about her comment. Her next words confirmed his suspicion.

"Doesn't he know about Josh?" LeeAnn asked,

wide-eyed with feigned disbelief. "He was your husband, for goodness' sakes."

"I really don't like to talk about that time in my life," Liz said, her voice tight. "You know that."

"Sure, but what I don't understand is why," LeeAnn said anyway, persisting in keeping the topic alive. "Josh was an amazing guy. It was tragic that he died, but you can't just pretend he never existed. You should be keeping those memories alive."

"Don't try to tell me how to live my life," Liz snapped. "And not in front of people you don't even know."

"Liz is right," her mother said, trying to smooth over the awkward moment. "This isn't the time or the place. Sweetie, if you'll just give us a key and point us in the right direction, we'll head on over to the house and unpack. I brought a cooler with some of your favorites. I thought we'd eat in tonight so we can relax after that drive."

Aidan watched Liz's expression. She didn't seem especially ecstatic about the plan, possibly because she knew the topic of her late husband was likely to be part of the evening's conversation.

He caught her gaze. "I could ride over with them and show them the way," he offered.

"Oh, we couldn't ask you to do that," her mother said. "How would you get back?"

He smiled. Clearly she hadn't been in town long

enough to see how close downtown was to everything. "I'll walk back. It's not far."

"Well, if you wouldn't mind, that would be helpful," she said, her tone more gracious than before. "Thank you."

Liz gave her mother a key to the house, then leaned in close to Aidan to whisper, "If my dogs attack them, don't try to stop it."

He laughed and held open the shop door. "Ladies."

Fifteen minutes later he'd deposited the three women inside Liz's house, calmed the barking dogs, discreetly avoided answering a single one of the myriad questions posed about his relationship with Liz and walked back to Main Street.

"They're safely tucked away at your place," he told Liz as he returned to Pet Style. "They're a curious bunch, aren't they?"

She groaned. "What did they ask you?"

"I believe my preference for boxers or briefs came up at one point."

Her eyes widened with dismay. "I'm going to kill them. I really am."

He laughed at her reaction. "It's okay. They didn't go quite that far."

"But close enough," she said wearily, then gave him a plaintive look. "Can I spend the night with you? Maybe the whole weekend?"

His jaw dropped, even though he knew she was only teasing. "I wouldn't say no."

She chuckled, as he'd intended. "Of course you wouldn't, but I suppose I can't escape my own family just by hiding out. What on earth was I thinking when I invited them to come for a visit?"

"That you wanted to see them?" he suggested. "Or wanted them to see where you live and how wonderful it is?"

Her eyes lit up. "Ah, yes, that was it." She sighed heavily. "I think it was probably a bad idea. LeeAnn especially is much more excited about meeting you than she's likely to be about anything else Chesapeake Shores has to offer. She's already criticized half a dozen things about the town and the store and they'd only been here about fifteen minutes when you walked in."

"I could join you for dinner, keep their attention diverted," he suggested, thinking that would serve his own purposes very nicely. Plus it might give him more insight into Liz and the marriage she was so clearly reluctant to discuss.

"I think you've already stirred up enough speculation for one day," she said. "But thanks."

"Are you sure you want to turn down someone who's offering to sacrifice themselves for the cause of keeping the attention off you?"

"Trust me—the attention will always come back to me. They've come with an agenda. They want me to come back to North Carolina, or at least my mother does. Nothing about Chesapeake Shores or my life here will meet their expectations."

"Not even me?" he asked with a grin.

"You're just a complication. I can't explain you away, and, in case you couldn't interpret that expression on my mother's face, she doesn't think I should be done mourning yet. In their eyes Josh was a saint."

There was an unmistakable edge in her voice that caught his attention. "He wasn't?" That would definitely explain the heartbreak she'd experienced.

For an instant it looked as if Liz might answer honestly, but then her expression closed down. "I was taught not to speak ill of the dead."

"Which says quite a lot just on the surface of it," Aidan commented. "Maybe it's time you did talk truthfully about your past. I'm getting a very strong feeling you've been glossing over the truly important parts."

"Aidan, please, not now," she pleaded. "Having the three of them here is stressful enough."

Reluctantly, he backed off—again. "By the way, I had a message from Bree that she'd left a ticket to the playhouse for me for tomorrow night," he told her.

"Did you now?" Liz said, looking amused. "Something tells me I'll be seeing you there."

"She left a ticket for you, too?"

"Four, as a matter of fact. You can play buffer then, assuming any of us is still alive by tomorrow night."

He laughed. "I have great faith in your restraint."

"Really? I can't imagine why. This is the first time you've seen me with my family. They can drive me over the brink faster than any O'Brien you've ever met."

"Then I'll look forward to tomorrow night," he said truthfully. He had a feeling it would give him yet more insight into Liz's past and whatever secrets she'd been so determined to keep. He'd already picked up more just this afternoon than she'd obviously intended.

Liz dallied over closing the store for as long as she thought she possibly could without causing a major uproar when she finally did get home. As it was, there were bound to be weighted remarks about how hard she was working. They wouldn't be worded as compliments.

When she walked into the house, the dogs were nowhere in sight. She could hear them barking frantically from the laundry room by the kitchen. She found her mother and sisters gathered in the kitchen. Pots of vegetables were simmering on the stove, and a casserole was apparently in the oven.

Ignoring the chatter, she opened the door to the laundry room. Both dogs and the cat bounded out and raced past her, clearly intent on getting far away from their captors.

"Why did you put them in there?" she asked, trying to keep her anger in check.

"We didn't think you'd want them running all through the house," her mother said. "Who knows what damage they might do."

"Didn't it occur to you that I was the one who'd left them out in the first place?" Liz asked. "Please don't shut them up like that again."

Her mother blinked at her hard tone. "Sure, honey, if that's what you want. Let's not get the evening off to a bad start over something so silly."

Liz was about to argue that any mistreatment of her pets was hardly inconsequential, but managed to stop herself. "You're right. I've been looking forward to playing cards or Scrabble and having some fun the way we used to."

"So are we," her mother said. "Now, why don't you change your clothes and take a shower. That'll relax you. Dinner will be ready in about twenty minutes."

Since changing and a shower meant she could escape from the kitchen, Liz seized on the suggestion. "Thanks, Mom. I won't be long." She forced a smile. "Dinner smells delicious."

"Wait till you see dessert," Danielle said. "She made a red velvet cake *and* a lemon meringue pie. I intend to eat some of each. I haven't allowed myself even a taste of dessert for what seems like forever. If I don't lose the last of this baby weight from having Kit six months ago, I think Nate'll probably pack up and leave."

Liz opened her mouth, but one glance at her mother had her clamping her lips together and leaving the room. *Don't start a fight,* she cautioned herself for the second time in a couple of minutes. *Not on the very first night.*

When she came back fifteen minutes later in shorts and a tank top, her feet bare, she drew a critical glance from her mother, but she ignored it. This was, after all, her home. She could surely dress as she wanted on a summer night. LeeAnn and Danielle, both wearing proper starched sundresses, eyed her enviously.

Dinner actually went surprisingly well, Liz thought, as the conversation covered the recipes for her mother's corn pudding, her baked chicken and noodle casserole, and the fresh green beans and sliced summer tomatoes that she'd brought from her own garden. As they had for years, all three sisters teased their mom that she was leaving out ingredients when she passed along her recipes, just so theirs would never live up to hers.

"I would never do such a thing," Doris Benson claimed, but there was a twinkle in her eyes when she said it. "After I'm gone you can go through my recipe box to your heart's content and you'll find it all written down exactly the way I've told you."

"Sure," LeeAnn said, grinning. "I imagine you covered your tracks pretty thoroughly. It's Grandma's recipe box I want to see."

Liz laughed. "I never thought of that. Now, exactly where did you hide that, Mom?"

"If it even exists, and I'm not saying it does, you'll find it long after I'm gone," her mother retorted. "That is if you don't just throw all the contents of the house into a Dumpster the way I hear Ginny Walker did with her parents' things." She shook her head. "I've never before heard of such disrespectful behavior."

"Mom, Ginny lives clear across the country. I'm sure she saved things that held real memories for her and dealt with the rest the best way she knew how in the little time she had to clean out the house and get it on the market," Danielle said. "You can't fault her for that."

"Well, I do," Doris said stubbornly. "You treat my things that way and I'll haunt the whole lot of you."

"Now there's a fun thought," LeeAnn said, giving Liz a conspiratorial wink. "I can hardly wait. How about you?"

Since having her mother alive and kicking under her roof was problematic enough, Liz couldn't imagine that having her haunting presence around would be much worse. "Think of the reality show we could do," she said lightly, drawing a scowl from her mother, but chuckles from her sisters.

For just a minute, it seemed a little like old times, back before they'd all gone their separate ways, then gotten married and moved on with their lives. Liz took a moment to indulge in the nostalgic thought, but her mother interrupted, snapping her back to the present.

"Let's talk about this Aidan Mitchell person," she said. "I'm surprised at you, dating so soon after losing your husband."

"Who said anything about dating?" Liz asked, her shoulders tightening with immediate tension. "We're friends."

"Any benefits?" LeeAnn asked hopefully.

"I don't like the sound of that," Doris Benson said, seemingly unfamiliar with the term, but grasping that she wouldn't approve.

Liz frowned at her youngest sister. "Really, LeeAnn, do you have to stir the pot?"

"It is fun," LeeAnn said unrepentantly. As the youngest, she'd always delighted in getting her big sisters to lose their cool. Tattling about their boyfriends had been one of her favorite forms of entertainment until both Liz and Danielle had threatened severe retaliation.

"My point is," their mother said, "that you should still be mourning the loss of your husband, not cavorting around with another man."

"Nobody's cavorting, Mom," Liz said tightly. "And I think over a year is plenty of time to be in mourning." She was not going to say that maybe Josh hadn't deserved even that much, at least not from her, but once again she bit her tongue. At this rate she'd need stitches in it before they left town.

Why ruin their illusions at this late date? she told herself sternly. It was bad enough that her own had been shattered. Maybe, though, if she'd confided in them from the beginning, the burden of Josh's infidelity would have been easier to bear and she'd have had the emotional support she'd denied herself. In her twisted thinking at the time, though, she'd thought she'd failed at marriage and hadn't wanted anyone to know just how badly.

"He was the love of your life," her mother persisted. "You're not even around to go to the cemetery and keep flowers on his grave."

"I'm sure his parents do that," Liz said, refusing to allow her mother to heap more guilt on her shoulders. "Even if I were there, I wouldn't be spending my time at his grave. Nobody does that."

"I still visit your grandparents' graves," her mother said.

"Every Christmas and Easter," Danielle reminded her. "You take a wreath at Christmas and a lily at Easter. It's not as if you're praying over them every day, the way you seem to want Liz to do."

Liz regarded her gratefully, appreciating the unexpected support.

Danielle acknowledged her with a wink. "I'm just saying."

Doris frowned at both of them. "I go more than that," she insisted. "I stop by Josh's grave, too. The headstone's real pretty." Once again, she regarded Liz with disapproval. "I still don't understand why you left the choice to his parents."

"Because I knew it meant more to them," Liz said, as she had about a hundred times after Josh had died. Nothing had seemed worth arguing over back then. "Now could we please change the subject?"

As soon as she saw the glint in her mother's eyes, she quickly amended, "And not to Aidan."

"Well, is there anything you do want to talk about?" her mother asked with a huff.

"How about your first impressions of Chesapeake Shores?"

The three women exchanged looks.

"There's not much to it," Danielle ventured.

"Of course, what there is seems to be charming," LeeAnn said, sending a defiant look in their mother's direction. "And the bay really is beautiful. It's so peaceful."

"When you've been to the Outer Banks as much as we have, the bay doesn't seem like much," her mother contradicted. "I could understand if you wanted to live by the ocean."

Liz sighed. "This is perfect for me. Maybe once you've had a chance to walk around tomorrow and visit some of the shops and have lunch by the water, you'll start to see it. Tomorrow night we have tickets for the local playhouse."

"Oh, sweetie, do you really want to spend some of our limited time together at some little community production?" her mother asked, her disparagement plain.

"The woman who wrote this play and runs this little community playhouse," Liz replied tartly, "has had plays produced on Broadway and in Chicago. Her works have been well reviewed by some of the most respected critics in the country. And several people in the cast perform in New York on a regular basis."

Her mother looked taken aback by that. "You don't have to take that tone with me. I didn't know," she said defensively.

"Could you just promise to be more open-minded?" Liz pleaded. "I love it here. The town is charming and the people have been very good to me. I hate that you don't even want to give it half a chance."

LeeAnn reached for her hand and gave it a squeeze. "We'll try harder," she promised.

Even Danielle nodded. "Of course we will. And if more of your friends are like Aidan Mitchell, we can't wait to meet them, too."

Liz noted that her mother made no such promise, but two out of three made the prospect of facing yet another day with her family almost bearable.

When Aidan arrived at the playhouse, he found his seat next to four empty spots, just as Liz had predicted. He glanced around and realized that they were surrounded by O'Briens. Mick and Megan were three rows in front, along with Nell and her husband, as well as Bree's husband, Jake, and her older sister Abby with her family. Kevin and Shanna were in the next row with their kids, along with Thomas, Connie and Sean. Just in front of Aidan were Jess and Will, Mack and Susie, along with Connor and Heather. Though a few other people were interspersed with them, Aidan assumed they, too, were O'Briens.

Susie promptly turned around and gave him a broad grin. "Expecting anyone special?" she asked, nodding toward the vacant seats.

"Your guess is as good as mine," he told her, refusing to confirm her apparent theory. "Bree only mentioned that she was leaving a ticket for me."

Susie didn't look as if she believed him. Suddenly her eyes lit up. "Thought so," she said triumphantly.

Aidan didn't have to turn around to know Liz was coming down the aisle with her mother and sisters.

"Look who's here," Susie said in a voice meant to carry to everyone in the family.

All O'Brien eyes focused on Liz, then Aidan. A satisfied murmur seemed to circulate that had him flushing and Liz looking as if she wanted to bolt.

The only person who didn't look happy by this

turn of events was Doris Benson. She looked as if she'd swallowed a particularly sour bite of lemon.

"You again!"

"Good evening," Aidan said, stepping aside to let them into the row. "Nice to see you all again. I hope you're enjoying your visit."

Liz's mother ignored him as she marched into the row and took her seat. Danielle and LeeAnn gave him apologetic looks, but were quick to make sure they got into the row ahead of Liz, leaving her to sit beside him.

"This is just great," she murmured with a moan. "I'll be up half the night listening to yet another lecture about how I'm disrespecting Josh's memory."

He frowned at her heartfelt dismay. "Seriously? After all this time?"

"Saints are meant to be worshipped for eternity. Hadn't you heard?"

Aidan blinked at her bitter tone. He could see the strain around her eyes and in the set of her lips. On impulse, he took her hand in his and realized hers was freezing even though it was a warm night. When she tried to pull away, he held tight and massaged gently until he could feel some warmth returning.

"That's better," he said at last, but he didn't release her hand.

She gave him a wry look. "That's what you think. Maybe you should come by the house so you can share in the pleasure of the postevening conversation."

"Happy to do it, if it would make things easier for you," he told her.

She looked into his eyes for what seemed like an eternity, then shook her head in apparent disbelief. "You'd really do that, wouldn't you? Even though you don't owe me a thing and there's nothing going on between us."

His lips curved slightly at that. "Oh, sweetheart, there's something going on. I think you're the only one who hasn't figured that out yet."

Just then, with perfect timing, the lights went down and silence fell in the theater as the curtain slowly rose.

Aidan had absolutely no idea what the play was about, though he was certain from the frequent laughter and applause that it had to be good. The only thing he knew he was going to remember about the night, though, was that Liz never again tried to remove her hand from his and that nothing he could recall had ever felt quite so right.

⇒ 16 ⇐

Liz couldn't believe she'd spent two hours holding hands with Aidan in public, especially with her mother just three seats away and the O'Briens all around them. There wasn't a doubt in her mind that every single person nearby had been aware of what was happening.

Even so, she hadn't been able to make herself jerk her hand away. It had felt way too good to have that connection with him, to remember what that current of sizzling electricity between two people could be like. Why it had to happen now and with this enigmatic man was beyond her, but it had. More and more, she was starting to think it would be self-destructive folly to ignore the possibilities. She had to find some way to put the past behind her and open her heart.

When the lights came up at the end of the play, she cast a panicked look in Aidan's direction. He winked, but he did release her hand.

Susie turned around immediately. "You'll all be at the inn for the after-party, right? I know Bree is expecting you to come."

Liz was about to shake her head, but several other O'Briens joined in issuing the invitation.

"You have to come," Shanna said. "It's Bree's big night. All of her friends should be there."

"It would be rude not to attend," LeeAnn said.

Even Danielle implored her to say yes, a hopeful note in her voice that was far too telling about the lack of fun in her life these days with three demanding children and an inconsiderate husband.

Liz conceded defeat. How could she possibly say no when it meant so much to them. This was supposed to be their vacation, albeit a brief one. They deserved to have a little fun, even if some of it was likely to come at her expense. And, who knew, perhaps getting to know her friends would help to convince them of what a great place she'd chosen for her future.

If that possibility weren't enough to persuade her to attend the party, there was the fact that it was bound to be better than going home to face the music with her mother. She forced a smile for Susie's and Shanna's benefit. "Sure, we'll be there, at least for a little while. I definitely want a chance to congratulate Bree on another great production."

Clearly satisfied at having accomplished one mission, Shanna turned her attention to Aidan. "And you?"

Never taking his gaze from Liz, he said, "Wouldn't miss it. Sounds like the perfect way to cap off a surprising evening."

Liz promptly pulled him into the aisle. "Please don't . . ."

"Don't what? Come to the party?"

"No, of course you should come, but don't do anything to give people the wrong idea."

His lips quirked in a worrisome way.

"Wrong idea? As I suggested earlier, I think you may be the only person who sees it that way."

"Aidan," she pleaded. "Not with my family here."

Apparently her genuine distress finally registered, because he gave a slow nod. "But you and I are going to have a long talk once they're gone. It's time we get everything out on the table."

Liz didn't even try to hide her shock at his words. She wasn't sure which she found more startling, having him call her on her secrets or his hint that he was finally going to reveal his. Perhaps he saw it as a one-sided conversation.

"Are you really ready to open up with me?" she inquired.

He nodded. "I think it's time. There have been way too many secrets for way too long. We need to clear the air so we can move forward."

"Okay, then," she said, though the promise filled her with trepidation. Could she really open herself up the way he was obviously expecting? Could she explain why she had so many doubts, about herself, about him, about relationships in general?

And what would happen once she'd bared her soul?

Of course, the one thing that made that prospect less terrifying was that Aidan was clearly willing at last to do the exact same thing. Was it possible that once they had, they could move on together? Or would stripping away their illusions tear them apart?

Tables in the dining room at The Inn at Eagle Point were overflowing with delicious appetizers and desserts, but Aidan only had eyes for Liz as she made her way around the room, laughing with her friends, even with her sisters and her mother. She seemed surprisingly at ease, given her earlier tension.

"Everything okay?" Thomas asked, coming up beside him, his gaze following Aidan's to settle on Liz.

Aidan nodded.

"You worried about how she's going to react to the news?" Thomas asked, surprising Aidan with his perceptiveness.

Aidan turned to look at him. "No more than you must be about the truth coming out. You have a lot more at stake with the people in this room than I do. I could totally understand if you wished I'd never come to town."

Thomas regarded him with what looked like genuine dismay. "Aidan, I won't deny that this is going to stir things up and that I'm going to face some unwelcome scrutiny." His expression turned rueful. "I imagine Ma is going to have quite a lot to say. She'll never in a million years believe that I didn't have an inkling that I'd fathered a child."

Aidan gave him a sympathetic look. He'd only been around Nell a couple of times, but he knew the hold she had over her sons and how much they wanted her respect. "For what it's worth, I believe you about that. I think my mom made a conscious choice to keep it from you. I may never totally understand why she did what she did, but I don't think you deliberately turned your back on us."

Thomas looked relieved. "Thank you for that." He smiled. "Not for being willing to defend me with Ma, but for believing in me."

Aidan shrugged. Faith in Thomas hadn't come easily or quickly—there had been years of anger and resentment to overcome, after all—but he'd spent enough time with him recently to accept that he was as honorable as his mother had clearly believed him to be.

"Any idea when the results will be in?" Aidan asked.

"They told me we should have a preliminary report on Monday if there's no obvious match based on blood type, but it could take longer for a detailed workup of the DNA results."

Before Aidan could express his frustration, obviously shared by Thomas, Connie appeared and inserted herself between them. "No shop-talk," she scolded, clearly assuming that they'd had their heads together over a far different topic.

Thomas leaned down and pressed a kiss to her cheek. "Now, why would I talk shop when I have an opportunity to be out on the town with the most beautiful woman in the room?"

A blush tinted Connie's cheeks, even as she laughed. "And that is exactly the sort of outrageous blarney that convinced me to marry this man," she told Aidan.

Aidan couldn't help wondering if that innate Irish charm had been directed toward his mother, as well. Had she fallen for it as readily? How could she not? As smart as she'd been, she was as susceptible to sweet talk as most women were. And at eighteen or nineteen when she and Thomas had known each other, Aidan could imagine that hint of an Irish brogue that appeared from time to time with all of the O'Brien men had seemed extraordinarily appealing.

He couldn't help wishing he'd seen the two of them together just once, experienced the bond that had connected them and resulted in a child. Oddly, he found himself envying his friends whose parents were divorced. At least before whatever acrimony had caused the split, there must have been a few good memories they could treasure.

A glance at Thomas suggested he had some idea of what Aidan was thinking. Whatever answers he could share about the past wouldn't be revealed tonight, though.

"Liz looks as if she'd welcome some company," Thomas told him.

Connie elbowed him in the ribs. "Meddling is Mick's territory, not yours."

"It was just an observation," Thomas told her, then winked at Aidan. "And taken in that spirit, isn't that so?"

Aidan laughed. "Absolutely. Enjoy the party."

He left them and headed in Liz's direction, snagging a couple of flutes of champagne on the way. By the time he'd caught up with her, she'd reached the French doors that opened onto a terrace. He joined her outside and silently held out a glass.

"Thanks," she said, meeting his gaze for an instant's connection, then quickly looking away as if afraid to allow that connection to last more than a heartbeat.

"You thinking about making a run for it?" he asked, nodding toward the lawn just past the terrace. It sloped away toward the bay.

"It crossed my mind," she admitted.

"You seemed to be successfully evading your family even indoors."

"I can thank the O'Briens for that. Megan has my mother cornered. Shanna has taken on Danielle, and Jess is showing LeeAnn around the inn." She grinned at him. "I sense a plot."

"What sort of plot?"

"I'm here on a moonlit terrace alone with you, aren't I? It was Susie's idea that I come out here, by the way. The only thing they haven't done is lock the terrace doors behind us."

Aidan laughed and glanced around, noting that the doors were still wide-open. "They probably didn't think of it."

She lifted a brow. "Do you honestly think they leave much to chance?"

"Probably not," he conceded, then set his glass of champagne on a white wrought-iron table and took a step closer.

Her eyes narrowed. "What are you doing?"

"I'd hate for all that careful planning to go to waste. How about you?" He reached for her glass and set it down.

"Didn't you just hand that to me?" she said, her eyes following the champagne with longing.

"And now it's in the way," he said, stepping even closer. He stroked a finger along the curve of her jaw and felt her tremble. "I can't imagine how I've waited so long to do this again."

"Aidan."

It was just his name, part plea, part protest, but it set his blood on fire.

"Yes, Liz," he whispered, tilting up her chin and gazing into the depths of her eyes, watching them darken with unmistakable passion. She could deny it all she wanted—to him, to herself—but she was as desperate for another kiss as he was.

"Aidan." This time it came out as barely more than a sigh.

He didn't waste breath on answering, just covered her mouth with his and felt the impact of the kiss rocket through him like jet fuel that had just been ignited.

Liz clung to his shoulders and this time she was the one who moved, inching closer as if she

305

couldn't bear to have even a hair's-breadth of space between them. Her lips parted, her breath turned ragged and the air around them seemed to crackle with the snap and heat of an unexpected blaze.

Aidan threaded his fingers through her thick hair, knowing that her careful topknot was toppling in a way that no one inside was likely to misconstrue. He needed to feel those silken strands, to see how they looked when wayward curls framed her face. It would be easy enough, then, to imagine how she'd look after making love, flushed and tousled and beautiful.

The sound of voices grew closer, cutting into his thoughts with the effect of ice water splashing over heated bodies. Liz stilled, but when she would have pulled away, he kept her in place, hoping whoever had thought to come outside would turn around and go away.

Sure enough, there was a knowing masculine laugh, a hurried exchange, and the voices faded. The intrusion had lasted less than a minute, but it was enough to bring them both back to reality.

"You were obviously wrong," he said, still keeping her encircled in his embrace.

"About what?" she asked, looking up at him with a dazed expression.

"About there not being any more kisses. I warned you they were pretty irresistible, that *you* are definitely irresistible."

She smiled. "I never said they weren't good kisses," she reminded him.

"Just that we couldn't repeat them."

"Exactly."

"Like I said, you were wrong."

"I think I was referring to the wisdom of repeating them, not to your ability to sneak one in."

He stood back with an expression of mock indignation. "There was nothing sneaky about that kiss. We're out on a terrace all alone in the moonlight. We're drinking champagne."

"I had one sip, hardly enough to cloud my judgment."

He chuckled. "So you went into that kiss with no excuses," he taunted. "That's even better."

She tilted her head and studied him. "You have an argument for everything, don't you?"

"When I need one," he said. "My point is that all the signs were pointing to a romantic encounter."

Amusement sparkled in her eyes. "So, if I didn't want you to kiss me, I should have made a dash for it when you first appeared with that champagne."

"A wise woman who truly didn't want to be kissed would have," he agreed.

"This theory of yours works out rather conveniently for you," she noted. "All of the responsibility falls on me."

He grinned unrepentantly. "Amazing how that works out, isn't it?"

To his surprise, she chuckled and moved closer to rest her head against his chest. "I honestly don't know why I keep fighting this so hard," she said. "In my mind, pushing you away makes all the sense in the world, but when you're this close, getting even closer is the only thing that makes sense."

Though her words were music to his ears, there was a note of regret in her voice he couldn't ignore. He hated that what felt so right to him still filled her with so much conflict. How could they possibly move past that?

"Liz, tell me what you really want. If it's not me, I can walk away."

"You didn't before," she reminded him.

He smiled. "I wasn't convinced then. Convince me."

She looked into his eyes. "I don't know how."

"Because it's not true?" he suggested quietly.

Her sigh was heavy and heartfelt. "Because it's not true," she acknowledged in a whisper.

"As long as I know that, we can figure out all the rest," he told her.

"I wish I could believe that."

He ran his fingers through her hair again, then caressed her cheek lightly. "Believe it, sweetheart. I do."

He wasn't entirely sure why or how he had so much faith with so many things left unsaid between them, but he did.

Liz woke up on Sunday morning to find the foyer filled with suitcases. She found her mother and sisters already in the kitchen, filling a Thermos with coffee. She eyed them warily, poured herself a cup and sat down, looking from LeeAnn and Danielle, both of whom deliberately avoided her gaze, to her mother.

"I gather you all are anxious to get on the road," she said carefully. "I didn't think you'd be leaving this early."

"Mom's idea," LeeAnn said, casting a hard look toward their mother.

Liz sighed. Of course it was. She'd lain awake the night before trying to figure out why her mother hadn't said a word on the ride home from the party. Now she knew. She'd seen or heard something that had sent Liz's disapproval rating into the stratosphere. That's what all the whispers she'd heard coming from the bedrooms had been about.

"Whatever's on your mind, Mom, why don't you just say it to my face?" Liz suggested. "You've obviously already filled in Danielle and LeeAnn."

Her mother's back stiffened. When she finally turned around, there were tears in her eyes. "I am so disappointed in you," she said. "You're just not the woman I raised you to be."

Nothing she might have said would have cut through Liz more. She'd told herself over the years to ignore her mother's nonstop guilt-inducing remarks, but how could any daughter live with knowing what a constant source of disappointment she was? She sometimes thought the one thing she'd done right in her mother's eyes was marrying Josh March. Quite possibly that was why she'd never wanted her to know the truth about their marriage, a truth she herself had discovered way too late.

"What is it I've done now?" she asked, though the answer was obvious. It had something to do with Aidan.

LeeAnn regarded her sympathetically. "Don't listen to her, Liz. There is nothing wrong with moving on with your life. And Danielle and I both like Aidan. We really do."

"A man like that?" their mother snapped. "One who'd take advantage of a grieving widow?"

Liz stared at her mother in shock. "Nobody is taking advantage of anybody, Mother. And I am not a grieving widow. I'm sorry Josh is dead, but our marriage would have been over anyway."

"Don't be ridiculous," her mother said. "That man adored you and you never showed him the respect he deserved."

Liz knew she was at least partly responsible for her family's misguided view of her marriage. She'd never wanted them to know the truth. She wasn't sure if she'd been protecting their illusions about Josh or whether she'd feared just this, that somehow she'd be the one in the wrong for the failure of the marriage. That once again, she wouldn't have measured up to her mom's impossibly high standards. Ironically, they only seemed to apply to Liz. LeeAnn and Danielle had always gotten away with everything with little more than a scolding and a chuckle.

"Maybe I did make mistakes," Liz said defensively, tired of hiding the truth. "In fact, I'm sure of it, but the worst might have been trusting my husband."

Her mother looked shocked. "How could you say a thing like that? Josh March was a fine, decent man."

Exhausted by the long-running charade, she said quietly, "I say it because it is true. Josh was cheating on me, Mom. He had been for months. At least with the woman I found out about. Maybe he'd been at it even longer."

The bitter words hung in the air. Liz noted the shock and disbelief on her mother's face, but LeeAnn and Danielle exchanged a telling look, proving that they'd somehow suspected not everything had been perfect in Liz's world.

"I don't believe you," her mother said, her voice icy.

"The night Josh died—our anniversary, by the way—I was talking about having a baby and he told me he wanted a divorce, that there'd been somebody else in his life for a long time. Does that give you some idea of what a great guy he was?" she asked, bitterness rising to the surface and spilling out.

LeeAnn gasped. She stood up and enveloped Liz in a fierce hug. "That son of a . . ." She glanced at their mother and edited herself. "That stupid son of a gun."

Liz almost smiled. Even at a moment like this, they were still fighting for their mother's often-withheld approval.

"I am so sorry, Liz," Danielle said, looking genuinely shaken. "You should have told us."

"Really? When? At the funeral home when everyone was extolling his virtues? Maybe at the cemetery, when I thought for sure his mother was going to throw herself into the grave? Or back at the house when everyone was speaking in low, reverent whispers?"

Danielle flushed with guilt. "No, not then, of course, but after that, or when we were alone together, just the three of us, you, me and LeeAnn. We're your sisters. We could have listened and given you the kind of support you really needed."

Liz sighed. "I'm sorry. I guess on some level I was trying to protect Josh's memory for the people who loved him. Just because I was dis-illusioned, I didn't think everyone else needed to be. Besides, I didn't really have time to come to grips with any of it. Everything happened so fast.

He made his big announcement, I tossed him out of the house, and then he died, all within a couple of hours. I was in shock on way too many levels."

She turned to her mother then to see what her reaction to all of this was. Doris was sitting at the table clutching a cup of coffee with a white-knuckled grip, her complexion pale.

"I knew," she said, her voice shaking.

Liz stared at her blankly. "Knew what?"

"About Josh seeing someone else. I saw them, more than once. I didn't want to believe it. Your father was so sure I was imagining things. He had a dozen perfectly reasonable explanations for what I'd seen." She drew in a deep breath. "Since you seemed so content, I told myself I had to be wrong, that I didn't have enough proof of any-thing to risk stirring up trouble for you."

"You were protecting Josh, not me," Liz said, her tone flat.

"Absolutely not. I kept quiet because I didn't have proof. I did it for the sake of your marriage. I was sure if there were problems you'd work them out. You never said a word about any trouble, so I blindly let myself believe there wasn't any that you couldn't overcome."

"If you thought he might be cheating, how could you go on acting as if he were such a saint?" Liz demanded.

"Because I wanted so badly to believe I'd been

wrong. I know it doesn't make sense but I wanted to believe you were truly happy. That's how you were acting."

"Then be happy for me now," Liz pleaded. "Aidan could be the one who can help me to move on. I don't know that for sure, and you'd better believe I'm going to take my time until I do know, but I want you to give him a chance, too." She gave her mother a hard look. "I think we can agree that you owe me that much."

Her mother sighed. "You're probably right. I will try. We certainly heard nothing but good things about him at the party last night." She smiled. "Your friends had quite a lot to say about what a fine man he is. Mick O'Brien certainly sang his praises."

Liz could just imagine. "Will you stay a little longer, then? Maybe go to Sally's for breakfast? Aidan's usually around. So are a few of the other people you met last night." Then she added the lure most likely to appeal to them. "There are waffles and French toast on the menu with genuine Vermont maple syrup."

"Count me in," Danielle said eagerly.

LeeAnn regarded her with amusement. "So much for dieting."

"Oh, to heck with it," Danielle said. "I had a baby. My husband needs to get over it."

Liz looked around at her sisters and her mom, all of them suddenly sporting new attitudes.

"Wow, it's a whole new day for the Benson women!" she said.

A surprising spirit of camaraderie filled the room. Even her mom seemed to have been infected.

"Power to us!" her mom said with real spirit.

Liz stood up and pulled her into a hug. "I love you, Mom."

Danielle and LeeAnn joined them. "Us, too," LeeAnn said.

Once again, her mom blinked back tears. "You know you were telling us about the magic that seems to happen in Chesapeake Shores. I have to admit I thought you were crazy, but I'm starting to believe you. I haven't felt this close to you girls in years."

Liz shrugged. "What can I say? This town is all about family. Apparently that affects even those who aren't O'Briens."

⇒ 17 ⇐

Aidan was just coming back from his run with Archie on Sunday morning when the dog spotted Liz and her family crossing the town green. Though he held tightly to the dog's leash, he was no match for Archie's determination to break free.

As the Aussie shot off in their direction, all he could do was shout a warning. "Archie, get back here," he commanded, then added, "Liz, watch out!"

She was already laughing when the dog jumped up and began exuberantly licking her face as if he hadn't seen her in weeks. Her mom and sisters took several careful steps back and watched the scene warily.

"It seems as if you're awfully well acquainted with Aidan's dog," LeeAnn said, already reaching out to scratch Archie's head. He abandoned Liz in favor of making a fresh conquest.

Aidan loped over to join them, nabbing the leash Archie had yanked from his hand. "Sorry," he apologized, then shook his head as the dog unabashedly moved on to seek attention from both Danielle and Mrs. Benson. "Apparently he has a real thing for the women in your family."

"He's fickle," Liz said. "No question about it. Cordelia would be mortified. She thought she'd trained him better than that before she turned him over to me."

Her mother regarded her with surprise. "He was yours?"

"Just a houseguest," Liz explained. "Then he adopted Aidan."

Her mother's lips quirked. "I imagine you had no say in the matter?" she asked Aidan.

"Not much," he agreed. "Between Archie and your daughter, I was pretty much doomed. They were very persuasive."

Her mother smiled. "Liz was the same way with every stray that came to the door back home. We'd have been overrun with them if she hadn't had a way of persuading all the neighbors to take them in. I doubt there was a home in the area that didn't have a pet she'd talked the owners into adopting."

"So it's not a recent development," he concluded.

"Heavens, no. Though I wasn't happy that she gave up teaching, it's little surprise to me that she's doing something related to animals."

Aidan noted that Liz seemed as surprised as he was by the accepting tone of her mother's comments. He also noted that she seemed uncomfortable with the sudden shift.

To change the subject, he asked her, "Are you on your way to breakfast? I noticed when I left for my run that Sally's is filling up fast."

Liz nodded. "I persuaded them not to take off at the crack of dawn and stay for breakfast. It didn't require much persuasion once I told them about Sally's waffles and French toast."

"Outrageously delicious," he assured them.

To his shock, it was Liz's mother who said, "Would you care to join us? I'd like to make amends for treating you so badly."

Aidan regarded her with shock. "You never mistreated me," he said. Oh, she'd made her displeasure with his presence in Liz's life clear, but she'd never been outright rude to him. Good Southern manners—or Liz's immediate defense of him—had kept her from crossing that line.

"Maybe not overtly, but my behavior was deplorable and you didn't deserve my suspicions," she said. "If it's not too late, I'd like to get to know you better. Mick O'Brien said some very nice things about you last night. So did everyone else I met."

Still startled by the attitude adjustment, he turned to Liz, who merely shrugged. LeeAnn and Danielle were clearly amused.

"Then I'd be happy to join you," he said. "Just let me take Archie upstairs and change out of my running clothes. I've tried leaving the dog outside Sally's, but he looks so sad when he watches me through the glass that everybody thinks I'm heartless."

"Well, it's obvious to me that he adores you," Mrs. Benson said, that rare note of approval still in her voice.

"I won't be long, but go ahead and order without me," he suggested.

"We don't mind waiting," Mrs. Benson said, clearly determined to be cheerful and accommodating. "Take your time."

As Aidan headed upstairs, he couldn't help wondering what the heck had gone on among these women after he'd said good-night at the party. The atmosphere had gone from frosty to warm overnight. Maybe it didn't really matter. Whatever had changed finally seemed to be working in his favor.

"Boy, when you decide to be more open-minded, you throw yourself right into it, don't you, Mom?" Liz said, regarding her mother with astonishment.

"Well, there's not much time left, and Aidan seems to be important to you, so I figured I'd better not waste a minute."

"And we're always happy for a little eye candy," LeeAnn chimed in.

"Amen to that," Danielle added.

Liz laughed when their mother regarded them with disapproval.

"Girls! Behave yourselves," she scolded. "You're grown women with husbands and children."

Danielle, for once, didn't look even slightly intimidated. "Are you seriously trying to tell me that you haven't noticed what a hunk Aidan is?"

A guilty flush stained their mother's cheeks. "Whether I have or I haven't, I'm not so indiscreet that I'd blab about it."

"She's noticed," LeeAnn said triumphantly. "I mean, Dad's a good-looking guy for his age, but Aidan is swoon-worthy, right, Mom?"

Their mother shook her head. "I sometimes think you must have been raised by a pack of wolves. Daughters of mine would never say such inappropriate things about their own parents."

LeeAnn nudged her with an elbow. "Just admit it, Mom. You finally see what we see in Aidan, don't you?"

"He's an attractive man," she conceded grudgingly. "But it's character that really counts."

"Amen to that," Liz said in heartfelt agreement as she led the way into Sally's and claimed the last available booth in the crowded café.

Fortunately they were several tables away from the various O'Briens, who were already eating, though no place would be far enough away from their prying eyes and smirking gazes once Aidan arrived.

When he walked in the door, she noticed him looking around for an extra chair, but there were none to be had. Her mother obviously noticed that, too. She waved him over.

"Just squeeze right in beside Liz and LeeAnn. They don't take up much space."

Grinning, he glanced at Liz. "Is that okay with you?"

Before she could reply, LeeAnn was already sliding over toward the wall.

"Come on, big sis. Make room for the man." A huge grin spread across her face. "Or you could let him sit in the middle. That would be cozy."

Liz slid closer to her sister. "This is fine, thanks."

"Darn! I was hoping to have a real story for my

husband about getting up close and personal with his football hero."

"I doubt he'd have been overjoyed about that," Liz said.

"Oh, he'd have been no more upset than you," LeeAnn taunted. "I notice it only took you about two seconds to make sure I didn't get that close to your guy."

She turned to her sister with a frown. "Will you stop that, please! Aidan is not 'my guy.' "

To her surprise, she heard a chuckle from her mother.

"I swear this takes me back to when you were teenagers. LeeAnn knew exactly how to get under your skin. Apparently she still does."

Hiding her own smile, Liz challenged her mother. "Are you any better at controlling her now than you were then? Or do I have to come up with some way to keep her quiet so we can enjoy our breakfast in peace?"

"You girls are old enough to fight your own battles," her mother replied. "Aidan, do you have siblings?"

"No, ma'am. I was an only child."

"Then you have no idea what you missed," she told him.

"You mean the constant squabbling?" Liz asked.

Her mother gave her a chiding look. "I was thinking about the bond the three of you share.

321

No one knows your history the way the three of you do."

Liz turned to Aidan and was surprised to see a hint of real regret in his eyes.

"You're right," he told her mother. "I can't imagine what that must be like."

Since Liz knew the way her mother's mind worked, she decided to forestall all the likely questions about Aidan's parents. That would definitely lead down a path it was best not to follow. She knew from experience how upsetting that would be for him.

She held up her menu. "Have you had a chance to look over the specials yet?"

"I was leaning toward the waffles before we ever came through the door," LeeAnn said at once. "And once I got a whiff of that aroma in the air, I was completely sold."

"Ditto for me," Danielle said.

"Mom?" Liz asked.

"I probably ought to have the oatmeal," she said without enthusiasm.

"Mom, this is a special occasion," Danielle said. "If I can treat myself to waffles, so can you. You can go back to being healthy when we're back home."

Liz saw her mother's expression shift from disappointment to resolve.

"You're absolutely right. I've eaten enough oatmeal this past year to soak up every ounce of cholesterol in the state of North Carolina. I'm having waffles with butter and syrup and I'm going to enjoy every bite."

"Way to go, Mom!" LeeAnn said. "And we promise not to tell Dad."

"Oh, phooey on that," she retorted. "Do you think he's been eating bran flakes and a banana every morning while I've been gone? I imagine I'd find the wrapping from a whole pound of bacon in the trash, if I looked." She sat back, hesitated, then said, "Come to think of it, I want bacon with my waffle, too."

Liz stared at her with surprise. "Mom, when was the last time you had bacon?"

"A week ago," she replied without a hint of apology, then added piously, "Not for breakfast, of course."

"Of course not," Danielle mocked, laughing. "But how can you possibly have a BLT without the bacon? You know perfectly well once the summer tomatoes start ripening, Mom's disapproval rating for bacon goes right out the window."

"Of course it does," her mother declared. "You tell me if there's anything better than a ripe tomato and bacon sandwich on a hot summer day? I doubt you'd turn one down."

"Never have," Danielle quickly agreed.

Liz turned to Aidan. "I don't imagine you had a garden growing up in New York."

He smiled, his expression nostalgic. "You'd be

wrong. My mother commandeered a part of the roof on our apartment building and planted tomatoes, peppers and herbs. You'd be amazed at what can be grown in such a small space." He looked at her mother. "If gardening's one of your interests, I think the two of you would have had a lot in common. I still miss those BLTs she used to make when I'd come in from playing."

To Liz's shock, her mother reached across the table and patted his hand. "I've left a half dozen ripe tomatoes from my garden with Liz. You make sure she gives you a couple."

"Or she could make you a sandwich herself," LeeAnn suggested slyly. "They do say that the way to a man's heart—"

Liz cut her off. "We need to order breakfast," she said hurriedly, gesturing for Sally.

Aidan leaned in close and whispered, "I'll be looking forward to that sandwich."

"Maybe you should get my sister to make it for you," she replied tartly.

"She's leaving. You'll be right here."

"I can give you a couple of tomatoes and you can make your own."

His hand somehow landed on her thigh, even as he managed to maintain a completely innocent look for the benefit of everyone else at the table. "Not the same, sweetheart. Besides, it's about time I found out whether you can cook."

"A BLT hardly qualifies as cooking," Liz said

with a laugh that came out more as a croak when his sneaky, clever fingers wandered just a little farther up her thigh. Since there was not much she could do to express her distress short of slapping at his hand and causing a scene, she sat back and enjoyed the sensation, praying that no one would notice the heated flush that surely must be climbing up her neck and staining her cheeks.

She vowed, though, to get even with him later. In fact, she had a couple of fascinating ideas that ought to work quite well. Not a one of them involved fixing him a meal.

Aidan knew he'd been testing Liz's limits over breakfast. It was the most fun he'd had in a long time. He'd also detected a glint in her eyes that suggested he'd pay later for his impudence. That promised to be fun, too. Her attitude toward him —toward *them*—was slowly loosening up. He intended to take full advantage of that.

After breakfast, he walked back to Liz's with the women and said goodbye as they drove off to return to North Carolina. He noted that Liz actually seemed sorry to see them go.

"The weekend went better than you'd anticipated, didn't it?"

She nodded. "It had its share of surprising moments," she told him. "I think maybe we finally put some things from the past where they belonged, behind us."

"Your mother certainly did a turnaround when it came to me," he commented as they walked back across the green so Liz could open the store. He glanced her way. "So did you, or am I wrong on both counts?"

She smiled. "Oh, your charm definitely paid off with my mother."

"But?"

"I think what really did it for my mom was convincing her that it was okay for me to stop grieving my late husband."

"How did you accomplish that?" he asked as she unlocked the door to Pet Style.

Liz sighed. "Maybe that's something we should discuss when we can really relax and talk." She seemed to hesitate for a very long time before meeting his gaze. "We could have those BLTs later."

"Are you cooking?"

"I can microwave the bacon and slice the tomatoes," she told him, sounding as if she were making a magnanimous gesture. "But you have to make your own sandwich."

He laughed. "It's good to know where the line has been drawn. Should I bring wine, dessert? Maybe my own bread?"

"Actually it wouldn't hurt for you to pick up a loaf of white bread. I know whole grain is very healthy, so that's what I have at home, but proper BLTs should be made on plain old white bread slathered with mayo."

"Agreed," he said at once. "What time? Six-thirty? Seven?"

"Make it seven, so I have time to shower and change after I get out of here."

"Done."

"And maybe you should bring some wine, too. If we're going to have a particularly heavy conversation, I'm going to need it."

Aidan frowned at that. "Liz, I know we've promised to bare our souls and all that, but if it's going to be that difficult for you, I can wait for answers."

She shook her head. "No, now's the time. We need to get this stuff out in the open. It's the only way we'll ever know if it's even possible to move on. In case you haven't noticed, I have a lot of hang-ups about that. I've made some progress recently, but I'm not 100 percent certain they're behind me."

She lifted her gaze to meet his. "How about you?"

"Not even close," he admitted. Worse, if full disclosure was on her menu for tonight, he couldn't share everything anyway. He'd made a promise to Thomas, and no matter how badly he wanted to be open and honest with Liz, he couldn't do that until they'd found out the truth and agreed that the time had come to share it. He had a feeling the delay, reasonable though it might be, was just one more thing he'd wind up holding against his father.

• • •

Liz's nerves went a little crazy every time she thought about her plans with Aidan. She knew it was time to be open and honest with him about her past, but the thought of telling him about that terrible night, the humiliation of discovering that her marriage was a sham, then the tragic accident that had followed made her sick to her stomach.

"You look a little green," Bree commented, coming into the store just before closing. "Too much champagne last night?"

"No, it was a wonderful party," Liz said, forcing her brightest smile. "You deserved to have a celebration. The play was brilliant and the food and champagne lived up to that high standard. No Broadway after-party could have been nicer."

Bree waved off the compliments. "You and Aidan seemed to be getting closer," she said casually. "There were reports of a romantic rendezvous on the terrace."

"Do the members of your family not have better things to do than spy on me?" Liz asked testily.

"Not lately," Bree said with no hint of apology in her voice. "Dad's gotten his own kids married off, as well as Uncle Jeff's and even his first granddaughter. He's at loose ends for the moment, at least until Carrie's love life shows signs of heating up. I don't think he's in a big rush for that to happen, not until he's sure she's not going to let that cheating, hotshot fashion designer back into her life."

Liz gave her a wry look. "Maybe I should encourage her to do just that and get the heat off me."

"Don't you dare," Bree said. "Marc Reynolds really hurt her. I don't think any of us realized how much till Carrie came back here and started moping around at loose ends."

"Okay, I won't use your niece as a diversionary tactic," Liz agreed. "What else might work?"

Bree's eyes lit up. "You could tell me if the kiss was as hot as the reports made it sound."

Liz laughed despite her frustration. "That's not a diversion, that's capitulating to your prurient interest in my love life."

Bree gave an unapologetic shrug. "It would work, though."

"Too bad. Did you have a reason for stopping by, other than tormenting me, I mean?"

"Not really. What are your plans for this evening? I imagine you're ready to relax now that your family's gone back to North Carolina."

"Relaxing is definitely at the top of the agenda," Liz agreed.

Bree studied her. "And what else? The idea of a nice shower and a good book would not put that blush in your cheeks." Her eyes immediately sparkled with delight. "We're back to

Aidan, aren't we? You have plans with him."

"Not talking," Liz declared. "And do not get any ideas about parking outside my house to see if he shows up. Or hanging around here to see if I go upstairs. Or coming within a hundred feet of either one of us, for that matter." She thought that ought to make her point clear.

"You sound as if you think you might need a restraining order, for goodness' sake."

"Do I?"

"Sweetie, we love you. We want you to be deliriously happy." Bree shrugged. "It makes us a little nosy, but we're not stalkers." A grin spread across her face. "Of course, there are a lot of us all over town. We tend to see things, even when we don't go looking."

"And you've taken the skill of texting to new heights," Liz said, knowing it was the method of choice for the O'Brien meddlers.

"We have adapted to technology," Bree agreed. "Even Dad, more's the pity. Mom keeps threatening to take his cell phone away from him and toss it in the bay, but Uncle Thomas would have a conniption and Dad would only replace it."

She reached across the counter and gave Liz's hand a squeeze. "Whatever you and Aidan are up to tonight, have fun."

Liz wasn't sure how much fun the evening would be, but it would be a turning point, no question about that.

●●●

Thomas hoped like hell that tomorrow would bring the quick and final proof that Aidan was not his son, but he knew it was unlikely. From the moment he'd first seen the boy, there'd been something about him that felt familiar. Sure, now that he knew he was Anna's son, that was part of it, but it was more. He'd felt that same stubbornness and grit that all the O'Briens shared.

At first, of course, that possibility hadn't even crossed his mind, but now it seemed so obvious.

Ever since Aidan had told him of their supposed connection, Thomas had been wrestling with his conscience. Had he known on some level back then that Anna was carrying his baby? Was that why he hadn't fought harder to keep her from leaving town? Surely he hadn't been that self-absorbed or shallow, but the truth was, he had been single-focused back then and for a lot of years after that.

His career had cost him two marriages. He couldn't deny the truth of that. And the only reason he was so happy now with Connie was because she understood him in ways neither of his other wives had. She was patient with his absorption with work and tolerant with the time it took away from their family.

Of course, he'd made more compromises with her than he had in either of his other relationships. He'd moved home to Chesapeake Shores. He worked from the house when he could. And he welcomed his wife's involvement in the work that had been his life's passion. In fact, it was that shared interest that had brought them together in the first place, despite quite a few obstacles and objections.

Though he'd tried for the past few days, he couldn't conceive of how the news that he had a son would disrupt his world. Despite what he'd told Mick about Connie accepting that he'd had a relationship with Aidan's mother, he knew that an old flame wasn't the same as having a grown son who would connect them forever.

She liked Aidan, though. Whatever her reaction to the relationship, Thomas thought he could count on her dealing with it in the same calm, evenhanded way she'd dealt with most of the rough spots in her life. She felt as strongly about family as he did. Surely her heart was big enough to embrace Aidan as part of that group.

He was pondering all this as he sat on the porch, an Irish whiskey in hand, when she came out and wrapped her arms around him from behind.

"You okay?" she asked, leaning down to whisper in his ear.

"Fine," he said. "Where's Sean?"

"In bed, more than likely reading a book even though I told him to turn off the light and go to sleep," she said, her voice threaded with laughter.

"I'd fight him harder, but I like that he loves to read." Her amusement faded quickly and she regarded him with concern. "You've been awfully quiet all evening."

"I have a lot on my mind."

"Are you thinking about the shock of discovering that your old college flame was Aidan's mother?"

"It was a shock, that's for sure," he said.

She came around and sat beside him, pulling her chair close enough to hold his hand. Her fingers caressed his knuckles, which had been roughened by so many hard days on the bay on the foundation's research boat.

"There's more, isn't there?" she asked softly.

Thomas gave her a sharp look. "What makes you ask that?"

"He's an O'Brien," she said flatly, keeping a close eye on his face as she awaited a reaction.

"You know?" He supposed he wasn't that surprised. Connie knew him better than anyone on this earth except maybe Nell.

"Not until this minute," she said. "Not for sure, anyway. You told me he looks like Anna, but I see you every time I look into his eyes. You and Mick and Jeff, you all have those smiling Irish eyes they talk about in the song. So does Aidan."

"I don't know for sure," he said, startled by the complacency he heard in her voice.

She smiled at him. "Yes, you do. You don't need a DNA test to tell you the truth."

"I'll await the results, just the same," he said stubbornly.

"Of course you will, because science matters to you."

"It doesn't lie."

She frowned at that. "And you think Aidan could be lying?"

"Anything's possible."

"You know better," she chided. "If I can see the truth, I know you can, too. Why are you so afraid to admit it?"

"It's going to change things," he said.

"Such as?"

"Us."

She shook her head. "Not a chance. I'll love your son the same way you've loved my daughter."

"Ma's going to lecture me from now till eternity."

Connie laughed at that. "More than likely, but she won't stop loving you. And she will open her heart to Aidan. If you think otherwise, you're not giving Nell enough credit. She'd be insulted by that."

She gave him a good long look that Thomas was sure could see into his soul.

"Want me to tell you what's really worrying you?" she asked.

"Because of course you know," he said, amused by her certainty.

"I do," she said. "You don't want Mick or Jeff to

think less of you. As much as you've feuded with your brothers over the years, the three of you have an incredibly strong bond. You need their respect, just as they need yours."

"I don't give two figs what Mick thinks," Thomas claimed, then sighed. "That won't stop me from having to listen to his opinion, though."

"No, it most certainly won't," she agreed. She placed a hand on his cheek. "It's going to be okay, Thomas. We'll work through it. So will you and Aidan. And with his mom gone, I think it's possible that he needs a father in his life more than he realizes."

"He says otherwise," Thomas told her, aware that it had been anger over all the years lost talking.

"I'm sure he does. He is an O'Brien, after all. They never admit to wanting something if they're afraid they might not get it. He's keeping his feelings for Liz close to the vest for the same reason."

He drew her out of her chair and onto his lap. "Have I told you lately how very much I love you and how lucky I was the day you came into my life?"

"You have," she said, her head on his shoulder. "But it's something I never tire of hearing."

"I love you, Connie."

"Right back at you."

Thomas sighed, and for the first time in days thought maybe everything really would turn out to be all right.

⇒ 18 ⇐

Aidan was waiting on the porch when Liz got home from the store. It was after seven, so he'd begun to wonder if she'd changed her mind and decided to ditch him and all the soul-baring. Archie barked enthusiastically at her arrival, as did the dogs inside the house. Her animals had been in a frenzy for the past few minutes ever since they'd heard Archie outside. He'd heard them scratching at the door, too, and envisioned owing Liz a paint job.

"Sorry about the commotion and the extra guest," Aidan apologized. "Archie wanted to visit his friends."

"Did he really?" she said, weariness written all over her face. "He told you that?"

"You'd be surprised by how well he communicates." He studied her as she opened the door. "You okay?"

"Exhausted, to be honest. And annoyed. I was all set to leave by six-fifteen. I'd closed out the register and even filled out a deposit slip. Just as I was about to turn off the lights, a tourist came by and knocked on the door. Since I try not to turn away prospective business, I let her in."

"Why, if you were already closed? Couldn't you have explained that to her?"

"Prospective business, remember? She'd been in earlier and expressed an interest in one of Matthew's custom doghouses. Crazy me, I assumed she'd decided to order one. Instead, she started debating with herself all over again about whether she wanted to spend the money or not. I'm pretty sure she thought if she wore me down, I'd drop the price, but I finally told her flatly she'd have to negotiate that with Matthew. I gave her his card and practically pushed her out the door." She looked guilty. "I doubt I'll be seeing her again."

Aidan chuckled. "Sounds to me as if you displayed amazing patience, and dumping her off on Matthew was ingenious. He does get the biggest slice of the doghouse profits, after all. Why shouldn't he handle some of the aggravation?"

She smiled at last. "I doubt he'll see it that way, but I'm sure he's dealt with more than his share of difficult, demanding customers, to say nothing of having his uncle Mick as his boss. Just like his uncle, though, he has all that O'Brien charm to fall back on, something I'm lacking."

Aidan could see the exhaustion around her eyes. "Would you rather postpone dinner? We can do this another night."

She shook her head. "No, come on in. It won't take me long to change. A quick shower should revive me."

He caught her gaze. "We could share it. That

would put some color back in your cheeks."

She laughed. "I'm sure it would, but we have a whole lot to work out before you get to see me naked."

Aidan doubted that the one-sided conversation he anticipated happening tonight was going to get them to that point. "You sure about that? Sometimes it's better to just jump into these things than it is to talk them to death."

"I'm not surprised you'd think so," she said, clearly amused by his self-serving suggestion. "But I need the talk, Aidan. I need to work through about a million issues that are in my head. Most of them have nothing to do with you personally, but they're there, and they're real for me. Dealing with them is the only way we'll ever be able to move forward."

"A million, huh? I guess we'd better get started, then. You take your shower and I'll have the sandwiches ready when you get to the kitchen. I assume you're hungry."

"Starving, actually," she admitted, giving him no argument at all about commandeering her kitchen. "Thanks."

With all three dogs and one suspicious cat watching his every move, Aidan made three BLTs with a couple of the perfect tomatoes that Liz's mom had left. Admittedly, while standing over the sink, he ate a half of one tomato with only a little salt sprinkled on it. If it was possible to capture summer in a single food, this was it for him. There had been enough fresh tomatoes from his mom's rooftop garden to last through the summer and into fall, even after sharing them with all the neighbors.

With the sandwiches made, he looked around and found an unexpected treat to cap off the meal, a container of homemade chocolate chip cookies. Of course, he sneaked a sample of those, too, then put the rest on the table, along with two glasses of iced tea. He'd discovered the pitcher of sweet tea for Liz already made and chilling in the refrigerator. Since he wasn't a convert to that yet, he zapped a tea bag in a cup of water in the microwave to make his own unsweetened tea.

When Liz got to the kitchen, wearing another pair of those impossibly short shorts and a tank top that exposed way too much bare skin for his comfort, Aidan tried to focus his attention elsewhere to keep from sweeping her into his arms.

Instead, he directed his attention deliberately to a last check of the table. He thought he'd done a halfway decent job with the simple meal's presentation, using colorful Fiesta Ware plates and bright napkins he'd found in the cupboard. Liz smiled when she saw the clashing colors that somehow worked.

"Trying to impress me? Paper plates would have been fine for such an informal meal."

"I like these," he admitted. "They seem to go with summer."

She looked at the table quizzically, then nodded. "They do, don't they? I've found most of them in antiques stores one by one, so they don't match, but I think they're cheerful."

Aidan had noticed something while he was preparing the meal and searching for things in her cupboards. They were surprisingly bare. He'd found only a few cooking utensils, even fewer pots and pans, and what looked to be a set of four discount-store wineglasses and four matching tumblers. He'd realized then that he hadn't noticed any fancy china cabinet in her dining room or matching furniture in the living room, not the sort of carefully chosen sets that most women would have after the end of a marriage. The sparse, slightly worn furnishings didn't add up.

He took a bite of his sandwich and closed his eyes. "These really are the perfect tomatoes, nothing like the red sawdust you buy in the produce section of most grocery stores, even at this time of year."

Liz gave him an approving look. "I'll report back to my mother that she made you swoon."

"I'll put it in writing, if you like."

"I don't think that's necessary," she said before taking her own first bite.

Aidan noticed it brought an immediate smile to her lips.

"Pretty good, huh?" he said.

"No need to beg for compliments. You did a

great job. You can be the official BLT maker around here from now on."

"Works for me," he said readily. "Do you think your mom would ship you more tomatoes?"

"I'm sure she would, but I've had pretty good luck at the farm stands out on the highway. And you might not want to suggest to Sally that my mom's tomatoes are better than hers. Hers are grown organically and delivered three times a week by a local farmer. She prides herself on using produce from nearby farms. So does Brady."

Aidan nodded. "Good for them. My mother would have loved that. She was into that whole farm-to-table movement to use whatever's available locally."

They ate quietly for several minutes until Aidan couldn't stand the silence any longer. "Can I ask you something?" he said.

She glanced up from her last bite of the sandwich and nodded. "Isn't that what tonight's supposed to be about?"

"I suppose, in a way, but I'm not sure how this fits in to the rest."

"Just ask," she said, pushing the plate aside and studying him warily as if afraid of where he might be heading. She put both hands around her glass of tea as if needing something to do with them to keep him from noticing how jittery she'd suddenly become. All three dogs seemed to sense her distress, because they moved closer, creating a protective circle around her. Even the cat got on board, jumping into her lap to purr contentedly.

Her obvious case of nerves was almost enough for him to back off and leave the heavy stuff for another time, but as she'd said, tonight was supposed to be about filling in some of the blanks in their lives.

"It dawned on me earlier that these dishes, the furniture you have, none of it looks as if it was something you might have gotten at a fancy bridal shower or to start your married life. Not that it's not cozy and exactly right for you," he added quickly, hoping not to insult her with the observation.

To his relief, she smiled.

"I sold every stick of furniture from my house in North Carolina," she explained. "I put my fancy dishes and the outrageously expensive crystal on consignment in a local shop and moved here with my clothes and not much else. I did keep my silver because it was an heirloom from my family, but I packed it away and left it with my mom."

"Why?"

"I didn't want anything that would remind me of that time of my life," she said, a startlingly bitter note in her voice.

It wasn't the first time that Aidan had seen through her veil of apparent grief and suspected her marriage hadn't been as rosy as she'd led everyone in town to believe, but the depth of her bitterness was new.

"Then you really, really wanted a completely fresh start," he said carefully.

"Down to every detail," she said. "I've told you how I found the dishes. I've done the same with the furniture and accessories, adding things as I found them. I've been in every antiques store, junk shop and consignment place within a hundred-mile radius of Chesapeake Shores." She gave him a surprisingly defiant look. "My husband would have hated every piece in here."

"And that mattered to you?"

She nodded. "When I got married, we did it all his way. We had the over-the-top wedding with at least a hundred of the guests turning out to be people that I'd never set eyes on before. They were all business associates and top corporate clients at his firm. We moved into a house in the best neighborhood and filled it with high-end furniture, set our table with expensive china and crystal. It was all about appearances. Josh was an up-and-coming lawyer hoping to make partner. Material things—the *best* material things—were proof that he was successful. It wasn't till the end that I realized none of that was a substitute for the one thing we didn't have."

"What was that?"

"Honesty." She held Aidan's gaze. "Are you beginning to see why I don't know if I'll ever be able to trust anyone again? The person I believed in the most betrayed me. I told you once before that he shattered my heart, and that's true. He also stole my ability to believe in people. How can I even think of moving on with all of those doubts crowding in every time I start to have faith in someone?" She leveled a sad look at him. "Especially someone who admitted he had secrets he's keeping from me?"

She regarded him with regret. "Trust is such a fragile thing, especially for me these days. It's ironic really because I used to see the good in everyone. I trusted everyone." She sighed heavily. "Not anymore."

There were tears in her eyes as she spoke. "I'm sorry, Aidan. I like you. Maybe it's even more than that, though I've fought incredibly hard to make sure nothing happens between us. I don't want to fall in love ever again, but you've still managed to slip past my defenses. I can't deny that, but I just don't see it turning out well."

She stood up, her hands visibly shaking. He knew if he reached for them, they'd be ice-cold.

"I'm sorry," she said again, her voice little more than a whisper. Her shoulders squared, her back stiff with pride, she walked out of the kitchen, leaving him shaken.

Aidan stared after her, debating whether he should follow. He needed a minute, though, to think first. He needed to come up with an argument to counter her very real fears, but how could he do that when even now he so clearly didn't know the whole story?

His imagination ran wild, trying to piece together what might have happened to her. It obviously went way beyond losing her husband in a tragic accident. Being grief-stricken was one thing. What he sensed pouring out of her, weighing her down with such pain, was so much worse. Whatever had happened seemed not only to have stolen her ability to trust another man, but had shattered her faith in her own judgment.

As he thought about what might have happened and how best to handle it, he busied himself cleaning up the dishes, washing them and putting them back into their lonely spots in the cupboards. He was still trying to make sense of what she'd said when he heard her coming back. He stilled as he waited, not knowing what to expect.

"I thought you'd leave," she said.

He couldn't tell with certainty if that note he heard in her voice was regret that he'd stayed or relief. He turned to face her and discovered that, while she'd dried her tears and seemed more composed, the old distance was back in her eyes. That barely banked distrust with which she'd viewed him almost from the day they'd met had returned, not because of anything he'd actually done, but because she'd lumped him in with her husband and apparently all males. Her wounds clearly ran a lot deeper than he'd ever imagined.

"I apologize again for the outburst," she said stiffly. "Maybe it would be for the best if we just forgot all about this, Aidan."

"For tonight?"

"For good," she said flatly. "I'm obviously not ready for a relationship. I thought maybe, if I opened up . . ." She shook her head. "It's not going to happen. I may never be ready."

He drew in a deep breath and came to a decision. He stepped closer and risked a light caress of her cheek, just a tiny reminder of the undeniable sparks that shouldn't be dismissed so easily. He felt her skin heat, proving his unspoken point.

"Then you need to explain to me why," he said softly. "Please, Liz. You can take your time, but I need to know. This is too important."

Then he did the only thing he could think of to do. He sat back down, kept his gaze on hers steady and unrelenting, and waited.

Liz studied Aidan with dismay. It was evident he wasn't going anywhere. That stillness and patience should have been annoying, but a part of her admired it. On some level she saw it as proof that his emotions were honest, his feelings for her real, if barely tested.

She didn't want to talk about the past. No matter what promises she'd made to Aidan earlier, she didn't want to revisit that time in her life. And yet, with Aidan regarding her with such compassion, how could she remain silent?

To buy time, she poured herself another glass of sweet tea, then finally, knowing she couldn't put him off forever, she sat across from him at the scarred kitchen table that reminded her of her life, a little battered and bruised, but—at least she hoped so—strong enough to survive.

When she still didn't speak, she sensed Aidan's growing impatience. He was studying her with that same confused expression she'd seen too often when family members hadn't understood the way she'd handled herself after Josh's death. They'd been even more shocked than Aidan when she'd removed every trace of the years she'd spent with her husband.

"Liz, talk to me," Aidan said at last, breaking the silence. "Your husband died in an accident. Let's start with that. It's a terrible loss for anyone to face, but plenty of people do fall in love again after a tragedy."

She took a deep breath and forced herself to respond. "It wasn't that simple and straight-forward," she told him, regretting more than she could say that it hadn't been. There were whole books on coping with grief. Surely one of them would have struck a chord and given her the skills to move on. Instead, that night's tragedy was all tangled up with a whole slew of complex emotions. Outrage, anger and disillusionment were just a few.

Aidan turned his chair to face her and took her hands in his. "Then tell me how it was," he pleaded. "I really want to understand. Maybe it will even help you if you get it out in the open."

His gentleness touched her in a way nothing else had. Liz had kept the story inside for so long now, she wasn't sure she could find the words, wasn't sure she wanted to. Even with all she'd revealed to her mother and sisters just this morning, there had been more that she'd kept to herself, mostly how unworthy Josh had made her feel with his devastating revelations.

But now, with Aidan regarding her so hopefully, his voice laced with that now-familiar compassion and caring—the same emotions she knew had led to him giving Archie a home—she knew that perhaps it was finally time. It wouldn't change how she felt about starting a new relationship, but maybe revealing the truth, sharing it with a friend, would ease the weight in her heart.

"I loved my husband more than anything," she began slowly, allowing herself to remember that. There had been good times, way back at the beginning. She'd deliberately buried most of those memories along with her husband.

"Josh and I fell in love in high school," she continued. "We were together all through college and got married a week after graduation. He went on to law school and I started teaching. He landed a job right away with a top law firm. I thought our life was just about perfect."

"It sounds as if it was," Aidan said.

"We'd even been talking about having a baby. Or maybe I'd been talking and he just hadn't said no. Sometimes I didn't listen, at least that's what he told me that last night. And sometimes I saw only what I wanted to see, the perfect marriage. My family certainly saw it that way. To them, marrying Josh was the smartest thing I'd ever done."

She blinked back tears. "I guess that's why I didn't see it coming. We had this nice dinner. It was our fifth anniversary and I'd gone all out cooking things he loved. I'd bought an outrageously expensive bottle of champagne to celebrate. And then, over dessert—his favorite red velvet cake made from scratch—he told me."

Aidan frowned. "Told you what?"

She gave him a chagrined look. "That he wanted a divorce. That he'd been seeing someone else for almost a year." She gave Aidan a bewildered look. "A year, and I'd been oblivious to it. What kind of an idiot does that make me?"

"He was the idiot!" Aidan said fiercely. "What kind of man makes an announcement like that out of the blue, especially during an anniversary celebration?"

"The kind who'd apparently been waiting for

me to catch him," she said bitterly. "Like I said, I was happy and oblivious. I gather he'd been dropping clues. All those late nights at the office, whispered phone calls that he claimed were about business, even a couple of overnight trips. I trusted him absolutely. I just took his word that they were part of the job, a requirement for getting ahead and making partner." She shook her head. "I was so blind and naive."

"You thought you were married to someone you could trust," Aidan reminded her.

"Well, obviously I was wrong about that. And he'd run out of patience with my naïveté, so he hit me with the news. There was no easing into it, just the hard cold facts. He was in love with someone else and they wanted to get married because she, *she,* was having his child."

Even now she could feel her heart breaking all over again at that. That woman was having the baby she'd wanted so desperately! She was sure that pain was still written all over her face, because Aidan looked as if he wanted to smash things.

"God, it was so awful," she told him. "It was as if I snapped mentally as the truth sank in. I told him to get out, right then, that I never wanted to see him again. It was the worst sort of betrayal I could imagine, and I'll admit I was pretty irrational."

"I think you had a right to be," Aidan said.

His understanding was surprisingly soothing, but she didn't deserve it.

"Wait," she warned. "The story doesn't end there. I knew it was pouring rain, that the roads might be turning icy, but I couldn't bear to look at Josh for another minute. He tried to reason with me. He said he didn't want to leave me until I'd calmed down, but I didn't see that happening anytime soon. I practically shoved him out the door."

Tears flowed down her cheeks as she remembered what happened next. "A half hour later, a policeman came to the house. Josh had been going at a high rate of speed. His car had run off the road and hit a tree. He'd died instantly."

Shock spread across Aidan's face. "That's when he died? Right after you'd fought? Sweetheart, I am so sorry," Aidan said.

"I don't deserve your sympathy," she said.

"Why on earth not?"

"I sent him out there that night," she said simply. "He died because of me."

"He died because he'd made a whole slew of stupid decisions and you justifiably called him on them. What happened after that was a tragic accident you couldn't possibly have foreseen," Aidan corrected.

"I knew how bad the roads were," she insisted, refusing to cut herself any slack. "There'd been warnings on the news. I'd seen them while I was cooking."

"I seriously doubt the local news was on your mind after hearing that your husband was involved with another woman and that she was carrying his child."

Liz still refused to let herself off the hook. "It was my fault," she repeated stubbornly. It was a refrain that had run through her head every night since the accident.

Aidan, bless him, didn't look convinced. "Didn't you say speed was involved? Were you in the car pressing down on the accelerator?"

"No, but—"

"No buts," he said firmly. "The accident was not your fault. He was on the road alone. He saw the conditions firsthand. He could have slowed down or pulled over. Instead, he chose to speed up."

Liz sighed. It was comforting to hear him say the words, even if she couldn't accept his quick defense of her actions that night.

"The bottom line is that two days later, I buried my husband and no one ever knew the truth, that he'd been leaving me that night. Nobody ever questioned that I wanted a small family-only funeral. They chalked it up to grief and let me have my way. The truth was, though, that I was terrified this other woman would show up if there was any announcement in the paper. I had no idea what I would do if that happened. I was terrified of making a scene."

She lifted her gaze to his. "To this day I don't

know if his parents know about the woman, if they know that they have a grandchild by now. Our parents knew each other, but they weren't close. After the funeral I don't think they were ever in touch. They've barely said two words to me since then. His mother called once to ask how I was doing, but I think she sensed that there were things I hadn't revealed. Maybe she didn't want to know. Or maybe she knew and felt pity for me."

Liz shrugged at the way one huge part of her life had just vanished that night, not just Josh, but an extended family, even friends who'd been more his than theirs.

"It's hard to imagine that no one said anything," Aidan said. "That no one warned you."

"My sisters certainly would have, if they'd known," she agreed. "But even after I told them this morning about the cheating, they didn't mention anything about a baby. Either the Marches don't know they have a grandchild or it's been handled very discreetly. The woman was a colleague at the law firm. I'm sure they closed ranks to protect her. That's one of the blessings of being in a big city. It's easier to keep secrets."

Aidan squeezed her hands. "I am so sorry, Liz. I can't imagine how difficult it must have been for you."

"No, you can't. Acting like the bereaved widow was horrible. It still is. I'm living this terrible lie. What kind of person would I be if I admitted that

I hated my husband for what he'd done? So I pretend we had this loving marriage right up until the end."

"It's not a pretense, at least not for you," Aidan corrected. "Up until that night, he'd been the love of your life. Just because you'd learned about his betrayal doesn't mean that you haven't been mourning him, or at least what you thought you'd had together."

"But I've been deceiving people all this time, because it was too hard to face the truth, that my husband had betrayed me. I've been keeping up appearances, just the way he would have if the tables had been turned. Ironic, isn't it, since that was one of the things I liked least about him."

"Whether it was out of some misguided sense of guilt or out of love, maybe you felt you owed it to his memory," Aidan suggested.

She regarded him wryly. "That sounds very noble. I'm afraid it was something else, though."

"Such as?"

"I just didn't want people to know I wasn't good enough for him," she said, a catch in her voice.

Aidan looked shocked by her words. "Oh, sweetheart, a man doesn't cheat because the woman in his life isn't good enough. He cheats because he's a jerk who likes knowing he's still attractive. It's about his ego."

"Have you ever cheated?" she asked. Because she was watching him so closely, she thought she detected a faint hesitation before he replied.

"Never," he said, his voice firm. "I've broken off relationships, but I can honestly say I've never cheated on a woman I've been seeing."

Liz should have felt reassured by his words. And if it hadn't been for that momentary hesitation she would have been. There was a story behind that, a warning that even though she was feeling closer to Aidan right this minute than she had to anyone for a very long time, it would be dangerous to trust him. She might have shared her most shameful secrets with him, but he'd shared none of his. While she'd missed all the obvious signs of lying and cheating with her husband, she was smarter and more suspicious now. She'd never ignore what *wasn't* said again.

⇒ 19 ⇐

Aidan didn't want to leave Liz alone, no matter what she said. He finally understood the burden she'd kept secret from all of her friends, the reason she'd so determinedly kept him at a distance.

Now, though, all that mattered was trying to make her see that she wasn't responsible for the way that horrible night had ended. She was clearly wrung out from all the revelations she'd shared. It physically pained him to see the unwarranted guilt she was carrying around. He understood that his absolution wasn't what she needed. She needed to let herself off the hook. Until she was able to do that, she was destined to live in this dark place, punishing herself for something that had never been her fault.

"Aidan, you should probably go," she said, that familiar distance back in her voice. "I care about you, more than I wanted to, more than I should have, but at least now you understand why there can't be anything between us. It's not about you. It's all about me."

"It's at least a little bit about me," he said. "Your husband was hiding things, important things, so secrets are obviously a big deal for you. And you've figured out that I haven't been 100 percent forthcoming with you. I can see why that would trigger all sorts of alarms for you."

She regarded him with surprise. He had a feeling it wasn't because there were things he hadn't shared, but because he'd admitted to as much.

He gave her a rueful look. "Given everything you just told me, I totally get why you'd be suspicious of any man who came into your life, especially one you suspected was being less than candid."

She nodded in acknowledgment. "If I'm ever going to trust anyone again, there can't be any secrets between us, not even little ones that probably wouldn't matter to most people." She regarded him wistfully. "Yours aren't little, though, are they?"

He shook his head. His was huge. In fact, his whole identity wasn't what anyone in this town thought it to be, at least not entirely. He was still Anna Mitchell's son, but there was so much more to it.

"That's what I mean," she said. "I know better than anyone what sort of damage that can do."

Aidan understood that from personal experience, though he wished he didn't. "I see exactly where you're coming from. I've lived with a lot of secrets in my lifetime, not mine, but around me. Things I didn't discover until recently, in fact. It changes the way we feel about the people we're supposed to be closest to." He thought of his mother and how much she'd kept from him—and from Thomas—and how it was affecting their lives to this very day.

"If you know that, then how can you expect me to ignore the fact that there are things you're not telling me?" Liz asked. "I don't want to wake up someday and realize the man I'm with is practically a stranger."

"I can't ask you to ignore anything," he conceded with regret. "I will ask you to be patient, though. I want to tell you everything, but I'm not able to."

She frowned at that. "What's preventing you?

Or is that just a convenient excuse because you don't really want to be open and honest? Are you afraid people will think less of you if these secrets come out?" Her expression turned wry. "I know a whole lot about that. It's the reason I've kept quiet. Not even Bree has heard the story I told you."

"She'd be on your side, the same way I am," he assured her.

"I'm not willing to take that chance."

Aidan understood her hesitance and her reluctance to believe in him. He could hear how flimsy it sounded to simply say he wasn't at liberty to talk about his secrets. If he were in her shoes, he wouldn't buy it, either.

"Will it help if I promise that you'll be the first person to know everything as soon as I can talk about it?" he asked. He thought of the initial blood test report. "Everything will be resolved soon, maybe even as early as tomorrow."

She looked genuinely torn, as if she desperately wanted to have faith in him, but feared that she'd be burned yet again by trusting the wrong man.

"Not good enough," she said at last. "I think you should go. And maybe we shouldn't spend any more time together for a while."

Aidan would have asked how long, but he already knew the answer. She didn't want him around until he was ready to disclose everything he'd been holding back. Even then such a big secret might be more than she could handle. He could hardly hold that against her. There were plenty of days when he had no idea how to live with the truth himself.

He nodded and stood up. Before getting Archie's leash and calling to the dog, he leaned down and pressed a kiss to Liz's forehead.

"This isn't over," he vowed. "Not by a long shot."

She gave him a sad look that spoke volumes. "I think it is."

And then she turned away, as if she couldn't bear to see him leave. Archie whined as Aidan tugged him toward the door. Even the dog seemed to sense that something had shifted here tonight, and not in a good way.

To Aidan's dismay, Thomas called him first thing on Monday morning to report that the blood test had been inconclusive. It hadn't ruled Thomas out as Aidan's father, but only the full DNA analysis on the swabs taken by the lab could prove definitively if they were father and son. Or not.

"I know we were both hoping for answers, but maybe this delay is good news," Aidan suggested, though he had a hard time believing that himself, not with his relationship with Liz hanging in the balance. "It means you haven't been ruled out as my father."

"It actually is good news," Thomas said.

Aidan was startled by his ready agreement. "You think so, too?"

"Shocking, isn't it, after my initial reaction?"

Aidan could almost imagine the smile as Thomas said those words. "What's changed?"

"Well, for whatever it's worth, I'm coming to grips with the idea that I have a grown son," Thomas explained. He hesitated, then said, "I know we weren't going to speak of this to anyone until the results are in, but my wife has already guessed. She says it's impossible to miss that you're an O'Brien."

Aidan was stunned, not because they'd talked about it, but because Connie saw what Thomas had refused to accept. "She believes me? And is she okay with the news?"

Thomas laughed. "Here's the thing you should know about my wife. She's tough. She raised a daughter mostly on her own. She took a long time coming around when we first started seeing each other. She'd done okay by herself. I was older. I was twice divorced. I was an O'Brien, which you may have seen by now can be a blessing and a curse. I was only slightly more amenable to the idea of taking another risk on marriage. Her daughter pretty much hated me. Well, not me, but having to compete for her mom's attention and love. It almost broke my wife's heart. I think the fact that Jenny and I have reconciled our differ-ences has made her see families in a whole new light. Biological connections aren't the only ones that matter."

Aidan had a feeling there might be a lesson in the story for him. "What turned things around? I mean in terms of winning her over with all those hurdles you faced?"

"We got out of our own way and focused on the fact that we'd fallen in love. If there's one thing O'Briens believe in, it's the power of love and family. I might have failed at two marriages, but as Mick likes to point out, they were to the wrong women. Good women, both of them, but wrong for me. When the right one comes along, a smart man doesn't turn his back on her, no matter what obstacles might lie in the path."

He hesitated, then added quietly, "Looking back with twenty-twenty hindsight, I think your mother could have been the right one, but I met her at the wrong time in my life."

"I've tried to imagine you together," Aidan admitted. "I can see it, too. I wish I'd had the chance to see the two of you together just once."

"Aidan, you have no idea how much I regret that we all missed out on so much. Keep in mind, though, that I was pretty self-absorbed and driven back then. Still am, to some degree, but I've put some balance into my life, realigned my priorities, so to speak. I'd like to think I might have done the same back then, if I'd been given the chance."

"I believe that now," Aidan said. "You didn't finish telling me about your wife's reaction. If me sticking around Chesapeake Shores is going to cause problems—"

"Nonsense," Thomas said. "At least not for Connie and me. Certainly not for anyone else in the family, either. We embrace our own, however they come to be a part of us. Now, you put together another losing football team, and I can't speak for the rest of the town."

Aidan laughed. "I'm on it," he told Thomas. "In fact, I'm heading over to the school to find out just how many unofficial workouts I might be able to squeeze in before the school district comes down on my head."

"Good luck with that," Thomas said. "I'll be in touch about the DNA test as soon as I know anything. Then we'll figure out where we go from there."

Aidan considered letting the conversation end on that note, but for some reason he couldn't. "Do you have some time in the next couple of days? I'd like to talk about that book I've been reading, maybe make some plans for the fall projects for the group at school." He felt surprisingly awkward even making the suggestion and quickly added, "Unless you want to hold off on that."

"No reason to hold off," Thomas said, clearly enthusiastic, if perhaps a little surprised. "I'm working in town today. You want to meet for coffee at Panini Bistro in an hour? Or on the pier at Mick's? Sean's dying to go fishing. He'd go every day of summer vacation if I were here to take him."

Aidan liked the idea of spending time with Thomas and his son. It sounded so normal, like something they might have done when he was a boy.

"Does Sean know what's going on?" he asked, needing to know so he didn't inadvertently slip up and say the wrong thing.

"No, though something tells me he'll be ecstatic to have a big brother. He loves having a big sister, but a guy? And one who coaches football? He'll be over the moon. I won't tell him, though, till we know the truth. For one thing, I love that boy with all my heart, but he couldn't keep his mouth shut if he tried. For another, I don't want him to be disappointed if it turns out we're wrong."

"I totally understand," Aidan said. "I just didn't want to put my foot in it. But if you don't mind me being around him before we know, maybe I'll buy a fishing pole and you can give me a lesson, too." He couldn't help thinking that it would be a nice first father-son memory, even if the facts weren't in yet.

"I have an extra pole I'll bring along," Thomas said at once. "We'll be there in an hour."

"Great. That'll give me just enough time to stop by the school." And maybe a few extra minutes to stick his head in the door at Pet Style for a quick glimpse of Liz to be sure she was doing okay. No matter what she'd said about wanting to be left alone, Thomas's reminiscence about his courtship of Connie suggested to Aidan that backing off from a relationship that could really matter wouldn't be the O'Brien way.

Liz spotted Aidan at the door of Pet Style and was grateful that she'd left home early and gone straight to Sally's. She'd wanted to be in and out with her morning coffee before any of her friends arrived to cross-examine her about the dark circles under her eyes that even an expert touch with makeup couldn't conceal.

When Aidan realized the store was still locked up, he glanced toward Sally's, but to her relief, he turned away and jogged across the street to the town green and kept on going.

"Why don't you seem very eager to run into Aidan this morning?" Bree asked, startling Liz as she appeared seemingly out of nowhere and slid into the booth.

"No idea what you're talking about," Liz said, mopping up the coffee that had spilled from her cup when she'd been startled by Bree's unexpected arrival. "I just happened to notice he was out there."

"And knocking on the door of your shop," Bree said. "Yet you didn't tap on the window to get his attention. You looked oddly relieved when he went away without coming in here."

"You're imagining things."

"I'm not imagining that you look as if you've had a rough night," Bree said, holding Liz's coffee cup in the air and gesturing to Sally for a refill for Liz, plus her own cup. "Problems keep you awake?"

"Something like that."

"Let me be more specific. Problems with Aidan?"

Liz gave her a plaintive look. "Nothing I want to talk about."

Bree's expression turned momentarily triumphant at having her guesswork confirmed, but then she frowned. "What did he do?" she demanded.

Her quick indignation actually made Liz smile. "What makes you think he did anything?"

"Because he's a man, and they're sometimes incredibly stupid and insensitive. They don't mean to be. It just happens."

"Does Jake know you hold him in such high esteem?" Liz inquired, amused by Bree's assessment.

"My husband is an exception," Bree declared at once, but then her expression turned thoughtful. "Now, anyway. There was a time when he fell into that category, too."

"So it's thanks to what, your training, that he's evolved?"

Bree grinned. "Pretty much."

Liz sat back with a sigh. "I envy you," she admitted without thinking.

Bree looked startled. "Why?"

"Because you have this perfect marriage and an adorable little girl, plus an amazing career as a playwright. Not to mention a flower shop as a side business that you love. You grew up in this incredible town, surrounded by family."

"Oh, sweetie, believe me, it wasn't always that way. I couldn't wait to get away from here and out into the world. When I came home from Chicago as a failure after an apprenticeship at a regional theater, I thought my life was over. Jake hated the sight of me because I'd let him down on so many levels. It took us a long time and a lot of patience and hard work to get where we both are today."

Liz was startled. "I thought you were childhood sweethearts."

Bree nodded, her expression nostalgic. "We were and then I blew it. I won't go into all the ugly details, but when I got back to town Jake didn't trust me and rightfully so, though of course I didn't want to admit I'd done anything wrong."

"How did you get through that and turn things around, because you obviously have?"

"Like I said, it took patience, hard work and a whole bunch of meddling to get us to admit that we still loved each other. We had to figure out whether our priorities meshed. I needed to get my feet back under me, personally and professionally.

Jake needed to figure out if he could trust me again."

She gave Liz a knowing look. "Are you and Aidan having trust issues? Jake's something of an expert in that area, if you need to talk. He got through to Jenny when she was up in the air about giving Caleb another chance."

"How'd you know that trust was at the root of my issues with Aidan?" Liz asked, startled by her insight.

"Because you have this big Keep Out wall up around yourself. You've denied to anyone who'd listen that you have feelings for Aidan. It's clear to all of us how hard you're fighting the attraction. What I don't understand is if this is really about Aidan or more about you."

"It's me," Liz conceded. "Mostly. He hasn't exactly been reassuring, though. There's something he's keeping from me, something big. I don't want to get close with another man, only to discover he's been deceiving me about something important."

"Another man? Is that about your marriage?"

Liz waved off the question. "Not now, okay? The point is I won't risk my heart again, not when there are clear warning signs that something's not right."

"Have you confronted Aidan about your concern?"

"Sure. And he doesn't deny that he's keeping a

secret of some kind, but he refuses to let me in on it. He says he's made a promise and he has to honor that."

"Well, that sounds fair," Bree said.

"Unless it's a convenient lie," Liz said.

Bree looked startled by the distrust in her voice. "Oh, sweetie, if you think he's capable of lying to you, then you've got bigger problems to worry about. Trust is essential to any relationship."

"I know that," Liz said in frustration. "Probably even better than you can possibly imagine. So it seems we're at a stalemate." She sighed. "It's probably for the best. I don't need the complication of a relationship, anyway. I need to focus on Pet Style and building a life for myself here."

"A life without a man in it?" Bree concluded. "Even if there's one right here who makes your toes curl?"

Liz smiled. "I don't know that he does."

"Liar. The two of you set off more fireworks when you're in the same room than the town does on the Fourth of July." Her expression brightened. "That's coming up soon. There will be chaos down here on the green, but we can see them from my dad's, so there will be a huge barbecue there that night. You have to come."

"Is this another opportunity for you to throw Aidan and me together?"

Bree chuckled. "The party will happen whether either of you is there. I just don't want you to miss your first big fireworks show in town. You should celebrate with friends."

Liz couldn't deny that it sounded like exactly the sort of small-town celebration she'd been envisioning when she'd chosen to settle in Chesapeake Shores. Why deny herself that just to avoid a situation that might never happen?

"I'll be there," she promised. "What can I bring?"

"Just yourself, or you'll insult my grandmother. Nell's already started baking. Dad's in charge of burgers and hot dogs. It's a pretty simple menu. Add some sliced tomatoes and potato salad and we have a major picnic."

"What about your mom?" Liz asked curiously. "Does she make the potato salad?"

"Actually we take turns trying to keep her out of the kitchen," Bree said with a laugh. "Cooking's not her strong suit. Besides, she'll be working at the gallery all day. She'll get home just in time for a bite to eat before the fireworks."

Bree glanced at her watch. "Oops! We both need to run. Time's gotten away from us. Only ten minutes till our stores open."

They paid quickly and hurried out. On the sidewalk in front of Pet Style, Bree gave her a quick hug.

"Don't write off Aidan just yet," she advised. "The O'Brien consensus seems to be that he's one of the good guys, and, if nothing else, I do trust my family's judgment."

"I'll keep that in mind," Liz promised.

"I also trust the sparks he puts in your eyes," Bree added with a wink. "You should, too."

When Aidan arrived at Mick's pier, Thomas was sitting on what was apparently his usual spot on a bench. Sean was dancing around impatiently in front of him as Thomas slathered on suntan lotion.

"Mom already did this," Sean protested.

"So you've said. A little extra won't hurt," Thomas told him. "And wear your baseball cap."

"It's too hot."

As Aidan stood by, Thomas gave him a wink, then turned to Sean with a serious expression. "Maybe it's too hot to be out here at all," he suggested.

Sean's eyes widened with unmistakable panic. "No, it's not. It's perfect." He settled the baseball cap on his head, then even added yet another coating of suntan lotion to his nose. "I'll be fine."

He spotted Aidan. "Hi. I didn't know you were coming."

"Your dad mentioned you all would be here and that maybe I could get a fishing lesson."

"You've never been fishing before?" Sean asked, his expression incredulous.

"Never," Aidan confirmed, then amended, "Well, once, but it probably doesn't count since I didn't catch anything."

"That happens," Sean said wisely. "Don't feel

bad. I'll bet we're going to catch at least a dozen fish today."

"And how many do we keep?" Thomas asked.

"Just enough to eat," Sean said dutifully, then grinned. "I can eat a lot." He looked up at Aidan. "Want me to show you how to bait the hook? You're not scared of worms, are you?"

Aidan looked at the box of slimy bait and resisted the strong desire to gag. "Nope. Not a bit."

"That's good," Sean said approvingly. "But I could have done it for you, if you were."

Aidan glanced toward Thomas, who was watching them with an odd expression. Maybe it was just a trick of the light, but it almost looked to Aidan as if he might have tears in his eyes.

Liz heard the plaintive *woofs* coming from upstairs and recognized the sound. Archie had tired of being cooped up. She was sure that just like with a baby whose cries should sometimes be ignored so they learned to fall asleep, ignoring Archie's barks was the sensible thing to do. If he'd been at her house, she'd never have heard them, after all.

But he wasn't at her house with the companionship of two other dogs and a cat. He didn't even have his person around. At least she hadn't seen any sign of Aidan returning.

When she couldn't stand it another minute, she

put a closed sign on the shop door, ran down the street to the management office and asked Susie if she could let her into Aidan's apartment.

Susie regarded her with immediate curiosity. "Planning a surprise? A wicked little welcome-home surprise, perhaps?"

"Not the kind you're imagining," Liz scolded. "It's Archie. He's barking like crazy."

Susie stood up at once and grabbed a key off the rack in the back of the management office. "Do you think it's a burglar or that something's happened to Aidan?"

Liz flushed a little at having caused her to worry. "Actually I just think he's lonely."

"You want to rescue the dog because you think he might be *lonely?*" Susie repeated, her expression torn between amusement and incredulity.

"Okay, I'm a soft touch. Sue me," Liz said. "Are you going to help me out or not?"

Susie shook her head, but she did close up the office and follow Liz outside. "If this were anyone but you or anyone's dog but Aidan's, I would not be doing this," she muttered. "And if he blows a gasket, I swear I'll tell him you broke into the office and stole the key or held me down and took it, something so that I don't come off as being unprofessional."

"Just a liar," Liz said, amused by her righteous indignation and choice of alternatives.

"Better that, than having my father fire me."

"As if that's likely," Liz said. "Everyone knows what a fantastic job you do running that office. And O'Briens don't fire family."

"Worse, they'd just look extremely disappointed in us," Susie said as they climbed the stairs to Aidan's apartment.

Apparently Archie knew that a friendly human was on the way, because his barking grew even more frenzied. When Susie unlocked the door, he made a dash straight past both of them and down the stairs to a nearby patch of grass.

Liz and Susie exchanged a look, then burst out laughing.

"He needed a potty break?" Susie said. "That's what all the commotion was about?"

Liz regarded her with a chagrined expression. "Think of it this way—we just saved the wood floor from an untimely accident."

Relieved, Archie now stood at the bottom of the steps, tail wagging enthusiastically.

"Back inside," Liz commanded.

The dog just ran in a circle, yipping happily.

Liz sighed. She'd started this. She might as well finish it and kidnap the dog and take him with her.

"I'll get your leash." She grabbed it off the back of a chair, waited for Susie to lock up and followed her down the steps.

"Thanks for doing this. I guess I'm going to have a helper for the afternoon."

"No more than you deserve," Susie said,

grinning. "I sure do hope I'm around when Aidan discovers his dog has escaped and sought refuge with you."

Liz shivered at the reminder that she was now going to be forced to see the very man she'd all but banned from her life. Maybe she hadn't been half as serious about that demand as she'd meant to be since she'd just seized an excuse to break the rules herself. Of course the biggest broken rule of all was the one meant to protect her heart. Despite every best intention in the world and enough warning flags to stop a NASCAR race, she'd gone and fallen in love again.

⇒ 20 ⇐

Aidan was lost in thought as he walked home from Mick's carrying a bucket of seawater with a very nice rockfish in it. He had no idea how to go about cleaning it, but Thomas had promised to stop by in a half hour to give him a quick lesson.

It had been a good morning. Being around Thomas had been amazingly stress-free, probably thanks to Sean's exuberant presence as a buffer that kept them from getting into the one topic that both of them preferred to avoid, but probably needed to keep on discussing until it became more comfortable: how to handle the new father-son thing, if it turned out to be true.

As Aidan crossed the green, he glanced toward Pet Style, blinked and looked again. Yep, no question about it. That was his dog sitting just inside the door barking his fool head off.

Even as he stared, Liz opened the door and Archie made a dash across the thankfully deserted street and straight for him. Aidan barely managed to get the bucket with the fish out of the dog's path before Archie jumped up to lick his face, then caught wind of the fish and tried to investigate.

"Get your nose out of there," Aidan commanded. "That's my dinner and I worked very hard for it. Now sit!"

To his shock, Archie obeyed the command. That was a first, but definitely a welcome one. More shocking, though, was the fact that his dog—the one he'd left in his locked apartment—had been with Liz. How on earth had that happened? Did he have some sort of O'Brien gene in his blood, too, the kind that had him meddling to straighten out Aidan's love life? Was he an escape artist on top of that?

There was only one way to solve that particular mystery. He headed for Pet Style, uncertain of his welcome.

Liz was waiting for him just inside the door. Clearly she'd anticipated his arrival, but the way she was nervously clenching her hands together suggested she was as uncertain as he was. One glance told him she'd slept no better than he had, but he was wise enough not to mention it.

"This is unexpected," he said, nodding in the direction of the dog, who was now sitting docilely at his feet with a rawhide bone in his mouth. That was new, too. "You taking in boarders again? Giving them treats they probably don't deserve, because you're a soft touch?"

A blush tinted her cheeks. "Not exactly. I may have made an error in judgment, but when you hear the whole story, I think you'll thank me. I hope so, anyway."

Aidan listened as she described hearing Archie's barks, her rescue mission and the discovery that he'd only wanted to go outside to pee. He bit back a laugh at her chagrined expression. "Thanks for saving the floor."

"Susie appreciated that, too," she said, a smile tugging at her lips. "I promise I won't go into your apartment on a regular basis. We didn't snoop around or anything."

It bothered him that she felt the need to defend herself in that way. "I'm sure you didn't."

"But I wouldn't blame you for not wanting strangers just busting in whenever the mood strikes. And given how many questions you know I have about you, it wouldn't surprise me if you thought I might get answers however I can."

"First of all, you're hardly a stranger. Second, that's not who you are, Liz. I know that. You may not like waiting for those answers until they come from me, but you will."

She nodded vigorously. "Yes, I will." She paused, then added, "And, just so you understand, none of this was Susie's fault. I begged her to let me in, so please don't get her in any trouble."

"I wouldn't dream of it. I probably should just give you a key in case something like this comes up again. Now that Archie knows he can get your attention by barking, who knows how often he'll pull the same stunt. And I've been known to lock myself out from time to time. Sure, Susie's close by, but it'll be good to have a backup place to get a spare key in case she's out of the office." He realized he was fighting hard to convince her to accept a spare key, which should have been nothing more than a matter of convenience. He seemed to be viewing it as more than that, a first step to a new level of intimacy, perhaps.

So, it seemed, did she. In fact, she looked genuinely startled by the gesture. "Aidan, are you sure about that? Things between us are kind of up in the air right now. Do you really want me to have a key?"

He heard the genuine worry in her voice. He looked her directly in the eyes and held her gaze. "I trust you, Liz. I know you have your doubts about me, but I have absolutely none about you or your motives."

"Well, if you're really sure, maybe it would be a

good idea, just in case of another emergency, or at least what passes for an emergency in Archie's world."

"I'll bring a spare key by later," he promised. "I have a couple upstairs. Susie gave me a slew of them. I'm not sure how much entertaining she thought I'd be doing, but having them looks as if it'll come in handy, after all."

She peered toward the bucket he'd set down just inside the front door. "What's in there?"

"A rockfish," he boasted. "The first one I ever caught." He decided to take a risk, since the past few minutes seemed to have gone well enough. "It's more than enough for dinner for two. Would you like to join me? Just as a friend and as a thank-you for rescuing Archie today. We can make it an early dinner. You can still be home before dark. I won't consider it impolite if you decide to eat and run."

When he actually met her gaze, she was fighting a smile.

"That's quite an extensive and persuasive argument," she said.

He grinned. "I was trying to hit all the right notes. You know, light, casual, no expectations."

"Aidan, I don't know. We just decided—"

"You decided," he corrected. "And won't it be easier to overcome your distrust if we keep the lines of communication open?"

She sighed heavily. "Okay, as long as you

understand that this is just a friendly meal, nothing more."

"Absolutely," he said at once. "I promise not to make a pass at you or to bring up anything heavy or too personal. A little friendly chitchat. That's it."

He thought maybe she looked just a little disappointed that he'd ruled out making a pass, but maybe that was just wishful thinking on his part. Bottom line, though, if he could get her to agree to keep on spending time with him until he could tell her everything, perhaps she'd find some way to start believing in him.

Since healthy food was at a premium in his nearly empty refrigerator, Aidan had made a quick trip to a farmer's market just outside of town after Thomas had given him a lesson in cleaning the fish. The process had been messy, but he thought he'd done a decent job of it. Now he needed some side dishes to go along with it. Thomas had recommended the local produce and even told him how to cook it on the grill.

"You're a man of many talents," Aidan had told him.

Thomas had laughed. "Trust me, this is a new one. Mick has always held the family barbecues and Ma's in charge of all the other cooking. Connie seemed to feel that we should be equal partners in the kitchen. My skills are still pretty limited but we don't starve when it's my night to cook."

Aidan had determined right then to make it one of his goals, too. It seemed like something Liz might appreciate. She'd been impressed by his sandwich-making ability, after all. A whole meal might just knock her socks off. And he was still determined to get those socks—figuratively—and a few other articles of clothing off. Nothing in recent days had changed that mission.

He'd started the grill, put a foil packet of vegetables on the heat to roast and made a salad by the time he heard her hesitant tap on his door. Not that he'd needed the warning. Archie's reaction—barking and racing to the door and back—had been sufficient.

"Sit!" he ordered before opening the door.

Archie obediently sat, though it was clear that he was practically quivering with excitement over Liz's arrival.

"Stay!" Aidan said as he opened the door.

Liz stood in the doorway and regarded them with a shocked expression. "When did this happen? All the good behavior, I mean."

"If you're referring to Archie's, it's relatively new. I've always been well mannered."

She laughed and some of the tension in her shoulders seemed to ease. She came in and looked around curiously, proving that she really hadn't explored the place earlier. Not that he would have minded if she had. He wanted her to know him, not that there was much she might discover from his belongings. He even wanted to get those secrets he couldn't yet reveal out in the open, too.

"Would you like a glass of wine? I've opened a bottle of white, but there's red here, too."

"White's fine."

"Dinner's almost ready," he told her as he poured the drink for her. "I just have to put the fish on the grill. I think I can follow the directions Thomas gave me."

She regarded him with surprise. "Thomas?"

"I guess I didn't mention it before. I was fishing at Mick's earlier with him and Sean," he said, hoping he'd managed to strike just the right casual note for something that had felt momentous to him.

"How'd that happen?"

Here was one of those minefields he wasn't certain how to navigate without giving away too much. For most of his life he'd been open and honest. He'd even had a reputation for unbridled candor with the media when he'd been playing pro football. Now he was forced to walk on egg-shells every time he opened his mouth, at least when it came to this one topic.

"You know the after-school activity I've been assigned to handle, aside from football, is the environmental club, right?"

"I think you mentioned it. I guess I didn't realize Thomas was involved, but that makes sense."

"Can you imagine a better person to inspire these kids to treat the environment around here with care?" he said.

Liz studied him with a curious expression. "You sound impressed."

"Of course. He has incredible credentials."

"This is quite a turnaround," she said. "I used to think there was bad blood between the two of you. What I couldn't understand was why, if you'd never even met."

"Just one of those things," Aidan said with a shrug. "We didn't hit it off at first. Now that I've gotten to know him better, I'm seeing him differently."

The comment was true as far as it went. He could only pray it was enough to satisfy Liz. He watched her closely and noted that she seemed to have made up her mind to let it go.

She studied him. "So today was about bonding and talking about your plans for fall?"

"Exactly," he said. "Thomas is getting me up to speed on what projects the club has tackled in the past and what he'd like to see the kids focus on this year. He even thinks perhaps one or two of them might want to testify during the hearings this year on some proposed changes to the law that could adversely affect the Chesapeake. The fishing was just a bonus. When he found out I'd never been, he suggested I join him and Sean."

"He must love it that you're embracing his favorite cause," she said.

"The man has pretty amazing recruitment skills," he said wryly. "I don't imagine anyone living in the entire region could resist his arguments about protecting the beauty of our natural resources. Kevin's good at it and just as passionate, but Thomas seems to innately know the right buttons to push."

"Believe me, I know," Liz said. "He had half the town working one day back in March to clean up the shoreline. It was still chilly and it started raining, but not a single person left. Nell was right there alongside him, even though her husband and Mick were grumbling she was going to wind up with pneumonia."

Aidan smiled at the image of Nell defying the two men to work on a cause dear to Thomas's heart. It suddenly dawned on him that that petite dynamo was his grandmother. Of course, he'd known that intellectually, but the implication hadn't really registered until now. He'd seen for himself how wise and caring she was and suddenly found himself yearning for that to be directed his way. Since he'd been in town and met the O'Briens, he was realizing how much he missed those deep family connections he'd lost when first his maternal grandparents and then his mom had died.

Liz regarded him with an odd expression. "What was that look about?" she asked. "Something seems to have shaken you."

Aidan scrambled for a plausible answer. "I just remembered the fish. I need to get it on the grill before the vegetables burn."

"Need any help?"

"I've got it. Just give me a minute to run downstairs to the barbecue area. I'll be back with everything, hopefully cooked to perfection."

"Are you sure you don't want me to come along to carry anything?"

What he really wanted was a minute to gather his composure. "I've got it covered. Sit out on the balcony and relax. You've been on your feet all day."

"To be honest, that does sound heavenly," she admitted.

"Then do it."

And maybe by the time he got back upstairs, she'd have forgotten all about the questions he'd managed to stir up.

Liz was puzzled by Aidan's eagerness to get away from her all of a sudden, but the prospect of sitting outside on the warm night with a glass of wine in hand was too tempting to pass up. What she hadn't considered was the fact that Aidan's balcony was in full view of any passerby on Main Street. While it had been a fairly quiet day in town, tonight the street was bustling with locals and tourists out for an evening stroll before or after dinner at one of the nearby restaurants.

"Well, well, well, look who's making herself right at home on Aidan's balcony," Susie taunted from below. "Has he taken you prisoner after your earlier break-in?"

"I did not break in," Liz reminded her, then glanced pointedly at Jeff, who was standing right there with his nosy daughter. "Do you really want to go down that road?"

"Oh, Dad knows," Susie said. "Unfortunately he came in while we were gone. I had to explain where I'd been when I got back to the office. I'm still employed."

"There is a big black mark on her employment history, though," Jeff said sternly. Even from upstairs Liz could see the twinkle in his eyes.

"Right next to all the others," Susie said unrepentantly. "So, how come you're at Aidan's?"

Jeff gave her another disapproving parental glance. "How is that any of your business?"

"Inquiring O'Brien minds want to know," Susie said. "Do you really want to walk into the pub without knowing the full scoop? Uncle Mick will be all over us."

"And that is my brother's flaw," Jeff said. He glanced up at Liz. "Watch out for this crew. They may be my family, but there are times I'd like to disown them."

385

Susie kissed her dad's cheek. "Oh, you would not. Come on. It's obvious we're not going to get anything out of her now. Maybe I'll send Bree around. Or Shanna."

"Please don't," Liz called down. But, just in case her plea didn't register, the minute they'd gone she decided maybe it would be wise if she waited for Aidan inside, after all.

When he came in, he looked startled to find her curled up on his sofa. "Too warm outside?"

She shook her head. "Too crowded."

"On my balcony?"

"On Main Street," she said. "Susie had questions. When I declined to answer, she vowed to send others."

Aidan laughed. "I have noticed that they're a chatty group, and they all seem to wander past this time of night, either going home from their businesses, or heading around the corner to Luke's pub. Not a one of them has chased me inside, though."

"Because this is your apartment. My presence here raises questions." She sighed. "And speculation."

"And pressure," Aidan guessed.

"Pretty much."

"Then I suppose we should eat inside."

"It might be better," Liz said. "Though it's probably a little late for discretion. I imagine there are a whole slew of bets being placed at O'Brien's right this minute."

"Bets?"

"About whether I'll still be here in the morning."

She noticed that Aidan looked as if he was about to laugh, but then he clearly recognized that she was serious.

"You're not kidding?" he asked.

She shrugged. "Not so much. I gather it's considered a family sport."

Aidan shook his head. "This is a very odd family."

"Very," she agreed, then smiled. "But kind of wonderful, too. I love my mom and my sisters, even when they're making me crazy, but there's something different about the O'Briens. Maybe it's all those generations right here in the same town. They might butt into each other's lives too much, but it's obvious how much they love and respect each other."

"It's only wonderful until you're on the receiving end of all that well-meant speculation," Aidan reminded her.

"Yes, well, this is the first time I've actually experienced that part." She regarded him with regret, then conceded, "I could probably live without it."

Unfortunately it seemed it came with living in Chesapeake Shores, and up till now, it was the only downside she'd discovered.

Aidan couldn't help wondering if he dared to ask Thomas to request that the O'Brien troops back off by explaining that their well-meant efforts might be counterproductive. Instead, as his evening with Liz went on with no real tension, he realized that she seemed accepting of this community oddity. Maybe, if circumstances between them had been less awkward, she'd even have welcomed it. That gave him a renewed sense of hope that they could work through their issues once those DNA test results were in.

Dinner the night before had gone surprisingly smoothly, mostly because they'd done exactly as he'd promised and kept the conversation casual and impersonal.

Afterward, he and Archie had walked her home. They'd parted on the front walk. She hadn't invited him in. He hadn't taken advantage of the moment to kiss her senseless the way he'd desperately wanted to. He had a feeling it had required amazing restraint on both of their parts. He'd noticed that she'd stood staring after him for a long time before finally closing her front door.

That, he concluded, was another positive turn of events. She'd looked as disappointed and disconcerted as he had been by the abrupt end to an otherwise perfect evening.

This morning, though, he was restless and edgy and glad that he'd sent out a text to his team members to meet him on the green at nine o'clock.

He stood on his balcony and watched them assembling, giving each other boisterous high fives as if they hadn't seen each other in weeks, rather than days. He smiled, then set his empty coffee cup in the kitchen sink and went down to join them.

"How come we're here, Coach?" Henry asked. "And why'd you tell us not to bring pads or helmets?"

Aidan called the boys together before answering.

"Okay, guys, here's the scoop. We're going to be doing some unofficial drills and there are some pretty strict regulations on what we're permitted to do. We can focus on training and getting in shape, but we can't be doing full-contact tackling. We can use the field when it's available, but it's in use by a summer camp right now and for the next few weeks. I know you all are anxious to get started, so we'll work out here for a couple of days a week." He gave them each a hard look. "Try not to mow down any little kids who might be around, okay?"

"Got it," Taylor said. "The green is plenty big enough for me and Hector to practice passing."

Henry's eyes lit up. "Actually it'll be kind of cool to be right here in the middle of town. People can see for themselves how good we're getting."

"They'll see us make fools of ourselves from time to time, too," Taylor said. "I'm probably still dropping more passes than I'm catching."

"That's about timing," Aidan told him. "You

and Hector will work out a rhythm." He glanced around. "Now, I have some permission slips you'll need your folks to sign saying the school's not liable for any injuries and I'm going to do my best to make sure we don't have any injuries to worry about." He looked from one boy to the next. "Understood? The first one of you who tackles another player is heading home. Is that also understood?"

"Yes, Coach!"

The loud chorus was led by Henry. Aidan smiled, once again impressed by his impulsive choice of what had turned out to be exactly the right kid to be team captain.

He divided the team into groups and assigned them various running and passing drills, then stood back and watched them approach their assignments with enthusiasm and real determination. When he timed a few of the drills, he noted that they were running faster than they had when he'd first done the same drills before the end of the school year. Pleased, he called them back over.

"You guys have been practicing without me, haven't you?" he said. He tapped the stopwatch. "Excellent times today. I'm proud of you. On Thursday I expect you to do even better."

"Not till Thursday?" Henry asked, clearly disappointed.

Aidan noted the same reaction on all of their faces. "I truly appreciate the enthusiasm, but this is summer vacation. You need to have some fun. I know some of you might even have part-time jobs. Two practices a week are two more than we were originally going to have. Do some running and weights on your own in between. Once August rolls around, we'll kick it up a notch and we'll be back on the field in full gear. By then you'll be begging me to let up on you. Enjoy this pace for now."

Once more it was Henry who stepped in. "What did we say we were going to do this year?"

"Whatever it takes!" the team members shouted.

"And who's going to lead us to the state championship?"

"Coach Mitchell!"

"And what are we going to do when we get there?" Henry demanded.

"We're going to win!"

A shout went up that could probably be heard all the way around on Shore Road. Aidan smiled and gave Henry a well-deserved pat on the back.

"How'd I wind up with a team captain, a head cheerleader and an assistant coach all wrapped up in one?" he asked the boy, whose cheeks imme-diately flushed.

Henry had replaced the contacts he'd been wearing for practice with the glasses he preferred. He shoved them up the bridge of his nose and grinned back at Aidan. "Just lucky, I guess."

Definitely lucky, Aidan thought as he dismissed

the team and watched them head straight to Sally's. Anticipating that, he'd told Sally to put whatever they ordered on his tab and he'd be by to pay her later. It wasn't something he intended to do all the time, but he wanted them to know just how much he appreciated their commitment.

As he headed back to his apartment, Shanna stepped out of the bookstore.

"That boy of yours is remarkable," Aidan told her.

"I've always believed that," she said, then held his gaze. "But you've brought out something new in him."

"What's that?"

"Honest-to-goodness self-confidence." She blinked back tears. "Thanks for that."

Aidan felt his own eyes sting at her comment. This, he decided, was what coaching was all about, turning boys into confident young men. When he'd walked off a professional football field for the last time, he'd chosen his next career really wisely. And, he was increasingly convinced that, despite all of the upheaval that might come when the truth about his relationship to Thomas came out, he'd found the best possible place to practice it.

⇒ 21 ⇐

Once again Liz tried really hard to beat the usual crowd to Sally's on the morning after her dinner with Aidan. She knew perfectly well that Susie would have spread the sighting of her sipping wine on Aidan's balcony far and wide.

Sally gave her a knowing look. "You're entirely too predictable. You know that, don't you?"

Liz regarded her with surprise. "How so?"

"You're only in here at the crack of dawn when you don't want your friends in your business."

Liz winced. "It's obvious?"

"Hon, I've had this place a long time. You're not the first to think if you can get out of here without a cross-examination by an O'Brien, you'll be home free. I'm here to tell you, it never works. They'll hunt you down."

Liz laughed. "Maybe so, but I'll have caffeine by then, and a head start."

Sally handed over her coffee in an extra-large to-go cup along with a raspberry croissant. "Good luck with that," she said as she took Liz's money.

Before Liz could turn and make her escape, the door of the café opened and Bree came in.

"Sneaking off?" Bree asked, amusement glinting in her eyes. "I don't think so."

"Good morning," Liz said with forced cheer. "I have a big shipment coming in today. I need to get started early."

"I'm sure that's it," Bree said, nodding sagely. "I'm sure you wouldn't skip out on your friends just to avoid a few questions."

"Absolutely not," Liz said. "I have nothing to hide. My life's an open book."

Bree grinned and tucked her arm through Liz's. "Great, then let's sit down and read a few pages of that book together."

Liz laughed. What else was she supposed to do? Just last night she'd acknowledged that this fascination with other people's lives was part of the Chesapeake Shores and O'Brien charm. Of course, she'd also said she wasn't crazy about it, but right this second it seemed she didn't have a choice, not without offending a friend. She noticed that Sally gave her a commiserating look.

"Ten minutes," she conceded, following Bree to a booth. "That's all you get."

"Then I guess you'll need to talk fast. How'd you wind up at Aidan's last night? Are you two finally . . . ?" She wiggled her eyebrows suggestively.

"We are not," Liz said emphatically, then probably ruined the flat denial by adding, "And I wouldn't tell you that if we were."

"Which means I can't actually trust a word

you say on the subject," Bree said thoughtfully. "That's quite a quandary. What to do? What to do?"

"We can take turns spying," Susie suggested, arriving just in time to pick up on the gist of the conversation.

Bree looked almost as indignant as Liz. "We do not spy on our friends," Bree scolded.

"Okay, we ply them with wine till they spill the details," Susie suggested. "That works for me, too. Let's go to the pub after work tonight. We haven't had book club or a real girls' night in a while now."

Bree studied Liz with a serious expression. "How about it? You up for a girls' night?"

"Sure," Liz said at once, then grinned. "But I'll be drinking diet soda. Now, I really do need to get to the store." She stood up. "Feel free to continue your plotting. I've got your number. I intend to have my guard up."

Bree and Susie exchanged a look, then burst out laughing.

"Oh, you sweet innocent," Bree said. "We have tactics you've never even dreamed of. The military could probably use them."

"I'll look forward to watching you try," Liz said lightly.

Only after she was in her own shop, with the door securely locked behind her, did she draw in a deep breath. For a woman intent on keeping a huge chunk of her life private, she had a hunch she was in knee-deep trouble.

After ending the unofficial practice with the team, Aidan changed into his running clothes and headed back out, hoping to get in a good workout before it got too hot. Unfortunately as he followed a route along the bay up to The Inn at Eagle Point, he realized the only things saving him from the surprising late-morning heat were the old shade trees and a faint breeze off the water.

Making a last-minute decision, he turned off the road and decided to throw himself on Jess's mercy at the inn and beg for water. She'd been friendly enough when he stayed there and she was an O'Brien, after all. They had a reputation to uphold for being kind to strays.

He tapped on the side door into the kitchen and waited for Jess's chef to answer. Gail took one look at him and shook her head.

"You look like something the cat dragged in, then spent some time chewing on," she said, grinning. "I wonder what all the girls who've been swooning over you would say if they could see you now?"

Aidan tried for his most appealing smile. "I hope at least one of them would be sweet enough to offer me a bottled water."

"Ah, so that's what brought you to the kitchen

door, rather than traipsing through the lobby. You think I'm a soft touch."

"I hope so."

Jess walked in just then and shook her head at the sight of him. "Don't you know no good comes of trying to run on a hot summer day around here?"

"It's great exercise," Aidan said, defending himself. "And I thought I'd be back home before the temperature skyrocketed."

Both women exchanged one of those female what-do-you-expect looks that drove men nuts. Sadly, right this second, he deserved it.

Gail retrieved two bottles of water, one from a case in the pantry, one from the massive refrigerator. "This one now," she said, handing him the lukewarm water.

"Yes, ma'am." He turned to Jess. "Does she boss you around, too?"

Jess laughed. "Only in here. At most other times, she wisely remembers that I write the checks. Now, come on outside and sit on the porch with me. There's a nice breeze. You can cool down a bit before you head back into town." She gave him a surprisingly stern look. "Walking, if you have an ounce of sense."

"How does Will put up with you?" Aidan teased, then thanked Gail before following Jess outside.

Jess smiled at the question. "I wondered the

same thing myself for a very long time. He claims to love me. I guess love really does make people stop using their brains. Gram's always telling us to listen with our heart, not our head."

Aidan settled into a rocker and set it in motion, closing his eyes for a moment to enjoy the cooling effect of the breeze from the bay.

"May I ask you something?" he ventured after several minutes of silence.

"Sure," Jess said.

"Most everyone I've met in your family seems to believe love can overcome anything, is that right?"

She laughed. "Personally I think it's a character flaw, but yes. And since it's worked in my favor with Will, I'm really in no position to express my doubts." She gave him a penetrating look. "Is this about Liz? I've seen you together and I've heard all the speculation. Are you two an item?"

"Not exactly," Aidan admitted.

"Why not?"

"She needs someone in her life she can trust," he began.

Jess frowned. "And you can't be trusted?" she demanded indignantly.

"Settle down," he urged, smiling. "Of course I can be, but there are things about me she needs to know and I'm not yet at liberty to discuss them."

"Bad things?" Jess asked, "The kind that might be a deal breaker?"

"I honestly don't think so," Aidan replied. "The real issue is that I've kept them a secret. A lot of people would understand that kind of obligation, but it's especially hard for Liz."

"Because someone in her life lied to her about something important?" Jess concluded.

Aidan nodded. "But that's another of those things I'm not at liberty to discuss."

She nodded, her expression turning thoughtful. "That makes sense. She clams up when anybody tries to get too personal. We've all wondered about that, because she's generally so upbeat and open." She regarded him curiously. "So what are you asking?"

"Do you think we can get past this? Can love really conquer all that distrust and lack of openness?"

Jess smiled. "My husband and certainly my family would say yes, but that it might take patience and determination."

"I have those things," Aidan said. "I'll hang in as long as I need to. I may not know much and I have zero experience with the kind of love we're talking about, but I'm smart enough to recognize that Liz is worth waiting for."

"Good answer," Jess said approvingly. "I'm not in the advice business. That's my husband's territory. I will say this, though. Whatever this secret is, make sure she's the first to know when you can talk about it. She needs to hear it from you, not from the Chesapeake Shores grapevine."

"Thanks," Aidan said, meaning it. He now knew exactly what he needed to do. He needed to get Thomas's assurance that no one would find out the results of that DNA test before he could fill Liz in. Fortunately he had a little time to put that plan into place.

Back in town, Aidan showered, changed, grabbed a late lunch, then started making calls to try to locate Thomas. He missed him at the office in Annapolis, and Connie reported that he hadn't yet arrived home.

"Want me to have him call you when he gets in?" she asked. "Or do you want to try his cell phone, not that he ever pays a bit of attention to it when he's on the road. He usually gets my messages as he's walking up the driveway, too late to stop for the milk or whatever else I might need from the store."

Aidan laughed. "Sounds as if that could be deliberate."

"Don't I know it?" she said, laughing with him. "We've discussed it a time or twenty. Still, you could try. He might take your call."

Since Aidan wasn't a big fan of cell phones on the road, he refused. "Just ask him to call me when he gets in."

"Will do." She hesitated, then said, "Aidan, I know you must be on pins and needles about that test, but I don't have a single doubt that you're a part of this family."

Aidan was surprised to discover that his eyes were stinging at her reassurance. "Thank you. I don't want to disrupt anyone's life. I came here because I needed to meet my father, not to get anything from him, just to know more about who I am."

"Good heavens, no one is going to judge you for trying to get to know your father. Don't you know that our hearts will be open to you once the truth comes out? I realize it may not have seemed that way when you first told Thomas, but he was in shock. Now that he's had time to get used to the idea that he's had a son all these years, he'll accept whatever role you want him to play in your life. You're a grown man now, so it's between the two of you to decide what comes next. I hope you'll want to spend time not just with him, but with all of us."

His voice thick, Aidan said, "I see now why Thomas fell in love with you. You're pretty amazing."

"Not so amazing," she said. "I just love my husband and his family. And he's done the same with my daughter. It'll all work out, Aidan. I know it will."

Aidan replayed her words several times in his mind as he sat on the balcony and awaited a call back from Thomas. But rather than the phone ringing, an hour later there was a knock on his door. He found Thomas standing there, an envelope in hand. Aidan couldn't seem to take his eyes off that envelope.

"That's it?"

Thomas nodded. "You should have a report in today's mail, too."

"I never even thought to check," he admitted. "Have you read it?"

Thomas shook his head. "Connie thought maybe it was something you and I ought to do together. She told me you'd called. She said it didn't sound as if you'd seen the report." Thomas looked oddly hesitant. "What do you think? Shall we read this together?"

Aidan nodded and led the way inside. "I could use a beer. How about you?"

Thomas nodded. "I wouldn't say no."

Aidan came back into the living room with two bottles of beer and handed one to Thomas, then sat down across the room. They each took a long sip of beer, exchanged a look and then Thomas set his bottle aside and glanced at Aidan.

"You ready?"

Even though he was convinced of what they'd find, Aidan's stomach filled with butterflies. "Sure."

Thomas unsealed the envelope and removed two pieces of paper, one apparently a letter, the other a copy of the detailed results. He scanned the letter, then the paper, then regarded Aidan with tears in his eyes.

"You're my son," he said softly.

Aidan felt his own eyes fill with tears. After all these years, the truth was out there. He knew now exactly who he was—Anna Mitchell's son, to be sure, but an O'Brien, too.

He studied Thomas's pale complexion. "Are you okay with this?" He gave a scratchy laugh. "Not that you could change it, but I mean really okay?"

"It's taken some getting used to," Thomas admitted, then smiled. "But, yes, I'm okay with it. We have a lot of time to make up for, you and me, a lot of catching up to do. I find myself longing to see baby pictures, report cards, anything you have from the years I missed."

Aidan gave him a hard look that he had a difficult time sustaining. "It's too late for you to be setting curfews and disciplining me," he warned.

At last Thomas—his *father*—laughed. "I wouldn't dream of trying. Connie wanted me to invite you over for dinner, so we can tell Sean."

Aidan stared at him, surprised. "She really was confident of what that report would say, wasn't she? I mean, she told me she knew the outcome, but I thought she just wanted to make me feel better."

"My mother is the wisest woman I know, but

Connie is a close second," Thomas said. "I'm thinking she can help us decide the right way to tell the rest of the family."

Aidan nodded. "I only have one request. I need to be the one to tell Liz, and I need to do it before anyone outside of you, Connie and Sean find out the truth."

"Then let's have this dinner," Thomas suggested. "Then you'd better track down Liz, because I can almost guarantee no matter how we try to keep my boy quiet, he'll have the news all over town before morning."

It wasn't at all difficult for Aidan to imagine trying to contain news that big once a little boy was in on the secret that he had a big brother. And that sort of premature disclosure, Aidan thought, was exactly what he hoped to avoid.

None of the women got especially rowdy on book club night at Susie's, so Liz was unprepared for the level of raucousness they achieved at Luke's pub. Even with two of the pregnant women not drinking alcohol and she herself carefully sticking to diet soda for her own self-protection, the noise level around the tables they'd pushed together at the back of the room was pretty high.

While several of the other women had been targets of good-natured teasing over dinner and drinks, attention had come back time and again to Liz and her relationship with Aidan. It was mostly amusing to see the variety of tactics they chose to try to dig into her personal life. Bree had been wrong. So far, they'd tried nothing that she hadn't been prepared for.

She turned just in time to see Bree and Susie exchange a frustrated look.

"She's tougher than I expected," Susie admitted.

Bree nodded. "I definitely thought she'd crack before now. I think it's the lack of alcohol in her system. Do you think we could convince Luke to lace her drinks with vodka or something?"

"Not a chance," Susie said with real regret. "My brother values his liquor license and his reputation. He also tries to remain impartial in family disputes."

Bree's gaze went to the door of the pub and her eyes lit up.

"Ah, reinforcements!" she announced happily. "This should be fun."

Liz turned in time to see Mick walking in with Megan and with Jeff and his wife. To her shock, though, they barely spared a glance for the table of women and, instead, sat down at the bar. Heads together, they were whispering about something. Judging from their intense expressions, whatever it was appeared to be big—and not necessarily good news.

Bree's gaze narrowed. "What do you suppose that's about?" she asked, clearly puzzled.

"One way to find out," Susie said, standing up,

wobbling for a minute, then steadying herself. She grinned. "That last ale might have been one too many."

She crossed the pub and inserted herself between her parents. For an instant Jeff, Jo, Mick and Megan fell silent.

Then Mick's booming voice said, "Oh, go ahead and tell her. The whole family's going to know soon enough."

Megan jabbed him with her elbow. "Hush. Thomas swore us to secrecy, remember?"

At the mention of Thomas, Liz strained a little harder to try to hear the now-muted conversation. Unfortunately Megan's reminder had succeeded in quieting all of them, Mick included.

Susie returned to the table, her expression filled with frustration.

"Well?" Bree demanded.

"Aunt Megan shut them down," she grumbled. "All I heard was something about Uncle Thomas." She frowned, then added, "And something about Aidan, but that doesn't make sense. What could possibly be going on between Uncle Thomas and Aidan?" She turned to Liz. "Any idea?"

"None," Liz said, but her heart was suddenly pounding. Whatever it was, she had little doubt that it was the big secret Aidan had been keeping from her. And if it was so huge it could reduce even Mick O'Brien to silence, then it was clearly something a man should have shared with a woman he claimed to care about and want in his life.

With a sudden terrible sense of déjà vu, she got to her feet. "I need to get out of here," she said, pulling some cash from her purse and leaving it on the table. "That should be enough for my dinner."

Bree regarded her with alarm. "Liz, what is it? Do you know what this is about?"

"Not a clue," she said emphatically. "And that's exactly the point."

She was halfway down the block when Bree caught up with her. "You're upset," she said. "You shouldn't be alone."

"I'm not fit for company right now," Liz countered.

"Which is why you've got me. I'm not company. I'm a friend. You can vent to me or you can stay perfectly quiet and stew over whatever's going on in that head of yours, but you will not be alone."

Liz turned to her, ready to argue, but the stubborn set of Bree's jaw suggested she'd be wasting her breath. "Okay, fine. Whatever."

They were crossing the town green at a good clip when Aidan appeared out of nowhere.

"I've been looking all over for you," he told Liz. "We need to talk."

"Too late," she muttered. "Come on, Bree."

Bree exchanged a long look with Aidan, then gave Liz's arm a squeeze. "Listen to whatever the man has to say. Then you can carve his heart out if you want to."

Liz gave her a wry look. "Yours, too, for abandoning me?"

Bree chuckled. "I hope you won't, but yes. I think this is the right call."

Never once glancing in Aidan's direction, Liz kept right on walking. Though she doubted her strategy of silence would work, she was hoping he'd get the message and give up.

At the house, she turned on every light downstairs, greeted the dogs and cat, gave them each a treat, let them outside for a quick run in the yard, then poured herself a glass of tap water. Aidan waited patiently through all of it.

"Finished avoiding me yet?" he asked eventually as she stood at the sink, water in hand.

"I suppose," she said, resigned. "You haven't gone away yet."

"I'm not going to," he told her.

"So what's the big news, Aidan?" she asked him pointedly, looking directly into his eyes. "And how many people heard it before me?"

"I don't—"

She shook her head. "If you're going to try to tell me you don't know what I'm talking about, you're wasting your breath. Mick and Jeff and their wives just came into the pub looking thunderstruck. We all heard that it has something to do with you and Thomas, so what is it? Are you going to work for his foundation? Maybe giving him some huge grant that'll curry favor with all the O'Briens? What? Or are you going to keep denying there's something weird going on?"

Aidan looked directly into her eyes, then spoke so quietly it was difficult to hear him.

"Not weird, Liz, just a shock. At least to the O'Briens," he said. "Thomas O'Brien is my father."

⇒ 22 ⇐

Aidan's announcement hung in the air, leaving Liz with her jaw dropping.

"Your father?" she whispered when she could finally speak. "How?"

Aidan's lips curved slightly. "The usual way, I imagine. Those aren't details I particularly want to know."

She frowned at his attempt to lighten a monumental revelation. "You know what I meant. Thomas and your mother were together? Did you know that when you came to Chesapeake Shores? Is that why you came?" Her eyes widened. "It all makes perfect sense now, the way you reacted to him at first."

Rather than focusing on his momentous news and the emotions he must be feeling, she selfishly seized on the deal breaker for her. "You deceived all of us, didn't you?"

"I didn't deceive anyone," he said. "At least that wasn't my intention."

"You didn't share the truth with anyone, did you? It's a pretty big secret to keep all to yourself, especially when it affects so many lives here in town." She wasn't entirely sure how she felt about him right this second. The news itself was almost secondary to the fact that this man for whom she had feelings had kept her in the dark about something so huge, something that went to the core of who he was. And how must the O'Briens be feeling, knowing he'd played them?

"Could we go for a walk, maybe, and talk about this?" Aidan pleaded. "Or at least sit down on the porch? I want to explain. It matters to me that you understand exactly what happened."

"I know exactly what happened," she said stubbornly. "From the moment we met you were keeping something from me."

"Which I never denied," he reminded her.

"No," she said, relenting enough to admit the truth. "You didn't. But this is huge, Aidan."

He gave her a wry look. "Don't you think I'm aware of that? Liz, be reasonable. Put yourself in my place. Would you tell someone you've just met something this personal, especially when the person most directly involved—Thomas—didn't know? He had no idea I was his son, that I had any connection to him at all."

"And after we stopped being strangers," she

asked quietly, "after you claimed to have feelings for me, what about then, Aidan? What's your excuse for keeping silent then?"

She fought the tears clouding her vision. When she finally dared to meet Aidan's gaze, he actually looked angry.

"I know what you're doing, Liz. You're lumping my silence in with the affair your husband kept from you. That's hardly fair. I've admitted all along that there was something I wanted to share with you, but wasn't at liberty to discuss. It was an extremely private matter between me and Thomas. I wasn't even sure if I wanted to tell him and turn his world upside down. What would be the point at this late date? I hardly need a daddy."

She was momentarily stunned into silence by the bitterness she heard in his voice. He seized the chance to continue.

"Liz, when I came here, I dragged something that happened twenty-eight years ago right into the middle of the present. I didn't want to do that out of anger or resentment, but only if I thought it was the right thing to do. Why would I put you into the middle of that dilemma?"

On some level she knew he was right, recognized that he'd been grappling with an emotional minefield, but she wasn't ready to be reasonable. She needed time to think this through, to remember that this was Aidan, not Josh, and that just as Aidan had said, the circumstances were entirely different. "Please go."

"You want me to leave without giving me a chance to explain?" he asked, his expression at first incredulous, then angry once more. "How is judging me without knowing all the facts fair?" He gave her a disappointed look. "Maybe I'm not the one at fault here."

Her temper kicked in. "What is that supposed to mean?"

"You told me yourself you were oblivious to your husband's cheating. I'm starting to wonder if you just shut him down when he tried to solve whatever problems you had. Did you, Liz? Did you set up barriers that forced him to turn to someone else?"

The accusation, which hit far too close to the truth, stung. She lashed out instinctively. "How dare you say something like that? You weren't there. You don't know anything about it."

"I know what you told me," he countered. "And I see exactly what you're doing to me. You claim you care for me. You know I have very strong feelings for you that I believe can lead to something great between us. But you'd rather seize on what you think I've done wrong and send me away than give me even a minute to explain." He shook his head wearily. "Fine. If that's the way you want it, I'm out of here. I have more than enough on my plate right now without adding this."

Trembling with a mix of outrage and pain, Liz watched him go. It was just like that night with Josh. She'd sent Aidan away. At least it wasn't pouring rain tonight and Aidan was walking, not driving, but it felt the same, as if disaster loomed right around the bend, as if her life would never be quite the same again. In a split second past and present had gotten all twisted together.

She could tell herself from now till eternity that the fault was Aidan's, that he'd kept the secret even knowing how she felt about being left in the dark, but when she was all alone in her bed tonight, was that self-righteous indignation going to be any comfort at all? One thing for certain, she was going to have a whole lot of time to hear his harsh accusations ringing in her ears. He might have lashed out in anger, but he'd hit on some truths about her marriage that she'd hoped never to have to acknowledge.

Aidan didn't know what made him angrier— Liz's refusal to give him a chance to explain or the fact that the news, or part of it anyway, had somehow leaked out despite Thomas's assurances that he wouldn't say a word to anybody before morning. It was obvious Liz hadn't known the whole story, of course. She'd known just enough to lump him in with the man who'd betrayed her.

He was crossing the town green when he spotted Bree. She stood up and headed his way, then fell into step beside him. To his surprise, though, she didn't say a word.

He glanced over at her. "In case you were wondering, it didn't go well."

"I figured, since you weren't gone that long."

"What were you doing sitting out there at this hour? I know it's a safe town, but it's late, Bree. Shouldn't you be home with your husband?"

"Jake knows where I am. I thought you might want to talk, and in my family we try to be there for our own."

Aidan regarded her with surprise. "You know?"

She nodded. "Once Liz charged out of Luke's pub, my dad and Uncle Jeff saw no reason to keep quiet, despite their promise to Thomas. By the time I got back there, everyone knew."

"So, what's the general consensus? That I'm a deceitful, untrustworthy human being?"

Bree regarded him with shock. "Is that what Liz said?"

"Pretty much." He closed his eyes and sighed. "And I get where she's coming from. I really do. I've known all along how she feels about lies, but what could I do? I couldn't share something with her until Thomas was satisfied I wasn't lying and we could decide how we wanted to go forward. He has a wife, a son to consider." He looked to Bree for support. "I'm not the one in the wrong here, am I?"

"Not in a perfectly rational world, but that's not what you're dealing with, is it? Liz has some history that none of us, except you, know about. You obviously stirred up all those old feelings."

"That's exactly what happened, but I honestly don't see what I could have done differently. I came to town knowing the truth, but even I didn't know if I would ever share it with Thomas, much less anyone else. I just wanted to see my dad, maybe have a chance to find out why he and my mom weren't together."

"And now that you know him, know that you have this huge, crazy family, how are you feeling?"

"Overwhelmed, to be honest with you. Add in everything that's going on with Liz and it's been quite a day."

"I'll talk to Liz tomorrow when she's had a chance to calm down," Bree offered. "She loves you, Aidan. I can see it in her eyes, hear it in her voice. She may not want to—she may be terrified of all those big, messy feelings she has—but she does love you. Otherwise this wouldn't matter to her so much."

"Is that the Irish second sight I've heard so much about?" he asked, his smile wry.

"Nope, just the insight of a woman who's attuned to the way the people around me fight being in love. We've been known to go down kicking and screaming, looking for excuses to keep our hearts whole and safely locked away from any potential for pain."

"I don't need you to plead my case," Aidan told her.

She smiled at him. "Yes, you do, but even if you didn't, you're an O'Brien now. You get the full-court meddling all the rest of us have been treated to over the years. And you should know right now that Dad's already planning a big welcome-to-the-family dinner for Sunday. Gram will be making every Irish specialty in her repertoire, so you'll get a complete introduction into your heritage, at least on the culinary side."

That sense of being overwhelmed washed over him again. "Do I have to?" he asked, already knowing he was wasting his breath. Of course he had to go.

"Yes," Bree said emphatically. "Unless you want to risk offending your grandmother. Trust me—you do not want to do that. Nell doesn't make a habit of heaping guilt on us, but she can do it with one disappointed look."

Aidan sighed. He knew declining to come on Sunday would only be postponing the inevitable. Besides, a part of him wanted this, wanted to discover the other half of his heritage, to have family ties again.

"I'll be there," he said.

Bree smiled. "Good decision." She pumped her

fist. "I must have gotten a few of those guilt-inducing genes from Gram."

"You might not want to brag about it," Aidan said. "It's annoying."

She laughed. "Spoken exactly like one of my brothers. You're an O'Brien, all right." Her expression sobered as she held his gaze. "Welcome to the family, Aidan. I mean that."

"Thanks, Bree. And I mean that."

"Get some sleep. I'll do what I can with Liz tomorrow, but you might want to give her some space, let her come to you."

"Sure," he said, but he knew better. Liz wasn't going to come to him. For better or worse, she'd made her decision tonight and he doubted there was a thing Bree could say to change her mind. After all, the last time she'd been hurt this deeply, she'd left her hometown and her family to get away from the memories.

Pleading a summer cold she was determined to nip in the bud, Liz called her part-time employee first thing in the morning and asked her to cover the shop for the whole day. Tess was delighted to have the extra hours. She was saving up to buy her own car.

With that cowardly decision behind her, Liz went back to bed and pulled the covers up. The worried dogs hovered nearby. Her cat sprawled across her feet and purred loudly in what Liz supposed was meant to be a comforting gesture. Instead the noise was just getting on her last nerve, probably because she knew somewhere deep inside that she didn't deserve to be comforted.

The things she'd said to Aidan the night before had been unkind and unwarranted. Sure, he'd kept a big secret from her, even knowing how much she hated secrets, lies and deceptions, lumping them all into one basket with her cheating ex-husband.

But, she was forced to admit, this wasn't exactly the same. Aidan's secret might have shaken her confidence in him, but it wasn't about her, not really. It was about him having a father he'd never met before coming to Chesapeake Shores. She tried to imagine what that must have been like and couldn't. And now that the news was out and he was ready—and able—to share it with her, she'd shut him down. It was probably the most dramatic, life-altering news of his life and she wouldn't even listen. How had she allowed Josh's big lie to harden her heart like that? And, she wondered, how had she forgotten just how many secrets of her own she'd been keeping since coming to Chesapeake Shores?

Even though she'd reached the conclusion that she'd been wrong, she had no idea how to correct her mistake. The most obvious answer was to go to Aidan and apologize. A mature, rational woman who wanted a relationship with him would do exactly that. A woman who was scared to death of taking another risk, especially with a man who'd held back something important, no matter how valid his reasons—well, that was something else entirely.

The pounding on her door wasn't entirely unexpected, but it surely wasn't welcome. She dragged herself out of bed, pulled on a robe and padded to the door. She found Bree, Shanna and Susie on her porch.

"You're not at work," Shanna announced as if Liz might not be aware of the fact.

"It's about Aidan, isn't it?" Susie said. "You've broken up with him. Don't you know that hiding out at home won't help anything? I tried hiding out from Mack more than once. It was a waste of time. He always found me and then I just felt foolish."

Liz's gaze narrowed. "Are you saying I'm foolish?"

"Not at all," Bree said, aiming a warning glance at Susie, even as she pushed right past Liz and headed for the kitchen.

By the time the rest of them trailed along behind, Bree already had coffee brewing.

"Make yourself at home, why don't you?" Liz muttered.

Bree grinned. "Already have," she said, going into the refrigerator for cream, eggs and butter.

She emerged and reached for a loaf of bread on the counter. "I'm thinking French toast. That's good comfort food."

"Ooh, I love French toast," Shanna said, then patted her belly. "So does the baby."

Liz just pulled out a chair, sat down and rested her head on her arms on the table. The chatter swirled around her. Oddly enough, she found it comforting. Clearly they didn't hate her for sending Aidan away, though she knew sooner or later she'd hear what they did think about it.

"Liz, any syrup?" Bree asked loudly, as if she feared Liz might have fallen asleep on them.

"Cabinet to the left of the sink, middle shelf," Liz murmured without looking up. "There are strawberry preserves from the farmer's market in the fridge."

"Drink your coffee," Shanna said as she set down the cup. "You'll feel better. Bree's is strong enough to make your hair stand straight on end."

Liz did glance up at that. "Sounds divine." She took a long, slow sip, then sighed appreciatively. She looked at Shanna. "You ought to consider having her make it at the bookstore."

Shanna's gaze narrowed. "Did you just insult my coffee?"

Liz managed a faint grin. "I think I did."

"You know it's true," Susie added. "Shanna, not to be mean, but I've had plain old water that had more flavor."

"Gee, thanks," Shanna said, then laughed. "Okay, I make lousy coffee. We all know it. If I could work that stupid cappuccino machine I bought when I opened, maybe it would be better. Kevin had a knack for it, but he's not inclined to come in to make coffee for my customers before he heads off to work. I'm stuck with that old coffeemaker of his that picks and chooses when it wants to perk. Is it any wonder I don't charge for the stuff?"

"Any one of us could probably help with the cappuccino machine," Susie suggested gently. "Did you ever think to ask? We just thought you made bad coffee so the customers wouldn't linger too long."

"Fine," Shanna said, seizing on the offer. "From now on you can stop in and get the cappuccino machine going every morning. Your efforts will be rewarded with one to-go cup and my eternal gratitude."

Liz grinned as she listened. "And Sally's dismay," she reminded them. "She's sold a lot more carryout coffee since people on Main Street have tasted yours."

Shanna frowned at her. "Bite me."

"Ladies, ladies," Bree said as she set plates of French toast in front of each of them. "We did not come over here to discuss coffee. We came because our friend needs us."

Liz noted that three expectant faces were

suddenly focused on her. She hesitated, then said, "I'm not sure what to say. Thanks?"

"Say you're going to forgive Aidan," Susie encouraged. "He's crazy in love with you, and he didn't mean to hurt you by keeping this news a secret."

"He really didn't," Bree agreed.

"I know that," Liz admitted, shocking them all into silence.

"You know that?" Bree repeated. "Since when?"

"Since the rational part of my brain kicked in," Liz admitted. Her curiosity stirred. "How's the family taking the news?"

Bree grinned. "How do you think? Dad swears he knew all along that Aidan was an O'Brien. Of course, there's no way he could possibly have known, but you know Dad. He claims to have whatever it is the Irish have that makes them more intuitive than the rest of the world."

"My dad says Thomas is still stunned," Susie reported. "He had no idea he had a son. He denied it was possible when Aidan first confronted him, but the DNA results prove that Aidan is his."

"Thomas insisted on a DNA test?" Liz asked, startled.

"Well, sure, wouldn't you?" Susie said. "It might have hurt Aidan's feelings that Thomas thought he would lie about it, but nobody takes that kind of thing on faith. I guess that's what they've been waiting on before telling anyone. It's not the kind of thing you can just blurt out and then find out you were wrong. Imagine the uproar that could have caused, especially for Thomas and Sean."

"How's Connie taking the news that she has a grown stepson?"

"Mom talked to her last night," Bree said. "She says there was never a doubt in Connie's mind that Aidan was telling the truth. She claims she could see the O'Brien in him. I think it might be easier for her that Aidan's mom is gone, so there's no question of old feelings being rekindled between her and Uncle Thomas, but even if that weren't the case, I'll bet she'd be okay. Connie's steady as a rock. And they've already dealt with blending families because of Jenny and how hard it was for her to accept Uncle Thomas as her step-father. This is going to be a piece of cake, once the shock has passed."

Liz realized Shanna's gaze hadn't left her face.

"Okay, your turn," Shanna said quietly. "How are you dealing with the news?"

"You mean today or last night at the pub when I first figured out that something monumental was going on and Aidan hadn't told me?"

"Both," Shanna said at once.

"Last night I was just a shade worse than the shrew in Shakespeare's play. Nothing Aidan tried to say could get through to me. I wouldn't let him explain anything. In fact, I kicked him out."

"And broke his heart," Bree said quietly.

Liz regarded her with shock. "What makes you say that?"

"I waited for him to come back from here. I had a bad feeling that it wouldn't go well, and I was right. You really hurt him, Liz."

"He really hurt me, more than you could possibly understand," Liz retorted.

"Because he kept a secret that he felt wasn't entirely his to share," Bree suggested gently.

Liz made a face at her perfectly rational argument. "Yes, that. And some of the things he said to me. I probably deserved them, but that doesn't mean they didn't hurt."

She turned to Shanna. "You asked about this morning. When the dust settled and I could think like a sane person again, I saw that he'd only done what he thought was right for Thomas and anyone else directly involved. I wish he'd included me in that circle, but I was wrong to demand it of him. There was so much at stake for him, for Thomas, for all of the O'Briens, for that matter. I shouldn't have made it about me."

Bree looked delighted with her response. "And you'll go to Aidan and tell him that? Work all of this out? We so want you to be a part of this family, too, and if you and Aidan get married, we'll be cousins. How perfect will that be?"

Liz stared at her incredulously. "Boy, when you take a leap forward, you really make it a giant one, don't you?"

"Only way to go," Bree said. "Plunge in and go for broke. Will you?"

"One step at a time," Liz countered. "I have to see if this new, sane me is real. If I'm ever going to have a relationship with someone, trust has to be a part of it. I can't freak out over every little thing the way I did over this. It wouldn't be fair."

"But you are going to try," Bree pressed. "Starting today."

"I'll speak to Aidan and try to clear the air," she promised. It was as much of a commitment as she could make for the moment.

"And you'll be at the family dinner at Mick's on Sunday," Susie said as if it were a foregone conclusion. "It's going to be an official welcome for Aidan as an O'Brien."

"Let's see how it goes," Liz equivocated.

The only way she could go to an event like that was if she and Aidan had reached some sort of understanding, if he'd forgiven her for over-reacting and lumping him in with Josh. If he was the man she'd believed him to be, he'd understand, but she also knew how difficult it was to move on once harsh words had been spoken in anger. She'd already dismissed the things he'd said as an overheated reaction to her behavior. But if he couldn't forgive the accusations she'd hurled at him, it might be over between them, and she'd have no one to blame but herself.

Aidan's heart ached for Liz and what she'd endured, but he hadn't deserved the way she'd lashed out at him the night before. If there was so little trust between them, how could they possibly move on? And right this minute, he had other things on his mind, such as figuring out how he fit in with this new family that was opening its arms to him.

He found himself once again reaching out to Thomas, as a son might reach out to a father, for advice. They agreed to meet on neutral turf, along Shore Road.

"I'll bring coffee," Aidan told him. "I'd like to talk some more about where we go from here and the fallout from the big announcement."

"Happy to do that," Thomas said.

Aidan had anticipated being alone with Thomas, but when he arrived just before ten, he found him there with Connie and Sean.

Sean ran toward him and threw his arms around his waist. "Wanna go fishing? You can take me this time. Our dad has to go to the office later."

"Aidan and your dad need to talk," Connie said. "You can go fishing another time." She smiled at Aidan. "Don't mind us. Sean and I will be heading to the bookstore. We were just keeping Thomas company till you got here."

Relieved, Aidan watched them go, then sat down and handed Thomas a cup of coffee. "You were right about the grapevine," he said. "I was on my way to see Liz after I left your place, but before I got to her, she already knew something was up."

Thomas looked chagrined. "My fault. I thought I should tell my brothers. I told them the news was strictly confidential. Apparently it took each of them about ten seconds to agree to meet at O'Brien's. I doubt they'd have blabbed to everyone else, but the place was crawling with family. Liz was there with a bunch of the women. Apparently Susie picked up on just enough of her dad's conversation with Mick to stir up trouble. I'm so sorry." He regarded Aidan with real concern. "How'd it go with Liz?"

Aidan shook his head. "Not good. She threw me out of her house, refused to let me explain anything."

"I could speak to her, tell her you'd kept silent at my request," Thomas offered.

"I don't think that will matter to her," Aidan said. "She has some real deep-seated issues about trust. I knew that when I kept this from her."

"Still, I feel responsible for your being in that position."

Aidan shook his head. "I put myself in that position."

Thomas studied him. "So, what's next for the two of you?"

"I have no idea. I was wondering how things went on your end." He allowed himself a faint smile. "Sean seems to be doing just fine with the news."

Thomas laughed. "I told you he would be." His expression sobered. "Aidan, you do want to have a relationship with me now, don't you? I could understand if you have reservations."

Aidan gave the question some thought. The fact that Thomas was sensitive enough to have asked it really mattered to him.

"There were times in my life when I resented the man who hadn't cared enough to stay with my mom. Even when I first got to town and saw you with this huge family and with a wife and son, it stirred up those old resentments."

"Understandable," Thomas said.

"But wrong," Aidan told him. "You never knew about me, and that was my mom's decision, not yours. Maybe things would have been different if you'd known, but more likely there would have been another divorce in your past."

"I'd like to think otherwise," Thomas said, "but I can't deny the likelihood." He gave Aidan a lingering look. "You had a good life, though, didn't you?"

Aidan smiled, remembering. "For the most part, I did. The only thing missing was having a dad. There were times when that was huge, but in general I have no complaints. My mom gave me love and values and a good education. No parent could have been more supportive of my choices in life. Nobody yelled louder than she did when I was on the field."

Thomas smiled at that. "I imagine she was very proud."

"She was. I'm glad she got to see me play professionally before she died."

"She must have loved that." He gave Aidan a sideways glance. "I saw you play a time or two. I know how good you were and how terrible it must have been to have your career ended by an injury."

Aidan shrugged. "I think coaching was what I was meant to do all along. I'm happy here. I hope to stay."

Thomas looked startled. "Is there any reason you wouldn't?"

"If this turns out to be too much for everyone to handle, for you to handle, I'll leave. It was never my intention to complicate anyone's life."

"Nonsense," Thomas said emphatically. "Chesapeake Shores is where you belong. You're family, Aidan. Make no mistake about that. We'll work out all the rest in time."

And for the first time since he'd arrived in town with this dark secret in his heart, Aidan truly felt at home. Now, if he could only make peace with Liz, his future might very well be everything he'd ever hoped for.

⇒ 23 ⇐

Thomas approached Nell's cottage with a huge knot in his stomach. He hoped that for once the family might have honored his wishes and left it to him to tell his mother about Aidan, but he couldn't be sure. One thing he did know: she wouldn't appreciate learning this news from anyone other than him. Nell had always been an exceptionally tolerant and understanding woman, but she had her ways of making her displeasure felt. A simple look could be more gut-wrenching than any words she might speak. Even in his fifties, that look could make him feel like a kid deserving of a scolding from the person he respected most.

He found her in the yard working in her garden. The early-morning sun was already hot, but she seemed oblivious to it as she weeded. A wide-brimmed straw hat, a recent concession to the sun's effects, shaded her lined face.

"Hey, Ma," he said as he approached.

She looked up, a smile of pleasure spreading across her face. "Thomas! What brings you by here on a workday? You're usually out on some mission or another by now."

"I have another sort of mission for today," he

said. "Can you take a break and go inside, where it's cooler?"

She gave him a chiding look. "Since when has a little summer heat bothered either of us? I'll take a break, but we'll sit where we can see the water. It's soothing. Though it offends me to see a lovely Earl Grey ruined in such a way, Dillon brought out a pitcher of iced tea not long ago. Hopefully all the ice won't have melted already."

At her suggestion, Thomas glanced toward the familiar pair of Adirondack chairs that faced the bay, then smiled at the realization that everyone in their family seemed to have a similar set of chairs for enjoying the view and the breeze. The family's deep love of this setting had started with his mother, not him.

He watched as his mother rose stiffly from her stool at the edge of the garden, ignoring the hand he held out to help her. *Stubborn old gal,* he thought, amused. Her steps were surprisingly brisk as she crossed the lawn, then sat down and poured their tea into tall glasses, one of which had probably been meant for her husband, the man she'd loved as a teenager and been reunited with just a few years ago in Dublin.

"Something on your mind?" she asked, after the silence had stretched out too long.

"I'm trying to figure out how to get into this," he admitted. "It doesn't speak well of me."

She frowned at that. "Thomas, I love all of my

sons. Every one of you is an honorable, decent man. You've all made your share of mistakes, but that doesn't lessen my love for you one bit."

He smiled at her ardent claim. "Thanks, Ma."

"It's not something you need to thank me for. It just is. Now, tell me."

"You remember Aidan Mitchell?"

She gave him an odd look. "My memory hasn't gone yet. Of course I do."

He drew in a deep breath, then blurted out the news. "It turns out that he's my son, Ma. Your grandson."

Her blue eyes widened, at first with shock, then with something he recognized as real delight, the way she always reacted to a new addition to the family, whether spouse or baby.

Tears filled her eyes. "I have another grandson? That handsome young man is your son?" She shook her head. "I should have seen it right away. He has your father's eyes, just as you all do."

"It's your eyes we have, Ma." Thomas studied her more closely, looking for signs of dismay. "You don't look as if you're upset by this."

"Why would I be?" she asked, sounding perfectly calm. "I might be taken aback at the news coming out of the blue like this, but a new member of the family is always welcome."

Thomas had expected this reaction . . .

eventually. "No criticisms or lectures about irresponsibility?"

She gave him a long look. "I imagine you've covered that ground quite nicely on your own."

"I have," he admitted.

"Because you're a decent and honorable man, as I just said. I don't need to say another word in judgment. Tell me how this happened and how you finally found out after all this time." Her gaze narrowed. "Unless you knew years ago."

He shook his head. "Not a clue. I was as stunned as everyone else who's learned the truth." He settled back and sipped his tea, then told her about Anna and their long-ago love affair.

"She sounds like she might have been good for you," Nell said. "She clearly understood you very well and made what she thought was a selfless decision. I hope you're not blaming her for that, for keeping you from your son."

Thomas thought about it, about how much he'd missed, then shook his head. "I'm sorry I lost so much time with Aidan, but she was right. I was probably far too self-absorbed and driven to be a good husband and father back then. Heaven knows, I still hadn't gotten the knack for marriage the first two times I walked down the aisle, and those came later, when my career was already well established."

"And now? Are the two of you intent on

bonding as father and son? Will you do whatever it takes to make that adjustment?"

"Aidan's a little old to need a father interfering
in his life," he reminded her.

"No one's ever too old to need family," Nell
scolded, then added confidently, "You'll be there
in whatever way the two of you work out." Her
expression turned sad. "I wish I had more time to
get to know this new grandson of mine."

Thomas frowned. "You'll have years to get to
know him, Ma. We're both counting on that."

A smile chased away that fleeting hint of
sorrow he thought he'd seen in her eyes.

"Then I'll do my best to hang around for a good
long time."

Thomas reached for his mother's hand. Despite
her age and some hints of frailty, her hands were
strong from all the gardening she still insisted on
doing herself. That core strength and determination would keep her with them.

"I love you, Ma. Aidan will be at Sunday
dinner at Mick's for an official O'Brien welcome. I'm counting on you to make our favorite
dishes."

She gave him a questioning look. "Are you sure
he's ready for all of us?"

"Is anyone ever ready for that? The fact that he's
willing to show up proves he's got tough O'Brien
genes."

"It does, doesn't it?" She squeezed his hand.

"Congratulations, Thomas. He's lucky to have you as his father."

"I'm not sure he understands it just yet, but he's lucky to be a part of this family," Thomas said. "I thank God every day for it myself."

"As do I," she said, her words heartfelt. "As do I."

More than once over the next several days, Liz tried to catch up with Aidan, but for the first time since he'd arrived in town, he was surprisingly elusive. It was entirely possible that he was deliberately avoiding her. She could hardly blame him after the harsh, unreasonable words they'd exchanged.

On Thursday, she spotted him on the town green at one of the football team's unofficial practices. She stood by the shop door and watched him work with the boys, smiling at the way Henry, Hector and Taylor hung on his every word.

As she observed the interaction and saw how good he was at motivating the team, her heart seemed to open just a little more. This was a man who was meant to be a father, unlike Josh, who'd never shown the least bit of interest in being a parent. All those dreams about having babies had been hers alone. She saw that much more clearly now.

Steeling herself to confront Aidan and offer her apology the minute practice ended, she was thoroughly frustrated when three tourists walked into the shop just as practice was ending on the green. By the time the women left, her receipts for the day were considerably higher, but so was her level of frustration.

She scrolled down the contact list on her cell phone to Aidan's number, but when it came time to press the call button, she couldn't make herself do it. Arranging a meeting made it seem too stiff and formal. She thought a casual encounter would make it easier to get the words out despite her nerves, but at this rate the first time she saw him might be Sunday dinner at Mick's, and there wouldn't be a second of privacy there for the conversation they needed to have.

Bree walked into the shop as she was staring at her phone. "You okay?"

Liz sighed. "Not really. I've been trying to work up the courage to talk to Aidan."

Bree's expression immediately brightened. "He's right upstairs. I can cover the shop if you want to run up there and get things straightened out."

Liz shook her head. "That doesn't feel right, either."

Bree frowned. "What do you mean?"

"I have this idea in my head that we'll bump into each other, I'll be able to say my piece, and everything will be okay again. If I call or go up there, it will feel like some big deal."

Her friend didn't even try to hide her amusement. "It *is* a big deal, sweetie. It's the first step toward your future. This was your first huge fight. How you end it will set the tone for the rest of your lives."

"Oh, don't be so dramatic, Ms. Playwright."

"Mock me, if you will, but as a moderately successful playwright, I'm telling you it's the pivotal scene when the audience finally knows with certainty that the couple will live happily-ever-after."

"Gee, now there's the kind of moral support I need before I risk doing something completely out of my comfort zone," Liz responded. "It's an apology, Bree. If I turn it into something more, I'll freeze and never get the first word out."

Just then, loud, persistent barking echoed from upstairs. Liz frowned. "I thought you said Aidan was in his apartment."

"I thought he was."

"Then why isn't he quieting Archie down?" Liz asked. "This sounds as if something's wrong."

Bree gave her a sly look. "Don't you have a key for emergencies?"

Liz started to reach in the cash drawer for the key, then hesitated. "You have to be right about Aidan being there. He just finished practice. He must be home."

"Well, you're the expert, but Archie sounds pretty frantic to me," Bree said, tilting her head as if to listen more intently.

Liz couldn't deny that he sounded that way to her, too. It was definitely Archie's version of an emergency alarm. Or maybe that's just what she needed it to be to get her past her reticence to head upstairs.

"You go," Bree said. "I'll stay here."

"Why don't you go? I'll wait here," Liz immediately countered, then quickly added, "In case a customer comes in."

"You should go," Bree insisted. "Aidan gave you the key and you're better equipped to deal with Archie than I would be."

Liz sighed. She had no argument for that. "I'll be right back. If you hear me yell, it means we're dealing with something more than a typical Archie crisis. Call 911."

"Will do," Bree promised.

Despite the sense of urgency she was feeling, Liz dragged her feet as she climbed the stairs to Aidan's apartment. Just in case they'd been wrong about Aidan being home, she tapped on the door, then knocked harder. Archie's barking grew even louder.

Using her key, she opened the door carefully. Archie barreled right into her, clearly ecstatic about her arrival. Since he didn't immediately dart down the steps, but instead ran back inside, she followed him over the threshold, then stopped in amazement.

The apartment was filled with flowers. Vases of

a dozen different varieties and colors—large, small and everything in between—scented the small room with their sweet fragrance. The centerpiece of it all was a dramatic arrangement of out-of-season pink and white dogwood branches in full bloom. Aidan stood next to that display, his expression hesitant.

"Too much?" he asked.

Liz smiled. "That depends on what you were going for."

"I was hoping to dazzle you, maybe impress you with a gesture that would tell you just how sorry I am for causing you even a moment of pain."

Liz's eyes filled with tears. "I detect Bree's hand in this."

"It was 100 percent my idea," he swore. "But she does have a flower shop and excellent skill in arranging flowers."

"Where on earth did she find dogwood at this time of year?"

He shrugged. "You'll have to ask her. I imagine Jake's nursery has all sorts of resources for finding flowers out of season. She tried to talk me out of them, but I said they were too significant. We met when Dogwood Hill was in full bloom."

Liz smiled. "I remember. I'm sure it was easy enough to get Bree to conspire with you. She is, after all, a huge romantic, but what about Archie? How'd you manage to get him to cooperate?"

"I told him our future depended on it," Aidan said. "And I kept mentioning your name. It's like some sort of trigger for him. I say your name, he goes into a happy frenzy."

Even now, in fact, the dog was dancing back and forth between them. Liz could almost swear she saw hope in his eyes.

"Am I forgiven?" Aidan asked. "I wanted so badly to tell you everything sooner. I'm sorry that I couldn't."

Liz drew in a deep breath. "And I should have understood that. By the next morning, I'd already realized how wrong I was to expect you to handle any of it differently. Of course you had to respect Thomas's wishes." She gave him a rueful look. "And it's not as if I've been forthcoming about my past with most people in town, not the whole story, anyway."

"But you were with me."

"I did it on my timetable, though. I should have shown you the same courtesy and realized you told me as soon as it felt right. I have a feeling I'll be wrestling with trust issues for a very long time. I'm not happy about that, and I will work on it. I'm not going to let what happened with Josh shape the rest of my life."

Aidan stepped closer. "I hope you know by now that you can trust me, Liz."

"I'm starting to accept that," she said, knowing it was true.

"Can we work on that together from here on out?" he asked.

"Meaning?"

"I want to move forward together. I want a future with you in it. I want marriage and a home here in Chesapeake Shores and a family." He held her gaze. "I think I fell in love with you the very first time I saw you chasing after Archie on Dogwood Hill. You were so incredibly beautiful in the sunlight."

"You just became part of a rather large family," she reminded him with a smile. "Isn't that enough for you?"

"I want my own," he insisted. "I know it's probably too soon, but you need to know where I'm coming from, where I'm heading. You can set the pace to determine how quickly we'll get there."

The last bit of ice lingering around Liz's heart melted at the sincerity behind his words. "I want that, too. I love you, Aidan," she said, squeezing the words bravely past the giant lump in her throat. "I'm scared to death of that feeling, but I can't deny it. I've known for some time that you're a man worth loving. I was just too frightened of repeating past mistakes."

"I'm pretty terrified, too, if you want to know the truth, but this is right. I feel it in my gut. I think I have from the moment I set eyes on you. Keep in mind I didn't have two parents with a perfect marriage to set an example for me. I'm following my heart here, and I can honestly say I don't have a single doubt about us."

She met his gaze. "I have enough doubts for both of us," she told him candidly. "Not about us so much as about the whole forever thing, if that makes any sense."

"But we're agreed?" he pressed, clearly determined not to leave her an opening she could claim later. "We'll take it one day at a time until it feels 100 percent right to both of us, and then we'll get married and start that family?"

Liz swallowed hard, fighting panic, but then she looked into Aidan's eyes and felt Archie's encouraging nudge. "I think that sounds like an amazing plan."

When Aidan reached for her, she moved into his arms, tears streaming down her cheeks. He rubbed them away with the pad of his thumb.

"If you're so happy, why are you crying?" he asked.

"Because that's what I do when I'm deliriously happy," she said. "I also do it when I'm scared or sad. Sometimes I'm just a blubbering mess for no good reason."

He grinned. "Then I guess I'd better get used to it, because I plan to keep you very, very happy."

Given Bree's involvement in Aidan's plan to seduce Liz and convince her to marry him, Aidan was stunned that for once the news hadn't leaked and circulated all over town before Sunday dinner at Mick's.

As they walked into the foyer, Liz came to an abrupt halt and whispered in his ear. "Today should be about you and Thomas, okay? Our news can wait."

He regarded her with amusement. "Our friend Bree might have been astonishingly silent about the other day up to now, but do you honestly think she'll be able to keep the news to herself through an entire family dinner?"

"I can beg her to try," Liz said earnestly.

Aidan studied her. "It's because of Thomas and me, and not because you're already running scared?"

She stood on tiptoe and kissed his cheek. "Absolutely."

Startled by the public gesture, he laughed. "Well, now you've gone and done it."

"Done what?"

"The kiss, Liz."

"What about it?"

"Take a look around."

At least a half dozen O'Briens were standing close by, mouths agape. Obviously they'd congregated to greet Aidan and witnessed a whole lot more than they'd bargained for. Being O'Briens, they put their own interpretation on that kiss.

"That wasn't what it looked like," Liz announced loudly, and clearly to no avail, given the hoots that greeted the comment.

Susie and Shanna were the first to cross the foyer and give Liz enthusiastic hugs.

"You're a couple!" Shanna said happily.

Liz opened her mouth, no doubt to deny it, but before she could, Susie chimed in, "Don't even try to deny it. This is the best day ever, a new cousin and a new cousin-in-law-to-be!"

Aidan smiled at Liz's stunned expression.

"I kissed you on the cheek," she murmured, sounding desperate. "Does that say *engagement* to you?"

"No," Susie agreed. "It was the expression of pure delight on Aidan's face that told that story."

Within minutes, they'd been dragged into the living room for enthusiastic embraces from what seemed like a couple of dozen people, some of whom Aidan was sure he'd never seen before. It was Thomas who finally came to their rescue.

"Okay, everybody, back off. There's somebody we need to see." He scowled at the rest of the family. "In private."

Leading the way, he took the two of them to the kitchen, where Nell was bustling around with the assistance of Mick's oldest daughter, Abby, and her twin daughters, Carrie and Caitlyn. Caitlyn held a baby in her arms, but still seemed to be doing a deft job of stirring a pot of something that smelled delicious.

"Ma," Thomas said quietly, immediately stopping the buzz of conversation. "I'd like to reintroduce you to Aidan Mitchell, your grandson." He winked at Liz. "And to the woman I've been led to believe may have agreed to become his wife."

As Aidan stood there, feeling more nervous and exposed than he ever had before the first play of any professional football game, a smile slowly spread across Nell's face. She crossed the kitchen and put her hands on his face. She had to reach high to do it, her touch gentle and full of such wonder that it brought tears to his eyes.

"I can't tell you how much joy it brings me to have another grandchild to cherish," Nell told him. She turned to Caitlyn and Carrie with a quick wink. "Maybe you can teach those two how to be more respectful of their elders."

"Gram!" Carrie protested indignantly.

Caitlyn quickly shushed her. "You know she's just teasing. We were her very first great-grandchildren. She adores us. And I'm holding her first great-great-grandchild right here in my arms. Do you really think she's going to risk me keeping this sweet boy away from her?"

Nell laughed. She took one of Aidan's hands in hers, then reached for Liz's hand, as well. "I couldn't be happier about the news, any of it. I wish you both all the blessings and happiness you deserve."

Aidan felt that salty sting of emotional tears in his eyes once more. He'd shed more tears today than he had in years. Even at his mother's funeral, he'd been stoic and dry-eyed. There was something about the O'Briens, though, that seemed to bring emotions to the surface.

His heart seemed to catch once more when Nell gave Thomas a kiss, too. "Thank you for bringing more joy into my life." Her expression turned stern then. "But no more surprises, okay? I'm not sure how much my heart can take."

Laughter ricocheted around the kitchen then, and the solemn mood was broken.

"Gram, I'm starved," Carrie announced. "Isn't it time to get dinner on the table?"

"Do you think I don't know when my own cooking is ready?" Nell chided. She turned to Aidan and Liz. "Aidan, you carry the pot roast to the table. Liz, you can get the soda bread."

She directed the preparations in such a perfectly orchestrated way that Aidan could see where Bree had learned the directorial skills that went along with her ability to write a great play.

At the table, surrounded by his new family, Aidan bowed his head with the rest of them.

And when Nell thanked God for all their bounty and for bringing Aidan into their lives, his eyes welled up with tears yet again. He glanced at Liz and saw that she, too, was thoroughly emotional. As she'd told him, she clearly shed tears on any and all occasions, but the smile on her lips told him this was another of the happy moments.

As the prayer ended, he caught her gaze. Oblivious to the curious gazes cast their way, he mouthed, "I love you."

She beamed back at him. "I love you, too," she said, but her words rang out loud and clear.

And in that moment, surrounded by family, Aidan knew that everything would work out just as it should.

Center Point Large Print
600 Brooks Road / PO Box 1
Thorndike, ME 04986-0001 USA

(207) 568-3717

US & Canada:
1 800 929-9108
www.centerpointlargeprint.com

4-15